21st Century Demon Hunter

CHARLES D. LINCOLN

Burning Bulb
PUBLISHING

21st Century Demon Hunter
By **Charles D. Lincoln**

Burning Bulb Publishing
P.O. Box 4721
Bridgeport, WV 26330-4721
United States of America
www.BurningBulbPublishing.com

Cover designed by Charles D. Lincoln.

First Edition.

Paperback Edition ISBN: 978-1-948278-17-1

Printed in the United States of America

DEDICATION

This book is dedicated to several people who have made me hate life less.

To Chelsea LeSage, my partner in crime, my muse, and the one actress who could play Julie, thank you for your tireless dedication to bringing her to the screen and for constantly pushing me to conquer. Who knew, when I told you I had a character I had written a novel about, that I'd like you to consider playing, that all of this would happen? The changes you've had on my life since you sent me that first audition video have been profound in all the best ways. Thank you for being in my life and thank you for helping give life to a character I think of as my drunken, surly, violent baby.

To Brittany Black, who showed me adventure and chaos in equal parts, and showed me who I really was, deep down, and that I was actually quite okay with it. You will always be Diabolica Robotica to me.

To Leanna Stager, who kept me alive when I was on my way out of this world, who helped me become a filmmaker, and who helped me believe in myself when I was at my lowest.

To Michelle Bowser, who not only got me in touch with the publishers, but also gave constant feedback and asked the important questions when I initially was writing the book. That help was invaluable.

To Katie Dowling, my favorite All-Terrain Englishwoman and an awesome Austrian, who helped me when I needed it, woke me up to truths about myself, and who knows the value of suitcase champagne.

To my seventh grade teacher Miss Burke, the first authority figure to tell me I was good at storytelling, even before I actually was. She was the first adult to not try to discourage my creativity and that meant a lot.

To the cast and crew of the *21st Century Demon Hunter* webseries, who have all helped to make a little writing exercise into something loved by many. You all have no idea how much your efforts, acting, and enthusiasm have helped me. Casey, Madison, Rebecca, Anna, Christopher, Hanan, Adam, Shannon, Rachel, Vivian, Samantha, Camilla, Justine, Matthew, Madeline, Lola, Emily, Razor, Kevin, Marine, Cat, Robert A., Patricia, Sarah, Alina, Maya, Keith, Kasia, Natalie, Jake, Robert H., Dani, Linnea, Nikki, Krista, Nicole, Jasmine, Andrew, Lake, Vahni, Scarlett, Elissa, Piyali, Jeffrey, and everybody else who contributed to the madness.

Thanks to all of you. I love you all. Well, most of you. One of you done fucked up. You know who you are.

To Ms. Dixon, my second grade teacher who went out of her way to try to put out the spark within me, fuck you. You probably succeeded at doing that to untold numbers of potential creative types, but you failed with me. You were a shit teacher and an awful person. If you're still alive, I hope all of your dreams have turned to dust. And if you're not alive, good.

PROLOGUE
DISCONNECTED

Well, that got ugly in a hurry, Jerry thought to himself, as he took off his pants and shorts, the cop with a flashlight behind him, snapping on rubber gloves. This wasn't his first dance with the law and he knew how these pigs operated, especially when you were opposing their billionaire overlord and his unjust banking system.

They had been occupying the Brooklyn Bridge when the nets came down. He had no idea how many of them had been arrested, but he knew that the police had closed off the way both in front of and behind them before dropping the nets. This was probably his third time being arrested just for protesting since 2011 and he wasn't about to let them stop him now. He knew his rights and he knew that while there was a chance that the Mayor might try to make an example out of him and the others they arrested today, chances are, like all the other times, it was going to be thrown out of court. They had a right to protest the injustice they saw in the system today and they were going to expose it to the world, no matter how many hours or days in a cage he had to deal with.

"Bend over and spread your cheeks."

He bent over and cupped both cheeks of his ass as the cop did a little soul searching behind him. The first time he had ever been strip searched, he had felt violated afterwards. This was probably the sixth or seventh time and it bothered him a bit that he was used to it by now. Still, another thing to add to the massive list of ways his rights as a citizen and an American had been violated by the oligarchy that ran this city and this country.

"He's clean," said the cop to his partner.

Jerry knew he was going to be staying overnight in the holding cell until his arraignment in the morning. He was glad this happened on a weekday so he wouldn't have to be sent to Rikers. That's where the real criminals were and he was a bit afraid of them, to be quite honest.

Jerry, whose friends had always compared him to a younger Zach Galifianakis, had run away from home when he was a teenager and spent the first few months of his time in New York City, sleeping on the street and in squats. Now, years later, he had gotten himself to the point where he had a place in Bushwick (they had tried to call it East Williamsburg when he first saw the place, but he knew better) and a job that just barely paid enough to keep him in PBR's with the lights on. He had become interested in social justice after seeing one too many of his friends getting arrested for putting their feet up on the subway seat and then when the Occupy Movement took Zucotti, he was there until they forcibly evicted everyone in a very illegal late night raid.

He remembered the riot gear and night sticks and how they had tried to make sure the press didn't report what was really going on in there. It didn't work. They couldn't stop the spirit of rebellion, no matter how hard they tried.

Now, it had been a little over a year or two since that moment and here he was, naked in a cell, about to be arraigned for continuing the spirit of protest. Something he knew this country had been founded on.

He waited for the cops to give him something to wear, which was usually right after the strip search. This time, though, they seemed to be busy talking to someone on their walkie talkies about something.

"Are you sure?" one of them said, "You guys have been doing this shit all night and you know as well as I do it's just going to result in a shit storm of lawsuits tomorrow."

"You have your orders, Officer," said the voice on the other end of the walkie talkie.

"I know. And *you know* I'm going to keep bringing this up to you every time tonight. We're not supposed to…"

"If you wish to file a complaint, you know how to do so, Officer. Now, the representatives from the Mayor's office will be there in a moment to relieve you of your duties."

"Whatever," said the cop.

"Officer," Jerry said, becoming very aware of how cold the room was, "Can I…"

"Hold your horses, kid. There's some people here who want to talk to you about something."

"About what? And can I get dressed first?"

"I don't have a fucking clue. Just keep your mouth shut is my advice."

"Can I get dressed first, Officer?"

A door opened from the far side of the room and a man in what Jerry could tell was a ridiculously expensive three piece suit showed up, with an officer in what appeared to be riot gear with a fully tinted face shield.

"Hello again, Officers," the man in the suit, who didn't appear to be a detective, from how immaculate his suit was and how evenly slicked back his hair was, said. Seriously, the man looked like a GQ model more than anything.

The two cops, obviously tired of having dealt with this man however many times they had before, grunted at him and walked out of the room, the one that had inspected Jerry throwing his rubber gloves into a garbage pail and then leaving the room. The cop in riot gear looked out the barred window of the door for a few moments and then nodded to the man in a suit.

"Detective or Officer or whatever the fuck you are," Jerry started, "Can I get dressed now?"

The man smiled and looked at a file he took out of his also ridiculously expensive black overcoat.

"Jerry, my man, you've got yourself quite a rap sheet. Destruction of private property, resisting arrest, receiving stolen property…"

"I'm aware of that, sir. Now, can I please," Jerry started, before being interrupted by a face full of pepper spray from the riot cop.

He held his hands to his face and let out a scream, writhing on the floor.

The next thing he knew, his bare body was stomach-down on the cold concrete, as his hands were zip-tied behind his back.

"What the fuck?!? What the fuck?!?" Jerry started to scream, between coughing, blinded by the spray, and feeling only the cold of the floor, the sting of the spray in his eyes, mouth, and nose, and the anger at how much his rights were being violated, "This is so fucked! This is so…"

"Jerry," he heard the man in the suit say, above him, "I would advise you to shut up. Speak when spoken to or this will get a lot worse."

"Fuck you! You fucking pig! I know my rights."

He felt a sharp pain to his ribs and he brought his knees up to his stomach to protect himself. He felt another sharp pain to his back, aware that this was him being kicked. He wished he had taken the time to look at the riot cop's badge, because this was not going to stand when he got a chance to talk to his lawyer.

"Jerry? Are you going to cooperate?"

Jerry, seething with rage, a long line of snot dripping from his nose into his mouth, nodded.

"Good. Now, Jerry, I am Mr. Trent. I have a couple questions for you. I want you to answer them as honestly as possible," Mr. Trent said, his voice always even and confident, like he was making a speech at all times, "And if you give me any shit about wanting to speak to a lawyer first, you're going to be in a lot of pain. Is that understood?"

Jerry nodded. Still blinded, he felt the boot of the riot cop as he was kicked across the side of the face.

"What the fuck?!? I nodded!"

"Jerry, we'd prefer an auditory response, alright?"

"Y-Yes."

"Yes, what?"

"Yes…sir."

"Good, we understand each other, Jerry. Now, it says in your file that you've been arrested numerous times since you decided to come to my fair city. Is that true?"

"Yes…sir."

"Good. Now, I was looking through your records and I couldn't help but notice that each time you've come here, you've utilized legal aide. Reports also indicate that you haven't ever had any family visit you during your short stays with us. Is that correct?"

"What is this abo….I mean…yes, sir. It is correct."

"So, it's safe to say that if anything happened to you, Jerry, no one would miss you?"

"W-what…wait…what are you…"

A hood was put over Jerry's head and he was brought to his feet. He didn't like what the cop had been talking about at all. No one would miss him? What the fuck did that mean? And after he had been brutalized by this gorilla in riot gear, Jerry wasn't going to go down without a fight, hands cuffed behind his back or not.

Blindly, he tried kicking, only to feel a thick arm around his throat. Mr. Trent whispered to him, "Calm down, Jerry."

He felt himself being dragged in some direction or the other, still wearing only the zip ties around his wrists and the hood over his head. They were going to kill him, he thought; they were going to take him into a back room and shoot him in the back of the head and no one would ever know. He screamed, he kicked, but he was dragged across a cold, concrete floor.

Within a few minutes, the ground and air around him grew even colder. He was outside now, naked in the cold March air. He heard the doors of a van opening and heard other voices scream and moaning in that direction. He didn't know what was going on, but he knew that they were probably going to execute him and everyone else in that van if he didn't run.

"That's 40. 20 males. 20 females. We have what the priests need for the season. Let's go," he heard Mr. Trent say to someone else.

"Very nice, Mr. Trent, but, uh…His Honor has some reservations about…"

"Look, if His Honor doesn't want to know how his sausage is made, he shouldn't send one of you to check out the pig farm."

"Noted. Alright, Malone, put him in the…"

Jerry had heard enough and made a break for it, he tried to turn in the opposite direction of the voices and run, but within a couple seconds, he felt a sharp blow to the back of his head and then everything went black.

BOOK ONE
I LOVE LIVING IN THE CITY

CHAPTER 1

The first thing Kelly noticed about it was the smell of its breath. It was a rank, bloody smell, made ever the worse by how hot the air was coming out of what looked like a mouth.

The thing that should have stayed within an H. R. Giger painting turned to her, as she pressed against the wall, paralyzed by a primal feeling that was way beyond something as small as fear and very much in the realm of complete abject terror. It was the size of a mastiff, but completely without fur of any sort. In its place were black scales and what looked like jagged pieces of bone randomly ripping out of its hide.

It didn't so much crawl as shuffle itself on its uneven number of limbs towards her, its mouth filled with row upon row of crooked teeth. Teeth that resembled a human's more than any animal she had seen before. Teeth that were frighteningly white. Its yellow, bloodshot eyes, which she couldn't count the number of, were focused on her as it shuffled ever closer across the living room at her, the lower half of its body dragging behind the front part..

Her body trembled with terror; her tanned but distinctly Nordic face moist with sweat, drops of it trickling down her maroon and gold-colored University of Minnesota, Twin Cities t-shirt; her fingernails, painted a drab pink, breaking the skin of her palms; the blond ringlets of her hair sticking to the skin of her forehead; her bladder ready to give out at any moment.

This thing was making its way towards her, crossing the living room like something out of a nightmare. *This is it*, she thought and screamed.

"JULIE!!! OH MY GOD! JULIE!! WAKE UP!! WAKE UP!! WAKE THE FUCK UP!!!"

The door on the other side of the living room opened up and her roommate, Julie, emerged, her makeup thick and smudged; her dyed black hair uncombed, her evenly cut-bangs falling into her eyes; her black wife beater exposing two sleeves and a chest adorned with

9

tattoos, the beginnings of a beer belly slightly pushing it and the pair of black boyshorts she wore away from each other. She yawned, scratched her head with one hand while picking her wedge with the other, then looked around the living room with half-closed eyes.

"Wha? What are you yelling for? I'm really hungover. Can you…"

"Julie! Don't you see there's a fucking monster in the…"

"Oh *that*…."

"Yes*, that*!"

"Oh, don't worry about that. It's just…curious. It's from Hell. It's called a…uh…uh…I don't really remember, but I've never seen one of these rape or eat anyone, so it's relatively harmless. Just give it a Triscuit or something."

"Give it a fucking Triscuit?!?"

"Yeah, they love them."

"I don't care what it loves! Get it the fuck out! Get it the fuck out!"

"Fine, you big baby," she sighed heavily, and then whistled to the creature, "Here, boy!"

The thing turned and looked at Julie and then lumbered towards her. She forced a smile, and pet the thing on what was probably its head…or a hump…or something. It seemed to like that.

"Sorry, boy, but my roommate says I can't keep you. And the landlord will probably bitch too, now that I think about it. So…"

She walked over to the front door of the apartment and led the thing outside, yelling, "You're free now! Go! Go, be with the wind!"

Kelly shook her head in disbelief, when Julie walked back into the living room, saying, "Okay, I took care of it."

"Julie! You just let that thing stalk the streets?!?"

"Don't be so melodramatic. It's not stalking anything. This is Brooklyn. Someone'll just think it's a dog or a really big rat or something and probably take it in."

"I don't fucking think so! That thing was a fucking nightmare!"

"Oh, now, you're just exaggerating."

"If people see that thing, they're going to shoot it!"

"Well, that'd be a very bad idea for them. When those things get pissed off…Christ," Julie played with her hair a little bit and then walked into the bathroom, leaving the door open as she peed, continuing the conversation, "Besides, I'm sure if there are any problems, animal control will just take it to a shelter and then some child will adopt it and be the coolest kid on his block."

"And then it'll eat his family."

"I just told you, they don't eat people...At least, I don't *think* they do."

"You're unbelievable."

"Whatever. Are we finished here? I've got work tomorrow...I think."

She wiped, flushed the toilet, and ran her hands under the water in the sink for a little bit, as Kelly moved into the center of the living room, not wanting to put her feet where the creature had been, all too aware of the heat the floor was radiating.

"And what's this, 'It's from hell. Feed it a Triscuit' bullshit? I know you told me you don't have much experience with normal people when I first moved here, but in no way is that an acceptable thing to say to someone!"

"Well, if that's what *Cosmopolitan* says, who am I to disagree?" Julie said opening her door, the smell of incense wafting from the room, strongly.

"And do you mean *work* work or your other work?"

"*Work* work. The other thing I don't have any sort of schedule for. They're usually just like, 'Hey Julie, there's a rift between worlds. We need you to close it' or 'Hey Julie, something with tentacles just came out of my toilet and boned my mom, can you take care of it?' It's usually an on-call type thing."

"Is that how that thing ended up here?"

"Kinda. There was a whole thing and then this other thing happened and I was kinda drunk and..."

"You know what? I don't want to hear it. I just don't want to see anything like that here ever again! I swear I'll move! I can't take that sort of thing again!"

"Alright. Anything else?"

"No. Go back to bed."

"Fine."

"You know...I'm sorry...This is all just so weird for...I...I never even believed in god until I moved in here."

"Why do you suddenly believe in god?"

"Because of your job."

"Why would me being a bike messenger make you believe in god?"

"No, the *other* job."

"What does that have to do with anything?"

"Well, if hell exists, then heaven must too, right?"

"*Oh*. Well, that's an awfully optimistic way of looking at it. But you're assuming by 'Hell,' I mean a Judeo-Christian fire and brimstone type place of punishment. I mean, there is a fire and brimstone *place*, kinda a section, but it doesn't really have anything to do with sin or anything like that. It's really just one of a set of nine completely different dimensions, filled with some pretty fucked up shit. Plus none of them are actually called 'Hell.' I just call 'em that to make the concept easier for civvies to understand. Okay...That and I can't really pronounce what they're really called. Something with an M, I think."

"What?"

"I told you I can't really pronounce it. I can spell it, though, if..."

"No, you mean, to tell me Hell has nothing to do with the Bible?"

"Nope. Two different concepts. One's rooted in the belief in good and evil and the other's rooted in reality. But if it helps you sleep better at night, it totally means god's real. Santa too, if you want."

"Oh..."

"Anyway, good night. Do me a favor, and if you see the landlord, tell her that I'm still visiting my sister in Chicago. Long story."

Julie walked back into her room and shut the door. Kelly sat down on the couch, buried her face in her hands, let out a deep breath and then realized she had initially come out here to go pee. She started towards the bathroom, stopping to sigh and shake her head as she stepped over the large burn marks the thing had left on the carpet.

The only thought that filled her head was, *Fuck. if I gave her my thirty days right now, I can bet I'm totally not going to get my security deposit back.*

CHAPTER 2

Julie recognized the song that playing. She didn't remember who played it or what it was called, but she remembered she hated it. She could have sworn that she had heard it in a commercial somewhere where douchey-looking dudes were wearing nautical caps and riding sailboats with their Botoxed country club wives.

Oh, that was it. It was called "Sail Away" or something like that.

And sure enough, as soon as she thought that, the words "Sail away, sail away, sail away" started to play. Yup. She thought this was probably Enya or Enigma or something. *Nah*, she thought, it couldn't be Enigma, because they did that Gregorian chant stuff with the bass beats over them, that would end up getting used in lesbian sex scenes in stuff she'd watch when she was a teenager, whenever whoever was making the show couldn't afford to license Portishead songs, the go-to-music of lesbian sex scenes everywhere.

Either way, this "Sail Away" song was playing. Really, really loudly from somewhere she couldn't see.

She was going to say something to herself about how this was the oddest music to play at this volume, unless she *was* at a country club…well, maybe one for deaf people, but when she tried to speak, she couldn't hear herself.

Well, that was nothing new. She had been to loud shows at clubs a lot, anyway, so she put her fingers in her ears and tried to make the witty comment to no one in particular again, but still couldn't hear herself.

That was odd. It wasn't the Enya that was preventing her from hearing herself. There was just nothing coming out of her vocal chords when she'd try to speak. She even tried screaming, but nothing came out. Normally, this would be a reason to panic, but she had been in a situation like this before.

She had tried Ketamine once. That went poorly.

Sail away, Sail away, Sail away...

Figuring it best not to dwell on the lack of being able to communicate verbally, she realized she didn't recognize the room she was in. It was white. Very white. So incredibly white. Clean and pristine, there was a children's tea table set in the center of the room. It reminded her of that George Lucas movie he made before Star Wars. Not American Graffiti. The one in the future that sounded like the little sound promo before movies. *THX-something or other.* Not that she had seen it, but she had seen pictures once. And the rooms in that seemed plenty white. Like this one.

Of course, there were no tea parties in that movie, or at least, she didn't think there were. That would be a very odd dystopian future if he had put tea parties in it. Or maybe the Best Future Ever. But either way, there was definitely a tea party going on here, in front of her. Sitting at it were two people she recognized to be Jesus Christ and Theodore Roosevelt, holding the tiny tea cups with their thumbs and index fingers, along with a whole bunch of stuffed animals. Mostly bunnies with tentacles, swaying gently to the music. She knew, automatically, that one of them was named Munnehausen. This didn't confuse her as much as it probably should have.

Jesus Christ was all dressed up for the crucifixion, complete with dirty loincloth, a bloody crown of thorns, and matching stigmata that was doing a very good job of messing up the white tablecloth on the table, his skin covered in a thick layer of grime and his hair uncombed and matted with blood; Roosevelt, on the other hand, looked like he was ready to go on safari, in a hunting suit and coonskin cap, medals adorning his chest, a monocle above his famously thick mustache.

It was at that point that Julie's confusion grew, for under her chest, the lyrics of the song were floating in the air, like bubbles, but bubbles in the Times New Roman font, with a little white ball bouncing on the word that was being recited:

We can sigh, say goodbye to Ross and his dependencies

She really wasn't sure who Ross was, but she was convinced that whoever was providing her and the little bouncing ball with the lyrics was probably wrong. Julie shrugged and figured she might as well go get herself some tea, only to notice that she wasn't walking, but roller skating. And she was dressed like an angel in a really bad 2nd grade production of the Nativity Story. In fact, the angel outfit probably would fit a second grader a lot more comfortably than it fit her, the hem of the dress about halfway between her thigh and hips, a few inches of panties exposed. She found herself glad that she had remembered to shave.

Or had she? She actually didn't remember shaving, but a quick rub of her crotch revealed underneath the cotton of the child's underwear she was wearing, that it was, indeed, smooth. Before she could contemplate this situation, the two guests at the tea party got her attention.

Jesus looked at her and nodded, saying, "I greatly enjoy breath mints."

In response, Theodore Roosevelt met her eyes and said, in a voice that sounded more like Foghorn Leghorn than Theodore Roosevelt, "Did you know, I say, did you know? I am quite adept at fucking both bulls and moose."

"It's not mooses?" Jesus asked, glancing quizzically at him.

"Oh, no, dear sir. The possessive pronoun of moose is still moose. Much like our friend, the majestic otter."

"I had thought that tadpoles grow into frogs when they get older."

"You have to be quiet because, sometimes, I say, sometimes, sir, candy is made in Pennsylvania."

"Hershey Park?"

"Right off that there Hershey Highway!"

They high-fived each other. A studio audience somewhere applauded.

Julie made a face. This was not the type of conversation she'd expect Jesus Christ and Theodore Roosevelt to have. Okay, in truth, she was unsure what exactly they *would* talk about, but this was not it. Also, she was pretty sure the tentacled bunny's name was now Munchausen and she didn't expect Theodore Roosevelt to suddenly start shooting lasers out of his mouth. Lasers he used to fry a gecko that had materialized on the ceiling above her.

Oh, fuck, she thought, *I'm dreaming.*

CHAPTER 3

Julie woke up, back in her room in her apartment in Brooklyn, her pillow wet with drool, face down, above the covers, her right leg straight, her left leg lifted up at hip level, as though her bed was a lover she couldn't wait to give herself to. There was no Enya and she was dressed, not in an angel outfit, but as she had been the night before when Kelly had woken her up to bother her, in her wife beater and boyshorts. Her room, as usual, looked like a cyclone had hit it. A very drunk cyclone; empty beer cans, Absolut and Jager bottles everywhere, clothes, mostly of the black variety, all over the bed and floor, a red bicycle leaning against the room's lone window, the blood red shades duct taped to the windowsill, faded posters of The Casualties and The Exploited and The Ramones and a host of other punk luminaries (a large number of which started with "The") adorning the walls. The floor was carpet, a white that had turned grey long before Julie even moved into the apartment.

The room constantly smelled of incense, the vanguard in Julie's constant war to block the smell of stale alcohol.

She reached forward in the fog of her room to her dresser, flailing forward, blindly, her hand fumbling around briefly before awkwardly grabbing its quarry and bringing it back to her field of vision. She looked at her cellphone, a black Galaxy with a blue case, covered in 99 Cent Store Jesus stickers that she had found at Coney Island and glitter, which besides having another unread text from Lucy on it, told her it was 8:03am, an hour from when she was supposed to be at work, and grumbled to a world that couldn't hear her a quiet, "Fuck," before closing her eyes and going back to sleep.

CHAPTER 4

Julie woke up again. Over a dance beat, Christian Bale was telling her it was fucking distracting before taunting, "Oh, good!" That was her work ringtone. A call this early meant that she had overslept. Again. Fuck.

Her eyes still refusing to open, her body still in the exact same position she had been in earlier, she put the phone to her ear and made a grunting acknowledgement..

"Yo, J.U.G...What up? You comin' in today?" asked the voice on the other end, her main dispatcher, a Latino man by the name of Caesar. She didn't really like him. For someone who was supposed to be assigning her work, he occasionally seemed to be completely unaware of the actual geography of the Five Boroughs of Manhattan. He had a habit of assigning her pick-ups several dozen blocks from where she had made her last drop-off, something the other dispatchers, thankfully, never did. Days where Caesar was sick or on vacation were something of a treat for Julie.

"Uh...fuck...yeah...rough night..." she responded, using all of her strength to force herself to open her eyes. It took a herculean effort, quite honestly. Considering that most of the previous night had involved her cleaning out an abandoned bar, with a rift leading to the Third Realm, of a number of creatures that had tentacles where their heads should be and heads where their arms should be, all while on a combination of Jager and Molly, calling it merely a "rough night" was an understatement.

"Your ass is two hours late already! You're killin' me, yo! Killin' me! Get outta bed and come on down! C'mon, girl!"

"Sorry... I'll...I'll call when I'm downtown." The part about being sorry was also a lie.

She hung up the phone and cursed to herself again, before forcing herself to endure yet another of the trials of a demigod: this time, attempting to sit up. She gave a loud yawn, swatted her hair out of her face, and then stretched, her eyes trying to adjust to the morning, despite her taped down shades filtering out as much light as they could. Julie had slain many a demon in her life, but her oldest and most bitter nemesis was the dawn.

One long, thin, newly-tattooed leg found its way to the floor, soon followed by another. She stood up, picked the underwear from her butt yet again (these boyshorts were probably a size too small), and narrowly avoided stepping on her Exploited, Black Flag, and Catholic Saint-stickered laptop on the floor, instead knocking over an empty bottle of Jager, the bottle loudly rolling under her bed before being stopped short by something else glass, most likely another empty bottle of Jager.

She looked down at the floor, sleepily singing The Ramones' "Chainsaw," to herself, grabbed a pair of camouflage pants from near her feet, and sniffed the crotch of them to see if they were clean enough to wear today. She threw them on the bed and reached for a pair of black skinny jeans, repeating the sniffing ritual. These smelled lived-in. A mixture of beer and sweat. Not the worst fluids she had found on her pants over the years, but not really ideal for a day of hard bicycle labor.

"Oh ohohoh oh oh ah whoa whoa whoa

Oh ohohoh oh oh ah whoa whoa whoa…"

Throwing the black skinny jeans onto the floor, she reached for the camouflage pants. Of the two pairs of pants within reaching distance, they were very clearly the cleanest. She only remembered wearing them twice since the last wash and they didn't smell like she had spilled anything on them. They'd do. She had been too broke to do laundry for a few weeks, so this ritual had become a daily event on those mornings where she woke up in her own bed.

The day's pants decided, she maneuvered over the various obstacles the floor had to offer to a dresser covered in beer bottles and candles of various Catholic Saints, casually opening an empty drawer. Of course, she hadn't expected it to be empty, as this was where she usually kept her panties, but it did drive home the point of how long it had been since she had washed her clothes.

Oh well, she thought, slipping off her boyshorts, *Goes with the camo.*

She giggled to herself, and while looking in a mirror, to see if she had to pluck the area between her eyebrows again (she didn't), skipped ahead a few tracks on the Ramones album in her head and started singing,

"They're doing their best, they do what they can
To get them ready for Vietnam…"

CHAPTER 5

Julie managed to get herself to work eventually, picking up and delivering packages from people too lazy and rich to deliver them themselves. It was lower-rung job on the scale of employed society, but it was the only one she could think of that wouldn't fire her if she took a month off at any given time.

And she got to dress how she wanted, they didn't give her shit about her tattoos or piercings, and riding a bike around New York City was a nice way of learning where everything was in the five boroughs.

She, her two sisters, and her parents had moved around a lot as a child, but it was mostly small towns in the Midwest, and so when she was old enough to move out on her own, New York was her first priority. Her parents had met there and from their stories, especially her mother's, it always seemed so much freer and accepting than any of the small bastions of nowhere she had grown up in.

She had been a bike messenger for the last four years. The pay sucked and she was often broke, but it was better than being stuck in some office with a little noose around the pants suit uniform she'd have to come in everyday, chained behind a computer, working at her miserable, soul-sucking job until the day she finally settled down and squeezed out some other miserable, beaten-down salaryman's brats.

Nah, Julie had a life that allowed her to get the most fun from the least effort and there was still that family tradition she would engage in for extra cash and occasional thrills. Her dad had always made it seem like it was no big deal, but when she got involved, it was like being high while fucking in the driver's side of a speeding car, a speeding car that was heading towards a cliff while it was on fire. Both the cliff and the car. The adrenaline was overwhelming and she was hooked on it.

Like her own personal lap-attached Bat Signal, she had a second phone on her at all times that was only to be used to tell her she had a job in this very tradition. Vera, her kinda-sorta "other" boss had given it to her. Vera, an eccentric but friendly woman with thick accent that it took Julie two months to figure out was Boston-based, ran an agency that specialized in low-level supernatural problems. Julie had found out about the agency from Craigslist, thinking it was a prank or a scam at first, as did probably most people not experienced in the occult who saw it. Of course, it turned out that it was totally legit and Julie, having grown up dealing with this sort of thing, found herself with a second, way more enjoyable job.

Of course, the woman may have been able to tell Julie when there were supernatural low-level emergencies happening, but she couldn't seem to understand the concept of a decent phone plan, since the phone didn't make outgoing calls, except back to Vera's office.

She had told Julie that she would be glad to go for whatever plan Julie wanted if Julie would pay for the phone. Julie decided to just stick with the status quo.

CHAPTER 6

Her uneventful day at work went by quicker than it would for most people, probably because Julie had picked up some beer early in the afternoon, and gotten herself a pleasant buzz to make picking up envelopes at the hot, sticky, uncomfortable service entrance on 40th and 2nd Avenue, only to go back into the icy cold outdoors, and then deliver them to the hospital waiting room-like atmosphere of 300 West 57th Street's messenger center a little easier.

Sure, she wasn't really supposed to be drinking on the job, but she also wasn't supposed to be carrying a giant serrated knife or a baseball bat or any number of the things she had in her messenger bag, either. Or occasionally be on acid.

Those were definite no-no's. But considering that most messengers were criminals, musicians, or some combination of the two, her behavior wasn't any worse than any of her co-workers when she was buzzed.

The day at work turned to an evening at a Bushwick club so nondescript, it didn't even have a sign, where a bedroom acquaintance was playing a hardcore evening. They had about 10 people in the crowd, and they really sounded like they wanted to be Agnostic Front, in the worst way, but the guitar player, Mike, had a nice cock, big enough to hurt, but not too much, and she always loved getting into pits where big, sweaty bald guys thought a skinny little chick like her couldn't hang. Thankfully, since they did sound like Agnostic Front instead of one of the newer bands that had appropriated the genre description of "hardcore," she was guaranteed a bunch of sweaty bald guys, instead of a large number of white kids dressed like members of the Wu-Tang Clan, thinking the pit is a place for karate, while the backwards-baseball capped singer kinda scream-raps and bops up and down like he's on a pogo stick when he isn't gesturing with his hands like he's having a seizure. Sometimes, there'd even be a second backwards-baseball capped singer scream-rapping.

She always hated when some fourteen year-old in baggy jeans (and a backwards baseball cap that matched the singer's) would do a jumping sweep kick or some shit (she didn't even know if a jumping sweep kick was a real thing or not, but that's what it looked like, so she'd call it that) near her head and she'd have to take her steel toed Docs and give him a swift, angry kick right to the balls and a punch to the mouth. She didn't have patience for fourteen year-olds in baggy jeans doing karate. Or fourteen year-olds. Or even karate, for that matter.

Finishing up a song that sounded incredibly like Agnostic Front's "Existence of Hate" (but was apparently called "Watch Your Back"), the band said they were going to do something a little bit different and proceeded to break into a cover of The Exploited's "Maggie." This caused Julie to go extra crazy in the pit, which had now grown to a colossal 15 people, two of which were even fellow women. *Wow,* she thought, *they were even bringing in the chicks. This band was going places. Might even have a full 30 people next year if they kept this up.*

As the fast and odd beat started, leading into bass, leading into guitar, she ping-ponged herself, violently, between several men many times her size, smiling when face would meet shoulder or shoulder would meet big, beefy chest. She stopped charging at people during the chorus, jumping up on the back of some absolutely huge guy who seemed more confused than anything that she was on his back, and yelled along with the song, since it had always been one of her favorites (In fact, she was pretty sure the guitarist was doing this just so they could fuck again. The vocalist seemed to not be totally into it, using his heavy Brooklyn accent in almost defiant contrast to the original version's Northern English accent of vocalist Wattie Buchan).

"Maggie! Maggie! Maggie! Maggie!

You fucking cunt!"

The chorus over, she used the guy as leverage and propelled herself back towards another random bald guy, who connected with her with a big, meaty thud, drowned out by the sounds of the music. She repeated this process throughout the entire song.

After the song was over, Julie cheered louder than anybody else there, which wasn't that hard to do, since most of the big scary skinhead dudes seemed to think they were too cool to cheer an Exploited cover.

The vocalist looked at her, rolled his eyes and said, "I hope that fuckin' gets Mike laid tonight," before introducing another of their originals that might as well have been Agnostic Front covers, this one called "An Eye for an Eye."

Ah, so I had been right, she thought with a giggle. They were playing "Maggie" purposely for her. Well, that was nice, she guessed. Romance obviously wasn't dead in the New York Hardcore scene. Of course, had she been named Maggie, this probably wouldn't have been as romantic a gesture. *Well, maybe,* she thought. It wasn't like the song wasn't about a particular Maggie in particular (Former English Prime Minister Maggie Thatcher, to be precise) and not women named Maggie in general, although if she had ever dated anyone by that name and had had an ugly breakup, you can bet she would have played that at every opportunity at every dive bar she could find it on the jukebox... especially if this other hypothetical Maggie was there on any of the given hypothetical nights she was thinking of.

Remembering that she wasn't wearing underwear tonight, she figured she might as well wait until their set was over and then sit on Mike's lap in the bathroom for a little bit. She wasn't that horny tonight, but no one else in the club was that attractive to her (she liked slamming into big, beefy sweaty bald men in only the most platonic of ways), so she figured she might as well have a quickie to say thanks for the song.

As if in response, she felt a vibration on her hip that she immediately recognized to be her "other" work phone sending her a text.

Now, *that* was exciting. She looked down at the text.

Possession. Townhouse. Madison and E. 93rd

Mike's somewhat nice cock would have to wait another night. *Quickly, to the Batmobile.*

CHAPTER 7

It took her a little over an hour to get there by subway. Both the L and the connecting 6 she switched to arrived within minutes of her reaching their respective platforms. She had thought of just riding her bike up to 93rd, but she was too drunk to get there without swerving into a cab or something at this time of night. Or eventually would be when she drank the bottle of Jager she had swiped from the bar at the club when the bartender was arguing with somebody and had left it too close to the counter.

A quick glance at the rapidly swaying display on her phone told her it was 9:13 when she got to the townhouse. The bottle was half finished and all the ritzy stores on Madison, the ones that always gave her the stink eye whenever she'd deliver to them, dark and closed.

She was not walking straight at this point and it took her a few minutes to chain her bike up to a parking meter before ringing the buzzer of the building. She checked three times to make sure she had closed the lock properly before finally making the arduous, zig-zagging journey of 10 feet to the door. During this vast trek, a lamp post kept trying to veer into her path, but Julie was just too dexterous to be fooled by the machinations of such a malicious inanimate object. The first leg of the quest complete, she pressed the buzzer on the second try, missing the first time because the goddamn button kept moving.

A worried blond, middle-aged woman answered the door, swaying back and forth while standing in the doorway. She wore a sweater of a color that only middle-aged moms wore, pants that were pulled up to just below her breasts, and various gold jewelry that Julie found ugly, even if a voice in the back of her head kept telling her that each of those baubles were probably worth more than she made in 10 years.

"Whoa. Are you okay?" Julie asked.

"What? Who are you?"

Suddenly, Julie realized the woman wasn't swaying. Only her vision was. It was time to be professional. Pretend to be sober. *Steady your eyes, goddammit!*

"Hi. I'm Julie Golighty and I'm your rep-rep-representative demonol...demonologist...for the night."

"You're drunk."

"I assure you," Julie said, the "sh" sound in the word emphasized way more than she would have liked it to have been, considering she was trying to pretend to be sober, "that my s-services are rendered unto...Caesar, as...ummmmmmm...wait a minute, I know this one..."

The woman started to close the door, at which point, Julie stuck her foot in.

"N-no wait...you've gotta wait. Wait. Wait. Shhhhhhhh...let's not be rash here. I'm here to solve your demon problem...I can do it. I'm alright. I can do it. I've done it before twice as drunk as this."

"So, you often show up drunk when people's..."

"N-no. Not sure why I said that, but don't worry...ummmmm...there's a priest, right?"

"Yes, currently, in my daughter's room, there is a priest."

"You know, he's probably drunk too. Yup. Blasted three sheets to the wind. They always carry one of those little things...the little things...caskets in their pockets with alcohol in them."

"Flasks?"

"Yes! Flasks. Flasks. Flasks filled with alcohol! I know. You don't know. I know! I've seen a million of these."

"You have?'

"Yessss...I'm an expert! Expert de...demon...demonologist."

Julie, realizing after the fact that her pronunciation of "expert" was currently closer to "esper," nodded in a manner that almost knocked her over and then rolled up the sleeve of her leather jacket to show her left wrist to the woman. Next to a tattoo of a goat-faced serpent with six eyes were a tally of seven notches.

"S-seriously, every one of those....I...I...ummmm...hold on."

Julie quickly turned around and then vomited onto the sidewalk, the woman looking on in horror. It was orange. That was odd. She didn't remember mixing any orange juice into anything she drank the last couple days. *Hmmm. Very odd, indeed.*

Julie wiped her mouth with her sleeve and then turned to the woman and smiled.

"See? I'm all better now."

The woman narrowed her eyes, all the wrinkles of her face seeming to express rage, and grabbed a cell phone out of her pocket, dialing a series of numbers while staring daggers at Julie. This wasn't going how she had hoped it would have.

"Hello?" the middle aged woman spoke into her phone, "Yes! It's me, Mrs. Dawn Abernathy…What seems to be the problem?!? Well, for one, the employee you sent here is drunk. *Visibly drunk*. She just vomited on the sidewalk outside my home."

"I'm fine now. Threw all the…alcohol…up. All gone. Totally sober now. Gimme my chips."

"It is not gone! You're still holding half a bottle full in your hand!"

Julie looked down at the Jagermeister in her hand.

"Oh."

"What type of business are you…No, I understand that, but this is un…You are just telling me…Your *best* girl? I find that hard to…Seven confirmed? *Seven?!?*"

Julie pointed at her tattoo, drunkenly.

"So, you're saying that the alcohol *helps* her deal with what she's about to face?"

"That…that is totally it, you know," Julie slurred.

"Can she sober up a little before she…You realize the size of the lawsuit you're facing if she makes things worse, right? I swear that I will make sure you…Okay, I will let her in. This is *my little girl*, we're talking about here. If *anything* happens to her, I swear that you and this drunken employee of yours *will* pay…Okay…put her on? Fine."

The woman handed Julie her phone with strict instructions not to drop it.

Julie gave her a wobbly thumbs up and then put her ear to the phone.

"Ahoy-hoy."

"Julie, how drunk are you?" Vera asked, her accent heavy on the South Boston, "You can handle this, right? I don't have to call in Thomas, do I?"

"Thomas can suck it," she said, heavily slurring the "s" sound, "I-I got this."

"You sure you don't want to get a coffee or something?"

"Have I ever let you down?"

"Not per say, but..."

"Then lemme go all America on this thing's ass! Whoosh! No more demon! USA! USA!"

"I really wish you wouldn't say things like that in front of the clients."

"I have to tell you, Vera...Tonight, Mike's band, they totally sounded like Agnostic Front. Oh my god! It was like, 'Get your own sty...'"

"Julie?"

"What?"

"Julie. Just go get rid of the demon and you can tell me later."

"Okey-dokey."

Julie ended the call and put the phone in her pocket. The woman glared at her and Julie remembered it wasn't her phone, handing it back to the woman.

The woman, looking down at the floor, made a sour expression, and then clasped her hands at her hips, poking her wedding ring with her opposite finger. She sighed and then looked at Julie, her eyes red with tears. Almost under her breath, she gave in.

"I'm going to trust you with this. I'm going to trust you because nothing else seems to be working. Don't you dare hurt my baby further."

Julie nodded a nod that almost knocked her over and then said, "Ma'am, I'm good. Seven of these things I've done. Seven. Seven. Sssssseven..."

The woman shook her head in disgust and let Julie come in.

"Please, whatever you do, do not vomit on the carpet. I just had it cleaned after..."

"She peed, didn't she?"

"Yes, I had guests over and she just stood there in the living room and urinated herself in front of us all. It was horrifying."

"Seen it before. Which room?"

"Up the stairs. First door on the right."

Julie looked down at her hands, trying to remember which one was her right and which one was her left.

"This one," the woman said, sighing heavily, tapping Julie on the right shoulder.

"Knew that. Just testing you. Making sure *you* knew."

Julie slipped off her leather jacket and handed it, vaguely in the direction of the woman, saying, "Here, hold this. I don't want to get anything nasty on it."

Julie then began her trek up the stairs. This was not easy, as her feet and eyes seemed to have different ideas of where each step was.

Once or twice, she had to grab the banister to stop herself from falling.

Her vision began to flicker as she got closer to her destination.

No, wait, she realized, *that actually* is *the light bulbs.* They were flickering.

Typical. Minor league demons always liked to act like little fucking puffer fish and put up a big show for the civilians. Hovering beds, peeing in odd places, rude remarks about people's mothers. It was all for show. This would probably be easier than she thought.

She opened the door to the little girl's room, a blast of cold air hitting her in the face. It was, at least, 20 degrees colder in the room than it was outside. She wished she had kept her jacket.

But fuck that shit, it was showtime.

Inside the eerily blue-tinted room, an elderly priest held a crucifix in the face of a scarred and bloody little girl. The girl's pupils were rolled up into her head as her tongue flicked suggestively at the priest, a line of green drool running down her chin, adding to the many stains on what looked like formerly white pajamas.

She was tied to the bed, making loud growling noises, as the priest fought with all the spiritual power he had to keep her down.

Julie noticed the bed was levitating a good six or seven inches off the ground. Yup. This one was totally fucking minor league.

"I cast you out, unclean spirit!" the priest yelled, "It is he that commands you! It is God the Father who commands you! It is God, the son who…"

"FUCK YOU, FATHER! FUCK YOUR GOD! FUCK YOUR WEAK FAITH!"

"It is God, the son who commands you! It is the Holy Spirit that commands you! It is…"

"YOU WILL BURN IN HELL WITH YOUR WHORE OF A MOTHER! SHE IS BURNING, FOREVER, IN TORMENT, FATHER! WOULD YOU LIKE TO TALK TO HER, FATHER! SHE WANTS TO KNOW WHY HER LITTLE RICKY LET HER

DIE ALONE! SHE IS RIGHT HERE! WE WILL SHOW YOU HER CUNT!!"

Okay, then. Julie cleared her throat loudly, and stood there, tapping her foot with her hands on her hips.

The demon and the priest stopped their interaction and turned to stare at her.

"You cannot be in here! This is God's work!" the priest yelled at her, a look of absolute concern on his face, "Please! Your soul is in danger just being near the…"

"LET THE WHORE COME TO ME!!" the demon said, smiling a black and green smile.

"Please, you must leave! This is…"

"NO! WE WILL FUCK HER WITH YOUR CRUCIFIX! WE WILL FUCK HER OOZING GASH! WE WILL…"

Julie cleared her throat her again. And made a shush noise motion to the priest and the demon.

"WE WILL…"

Julie shushed the demon. It stopped talking.

She waited a moment or two to see if she had everyone's complete and undivided attention before speaking.

"Okay. First, *padre*: You're on the bench."

"What?"

"Apparently, this is taking way too long and the woman here wanted to call in someone who knows what they're doing, so you gotta go."

"What are you talking about? This is a delicate and dangerous process! You can't just have any layman off the street…"

"*Padre,* how many of these you done?"

"This is my second in thirty years! I once came across the demon Pazuzu in the deserts of…"

"No, you didn't. That was just a little minor bitch of a demon, like this one. They talk all big, but you didn't run into the Lord of All Fevers and Plague, or you'd know it by being very, very dead."

Julie was very impressed with herself for only slightly slurring her words during all this.

"What do you know of…"

"Seven, *padre*. Done seven of these before. So, why don't you go find yourself an altar boy or something and take five while the adult handles the big scaaawy demon."

"OH YES, FATHER! LEAVE HER ALONE WITH…"

"You," Julie said, wobbling a little more than she would have liked, "You! You shut the fuck up. I'll get to *you* in a second. '*Oozing gash?!?*' Eww. You're very, very…rude. Very rude. Potty mouth. So, you shut up."

"Are you inebriated?!?" the priest asked.

"Yes. Yes, I am," Julie responded, "Now, run along."

"Now, wait just a minute, miss! I will have you know that I am…"

"Holy shit! What's that in the hallway! Is the mother possessed too?!?" Julie suddenly yelled, looking back over her shoulder out of the room, jumping back from the door in fear.

"Where?!? I must see!" the priest said, rushing to the hallway to see what Julie was talking about.

His back turned to her, Julie whipped a stun-gun out of her messenger bag and shocked the priest. He fell over, convulsing in the hallway, as Julie closed the door behind him. He was probably still okay…kinda. As long as he didn't have a heart condition and what were the chances of an old man with a stressful job having one of those, right?

She took a swig of her Jager and then smiled at the demon.

"Hi."

The demon smiled back from within the body of the girl.

"WE ARE AMUSED BY YOU!"

"Wonderful."

Julie stumbled closer to the bed.

"DO YOU SEEK TO SHOCK US WITH YOUR WEAPON, TOO?"

"Nope. Won't need to."

"OH?"

"That's right. Not gonna need it."

"THEN YOU WILL DIE, SCREAMING!"

Julie rolled her eyes and yawned.

"ARE YOU MOCKING US?!?"

"Are you mocking us?" she said, in a voice intended to sound like a stupid person.

"WE WILL…"

"Shuddup."

Julie reached into her bag for a moment, fumbled about for a bit, and then pulled out a salt shaker. The demon looked at her, puzzled.

Julie, using one hand to steady herself against the walls, started pouring salt on the ground, in a circle around the bed.

"AH, WE SEE! SEND OUT THE HOLY MAN AND CALL IN A WITCH!"

Julie didn't respond. She was busy trying to make sure that, in her drunken state, what she was making was, at least, kinda circular.

"SO, YOU SEEK TO CREATE A CIRCLE FROM WHICH WE CANNOT LEAVE?!? HAHAHAHAHA!!! THAT WILL NOT GET US OUT OF THE GIRL! HAHAHA!! YOU STUPID, DRUNKEN WITCH BITCH, YOU ARE DOING NOTHING TO STOP US!!"

Julie finished the salt kinda-circle and then threw the salt shaker at the demon, conking it on the head.

It growled in rage at her. The demon, not the salt shaker.

"YOU STRIKE US?!? COME STAND INSIDE THE CIRCLE, WITCH! WHERE WE CAN…"

Julie stumbled her way into the circle and then folded her arms, staring right into the eyes of the demon-possessed girl.

"OH…"

The room shook as though there was an earthquake, the glass of the windows shattered, the bed frame rocking to its limits, and the demon roared. The tiny lights of the candles around the room grew to large fires, blackening the ceiling above them, and tinting the room red, as demonic laughter filled the air. Stuffed animals fell off shelves, a glass vase shattered, and dresser drawers emptied their contents.

Julie, unimpressed, looked around the room, nodded her head and then walked right up to the demon, slapping it across the face.

"That all you got?"

"WE WILL SWALLOW YOUR SOUL!!"

"Okay, did you seriously just quote *Evil Dead* at me?"

"*EGO TUUM DEVORABIT CUNNUS!*"

"Oh, getting Latin with our insults, eh?"

"*EGO FUTUO FACIEM TUAM!*"

"*E pluribus unum.*"

"*VOUS AUREZ ROTIR EN ENFER!*"

"*Le chien brun chassé le chat noir.*"

"*BYDD CHI DDIFETHIR SGRECHIAN!*"

"*Erin go bragh.*"

"*YOB TVA'YOO MAT, BLYAD!*"

"*Hab sosli' Quch, P'Tok!*"

"THAT IS NOT EVEN A LANGUAGE!"

"The internet would disagree."

"DO NOT MOCK US, WITCH! WE WILL DEVOUR YOU! WE RIDE THE VERY WIND OF YOUR DESPAIR! WE THRIVE ON YOUR NIGHTMARES! WE ARE EVERYWHERE AND SEE ALL! WE ARE LEGION, FOR WE ARE..."

"We are a bitch. That's what 'we' are."

"WHAT?"

"You heard me. Don't be coming at me all Wendy O. Williams when your ass is Katy Perry. You don't even have a body of your own. Look at you all hiding in a little girl."

"YOU HAVE NO IDEA OF OUR..."

"Of your *vagina*! Because you're a pussy. You may scare Max Von Sydow back there, but come on, *I'm drunk*. Like, really, really drunk. And I don't have time for this shit. I see things all the time that can take corporeal form without having to hide in little kids and I kick their asses. That makes me kinda, like, 'Straight Outta Compton,' and you, like, 'Please Hammer Don't Hurt Him.' No, no. You're not even 'Please Hammer Don't Hurt Him,' you're 'Ice Ice Baby.' I'm the fucking Sex Pistols and you're Avril Lavigne. I'm Slayer and you're Warrant. I'm Iron Maiden and you're Tygers of fucking Pan Tang. I'm..."

"I HAVE NO IDEA OF WHAT YOU SPEAK!"

"Ah ha! See? You said, 'I.' That's singular. '*We* are legion.' Psssh. Shuddup, bitch. You ain't Legion. You ain't shit. Stop using plural."

The demon's face contorted into a mask of rage, tempered with a light sprinkling of confusion. It glared at Julie, hatefully, and proceeded to projectile vomit in her direction.

She dodged it, gagged, and then proceeded to vomit on the demon. She really could not figure out what she had ingested that was orange.

"WHAT IS WRONG WITH YOU?"

"Didn't you hear me? I said I was drunk. That's like the second time tonight."

"I WILL..."

"Shuddup. Don't wanna hear it. Don't care. Was about to get laid when I got the text about you. You don't know. You don't have any idea. Shut up. Shut up."

The demon just seemed confused at this point.

"So, you're going to leave that little girl and fuck off, so I can go get laid."

"HAHAHAHA!!! SHALL I JUMP INTO YOU, INSTEAD, WITCH?"

Julie fumbled in her messenger bag for a bit again and then pulled out a green teddy bear that had seen much, much better days in its time. It was beaten up beyond belief, stuffing exposed all over, with one brown eye sewn on in a not-quite-symmetrical place. There was a rusted turn-key in the bear's stomach.

"Nope. You're going to jump into this," she said, turning the turn-key and then letting a tinny version of "Happy Birthday to You" play for a few seconds.

"HAHAHAHA!!! AND WHY WOULD I DO THAT?"

"Figured you were gonna ask that..."

Julie reached into her bag again and pulled out two tiny bells. They were about the size of silver dollar, two little brass bells with several millimeter-high Tibetan blessings and curses carved into every bit of their surface. The demon's face contorted with fear upon seeing them.

"YOU WOULD NOT!"

Julie nodded her head and rang the two little bells.

The sound they produced was small and almost gentle, barely a step above wind-chimes. But there was something awful, something ominous behind the tiny little bells.

The room around them started to turn dark. Everything outside of the circle they were in faded away until all around them was blackness. There was silence. Uncomfortable silence. The silence of the grave. The silence one imagines is only possible at the moment before an atomic bomb would destroy your city. The silence before the screams begin.

Suddenly, there was the loud rushing sound of howls on the wind, but the wind was not so much wind but wailing spirits violently thrashing through the air. The smell of sulfur assaulted Julie's nose. The room they were in was gone, replaced by undulating mountains of flesh and bone, reaching high into the blood red sky. A living land, where the very ground was miles and miles of exposed muscle, stretching and pulling constantly.

Shadows gathered all around the circle, the whispers of thousand of voices, speaking languages rarely ever heard by human ears, swirled around them in an unholy tornado of silent screams.

"THIS IS NOT SAFE! WE MUST LEAVE!"

"Not before you leave the little girl. I gots ta get paid."

"I WILL KILL HER! TAKE US BACK NOW!"

"Nope. You kill her, I just break the circle."

"YOU WOULDN'T! THEY'LL TEAR YOU APART!"

Julie started laughing. In fact, she was bent over from laughter, the way only someone really drunk can get.

"WHAT IS SO FUNNY, WOMAN?"

"That whatever's in the Third Realm will tear me apart. I've been here many, many times before. Bitch, I come here when I want to relax."

She rolled up her right sleeve to show some of her tattoos.

"WHY WOULD YOU HAVE A TATTOO OF A I'KLESF? YOU HAVE STOOD UP TO A I'KLESF?"

"Yup. Killed one that decided to venture into Greenpoint. Rare, but it happens. You, on the other hand, you're a little First Realm bitch. You don't even have your own form, so to come into my world, you've gotta jump into someone. Down here, though, they won't care if you're in a body. They'll just tear your ass up. Metaphorically speaking, obviously, as you need a body to have an ass. But, then again, right now, you *do* currently have a body, so... "

There was a shaking of the muscle-ground and there was a loud roar in the distance, the thud-squish sound of approaching footsteps growing loud.

"Oh fuck," Julie blurted out, a tone of true concern in her voice.

"YOU FEAR IT TOO! YOU MAY HAVE BEEN ABLE TO SLAY ONE IN YOUR REALM, BUT HERE, WHERE IT IS AT ITS STRONGEST..."

"No no no. That wasn't what I was upset about. I think the transfer between dimensions sobered me up. I don't feel drunk anymore. That doesn't happen all the time, but when it does, it sucks."

"WHO CARES?!? WE MUST LEAVE IMMEDIATELY! THERE IS NO TELLING HOW LONG THE CIRCLE WILL LAST!"

"You're right. There isn't. And you know, as a First Realmer, you're as much of a target down here as me and the little girl. More so, really. So...you might want to be moving into the teddy bear, right about now."

"I WILL NOT!"

The roar grew to an almost deafening level as the wet sounds of footsteps on flesh were joined by the sound of even more footsteps. There were, at least, three of them. And they were coming closer.

"PLEASE, WE MUST LEAVE! I WILL GIVE YOU ANYTHING YOU WANT!"

"Whoa. Just because I took you to the wrong hood doesn't suddenly make you a genie. You aren't granting me any wishes, so don't try to play that game. You know the deal. You leave the girl, you go in the bear, we go back to Earth. Otherwise…"

Julie started to nudge the salt with her boot. The demon screamed in terror.

"FINE! FINE! I WILL GO INTO THE BEAR! BUT DO NOT THINK THAT I WILL STAY THERE FOREVER!"

"Get to it."

With a loud rush of energy, the demon left the girl. Her body regained a human appearance, albeit one with several scars on her face, from whatever damage the demon had done while it was in her body. The girl didn't even open her eyes, so physically and spiritually exhausted that she'd probably never know she had been in another dimension while she had been out.

The bear in Julie's hands radiated a darkness that, to most people, would be overwhelming, but to Julie was nothing. She picked up the bear, it seeming to glare at her with malice in its plastic eye.

She turned the turn-key in the bear's stomach, which would normally produce a lullaby, but now allowed the demon to speak for as long as the mechanism turned.

"I AM IN THE BEAR NOW! TAKE US BACK TO EARTH! AND I…"

The demon's voice slowed down and then stopped, altogether, until she wound it up some more.

"PROMISE YOU THAT I WILL SEE YOU SUFFER SOME DAY! NOW, WHAT ARE YOU WAITING…"

This time, when it stopped talking, she patted it on the head. She reached into her bag again and pulled out one of the two bells she had previously used to shift worlds.

As she pulled out the bell, three hulking entities appeared over the horizon. The I'Klesf, which Julie could never pronounce properly, resembled large, black hooded skeletons, only the hoods were not fabric but congealed flesh, dripping off their huge bodies, each over 20 feet tall, black flame belching forth from each of their bodily orifices, their lower bodies a sharp contrast to their upper bodies, thick and muscular, with hooves, their thighs covered in coarse black needles that most people who saw them mistook for hair. These three were all males. She could tell because of the obscenely long snake-like genitals that hung down to their knees, covered in the same needles as their legs, but with a mouth at the end, complete with tongue and fangs (it should be noted that their testes were inside what looked like two Siamese-twin shriveled heads hanging under the "snake," complete with eyes and a mouth that constantly drooled out the excess black sperm they produced). She waved at the three demons and then proceeded to wind up the bear again, the I'Klesf charging at her now, with purpose.

"THEY ARE HERE! WE MUST LEAVE NOW!"

"Yeah...we should."

With that, she threw the bear out of the circle at the three rampaging demons.

"YOU BITCH! YOU BETRAYED ME! YOU…"

"Yup, I did. Suck it," she said, giggling to herself, before tinkling the bell, as two of the large demons descended upon the screaming teddy bear and the third charged towards her circle.

In the blink of an eye, she and the unconscious little girl were back in the room on East 93rd.

The girl was safe. The job was done.

Julie patted herself on the back and put the bell back into her messenger bag. It then occurred to her that she had been drinking a lot of alcohol tonight and her bladder was quite full.

She looked at the floor, where the demon had vomited, and put her hand on her stomach, thinking for a moment. She shrugged.

A few minutes later, Julie came down the stairs with a lot less effort than it took to get up them, the middle-aged woman looking anxiously at Julie.

"Is it over?"

"Yup."

"My Meghan is safe?"

"Yup."

"And this won't happen again?"

"Usually doesn't."

"And what happened to Father Renaldi? I was expecting him to come down and say something about you?"

"Oh...uh...the demon knocked him out...and totally peed on the rug in her room too."

"Oh dear."

"Well, that's what Home Depot is for, right? So, Vera told you who to make the check out to?"

CHAPTER 8

Jerry had no idea how long he'd been sitting here. His bare skin had been chained to something metal for what felt like forever. He still had the hood over his face, so he couldn't see what was going on, but his hearing had become sharper for it. He been moved once since the van and now found himself in what he assumed, due to the sounds of clanking metal doors and buzzers, was a prison. They had taken him here, sat him down and chained him to something, his hands still behind his back, the zip ties around his wrists biting into his flesh..

The place reeked of human waste, some of it his own, and the stink of an unfathomable amount of body odor. He was sitting on a cold, metal bench, pressed next to men on each side of him. From the bare flesh that rubbed up against his hips, he could feel they were naked, as well. He heard their begging and pleadings, the rumblings of their bodies for food, and the sounds and smells of their bodies no longer being able to hold whatever they had in them. He could hear, not far from here, the wails of women's voices, crying out in terror, just like he and his male fellow captives were.

There had been some sort of commotion not too long along ago. There were screams and a woman yelling defiantly for a bit.

Alarms had sounded loudly and he could hear the sounds of someone being beaten, viciously, the woman's former triumphant yells turning to her screams.

He heard a familiar voice about an hour later. It was Mr. Trent.

"So, what am I looking at here? Why was I interrupted in the middle of a very expensive dinner, Jacobs?"

"We have a problem, Mr. Trent."

"I assumed that. Otherwise, I wouldn't be here. Now, *why* am I here? This place smells like a monkey cage."

"I think you should see it for yourself."

"Jesus Christ, fine. Take me to it."

There were the sounds of footsteps for a few seconds or so.

"I see…How did this happen?"

"Well, security cameras show that Mr. Donaldson went into the cage with the females."

"You people and your urges. You can't just keep your hands and other parts to yourselves?"

"We've never had an incident like this in the 10 years before!"

"I don't want to hear excuses, Jacobs…My my, she bit it clean off didn't she?"

"Yeah. I don't ever wanna see that sort of thing again, I can tell you that, Mr. Trent."

"Did you know the Romans abhorred the concepts of oral sex? It was considered below a Roman man to allow someone under him to have the entire source of his power in their mouth."

"Didn't know that."

"Obviously, neither did Mr. Donaldson. So, which one of our guests did the deed? This one over here looks quite the worse for wear."

"Yeah, it's that one."

Jerry heard Mr. Trent take a few steps and then heard a weary sounding female voice.

"F-f-fuck you all. I-I'm not going to let you tr-treat me…like…this. I-I'm a person. I have a name…I have rights…Even if you can take away…everything else fr-from me. I still have my…dignity."

"That was quite the speech, Monica," Mr. Trent said, he chuckled to himself, "Whitney Houston. 'Greatest Love of All,' right?"

"F-fuck you."

"Hope it was worth it."

There was a very *loud* bang at the sound of a gun being discharged. There were screams everywhere and whimpers from all directions. Crying, Jerry found what urine was still left in his body running down his bare legs.

"Take that and dispose of it somewhere. I have a call to make."

Jerry, over the sounds of panic, could hear what sounded like a body being dragged away as Mr. Trent paused for a few moment and then began speaking into what Jerry assumed was a cellphone.

"Yeah, it's me. We have a problem. Our High Priest decided to get himself some the night before…No, I know there's no rule against that, but there should be. She fought back…He's dead. That's how bad…Yes, 'whoa,' is right…I'm aware His Honor isn't going to be happy about this…We certainly can't do the ritual tomorrow night anymore… Well, him, we're going to have to make it look like some sort of accident at home. We can't very well tell everyone how he died. The man was a respected pillar of the community. We can't tell his family that he was castrated by someone he was trying to…Exactly…Do you have other candidates?…I see…You make the calls…How long? Well, assuming you get someone by Saturday, since I'm very much assuming you won't be able to get someone by tomorrow, we're talking another week…I'm aware of that…His Honor can blame you for hiring someone who couldn't keep it in his pants for that…I'm also aware of that…They will be fine. Just get some IV drips. They're going to need fluids…Nah, humans can survive for three weeks without food. They'll live. But you are going to have to hydrate them, thus the IV drips. However, you have to find someone ASAP or this batch is going to go bad. The stars will only stay aligned for so long and I'm not sure His Honor wants to leave this to chance, considering what this year is…Right…Wednesday. You pay whatever you have to, but you make sure you get someone who isn't going to diddle the merchandise…Right…and don't forget the IV drips. We're going to need those by tomorrow. We weren't expecting our guests to still be our guests by then."

Having heard all that, his stomach seeming to sink through the floor, Jerry found himself doing something he hadn't done since he was a little boy: he began to pray.

CHAPTER 9

Struggling to carry the two Whole Foods grocery bags as she ascended the stairs, Kelly fumbled for the keys to the apartment for a good minute before finally being able to balance everything long enough to unlock the three locks and open the door, the horrors of the living room abomination from a few nights ago momentarily forgotten.

She entered the living room, only to find Julie laying stomach down on the couch, playing something on her little portable Playstation. Her hair was messed up and wet, her body covered in a layer of sweat that gave a sheen to her tattoo-covered back and arms. She was also naked.

"Hey," Julie said, not looking up from her game, "Did you buy toilet paper? We're out."

"Why are you naked?!?"

"What?"

"Why are you naked and sweaty on the couch?"

"Oh…uh…ritual."

"A ritual?"

"Yeah, you know, saving the world from the forces of chaos and stuff. Very, very important. Oh, my stars and garters, how important it was. Didn't, uh, have time to get dressed. Fate of all life as we know it and all."

Kelly sighed and shook her head before walking over to the kitchen area. She put her groceries on the counter, suddenly noticing the sound of the shower running. She marched back into the living room area, the carpet still showing signs of whatever that *thing* was that had been there the other night.

"Julie," Kelly started, "is someone in the shower?"

"Oh…that. Uh, yeah."

"Oh my god, were you *fucking* on the couch?"

"Uh…maybe."

"Holy shit, Julie! That's so gross! I sit on that!"

"Well, you know how these things go. You have a few drinks, you meet a guy…"

"Why…why are there two pairs of panties on the floor?"

"…and his girlfriend…"

"Why did you lie and say that it was a ritual?"

"That's a ritual…in some cultures…"

"Why didn't you go into your room and do it?"

"You've never fucked on the couch before? Heat of the moment? You meet a stranger or two and you're so into each other that you can't wait until you reach the bedroom? You've really never had that?"

"No, I haven't."

"Jesus, you're repressed. Next thing you'll tell me you've never fucked on the counter either."

Kelly looked at the counter she had just put her food on and made a disgusted face.

From the floor, Julie's cell phone went off. Her ringtone was a song about waffles, something about them being invented by Ghandi, so you should keep some handy.

Julie, without even stopping her game, extended her leg over the couch, opening her legs in front of Kelly, reached down with her foot, and grabbed her phone with her toes.

"Jesus Christ, I could have gone without seeing that," Kelly said.

"So repressed…didn't you have sisters?" Julie said bringing her leg back up on the couch and bending it backwards to bring the phone within reaching distance of her hands.

"No, I grew up with all brothers."

Julie, rested the phone on her shoulders, continuing to play.

"Hey, Daddy! How are you? …No, that's tomorrow, silly…True. I have trouble remembering the time zones too…But thank you very much. It means a lot that you called…Awww…I love you too, daddy…Yeah, Sammi's coming by tomorrow. She said she's going to take me out for dinner…I promise…No, I haven't heard from Perci in…Oh god, Daddy…Fine…I haven't heard from Persephone in a while. I think she's angry at me…She got all haughty taughty after she got that job with the Royal Family…I'll try, Daddy. I love you too, Daddy…Goodbye."

Julie smiled and let the phone drop from her shoulder on to the floor.

"That was your dad?"

"Yeah, he was calling to wish me a happy birthday."

"That's really nice of him."

"Yeah, he always makes such a big deal of my birthday. It's kinda goofy, but you know how dads get."

"Does he know what you do?"

"I don't think my sex life is much of his business."

"No, not your sex life. Your job. Your *other* job."

"Oh, of course he does. It's been the family thing for like forever. In fact, thinking of birthdays…"

CHAPTER 10

It was a March, in the middle of the 90's, in a suburban neighborhood like so many others in Middle America. The sky was blue, the fence was white, the house was yellow, and the grass was green. The sounds of children's laughter filled the backyard. It was Julie's 8th birthday and her parents had gone all out for her. Her father, a tall, middle-aged man with a solid jaw and wavy, strawberry blonde hair that fell upon his shoulders, stood on one side of the room, smiling at his daughter, who had the usual conical birthday hat on, as her friends sang "Happy Birthday" to her.

He wore black leather pants, black leather engineer boots, and a black buttoned down shirt open just enough to show his tattoo-covered chest.

The song ended and everybody clapped, little Julie blew out the candles and smiled at the adoration she was receiving.

He clapped for her and walked over, kissing her on the forehead, gently brushing her then-red hair with his palm, revealing that his wrist was covered in tattoos, as well.

One of her friends, a dark-haired girl named Suzy, looked at his wrist and asked, "Mr. Fairweather, are you a truck driver?"

"No, my dear. Why would you think that?"

"Because you have pictures all over your arm and my mom said that only truck drivers and sailors have those."

"Oh, Suzy, no no. These are...mementos."

"What's a memento?" asked another little girl, a platinum blond child with thick blue rimmed glasses.

"Well, Iris, it's a trophy of sorts. It's so I always remember my adventures. Whenever I've fought something and defeated it, I tattoo it onto my skin, so I always remember where I've been."

"Daddy, can I have mementos, too?" Julie asked, smiling widely.

"Of course you can, Juliette. When you're old enough, you can do whatever it is you want to do."

"I'm already eight, Daddy! When will I be old enough?"

"Well, it's funny you should ask that, because I have your present right here. Hold on, one second."

He got a mischievous glint in his blue eyes as he theatrically tiptoed to the gate of the backyard's fence. The children giggled at his exaggerated movements.

He winked at Julie as he got to the gate of the fence, then calling out, "It's time," to someone outside.

The gate opened, slowly, and a clown emerged. He was wearing a big bright red afro wig, a red circular nose, and a red big smile painted on his face. His jumpsuit was baggy and bright blue, with big yellow smiley-faces polka-dotting it. His red, oversized shoes made squeaky noises. He was juggling four red balls and riding a unicycle.

Suzy shrieked, "I'm scared of clowns, Mr. Fairweather!"

"Oh, there's nothing to be afraid of. This is a very special clown. Aren't you, Mr. Poggles?"

Mr. Poggles rode his unicycle into the center of the backyard.

"Of course I am, Mr. Fairweather," he said in a voice that could accurately be described as clowny, "I came here just to see a very special little girl. Which one of you is Juliette Fairweather?"

Julie raised her hand excitedly. Some of the children pointed at her.

"That's just great, Juliette!" Mr. Poggles said, in his wacky clown voice, punctuating his words with laughter that could also accurately be described as clowny, "Now, I'm going to show all of you a trick. I need a volunteer to give…"

His voice seemed to grow deeper and his eyes bugged out.

"me…THEIR…"

His voice grew louder and his posture stiffened up as he threw his head back. There was a loud cracking noise as his jaw split in half vertically, turning into a pair of preying mantis-like mandibles, blood dripping from the worm-like row of teeth underneath.

"SOOOOOOOOOOUUUUULLLLLLL!!!!!!!"

From the red-nose up, he was still a clown. Under his mandibles, his arms broke to reveal row after row of centipede-like short legs, each one topped by a reptilian claw. His stomach ripped open to reveal another mouth, this one with a long, black tongue, dripping with steaming saliva, lolling back and forth like a tail. Two giant bat-like wings, affixed with multiple eyes on the rotted leathery membrane of their expanse, burst from his back, as he roared loudly. The roar was more demony than clowny.

The children, all except for Julie, cried and screamed and ran for the back door of the house, which they found locked. Some of them wet themselves. Some of them just kept repeating cries for their mothers as Mr. Fairweather walked over to Julie, who was looking with her eyes wide open in wonder at what was in front of her.

"Okay, Juliette, this is your chance to be a big girl! Go get 'em. I can't help you with this. You've got to do it all on your own."

"How do I do it, Daddy?" she asked, as the thing that had been Mr. Poggles burned the ground around it, walking towards her with a murderous intent.

"That's up to you. You're a smart girl and I'm sure you'll do fine. Oh…one other thing…You like it here, right?"

"Yes, I do, Daddy."

"Okay, well, then just keep in mind if that thing eats any of the other children, we'll probably have to move."

"Again?"

"Yes, again. Don't blame your sister for that, it was her first time too."

"Stupid Sammi," Julie said as the clown-thing roared and reared back to charge at her.

CHAPTER 11

"Believe it or not, we ended up having to move anyway," Julie said, looking at the small tattoo on her right forearm of a mandible-faced clown, "Some of those kids' parents were really not very understanding. I mean, nobody died!"

Kelly just stood there, with her mouth open.

"So, what *are* you getting me for my birthday? I have an Amazon wishlist, if you haven't gone shopping yet."

CHAPTER 12

Julie woke up to the sounds of water dripping, her vision foggy and her head pounding. There was a metallic taste in her mouth. And she was cold.

A quick survey of her situation revealed that she was nude in a bathtub in an apartment she didn't recognize. There was an equally nude Asian girl cuddled up next to her, nuzzling her head into Julie's tiny breasts. Julie put a hand to her own mouth and it came back bloody. She pushed away the Asian girl, who snorted and turned over in the bathtub, drops of water now landing on her feet.

Julie stood up and stepped out of the bathtub, realizing she couldn't remember the girl's name or if this was her apartment. She looked in the mirror, to see her nose was bleeding. There was a little compact on the sink, right next to the mirror, two lines of a white powder she immediately recognized to be cocaine laid out evenly next to a credit card, registered under the name Jennifer Liu.

Julie leaned against the mirror, wiping her nose with her palm, looking at the fresh notch she had tattooed on her wrist, a souvenir of her little adventure with the possessed child the other night.

She couldn't remember meeting Jennifer or even what day it was supposed to be. This place was a shithole and she certainly wouldn't have laid down in that mildew covered bathtub while sober.

She leaned forward and snorted a line of coke from the compact, hoping it would help clear her head a little.

She sniffed loudly and then washed her face enough to get the blood off.

She sat on the toilet to pee and rested her head in her hands.

"Happy birthday!" a male voice said, from the doorway.

There was a skinny guy with some sort of obnoxious goth/industrial hairstyle where he had short hair, but really long bangs that were dyed the bluest blackest black possible, standing there as nude as she was, his pubic region shaved clean, his little pink dick

49

circumcised and flaccid. She still didn't remember him. She knew for a fact that this couple was not the couple she had met and taken home from the club yesterday. Or what she thought had to be yesterday, but could have actually been two days ago, since this guy did just wish her a happy birthday.

"Huh?" Julie mumbled, not even looking up.

"Today's your birthday, right? You told us it was…"

"Yeah yeah. Where the fuck am I?"

"Our apartment. Remember? I mean, you were really fucked up when we met yesterday, but…"

"I don't fucking remember you or…uh…"

"Jenny?"

"Jenny…over there. Where are my clothes?"

"Uh…all over the apartment. Wow, you really were…"

"Fuck. Did you cum in me?"

"Nah…I'm always safe about it. Listen, you're welcome to stay here for a…"

"Nope. Gotta bounce. Don't want to be here."

"Oh, I'm sorry. Did we…"

From the other room, Julie could hear the "Badger Badger Badger Badger Mushroom Mushroom" song she had set as her sister's ringtone go off. Julie sprang off the toilet, not bothering to flush, and pushed her way past whatever this guy's name was, and found her cellphone on an old, torn loveseat, a poster of Depeche Mode tacked to the wall above it. On the floor was another nude sleeping person, but since their back was facing her and they were as skinny and androgynous as everybody else here, she couldn't tell what gender the person was. Frankly, she didn't care.

Julie put the phone to her ear and grunted a greeting.

"Hey you!" Sammi said, in her heavy Midwestern accent, over the cell, "Happy birthday, sis!"

"Yeah. Thanks."

"Did I call at a bad time?"

"Kinda. When and where are we meeting tonight?"

"Uh…well, I thought we might get some Thai food. I know you love Thai f…"

"Yeah. That's great. Ummmm…Lemme text you when I'm more awake."

"Sure thing. Are you okay, Julie?"

"Don't worry about it. See you later."

She hung up the phone and started collecting her clothes, which were strewn about the living room

The goth/industrial guy walked up to her, looking a little embarrassed.

"Did we do something wrong?"

"Whatever, dude. Don't worry about it," she said, slipping on the pair of panties she found on the tv, stopping to make sure they were hers first.

She sneezed, a second later, yelling at him, *"Poshel na khui, suka, blyad!"*

Fuck. Was that Russian? That was Russian. Am I speaking in tongues again? Fuck, I'm speaking in tongues again! Sometimes, that happened after dealing with a possession. It only lasted a few weeks, but it was always annoying.

"What language was that?" he asked.

"One of them," she said, pulling up the black skinny jeans she figured were hers.

In a couple minutes, she was fully dressed, in jeans, a black G. G. Allin hoodie, Docs, and her leather motorcycle jacket.

"So, ummmm…you wouldn't want to exchange numbers?" the guy asked, "I mean, we all had a fun time last night…"

"Don't be such a woman, dude. It was what it was."

His face said that he was disappointed. Her face said she didn't care.

After a few minutes of making sure she had everything of hers, Julie walked down two flights of stairs, and then out a long hallway, into the brisk, March air. The sunlight hurt her eyes, so she slipped on some sunglasses and flipped her hoodie up.

She couldn't remember if she had brought her bike with her or not, and didn't see it chained anywhere out here, so she assumed she had just taken the subway. Of course, she could have brought it and lost it somewhere while fucked up, but whatever. She'd find that out whenever she got home. She realized she could have just gone back up and asked if she had taken her bike here, but she didn't want to deal with those people anymore.

She recognized this neighborhood to be Prospect Park, which was only about a 45 minute or so walk from her apartment or a 15 minute bike ride.

Fuck, she thought, *I hope I didn't lose my bike.*

Bummed out, Julie decided to walk to the Barnes & Noble she knew was around here and just sit and read. She bought herself an overpriced coffee at the café there and picked up a copy of *Naked Lunch*. She had read it, probably about 10 times before, but loved each time. She read until the sun went down and then texted her sister.

CHAPTER 13

Julie got off the subway in Manhattan at 50th Street, walking up to 9th Avenue, to a place called the Pure Thai Cookhouse. Sitting on a bench there, waiting, was her sister. Sammi was two years older than Julie. She was a tall, thin woman with long, straight brown hair (that had been the brightest red of all three sisters when she was a child) and a kind but sad smile. She had a strong jaw like their father and a small nose like their mother. She wore a black eyepatch, as she always thought the flesh-colored ones were creepy, and a bright red sweater, under a warm winter coat.

She stood up and greeted Julie at the door of the restaurant with a warm hug. Hugs from Sammi always felt like she hadn't seen you in years, so strong and comforting.

"Happy birthday, again!" Sammi said.

"Thanks, Sammi." Julie said.

Sammi hugged her again and kissed her on the forehead. Sammi nodded at the hostess and a smiling Asian waitress lead the two of them to to their table.

"Glad to see you're here, they were waiting for you to arrive before seating us. Also, good to see you decided to dress up," Sammi joked, Julie giving a half smile.

As they sat at their table, Sammi reached forward and handed her sister a card.

"I wasn't sure what you wanted, so I got you a gift certificate to Sephora. I mean, that raccoon thing you do with your eyeliner can't be cheap."

Julie took the gift certificate and held her sister's hand for a few seconds, before putting it in her jacket pocket.

"I seem to recall you doing this too, when you were in high school."

"No idea what you're talking about"

"Uh huh."

"And I'm sure you can buy more hair dye there," Sammi added.

"Hey, if I don't dye it, I look like the chick from the new *Spiderman*."

"Emma Stone?"

"No, the blond girl in *Amazing Spiderman*."

"That was Emma Stone."

"Really?"

"Yeah."

"Well, that's who I look like when I leave it natural."

"As opposed to looking like she does in *Zombieland*? I mean, you even have the bangs going on."

"I didn't know that was her in that movie."

"It is."

"Alright. So, let me just confirm this is you this time, right? That was really annoying."

"Well, if I was another demon, pretending to be me, you know I probably wouldn't tell you, but yes, it's me. Or would you like me to bring up the corgi incident?"

"Okaaaaay, yeah, real Sammi…"

"Good. We still haven't figured out who or what that was."

"Sick, sad world…and I don't want to think of the corgiplosion, so, uh, how's Hogwarts?" Julie asked.

"It's not *Hogwarts*. It's the Illinois University of Metaphysical Medicine."

"You know, that totally sounds like you made it up."

"Well, I didn't."

"That's what you'd say if you made it up."

"*Touché*…Well, I'm an officially licensed DMPM now."

"So, you're a Witch Doctor now."

"I guess if you want to put it that way. Hahaha. Yes, I am. You should have seen the ceremony, by the way. I gave the valedictory. Wish you could have been there."

"Yeah, money's kinda tight," Julie mumbled, "Did Perci go to it?"

"Yup. She took all the pictures, actually."

Sammi reached into her purse and pulled out her Smartphone. She fiddled with the buttons a little bit until she found pictures of her graduation, showing them to Julie.

There was picture after picture of Sammi in her cap and gown, looking very proud, surrounded by friends and classmates. Eventually, there was a picture of her and another cap-and-gown-clad graduate, kissing. The next picture, where they held each other tightly, revealed him to be slightly shorter than her, with floppy but short brown hair, and a lot of stubble.

"Who's that guy?"

"Oh, that's, uh, Brian."

"His intentions honorable?"

Sammi smiled and held up her left hand to show her engagement ring, a silver band with a large amethyst adorning it.

"Whoa."

"Yup. Met him in my Necromancy classes. He's a sweetheart. You'd like him."

"Probably not."

"Okay, probably not your type. He doesn't have his forehead pierced."

"A Prince Albert maybe?"

"A Princ...? Uh...ewwww."

"Hehe."

"Oh, you are such a menace."

"I try."

"And that's what's worrying me. You don't normally have to *try*. You're normally just a sarcastic quippy machine. Tonight, you just seem down. Out of it. What's up? It's your birthday! You should be happy. I'd think you'd be having some sort of wild party or the other, knowing you."

"Just not feeling it today. Woke up today on the wrong side of the bathtub."

"The what?"

"You probably don't want to know."

"I'm sure I don't...So, what is it? Are you just feeling old, miss 25 years old? My god, you're a quarter of a century old! How does it feel to be collecting your pension?"

"No no. Not feeling old. Just kinda..blah."

"Well, maybe if you got yourself a real job you'd feel more accomplished."

Julie rolled her eyes, "Oh, not this shit again."

"Julie, I'm not asking you to get a job at Walmart. It's just you're really, really skilled at the, uh, 'family business.' I was never good at that, like you and Persephone. You two have dad's gift for it. I don't see why you don't apply to a job for the Council. They have a New

York branch, you know. I could introduce you to Mr. Hawthorne. He runs..."

"Nah. That's just not me. I don't want any of that stuffy bullshit. Happy where I am."

"You don't *seem* happy, Julie."

"I'm fine, Sammi."

"You are *not* fine, Julie. I worry about you. You don't seem...is there anyone special in your life?"

"Nah. Don't need the drama."

"How about friends? You have *friends*, right? It's really important to have friends."

"Nah. I...I don't need a lot of people asking questions, you know? I don't know how to relate to normal people, anyway. I'm fucking weird, you know. Our whole family is."

"You know why you're like that, right?"

"Cause we moved around so much?"

"It's inevitable. You never really got the chance to make any lasting connection with people. It's perfectly understandable. But maybe if you applied for a Council job, you could meet some other people who do what we do."

"Nah, that's cool. I...*Bwytewch y cachu o fil o geifr!*"

"What the hell was that?"

"Oh, nothing. That's been happening. It's nothing..."

"*You're speaking in tongues?!?* Holy shit, Julie. How long has that been going on?"

"Just a couple days. Did a possession a few days ago..."

"You don't have your shots?"

"Nah, I try to avoid needles."

"Well, that's good to hear, but...*That's it!* You're coming into the clinic tomorrow and getting immunized."

"Ah, I hate Doctors...no offense."

"No. Just no. Not taking no for an answer, Julie. You have the spiritual equivalent of mono right now. What if next time, it's something serious? What if..."

"Some birthday this is turning out to be."

"You can't beat the Axis is you have VD. It's just a little prick and..."

"That's what she said."

"Oh dear," Sammi said, unable to keep a straight face anymore.

"Hey now!"

"Alright, *Hank*...man, remember how much you used to love watching that with dad? You were pretty young, but..."

"I remember. I'd sit on his chest and watch it, and he'd laugh so much. And then Perci would waddle on by and demand to sit with us."

"*You all* loved to watch that. Me? I was busy studying."

"It was all about Hank. Artie was cool, but Hank is what made it...So, when was the last time you spoke to Perci? The graduation? Dad was asking about her."

"Few days ago, actually. She said she wished you a happy birthday."

"Perci? Come on."

"Okay, no, she didn't. But she's doing really well."

"I heard."

"And she got set up through the Council, you know. If your baby sister can get work with them, I'm sure you can too. Also, changing the subject does not mean you don't have to come to the clinic tomorrow."

"*Anyway,*" Julie said, motioning for the waitress to come by and take their order. She was in the mood for some lump crab fried rice, ratchaburi crab, and pork noodle soup. In truth, Julie would have preferred pizza, but her sister always wanted to go someplace classy. So, when in Rome...

Her cellphone rang, this time the default ringtone. Julie looked down and rolled her eyes, letting it ring. Fucking Lucy.

"Aren't you going to answer that?"

"No. No, I'm not."

She turned to the waitress.

CHAPTER 14

The Council clinic was disappointingly bland. She knew the whole Harry Potter aesthetic was fictional, but would it have hurt them to put in some torches, maybe some owls, have some Danny Elfman-like music piped in, instead of some muzak song she couldn't identify (it was actually "You Light Up My Life")? It reminded her of the free clinic she went to on 9th Avenue that one time she had gotten Chlamydia. Same posters and everything. Same type of doctor coming out to talk about what insurance policies they accepted and how you could apply for assistance if you couldn't afford it. They even talked about the importance of practicing safe sex and not using other people's needles. Only difference was that the Council had special programs outside of Medicaid you could apply for. Oh, and the discussion of safe sex included a couple sentences about incubi and succubae.

They explained what Julie already knew, growing up with a sister in the field of metaphysical medicine: Most people were unaware that the world of the metaphysical worked very much like the world of the physical. Becoming possessed was very much the same as contracting any illness. It could only happen if your immune system wasn't prepared to handle it. The only difference between that and influenza was that possession affected your spiritual immune system. If your spiritual health was up to par, there was no way a demon could move into your body. Nor would things like werewolves and vampires be able to spread their illnesses to you. Then there were also STDs that were only spread by spiritual or demonic sexual contact. It wasn't that different from the regular world that regular people knew, really. But then again, the movies and books wouldn't be quite as interesting if, after surviving a scratch on the moors, the American tourist went to a clinic, got some shots, got a prescription for some Anti-Lycans and then that was the end of it.

She was a little annoyed that she had been totally sober for two days, even if her sister had surprised her with tickets to see "The Book of Mormon" after dinner. While the play had been hysterical, she really wanted to go to a bar or something when it was done, but so rarely got a chance to see her sister, she decided to tough it out all night, and into this morning, ultimately sleeping over at Sammi's hotel room for the night. Unfortunately, the hotel bar was closed by the time they got back in, so Julie spent the whole night awake, staring at the ceiling, and then, when she was sure Sammi was asleep, alternated between discreeting masturbating and playing her Vita until she passed out.

After this clinic shit was done, she planned on getting good and fucked up, although hopefully, she would actually remember who they were if she were to wake up with anybody tomorrow.

Yesterday morning wasn't something she was necessarily happy with. She had no problem going home with strangers, if she found them attractive enough, but she really hated not being able to remember meeting them. She didn't like not knowing where she was or who she was with. It always reminded her of moving to a new town as a teenager, having to start from day one, with no friends, and a new fake backstory to remember. She also didn't like not remembering what exactly had enticed her to go home/bring them home with her in the first place. Contrary to what some people had said, back in her high school days, she was very selective about who she slept with, even if she did have a longer list of partners than most people. Enjoying sex with multiple partners did not mean that she enjoyed sex with anyone with a pulse.

Bored, Julie scanned the room to see who else was there with her. There was an extremely attractive redhead with just stunning blue eyes, who was sitting two empty chairs away from her. Julie thought of moving closer to her and then suddenly remembered the same thing that she had remembered when she had seen that really hot guy at the free clinic: this was *not* the place to try to pick people up. It is entirely possible that he was just there to get the same things she was: a regular checkup and some shots. But it was entirely possible he was there to get ointment for his genital herpes. So, the brain won out over the libido this time. She was very proud of herself, actually.

"Julie Golightly," the nurse, a large African American woman with closely cropped hair, called, almost as if she had wanted to interrupt Julie's personal victory.

Julie sat up, smiled at the redhead (*remember where you are, dammit!*), and then walked into the little examination room her sister was sitting in. Sammi was wearing green scrubs with a white coat over it, slipping on rubber gloves, the nurse who had just called her name assisting her sister in the exam.

"Glad to see you came, Julie."

"Yeah, yeah, let's get this over with, Sammi."

"Okay, give me a moment."

Julie nodded at her sister and then scanned the room a bit, as the nurse began to take her blood pressure. She looked up at the diploma on the wall.

Samantha Athena Henderson
Doctor of Metaphysical Medicine

She smiled a little. It still totally sounded made up. Well, almost as made up as the last name.

CHAPTER 15

Later, after the sun had gone down, a black stretch limo pulled up Chamber Street, as though some rock star who was reaching the peak of his fame, just before his speedball-induced overdose cut him down at the magical age of 27, wanted to be seen by the various paparazzi awaiting him at some red carpet event or the other.

But there was no paparazzi, no rock star; Just Mr. Trent and his ever present bodyguard, Timothy O'Neil, standing around, waiting on the steps of City Hall. Timothy, as usual, was wearing his SWAT drag, the tinted visor covering his face completely. Mr. Trent decided on dressing Timothy like that. It helped around the city authorities to have someone who looked like he belonged there. Timothy was many things, but he had never been much of a master of disguise, so the tinted visor and full body outfit were quite helpful.

Mr. Trent was fresh from a meeting with the Mayor's aide, William Malone (never the Mayor. Never, ever the Mayor. His Honor never wanted to see how the deeds were done. He just wanted to reap the benefits. Very typical, very human response) about how things were progressing, And now that they had hired someone new for the ritual, it was time to get the show back on the road, as they said.

The limo stopped as Mr. Trent stood up and walked to the curb, a bit aghast that the person they had hired wanted to travel in such an attention machine. This was supposed to be a low-key job. *And here she is, parking a giant frigging limo in front of City Hall. Not noticeable at all*, he grumbled to himself.

The chauffeur nodded to Mr. Trent and then walked to the backdoor, opening it up, some sort of bubbly pop music blasting from the speakers. Probably that awful fucking 2 Hot for U bullshit.

Two tall figures exited the limo first, a man and a woman.
Great, she has a posse.

He didn't like them from the moment he saw them, their bleached hair styled annoyingly, the woman in a pixie haircut and the male in that stupid floppy Hitler-hairstyle that he saw so many times among young people these days, their skin porcelain white and their eyes as green as emeralds. They wore matching tailored snake skin suits and cowboy boots, which, to Mr. Trent, seemed very tacky, but to the two of them probably made them seem special.

He *really* hated their kind. Would probably explain why they had wanted this meeting to be so late.

They stood on either side of the door and then an incredibly expensive Bruno Malle shoe exited the limo. Then another one.

Finally, a very petite woman in a very well-tailored cream-colored pantsuit exited. She was a lot younger than Mr. Trent had expected her to be. He wasn't sure if it was magic or if she were really that young, since he was dealing with someone whose file said was an accomplished magician. It was an unfortunate side-effect of dealing with these types of people. You could never tell if they were really young or just really really vain. The files on her said that she was 21, but then again, the files on him said he was 35, and he was much, much older than that.

Her smile was pleasant and kind, her long, straight red hair, flowing over her shoulders and touching her hips. She had white gloves on and a carnation on the lapel of her pants suit.

"Mr. Trent," she said, in a soft, posh English accent, extending her hand.

"Ms. Roberts," he said, walking towards her to extend his hand.

He reached forward and, as he touched her hand, suddenly knew what it was like when people used those prank handbuzzers, as his body was shook by a wave of what he assumed electricity felt like, causing a scream to escape his lips, and him to fall to his knees. Only this was magic, and it was about a hundred times stronger than what he imagined one of those felt like. He knew, for certain, if he had been an ordinary man, that would have killed him, fried his insides stone dead.

"Oh, terribly sorry about that, Mr. Trent," she said, giving a slight curtsy. Her snake-skin clad posse smiled.

He was angered by this.

"Just what was that about, Ms. Roberts?!?"

"I just wanted the Prince of the Fifth Realm Makai House of Temen-ni-gru to know that I shall be watching him closely."

"You knew?"

"I've had, shall we say, encounters with your kind before. No matter what form you decide to take, I can *always* sense your presence."

"So, you came here to fight me?"

Mr. Trent frowned and tensed his muscles, the ground under him beginning to smoke, the smell of sulfur suddenly filling the air. Timothy began to glow a faint red. They were standing out on the street, outside of City Hall, but he would be damned if he'd let this little human bitch...

"Oh no," she said, laughing a gentle laugh that seemed to change her entire demeanor, "I came here to do business."

Mr. Trent stopped tensing and the air around him became breathable again. Timothy stopped glowing.

"I don't think I understand what your game is, Ms. Roberts."

"I just wanted you to be aware that I am aware of who you are and of what you are."

"I'm not sure how necessary that is, considering I already knew your credentials from your file."

"Ah, but aren't such things dreadfully impersonal?"

"And your little magical electrocution trick wasn't..."

"Now, now, Mr. Trent, you must understand that this ritual you wish for me to perform does carry its own dangers for me, as well. As I understand it, my predecessor met with a most untimely end."

"He had his hand in the cookie jar."

"So to speak, yes. But you do understand a delicate lady such as myself has to be careful."

"Understood, but...uh...Let's not make it a habit, alright?"

"Of course."

"So, these...two?" Mr. Trent motioned at the two twins, who had been leaning against the side of the limo, watching the whole thing with smirking looks of amusement in their eyes. Mr. Trent did very much not like them.

"Oh, they are here merely to perform a task I need performing."

"Does it have to do with the conditions you asked for?"

"Very much so. Christopher? Serenity?"

The two twins popped off the limo and stood in front of her.

"Right here, missus," said the male, Christopher, his accent, in contrast to the proper accent of Ms. Roberts, a strong East End dialect, the "t" in "right" and the "h" in "here" silent.

"Right right," said Serenity, the female in the same dialect, giving a mock salute.

"Yes, I trust that you two know what you have to do."

"We get that, yeah, but," Serenity said, scratching her head, "We was kinda hoping we could, like, do all that tomorrow."

"Tomorrow?" Ms. Roberts asked.

"Yeah, like, we ain't been in this city since the Twin Towers was up," Christopher explained. "Thought we might see the sights, like."

"Get a bite to eat too," Serenity added in.

"Famished, I am."

"Aye. Plus, there is the Sanrio Store."

"Here we go…"

"What?"

"Not saying a bloody thing."

"Right."

"So," Ms. Roberts said, sighing, "Anything else you two wanted to do? See the Statue of Liberty, perhaps? There is also the Empire State Building and the Stock Exchange."

"No worries on that. Planned on doing me stocks over the mobile," Serenity said, whipping out her cellphone. It was a Hello Kitty phone.

"Indeed," Ms. Roberts said.

"Yeah, so would it be possible for us to just see the sights tonight, take a peek up the old girl's skirt, so to speak?" Christopher asked.

"Serenity, Christopher…you know I hold you both in the highest esteem. That's why I am able to remain so composed at the moment."

"So that's a no go, yeah?" Serenity asked.

"That is, indeed a no go. Am I correct in assuming you know the mission?"

"Aye."

"And you know how to sniff out, as it were, the target? Correct?"

"Aye."

"Then you two should get to it."

"Right right, Ms. Roberts."

"And if it makes you feel any better, I am sure you'll find plenty of illicit activity wherever she may be."

"Not talking the pony, yeah?" Christopher asked, Mr. Trent having no idea what that even meant.

"Not talking the proverbial pony, Christopher. Just remember. Only *watch* tonight. Do not, and I repeat, do not engage her."

"Right then, let's get to it."

"*Ja wohl, mein Führer*," Serenity said, nodding, with a smile and a bad German accent.

Christopher saluted with a smile and the two twins walked off into the night.

Mr. Trent shrugged his shoulders and said, "Those two seem like a handful."

"Quite far from it, actually. I trust that the conditions of my employment will be extended to them as well."

"They already get full cooperation from the NYPD for..."

"Yes, I am aware the Hierarchy has branches in New York. However, I want special cooperation. I know there are certain rules they must abide by. I would like a waiver of those rules. Within reason, of course. Nothing that I, myself, am not entitled to."

"Now, wait a moment here, Ms. Roberts..."

"I believe I did discuss that with your..."

"That could be asking a bit much, what with..."

"Full cooperation was the deal, Mr. Trent. Unless you'd like to find an alternate candidate for the Ritual."

"Fine," he said, sighing heavily and running his fingers through his hair, "They'll get it."

"Excellent."

"So, uh, I guess you're probably pretty tired and will want to get back to your hotel room for the night. I can meet you first thing in the..."

"Oh, no. I want to see the workspace you've provided for me."

"I guess we can do that, but it really reeks in there."

"And why is that?"

"What do you mean, 'why?' Because you've got 40, well, 39 now, humans in a confined space. You people don't exactly smell like roses in your natural state."

"Mr. Trent, I want you to take me there, immediately. I am not sure if I am pleased with what you're telling me."

CHAPTER 16

Julie, still feeling a little under the weather from her shots, walked down from the Myrtle Avenue stop on the M to the bar she had been planning on checking out tonight. She had heard they had fire eaters and she always liked fire eaters.

She had stopped by her apartment after her time at the clinic, relieved to see her bike was at home, but she didn't want to risk tying it up anywhere in this neighborhood. The Real Estate agents could try to pretty it up for the suburban white kids all they wanted by calling it East Williamsburg, but this was still Bushwick, so she wasn't about to leave anything valuable lying around here where anyone could just steal it.

The bar was only a block from the train, so it was easy to find. She showed her ID and entered, recognizing the music playing as being Babes in Toyland's "Real Eyes." The place was pretty crowded, but while she was feeling weaker physically, mentally, she was in a lot better place than she was yesterday, especially now that she was only a couple minutes from alcohol-time.

There was a special of 5 shots for $10. That was certainly not a deal she was going to pass up, so she got herself 5 shots of tequila, downing them all in less than a minute. There was that nice, warm sensation in her chest that she was so very fond of.

There were no fire-eaters as of yet, but she did see a group of people who seemed more dressed up than usual talking to each other in the front of the room, so that was probably them.

She scanned the room, to see if she might be going home with anybody tonight, but nobody floated her boat. She ordered another 5 shots.

After downing them, she couldn't help but notice a large hand on her inner thigh that certainly wasn't there a minute ago.

She looked down to see that, yes, indeed there was a hand. She followed the hand to a well-muscled wrist which lead to a thick arm which lead to a large bald man with a goatee, sitting next to her, smirking at her.

"What's your name, honey?"

"Pardon me, but you seem to have misplaced your hand," Julie said.

"I don't think so. I think it's exactly where it needs to be."

"If you don't mind losing it."

The man smiled, the very strong smell of his alcohol-induced breath hitting Julie right in the face.

"Let's stop pretending, honey," he said, squeezing her thigh with his hand, "You just downed 10 shots in two minutes. If that's not a girl looking to lube herself up for something, I don't know what is."

"Lube myself up? Damn, you are fucking charming, dude."

"C'mon. Let's not pretend. I bet if I move my fingers up a little bit, it'll come back soaking."

"Wow. You really talk like this."

"Just being honest. You bitches are always saying how you want 'nice guys' who aren't gonna lie and, well, here I am being honest."

"Well, you're just every woman's dream, aren't you?"

He smiled, and started to slip his hand up her thigh. She leapt off the barstool, his hand, still wrapped, tightly, around her thigh.

"Okay, seriously, get your hands off me right now!"

"Or what? You gonna call to the bouncers? Go ahead. Luke's my fucking bro from way back. You got enough holes for the both of us."

He moved his hand against her crotch.

She gave the guy an open palm strike right to the nose. There was a loud cracking noise, and the guy, who, now standing, was easily 6' 5", and built like a small European car, staggered backwards, his eyes watering and his nose bleeding.

"Fucking bitch broke my fucking nose!" he said, blood seeping from the hand he had over his face.

"Guy fucking grabbed me! You all saw…" Julie started, before the guy took a swing and hit her right in the jaw. She fell over, her ears ringing, her jaw aching.

Instinctively, she grabbed a beer bottle off the bar and smashed him in the face with it. He stumbled backwards, as she leapt forward, kneeing him with all of her strength in the balls. She kneed him again and again and again, in rapid succession, slashing at his face with the jagged end of the bottle.

She felt a hand wrap around hers as the bouncer ran over and took the beer bottle from her. She headbutted him, shifting his nose to the side with a squishy cracking noise. Stunned, he had enough time to see Julie spin around and punch him in the temple, extending the middle knuckle of her fist to do extra damage. He fell to his knees and she kicked him in the face, a stunned silence falling over the bar.

The bald guy started to get to his feet, only for Julie to kick him straight in the face, knocking him straight back down, a tooth flying from his mouth. She gave a war cry and started stomping on his crotch a good seven or eight times before reaching down and grabbing his already bruised manhood and digging her nails into it as he screamed, her fingers drawing blood. As she did this, she repeatedly headbutted him, before finding herself in a chokehold as the bouncer stood up again.

"Call the fucking police! This bitch is trying to kill him!"

"Fuck you! Fuck you!" she yelled slipping out of the chokehold, striking the bouncer behind her with a headbutt.

"Call the fucking police!"

"I'm out! Alright?!? I'm out!" Julie yelled, slipping out of the chokehold, and then putting her hands up, while walking towards the exit.

"Nah, doesn't work that way! Tone, call the police!" he said, trying to block her way out.

"You put your fucking hands on me, I *will* fucking kill you," she yelled at the bouncer, pushing her way out of the bar, a crowd of murmuring people gathering around the fallen body of the man she had beaten.

Julie flipped up her hoodie and walked off into the night, hoping nobody had taken any cell phone footage of her performance.

On the far side of the bar, amongst all the confusion, the twins smiled to each other.

"Doesn't take that one long to bring the show, eh?" Christopher commented.

"She seems fun," Serenity giggled.

CHAPTER 17

Jerry screamed in pain as the flesh on the back of his thighs tore as he was forcibly pulled from the bench he had been on. He had been in one position for so long and had been gelled there by his own waste, so when he had been forced to his feet, his skin didn't want to cooperate with what the rest of his body was doing.

He didn't know what was going on, as the hood was still over his head, but he was being lead off somewhere. His body, deprived of food and fluid for days, didn't have the strength to fight anymore. Even the scream had taken a lot out of him.

He figured this was the end. Whatever the big plan had been for them all was now. The screams all around him, as he felt flesh pressed against his body while he was being lead somewhere, herded like cattle, his hands still tied behind his back, being brought to the man with the big hammer, were more subdued than he would have thought they would have been in these final moments.

He was stopped at one spot and, his legs barely able to stand in the first place, he fell to a kneeling position as his knees were kicked out from under him. He heard authoritative voices yelling at others to get on their knees. He could only imagine this meant they were all going to be killed execution style. More than anything, he wanted someone to hold his hand.

His face was pressed to the floor in front of him, his position gone from one of kneeling to one of bowing.

Much to his surprise, there was no bullet to the back of his head. Instead, the hood was removed from his head, blinding him with an assault of white light.

He screamed again, from the pain of the light.

It seemed like forever before the light became blurry shapes and then another lifetime before the blurry shapes became a location.

He was in what looked like a high school gym but was most likely a prison courtyard. In front of him was what looked like a stage with a microphone setup. There were a dozen guards standing there, in full prison riot gear, several of them even holding a fire hose.

All around him were naked men and women, their bodies smeared in blood and feces, all bowing before the stage.

He could see the man he would recognize as Mr. Trent standing on the stage, looking at all of them, a look of disgust in his eyes, and a handkerchief to his nose.

"Oh my," said a female voice entering the room from behind where Jerry was. He wanted to turn around but figured that they'd probably punish him for changing positions.

"This place *is* quite ripe," she said, walking in front of them, clad in a cream-colored pantsuit. She was young and pretty and English. He wasn't sure what she was doing here, but he was struck with terror at the thought that maybe this was Mr. Trent's girlfriend here to fulfill some sort of weird fetish.

"Not to worry, though," she said, and was suddenly surrounded by a gentle blue light. Under her, and Jerry, at first, thought he was hallucinating, flowers grew, bright and beautiful, of many colors, a whole bed of flowers that seemed to grow with every step she took towards the stage.

One of the guards pulled out a folding chair for her and set it up on the stage, she sitting down, with her legs crossed, a pleasant smile on her face, the flowers around her making the stage look like some odd garden had been placed there as part of a very elaborate play.

"Hello," she said, addressing Jerry and the others, through a mic handed to her. A guard holding a pitcher of water and several Dixie Cups stood next to her, "My name is Ms. Roberts, but you may all call me Ms. Roberts."

"Say, 'Hello Ms. Roberts!'" one of the guards yelled, kicking Jerry in the ribs.

"Hello, Ms. Roberts," Jerry and the other bowing prisoners said.

"Now, before we begin," Ms. Roberts said, "Do any of you know how to make tea? I very much could go for a spot of tea at the moment. Raise your hand if you can."

"Their hands are zip-tied," Mr. Trent told her.

She sighed heavily and then instructed the guards to free everyone's hands. This took about a minute. During this minute, she would check her cell phone and roll her eyes.

Finally, all the prisoners' hands free, she asked again, "Now, who knows how to make tea?"

Jerry saw three people timidly raise their hands, while continuing to bow.

"Excellent," Ms. Roberts said, "After this is over, someone will take you to a kettle and…"

"We don't have a kettle," one of the guards said.

"Excuse me?" Ms. Roberts asked, sounding indignant.

"We don't have a tea kettle. And if we did, it doesn't sound advisable to be letting the prisoners have access to scalding hot water."

"I believe that is my decision to make, Officer…"

"I'm not NYPD, ma'am. Private contractor. Name's Team Leader Edward Drake."

"Well, Team Leader Edward Drake, tell me: Are you private contractor types too manly to engage in the simple pleasure of tea?"

"No, ma'am. We just don't have a kettle. Nor a stove to put one on."

"My god, are you people living in the Dark Ages? Please do tell me you have a water heater."

"No, ma'am."

"Are you telling me there's nothing in the budget for anything other than a coffee maker."

"No, ma'am. We don't have one of those, either. There is a vending machine…"

"A vending machine? Seriously, Mr. Trent, that's the extent of your hospitality towards your valued guests? I'm to quench my thirst with…what, a can of the carbonated beverage of my choosing?"

Mr. Trent sighed and said, "Can we get to the matter at hand, Ms. Roberts?"

"The matter at hand is that if you intend on this going off to your satisfaction, you will make sure I am able to have tea like a civilized person, Mr. Trent."

Jerry couldn't believe that this was what they were arguing about. After the days of shame and humiliation and pain and hearing that poor girl be executed, they were arguing about fucking tea time! It filled him with an impotent rage. He knew he could do nothing about it, but

71

wait for Evil Mary Poppins there to deign to pay attention to him. On the other hand, if she was talking to Mr. Trent in that way, maybe it might be best the longer she didn't pay attention to him.

"I will have it fixed by tomorrow, Ms. Roberts," Mr. Trent said, visibly annoyed.

"That's all I ask," she said, before turning to the prisoners, "Well, once the situation is fixed, we will figure out which one of you will be responsible for my tea. In the meantime, as I said earlier, I am Ms. Roberts, and I will be the one in charge of a very special activity that you will all be participating in, several days from now."

She stood up and walked over to the edge of the stage, the flowers around her continuing to grow at an unnatural rate.

"Now, let's get some things clear, shall we? Good. Now, I am sure all of you know about what happened to my predecessor. He tried to use one of you in an untoward fashion and one of your number fought back, killing him. Now, I'm sure to many of you, she is a shining example of bravery in the face of adversity, but let me tell you a little bit about what happened next.

"After she was executed, her body was taken from here and left in a dumpster in an area of the city known for its high prostitution activity. She was found, but no one was there to identify her, so it was assumed that she was merely another lady of ill repute that fell into the clutches of the wrong client. With no family to identify her, she was classified as a Jane Doe. Currently, she sits in a drawer at a city morgue. In a few days, when no one claims her, she will be taken to a Potter's Field and buried in an unmarked grave. No one will ever know that she was brave enough to fight back. No one will ever know what her hopes or her dreams were or who she loved or what she believed in. She will simply be, in the eyes of the public, another piece of refuge.

"I tell you this because I want to make it clear that, though my predecessor intended on killing all of you after our task was complete and I do not, that I am *not* your friend. *I am your owner.* You are property of the State now. Any rights you might have had in the outside world disappeared the moment you met Mr. Trent. For all intents and purposes, you are slaves now. Your lives are completely disposable and any disobedience will be met with swift retribution. Retribution that we will 'get away' with, because, quite honestly, you are no longer people. You are cattle. You are tools. You are property. There is a reason why *I* am up on the stage, looking down at each of you, while *you* are naked as the day you were born, bowing, covered in your own filth. None of you could play by the very simple rules that society requires of its members. Failure to comply with those very simple rules results in punishment. All of you were disobedient and now you are being metaphorically spanked."

Jerry couldn't believe what he was hearing, even after everything he had been through.

"Now, if any of you have anything to say that, I encourage you, without fear of harm, to express to me exactly what you feel."

Jerry tried to open his mouth to say something, so filled with rage at what was happening that he didn't care about being buried in an unmarked grave as punishment, but much to his horror, he couldn't open his mouth. It was like it was glued shut or something, but that couldn't be right, since he had just spoken a few moments ago.

Then he saw the most horrible thing he had ever seen in his life. Several of the other people bowing had no mouths. It wasn't like they were sewn shut or their lips were cut off. No, they had no mouths, it was smooth uninterrupted skin, their eyes filled with panic, and their screams muffled. He felt his face, only to find that his mouth was gone too.

He was filled with the strongest terror he'd ever felt in his entire life. Somehow they had taken his mouth away. If they could do that, what else couldn't they do? He started screaming, finding himself unable to stop, but the skin covering his teeth made nothing but a muted whimper come out.

He thrashed at his face, trying to dig into the skin covering his teeth with his nails, clawing at himself like an animal caught in a trap.

He could hear Ms. Roberts giggling to herself, as though she had just heard the world's most polite joke.

"Now," she said, smiling, "I admit, that *was* cruel. But I wanted you to be aware that I can quite literally do anything I wish to any of you, anytime I want. I do hope the lesson has been learned."

She sat down on the folding chair again, crossing her legs, and pouring some water into a cup.

"And now for the good news. Once what I need you for is done, I will make sure that all of you have a vital job at a fair salary, serving the people of New York in a way that you find comfortable and fulfilling."

"You're going to give us jobs?" a female prisoner asked. Jerry was surprised and relieved to see he had a mouth again.

"Yes, we are. My predecessor would have killed all of you, but I think you are all a vital resource that can greatly improve the lives of your fellow New Yorkers."

"You're going to let us go?"

"Yes, I will allow you to leave here. Of course, you will not be free. Your old lives are over. You will not be returning to making trouble for law enforcement. But you will be allowed to live lives that benefit everyone, yourselves included."

She looked at the girl, "You, stand up. Come up to the front of the stage. You must be thirsty. I am going to provide everyone here with water, so you may hydrate yourselves and get clean. Also, both the male and female cells will be provided with a bucket each, so that will no longer have to make your waste all over the bunks and yourselves."

"Applaud!" the order was given. Jerry, the girl standing, and all the others applauded.

Ms. Roberts motioned to the girl to walk to her. The girl, visibly embarrassed by her nudity in front of the other prisoners and Ms. Roberts, walked timidly up to the front of the stage.

Ms. Roberts had her turn around, with her arm down at her sides, so that her nudity would be plain to everyone.

"Oh my," Ms. Roberts said, pointing to blood on the girl's thighs, "It appears someone here has their menses."

The girl silently nodded, tears in her eyes.

"I'm sorry, I didn't hear that."

"I...do..." the girl whispered.

"You do what?"

"Have...my...my...period..."

"Speak up," Ms. Roberts said, holding the mic to the girl.

"I have my period," she said, her voice trembling.

"I imagine that must be uncomfortable."

"Y...yes."

"And it appears that you've had a bowel movement all over yourself in the last few days. Is that true?"

The girl nodded, crying.

"Can't hear you."

"I have...I shit myself."

"I would think if you're old enough to have your menses, you'd be old enough to be potty trained. I guess not. But don't despair. We will clean all of you up, one by one. And..."

Ms. Roberts stood up and looked at one of the male prisoners who had started to get out of the bowing position. A look of anger crossed her face, she yelled, "I did not tell you that you could change positions!" and the man's body was thrown from the ground as if an invisible force picked him up and tossed him towards the ceiling. Only thing was in mid-air, the man's body split in half, right down the middle, the two halves of his body flying towards the opposite walls, his organs spilling out somewhere in the middle, showering Jerry and a few of the others who were now cowering.

The girl on stage curled up into a fetal position, shaking. Ms. Roberts, regained her composure, and patted the girl on the back.

"There, there. Now, are you thirsty?"

"I'm...really...thirsty."

Ms. Roberts held the cup out to the girl and then snatched it back when the girl reached for it.

"Do I get a, 'Thank you, Ms. Roberts?'"

"Th-thank you, Ms. Roberts."

Ms. Roberts nodded and gave the girl the cup, which she downed in one gulp. She was given four refills and then taken to the back of the stage, where she was hosed down by one guard while three others scrubbed her body until it was clean. Her wounds were dressed and she was returned to her original position, where she was made to bow again.

One by one, they were lead up to the stage, where Ms. Roberts pointed out their lack of control over their bodies, or made to describe the mistakes they had made that lead up to them being here, or in the case of one man who got an erection upon being onstage, being made to violently beat his penis down until it entered a flaccid state again, or, in Jerry's case, told to relay to everyone how his dreams had all failed. And then, they were to thank Ms. Roberts, before being given water and cleaned.

And slowly but surely as everyone's spirits broke under the psychological weight of everything that they had experienced and been subjected to by this point, Jerry found himself starting to actually feel thankful towards Ms. Roberts.

CHAPTER 18

In Crown Heights, a half hour walk from East Williamsburg, the bald man who Julie had beaten had refused medical help and wandered out of the bar. He was furious, hoping he'd run into her somewhere, or, at the very least, someone else he could take out his frustrations on.

He walked down an isolated street, smoking a cigarette, his crotch still burning with pain, his sinuses fucked to all hell, and his broken nose, unbandaged.

"Fucking cunt!" he yelled at no one in particular and punched the window of a parked car.

The window shattered, but he was not even bothered by his now bleeding hand, so filled with rage was he.

"My my my," said a Cockney male voice behind him.

"Ain't your day, innit?" said Serenity, standing next to her brother.

He turned around, anxious to hurt someone. Anyone.

"What the fuck you David Bowie-looking faggots want?"

"Real eloquent like, this one is," Christopher said, with a smirk.

"Guess getting his bullocks beat in by little bitty girl'll do that," Serenity giggled, "John Thomas not going to be saluting the flag again, eh?"

"Okay, that's it! You two are dead!"

"Not technically...but close," Chris asked, smiling. Serenity smiled with him.

That's when he saw their fangs.

And then never saw anything ever again.

CHAPTER 19

Julie wasn't sure how long she had been running from the bar. She didn't take the train, since waiting for the train was a good way to get arrested after what had just happened. She was worried. Would the police believe it was self defense? Would the bouncer, if he was the guy's friend, say she had started it? Would the police count her drunkenness against her? And if they drug tested her, would they detect the coke in her system? *Fuck fuck fuck fuck!* She punched a wall, bloodying up her hand, even more than it was. Only this time, it was her blood.

She stopped running, she looking around; to find herself in an area she wasn't familiar with. She looked at one of the buildings, seeing the numbers had hyphens in them. That meant she was in Queens. Fuck it.

She took a deep breath and decided it was time to just go home.

She looked at her phone to see what time it was, and smiled when she saw that she had a text from Vera.

Dimensional tear, 95 Baruch, Apt. 9J Manhattan

She wasn't familiar with the address, but whatever, that's what Google maps was for, and she could use a demon to fight tonight.

While she was the type to stand up for herself and would fight a human if threatened, in truth, she hated it. There were so many consequences for fighting one. Police got involved, lawyers, the possibility of jail; if it was in a small town, it usually involved her having to move. Demons? Demons were easy. What were they going to do? Kill her? She'd never met a demon she couldn't kill. Most, with her bare hands or teeth.

Fun fact: The minor Third Realm demons, the Asanai, who resembled furless sloths with wings and four sets of teeth, xenomorph-style, had blood that tasted exactly like strawberry ice cream.

Unfortunately, ingesting it gave you diarrhea for four days.

Julie had found that out the hard way. She had started looking up cholera on WebMD, at the time, wondering if she should maybe get to a hospital.

But damn, that was some tasty blood.

Human blood just put you at risk for Hepatitis or HIV. And wasn't anywhere near as tasty.

CHAPTER 20

Back in an expensive hotel room in Manhattan, two people who would disagree with Julie's opinion of human blood showered together. Serenity and Christopher embraced as they washed the blood off their bodies. Giggling, Serenity ran the sponge down her brother's stomach, as he scrubbed her back.

A sound from the next room indicated they had a Skype call.

"I think the missus is calling us," Christopher said.

Serenity nodded, gave her brother a playful kiss on the cheek, and then exited the shower, holding his hand.

It was Ms. Roberts.

"Evening," Serenity said, answering the call, laying down on her stomach, as her brother sat on her ass and toweled her off.

"Oh, dear," Ms. Roberts said, averting her eyes, "Can you two please wait until we're done with the call before you start engaging in incestuous activities."

"For the last time, Adam and Eve, we isn't like that, Ms. Roberts," Christopher said.

"Just real close we is," Serenity said.

"Shared a womb."

"Shared a womb."

"Whatever," Ms. Roberts said, rolling her eyes, and forcing a smile, "So, did you find the target?"

"Matherson's intel checked out. Easy-peasy," Christopher said, drying his sister's hair.

"Japanesey," Serenity added.

"Cut it, you," Christopher said biting her shoulder.

"Okay, Mimmy," Serenity said, giving him a light slap.

"Ahem," Ms. Roberts cleared her throat, "So, what was she doing tonight? Shooting up? Blowing sailors, perhaps? Or did you see her in battle?"

"Nothing like that, Ms. Roberts," Serenity said.

"Nope. She beat some bloke down, though," Christopher.

"Took care of him before the Sweeney showed," Serenity added.

"That we did. Think he was on angel dust, though. His blood burned a bit."

"That it did."

"A bit of custard on the pie."

"Seasoning for your pudding."

"Sometimes," Ms. Roberts added, "I have no idea what you two are talking about."

"*A la mode,*" Serenity giggled.

"So, the Peckham?" Christopher asked.

"The...peck...oh, Mr. Trent!" Ms. Roberts realized they were talking about.

"Yup. What's his story?" Serenity asked.

"Not gonna be trouble, is he?" Christopher added.

"Oh no, not at all. Demonic royalty. You know how they are. What's the good of being a prince when your father is immortal, after all?"

"Good point, that is."

"So, you saw her fight a human tonight," Ms. Roberts, "I take it if the two of you finished him off, he was quite the worse for wear."

"That he was."

"Good. You did provide your local chapter with information on where you left him, right?"

"Course we did. Rules is rules," Serenity said.

"Right. Don't want the local bloodsuckers cross with us," Christopher said.

"Their territory and all," Serenity interjected.

"Excellent. I'll have the local authorities take the appropriate measures," Ms. Roberts said.

"So, what about the bird?" Christopher asked.

"Do not directly engage her yet. Go to the second phase of the plan."

"That we will," Christopher assured her.

"Wonderful. Now, if you'll excuse me, I do think I should get some sleep. Big day tomorrow," Ms. Roberts said, "Good night, you two."

"*Buenas noches, mein Führer,*" Serenity said, saluting her.

They closed the laptop and, under him, Serenity turned around, facing her brother, stroking his bare stomach.

"So, we have a few hours to kill," Christopher said, smiling down at his sister.

"Sanrio store long closed right now, right?"

"You and the Sanrio store."

"Not leaving without a trip there, Mimmy."

"Stop calling me that."

"You'll always be my Mimmy."

"Yes, yes. Now, what ever shall we do tonight?"

She leaned forward, getting face to face with her brother, their lips almost touching, their arms around each other's bare skin.

"You in the mood for another bite to eat?"

"Not a sponge, love."

"Bit parched, I am. I swear that was angel dust. Not good for the constitution."

"Just burned a little for me."

"Not hungry?"

"I guess I could always watch. And then help you get clean again," she licked her brother's face, "Make sure you're all shiny and presentable-like, for tomorrow."

"Sounds like a plan. I like when you watch."

Christopher leapt off his sister, and walked over to the counter, taking the bucket that their complimentary champagne had come in, and then, turning his attention to the nude, unconscious boyish-looking male, who was tied to a chair in another corner of the room, splashed the boy with the melted ice water. He was probably not that far into his 20's, if that. Fair-skinned and blonde. Thin. O positive, from the scent of his blood. Uncircumcised. Didn't usually see that much in the States. Maybe a tourist. The floor of the room, under him, was covered in a clear plastic tarp.

"Wake up, lad," Christopher said, as the boy jolted awake, trying to scream through the gag in his mouth, "Playtime."

Christopher reached between the boy's legs and squeezed his testicles, showing his fangs off. He ran his fingers up the boy's navel, up to his chest, and then traced the shape of the boy's mouth, covered by duct tape.

Serenity reached under the bed and pulled out her violin, as her brother danced around the boy. She proceeded to play Beethoven's 7th Symphony's 2nd Movement, as Christopher slapped the boy across the face a few times, he becoming visibly aroused by the boy's pain.

Serenity smiled, her fangs popping out, a shudder running down her back, as she continued to play the song more intensely, her brother having ripped the boy from the chair, tearing through the thick rope like it was tissue paper, and throwing him to the floor. Christopher stroked himself a bit, his foot resting in the small of the boy's back.

"Oh, you bale Alphonse, you got me berlin all Geoff. Up the jam roll with you!"

He mounted the boy, entering him from behind, tearing skin from the flesh of the boy's back and shoulders with his teeth, her brother's face a mask of the boy's sweet, sweet crimson.

Her brother pumped away at the boy's struggling form, biting deeply into the boy's throat, tearing his jugular vein out, blood spraying everywhere, as he came, with a loud grunt into the boy's dying body.

Serenity's vision turned dark as she sank into orgasm, herself.

CHAPTER 21

Back at her hotel room in Chelsea, Ms. Roberts sat at her window, looking out the window, at the city her mother had talked about so much, listening to one of her favorite songs.

She was wearing a pink bathrobe, her hair up in a towel, drinking tea, her laptop open, but no windows save iTunes running, a picture of her mother, a proud, fun, cultured woman with curly brown hair, wearing an ushanka, her desktop photo.

"Sail away, sail away, sail away," she sang to herself in time with Enya.

It wasn't that different from London, really. The architecture was even similar. Overcrowded, dirty, and filled with relics and people who didn't know their place. Filling the streets like vast ant colonies without a queen, wandering aimlessly and purposeless. All convinced that they were the heroes of their own stories, when really, they were barely the extras.

Pretty much exactly like London. Yet, her mother loved it here.

Ms. Roberts remembered when she and her mother had sat together watching her mother's favorite movie, *Breakfast at Tiffany's*, over and over again.

Her mother had promised to take her to New York City once, but that hadn't happened for obvious reasons.

Her mother had apparently been here once when she was young and rebellious, trying to get away from her own super strict parents. Ms. Roberts didn't recall ever meeting her grandparents, but she had heard they were super religious Christians who probably would have greatly disapproved of their granddaughter regularly participating in human sacrifice.

Well, they didn't matter. Nor did the ritual, when it really came down to it. There was the plan and that was all that mattered. It could have happened anywhere. It just happened to be New York City where the first step of it was put into motion. The ritual was a means to an end. She had been hoping there would be some excuse to leave her responsibilities across the Atlantic to come here and put her plan into action, and when the offer to participate in the ritual was given, it took all her willpower to act nonchalant about it with the Mayor's representatives.

After leaving Mr. Trent's prison, she had stopped to take a walk down 5th Avenue in Manhattan. It was late, around the time Christopher and Serenity were off following their target, and all the stores were closed, but she made a point to stop by Tiffany's. She stood outside, like so many tourists before, looking inside the darkened window. Of course, unlike those other tourists, she had more than enough money to actually shop there, and it was on her "to do" list before she went back to England. Still, at that moment, she closed her eyes and thought of her mother and, despite the fact that she was only 21 years old, many years she had been planning this.

She looked at the open compact mirror on her desk expectantly for a moment, then sighed, and closed it.

CHAPTER 22

Back in Crown Heights, Mr. Trent stepped through the yellow police tape, serving as a warning to civilians to stay out of the darkened alley. Timothy waited in the car, as he wasn't appropriately dressed for this sort of occasion, and to take off his helmet would create a scene.

Mr. Trent showed off his credentials to any officers that questioned what he was doing there, as he walked towards a middle-aged cop with Lieutenant bars. He was a hard-faced man with a sarcastic smirk and brown hair who sort of resembled Dennis Leary, but with emerald green eyes.

He was standing over the bloodied body of the bald man who had harassed Julie earlier. The man's throat was very distinctly not where it was supposed to be and a great deal of his blood had seemingly painted the brick walls and concrete ground of the general area.

"Lieutenant Carcetti," Mr. Trent said, nodding.

"Oh, fuck me! Look at this," Carcetti said, in his heavy Brooklyn accent, "To what do I owe the fucking pleasure?"

"You're taking care of this one, right?"

"Why the fuck wouldn't I? It's a fucking vampire attack. You know that's where I come in, right? What I'm wondering is why the fuck you're here. I know you don't like us very much and you being here isn't exactly standard procedure."

"To be honest, I don't like any of you ape-derivatives, living or undead. I mean, I'd be lying if I said I didn't see you as the straight girls at the bar, making out with each other to try to impress your boyfriends, as opposed to my kind's hardcore diesel dykes."

"Clever and classy. You think of that one yourself?"

"Yup. Let's take a walk."

Carcetti spoke to one of his underlings, a human officer who had no idea of Carcetti's condition, putting the officer in charge of the scene while he was gone, and then he and Mr. Trent walked out of the alley, stopping by Mr. Trent's car.

Carcetti looked at Timothy sitting in it, and commented, "You know, you should probably roll down the window, so your dog doesn't suffocate."

Mr. Trent ignored the comment and pulled a manila envelope out of his overcoat, handing it to Carcetti, "This is who goes down for this."

Carcetti opened up the envelope, pulling out pictures of Julie riding her bike around the city.

"Fuck me. You know who this is, right?"

"Some human or the other. Juliette Ursula Golightly. The Mayor's current high priestess has some sort of vendetta against her or the other. I don't particularly care, as long as the ritual goes through without a hitch."

"'Golightly,' huh? Bit fucking obvious, don't you think?"

"I don't get it."

"That's from something. Before your time."

"*Nothing's* before my time."

"Apparently, humor is…Anyway, I'm telling you, *you* know her father."

"If I do, I wouldn't recognize him. They all look pretty much the same to me."

"No, no. *You know him.* He took out your brother, Raz'yel about 40 years ago."

"My brother was an asshole. In fact, all one thousand of my brothers were assholes. It's why I'm not around them anymore."

"Even the Vice President?"

"*Especially* the Vice President. And he's a *former* Vice President."

"If you don't mind me saying, he doesn't do a very good job of passing, what with the faces he's making in all of his pictures. Your other brother is a lot more photogenic. Just don't know why he hasn't killed Perez Hilton already after that whole bullshit with that human girl."

"Tell me about it. Anyway, the bigger question, to me, is not who her father is, but how do you know this?"

"Her dad's pretty fucking famous, with the Makai, with the Hierarchy, with the Council. Well, a better word would be 'infamous.' Her dad's Alexander Johannes."

"Johannes…Johannes…*Oh! That* Alexander Johannes! With all the tattoos?"

"Yup."

"Shit, I do know him. Well, I know *of* him. Man manages to piss off more than one world, his name gets out. So, how come I didn't know about this daughter?"

"Once he got himself a family, he started moving around a lot. Families are great targets. A man with three daughters and a wife has four glaring weak spots to anyone he might have upset in the past. Whenever they'd attract enough attention, they'd pack up and leave. Spent a lot of time in little nothing towns, in the Flyover States. You didn't notice his severely reduced activity in the last 30 years?"

"You are forgetting how old I am. I wouldn't notice 30 years. When I was born, this rock was still molten."

"As you keep reminding me, every fucking time we meet."

"And once again, I ask, how do you know all this? How would you even know about that brother, never mind what happened to him. The fight with Johannes didn't even happen in this realm."

"I may be just another fucking vampire in your eyes, but I'm a fucking vampire who also happens to be a Lieutenant in the NYPD. Ever since 9/11, we got ourselves all sorts of Homeland Security shit. Had a little pet project with surveillance on the Council. You know, anyone with the power to open up rifts between dimensions is not hard to get funding to monitor as a potential terrorist threat. So, we've been watching them."

"And the Clan Hierarchy, I imagine."

Carcetti smiled, and giggled to himself, "I ain't saying nothing. Although they haven't used the 'Clan' part of the 'Clan Hierarchy' in a few decades. Has a negative connotation these days."

"I bet. "

"Anyway, the Council had some pretty extensive files."

"I see. Is there any way…"

"Before you even ask, no, I can't show you them, since they upgraded their security after Anonymous managed to hack them, back in 2010. Magic shit now…which you'd think they would have done in the first place, but whatever."

"So…wait…so if this girl is Johannes' daughter then that means…Oh, hahaha, I see why Roberts has such a problem with her then."

"So, anyway, do we bring her in? I mean, we have witnesses at the bar that said they saw her fighting with this guy before the Twins had their way with him."

"Ah, so you already know about them."

"Of course, I do. The UK Hierarchy representative told me they were coming before they even got on the plane. And then they called up to report this. Just got a call from them about a kid in a hotel they were planning to do an hour or two ago. I got some guys going to clean that up in the morning."

"Okay. So, they're playing by the rules?"

"Yup. They're old world, anyway. Real Oliver Twist shit, for real. We have records from their last trip to the city, back in '82. They may leave bodies behind, but they know to not ruffle the wrong feathers. Never kill any tourists, never kill anyone with enough money for questions to get asked. Contacted all four local families: Sakkara, Yara, the Chinese, Picario. Frankly, these two got more respect for the rules than some of these new kids. I'm surprised half these newborn orphan shitheads don't run out into the sun to see if they sparkle, for fuck's sake."

"I see. Any idea why they're with Roberts, though?"

"Muscle is my guess."

"Mmm...So, about this Juliette?"

"Sounds pretty open and shut to me that she followed this guy out of the club and took him out. Initial fight was self-defense but this...this was a vengeance killing."

"Good, but not yet. There's something else Roberts wants first."

"Suit yourself."

"Believe me, it's not suiting myself. I could care less about Roberts or this Juliette Johannes or any sort of petty human feud. But if I want her to complete the job, it's part of her conditions."

"You remember when all people cared about was money?"

"No, I don't. As long as you hairless apes have been on this rock, you've always found some way to hold grudges against your fellow hairless apes. Before the first one of you even thought of trading services for goods, you were thinking of ways to bash your neighbor's heads in with the nearest blunt object."

"You're such a fucking romantic, you know that?"

"That I am."

"So, anything else before I get back to work? It's almost morning and I'd like to get this crime scene cleared before I burst into flames."

"No, just keep this Juliette in mind. In a few days, you'll have something else to pin on her. Then you can take her down."

CHAPTER 23

From somewhere, far off, like an itch that didn't need to be scratched until rubbed, Julie heard Portishead playing. It was "Glory Box." Subtle, just enough to set the mood. But she was having too much fun to really even care.

At the moment, she didn't know where her body ended and where Scarlett Johansson began. She knew her legs were wrapped, tightly, around the starlet's head, pushing her face into the warm, wet wonderland between Julie's thighs. And what a wonderland it was. After she had been with Nick Cave from the 80's, looking as simultaneously creepy and hot (or maybe hot because he was creepy) as he had when he was in The Birthday Party, who just had the most amazing dick she had ever felt, she found herself being devoured by Miss Johansson.

Julie was seeing stars, seriously; just an unbelievable torrent of pleasure that had her halfway to losing her voice. She was in someplace white, a bed, a cloud, a 2006 Prius. It didn't matter. All that mattered was the tongue that lapped up every drop of her pleasure. All that mattered were the teeth that bit into her tensed inner thighs. All that mattered were the hands that caressed her legs, her ass, her hips.

She felt a building up in her bladder, that feeling she got on the one occasion someone actually brought her to ejaculation, that feeling that, at first, felt like she had to pee, but was something so much more earth-shattering.

Scarlett Johansson's hands ran up and down her ankles, while they squeezed her ass, a finger teasing her anus, another slowly scratching her back, as Julie, unable to even moan at this point, silently opened her mouth, only to find it met by the animalistic kisses of 80's Nick Cave. His breath tasted of whiskey and cocaine. He bit her lips hard enough to draw blood, and Julie just let go, spraying for only the second time in her life, the world bleeding away into the oblivion of ecstasy. The sound of the blood rushing through her body, the only reality for a moment.

Her muscles spasmed, her clit throbbed, her fingernails drew blood, as she felt Scarlett's hands squeeze her breasts at the same time they ran down her thighs, her ankles, caressed her hips, massaged her buttocks, fingered her...

Wait a minute...Scarlett Johansson sure has a lot of hands.

Julie opened her eyes and looked down at 80's Nick Cave and Scarlett Johansson. She had about ten arms. He had six. That was a detail she hadn't paid attention to because she was enjoying herself too much.

Oh, fuck. That's right, I'm being killed.

She reached forward and put her fist through Nick Cave's face, his cranium splitting open like a ripe melon thrown from a window, the whole scene around her abruptly changing. She suddenly found herself with a large tentacle wrapped around her throat, fully dressed, back the bathroom of an apartment in the Baruch Projects in lower Manhattan. The tentacle was protruding from mid-air, where a rift had opened up between this world and the Second Realm.

The apartment and, in fact, the entire building itself was empty, the owner claiming that they were spraying for bedbugs, when in reality, it was a cover to get someone in there to fix the rift. It may have seemed weird that they had suddenly decided to spray late at night, but the tenants were so used to being completely ignored whenever the roof would leak or there were real bedbugs, roaches, or rats, that many were just happy to have something actually being done. Many assumed that this was just the owner's way of getting out of more fines from the city.

They weren't entirely wrong about that, but he was more worried about the shit he'd get in if the rift got bigger and sucked in the whole building. He had seen *Poltergeist*, after all.

She had fought these things before. They were parasites, nothing more. Like leeches, really. Fairly common whenever a rift would form between worlds. They looked like giant bloodshot eyes with tentacles. They were relatively easy to kill, so Julie had first fought one when she was 12 and had fought them dozens of time since.

And on one of those fairly common instances, she had discovered that when they tried to kill you, they wrapped their tentacles around your throat, which caused a reaction that put you in a hallucinogenic state, a place of pure pleasure, so that you never realized that you were even being killed.

So, being they provided an amazing sexual high, she always kinda let them try to kill her before she went to work.

It had never been that intense before, though. Her knees were still wobbly.

She realized she didn't have the strength in her arms to pull this thing off her, so she bit down as hard as she could, the world shifting into an epileptic nightmare of sexual fantasy and flesh. The feeling was enough to knock her off her feet, but the tentacle let go of her as the parasite jumped out of the portal, skittering, like an octopus on land, into the small living room, knocking over several items she couldn't see from the bathroom.

She got her bearings and spit the blood out of her mouth, into the toilet, feeling the shudder of orgasm, as the blood of this thing left her body.

She leaned against the wall, felt up her own collar for a little bit, noticed that her hair was soaked with sweat, and then, put a hand between her legs, feeling that she had managed to soak right through her pants.

Well, that's one pair of panties I'm going to have to throw away.

She heard more skittering in the next room and picked up her messenger bag, pulling out an ornate jeweled dagger from it. Closing the messenger bag, she stabbed at the rift, and pulled downwards, white light protruding from thin air, as the rift bound itself back together. She wasn't quite sure how that worked, something about stabbing reality to put reality back together, but like most things of a metaphysical nature, Julie wasn't really interested in the "whys."

With that out of the way, and no more little pests about to come out of the rift, she had to get rid of the one in the living room. She walked in, looking at the water damaged ceiling, and the peeling white paint of this room, portraits of Jesus lining the walls, a tv and an X-Box the centerpiece of the room, the window shades orange. This thing was here, somewhere, but she couldn't see it anywhere. She didn't hear it as the only sound was the radiator giving off steam.

The parasite had knocked over the little altar to St. Sebastian in the corner of the room, but there wasn't anything personal about that. Catholic Saints meant nothing to beings such as this, really. In fact, most of the world's religions were stunningly wrong, to be quite honest. This thing had no grudge against this man venerated by humans and humans only. This thing was just clumsy.

Julie scanned the room, trying not to move, still breathing heavily, very much aware that her pants were sticking to her thighs. Could it be in that pile of clothes over there? Could it be behind the tv? Could it be…?

She stopped and looked up at the ceiling. It leapt at her, all eight of its tentacles whipping at her wildly. She ducked, as it crashed into the wall, knocking down a portrait of Jesus, before again leaping at her.

She really kinda wanted to let it grab her again, but knew she eventually had the kill it, so she gave it a good swift kick in the eye, as it flew towards her. That alone sent a shiver of pleasure up her spine that almost took her off her feet. It definitely made her moan a little.

The thing used its tentacles to whip itself around the corner of the room, to spring itself towards the tiny kitchen of the apartment. She realized that with how small the kitchen was, unless it decided to hide in the oven, which was unlikely, it was going to try to make a play for the window, so it could get out of the building.

She rushed towards it, grabbing it by two of its tentacles, her knees buckling from under her, with a spasm of joy.

It fell to the floor with a loud squish, looking at her, probably trying to decide if it wanted to try to kill her again or go for the window.

Seeing an opportunity, Julie sat down on it, holding the knife downwards, so it stabbed directly into the cornea, its tentacles flailing wildly as it died.

Julie moaned loudly, as her body touched the dying parasite. This felt amazing, her genitals making direct contact with the creature, even through her pants. In fact, she was pretty sure if she hadn't been wearing pants, right now, her heart would probably stop from pure pleasure.

Once again, she was right there with the trip-hop beat of Portishead playing and 80's Nick Cave's amazing cock and Scarlett Johansson's many, many sexy arms until it all faded away, and Julie was lying there, on the floor of the kitchen, staring up at the ceiling until the sun came up, just enjoying the post sex glow, watching the parasite shrivel up in death until it turned to dust.

And when she was able to move around enough, she collected what was left of the dust, feeling a tingle go up her spine as she touched it.

Mostly to make sure there was no evidence of what had once been here, but also because she was curious what would happen if you snorted the dust.

She also realized she'd probably have to throw this outfit out, completely.

CHAPTER 24

Back in a hotel in Manhattan, at the same time Julie was dealing with the parasite and Mr. Trent and Officer Carcetti were conspiring, Samantha was awoken by the ringing of her cell phone.

"Hello?" she said, not awake enough at this hour to look at who was calling her this late. She was expecting either her fiancée calling her about an emergency back home or, even worse, some sort of law enforcement official calling to tell her that Julie had overdosed somewhere.

"Samantha?" said a soft, friendly voice with a slight Midwestern lilt to her voice.

"Persephone! Oh my god, how are you? Is everything alright?"

"I hope I'm not calling too late. You know how I get about time once I get to work. I was just calling to let you know that I'm going to be in Chicago on business soon. It's something that just popped up and I'm going to be very busy over the next few days, so I thought I'd…"

"I'm not in Chicago for the next week and a half. I'm in New York right now."

"Oh…Are you visiting *her*?"

"Yes, I'm visiting Julie. It was her birthday a couple days ago."

"I see."

"You need to stop that, Persephone. Julie loves you, you know."

"So, a week and a half? You're not spending the whole time with her, I hope? I don't see you as participating in whatever drug and sex parties I'm sure she.."

"No, I have Council business. There's a medical symposium at the end of the week. I thought I'd come here early so I could help her celebrate her birthday."

"I'd ask how that went, but you know I don't particularly care."

"Persephone…"

"Samantha. Whatever. You want to spend time with Juliette, that's up to you. I just choose not to."

"I really wish you'd reconsider."

"Not bloody likely. So…have you heard from dad recently?"

"Julie said she got a call from him the day before her birthday."

"Of course, *she* did. He doesn't even answer *my* calls. I keep getting his voicemail."

"Well, there's a reason for that."

"I don't care. It's incredibly rude that he would treat one of his children in this manner. But Juliette's always been the favorite anyway. Despite how hard I worked, despite how much knowledge I have in the field of demonology and metaphysics. Despite…"

"Persephone. It's not like that…It's…Look, it's late. It would take me a very long time to explain this to you and I'm barely awake. We can talk about it when you're here."

"You're right. I have to get back to work. I will be there in three days time."

"I have a rental car. Do you want me to pick you up at the airport?"

"No need. I'm sure it won't be difficult to have the Council arrange for accommodations."

"Alright. Goodnight, Persephone. I love you."

"I love you too. Good night."

CHAPTER 25

That was an awfully familiar bassline. And that was definitely a piano.

I'm just a Gigilo and everywhere I go

Julie looked confused. There was a man in a white tuxedo and top hat, with bleached hair, dancing around the kitchen of the Baruch Projects apartment she had fought the parasite in.

Life goes on without me

Julie scratched her head and looked at the man, convinced she had seen him somewhere before. In fact, she was pretty sure she had heard this song somewhere before.

He was now dancing on the ceiling. And he had a cane.

She was pretty sure this was not a parasite-induced sexual fantasy, in fact, this was the exact polar opposite of arousing, so she wasn't sure what exactly was up.

Cuz...

I ain't got nobody

And then he began to scat. And went back into the chorus.

"Uh...excuse me?" Julie started.

"Hey, baby! Hold on! Here comes the saxophone solo!"

And indeed, there was a saxophone solo. He danced some more.

"Seriously...uh...what is going on here? I'm used to weird shit. Trust me. I'm used to weird shit, but..."

He put his finger to her mouth to shush her, and the music stopped, and he yelled, in her face.

"*Hum-a-la-babe-a-la-zee-ba-la-boo-ba-la-hum-a-la-babe-a-la-zee-ba-la-bop!*"

And then, as the chorus played again, took off his top hat and took a bow.

"Hey, babe! The show has to go on, you know?"

"So, I've heard. You are...?"

"Whoa, you're shitting me! You don't know 'Diamond' David Lee Roth?!? Van Halen?!? Hot for Teacher?!? Woooooow!"

He did a split kick in the air.

"Wasn't the singer of Van Halen that lame guy who did the 'Right Now' song? I remember hating that song as a kid."

"Nah! Fuck that Van Hagar shit! You ain't telling Diamond David Lee Roth that you ain't heard the classics? Got it bad! Got it bad! Got it bad! I'm hot for teacher! Might as well jump! Hey-hey-hey-jump! I'm your ice cream man! All my flavors are guarantee-ee-ee-eeeeeeee-eee-eeed to satisfy…"

"Yeah, I'm going to leave now."

"Whoa…whoa…whoa…I have an important message from your father."

"Oh. Why didn't you just say that? Ooooh…now I know where I've heard your song from before. Christ, last time he did this, I had spent an hour trying to figure out who Marc Bolan was. Something about banging a gong."

"Who?"

"Exactly. I don't see why he doesn't just psychically project Wattie or Sid Vicious or Glenn Danzig or somebody like that."

"So, baby, Diamond David…"

"Yes, yes…what's the message?"

David Lee Roth turned into her father briefly. Although still dressed in the white tux and top hat. He waved and then he turned into Freddie Mercury, without a shirt, his mustache porno-proud.

Julie just frowned and sighed.

"Bicycle! Bicycle!"

And with that, Julie woke up,

"Seriously, dad? What the fuck?!?"

CHAPTER 26

Julie, confused, had a few drinks before leaving the apartment, contacting Vera, to let her know the job was over. She had another three messages from Lucy, which she promptly deleted without listening to, and one from work, wondering why she hadn't come in today. She called to say that she wasn't coming in because a guy had started with her at a bar and was sorry for not calling. They asked how many of his bones she broke and then said they understood and would see her on Monday. Then she went home, threw her clothes in the garbage, and then slept until early evening, dreaming of bicycle races with fat-bottomed girls and not believing in Peter Pan, Frankenstein, or Superman. *Goddammit, dad!*

CHAPTER 27

Serenity was bringing an inordinate amount of shopping bags into the hotel room.

"Mimmy, look here at what I got at the Sanrio store!"

"Serenity, bloody hell, stop calling me that! This is what we came all the bloody way to New York for? Not fulfilling whatever Ms. Robert's vendetta is. No, we came all this way so you could buy more Hello Kitty merchandise."

"You don't want to see it?"

"You're going to show it to me, anyway..."

Serenity nodded and pulled out a little pink bow, she put in the side of her hair.

She started dancing around, singing, "I Want to Marry a Lighthouse Keeper," for a few seconds, as Christopher gave a tired nod. Serenity, almost as happy as she was whenever she'd get to kill someone with her bare hands, giggled as she pulled a figure out of one of the dozen or so bags she had.

"Look at this!"

"Looks just like all the others."

"You said that when I showed you Dear Daniel."

"And he looked like all the other bullocks you show me."

"I cannot wait to get this home! Can we please hurry up and kill the girl?"

"Right right, let's let all our recon and Freddy-boy's work go to blazes because you've found another exhibit for our flat's museum wing."

"Oh, come on! You know why I love it!"

"Because you love daft things?"

"No! Because she's just like us! She's a twin born on November 1st and her papa was named George and..."

"Oh dear. You're going to go on about why she ain't have a mouth again, ain't you?"

"Because that way, she can be just as happy or sad as I am! And because she isn't bound to any one particular language."

"Bully for her."

"Shimizu-san said..."

"You realize you just put 'san' at the end of someone's name, right?"

"You're just angry because I keep telling you not to keep eating those sweets."

"Man should be able to enjoy a zebra cake in private."

"Not when that man ain't able to digest anything that ain't blood and that man spends the next hour in the toilet instead of out hunting with his dear sister."

"Can't help it if the Septics make some delicious sweets."

"Surprised you still got your fangs with how much sugar you shove down your gullet. Do you still got your fangs?"

She reached forward and stretched the skin of his lips into a smile, his fangs as deadly as ever.

He ran his fingers down the side of her face. She turned her head to smile at him, and suck on that finger.

"Now, my dear sister, are we ready to do Ms. Roberts' duty?"

"Adam and Eve!"

"Adam and Eve!"

CHAPTER 28

Julie woke up in her darkened room, her phone telling her that, besides getting another text from Lucy, which she deleted without reading, that it was after 8pm already.

She walked into the living room, Kelly sitting there with some hipster looking dude with a fedora and a curly mustache. They stared at her with open mouths.

"What?" Julie said, burping, and walking to the kitchen to get herself a bowl of Captain Crunch.

"Julie, I've got a guest!"

"Good for you! About time you had one!"

"You don't think you might want to put some…clothes on?"

"Oh…" Julie said, rummaging through the cabinets, stopping to look down, noticing she was naked, "Uh, not really."

"Hey, if this is a bad time," the hipster started.

"Nah, I don't mind," Julie said, shaking a box of Captain Crunch she found. It felt empty. Time for Plan B. There were Honey Nut Cheerios.

She poured herself a bowl and then took it and a can of beer into the bathroom with her, sitting on the toilet, eating the cereal, leaving Kelly and the hipster looking confused at what they had just seen.

Julie sat on the toilet, daydreaming, and eating the cereal, trying to figure out why her father had been bothering her with that particular Queen song.

After flushing and walking back into her room, she saw her phone had received a text. It was from Vera.

Damn, things were busy recently. Sometimes, she'd go as long as two or three weeks without a single text from Vera, and here she was with two in two days. Well, extra money was always good.

Minor Entity seen in warehouse, Long Island City, 45th Road Stop on the 7.

A minor entity seemed like exactly what she needed as a nice cool down. If she was lucky, it might be another little orgasm parasite.

She took a shower, got dressed, and then went to leave the apartment. Right as she was about to lock the door, it occurred to her that maybe she should bring her bicycle.

CHAPTER 29

It wasn't hard to figure out what warehouse the text was about, once she got to Long Island City. The air in this place was still. Dead. But that wasn't right.

A minor entity wouldn't have an effect on the air like that.

This felt different. Julie felt chills going up her spine. For the first time in a while, she was glad she wasn't drunk, even though she had brought some Smirnoff with her

The warehouse was dark, still, silent, like a statue. The security booth was empty. The gates to the place were open, the chains holding them shut laying on the sidewalk outside the fence. There was a small city of crates that gave the place its landscape, levels of scaffolding above her.

Julie held a flashlight, shining between the crates. She knew *something* was here. She could feel it. Strongly.

She started up a flight of steel stairs, her steps echoing throughout the warehouse, until she found herself on the scaffolding above the landscape of crates below. If this was a movie, this would be the part where the stupid girl would start calling if anybody was there. Julie wasn't a stupid girl.

She looked over the railing at the tops of the crates below, scanning her surroundings. She wished she had bought that special edition of Call of Duty with the night vision goggles from a few years back right now. But that thing had cost like $150 and why would she spend that much money on a game, right?

Because night vision goggles! Duh!

So, here she was, every fiber of her being telling her that this was a worse idea than usual, and that she should probably leave. This was a rare feeling in her.

Maybe she was wrong. Maybe she should've gotten drunk first. Some liquid courage would help right about now.

She took a step forward and noticed her boots were sticking to the scaffolding.

She turned her flashlight towards her feet and saw that the scaffolding ahead of her was covered in blood. That was probably where the security guard went.

Whatever this thing was, it was capable of dragging a man up several flights of stairs before killing him, or maybe it chased him up here. She wasn't sure which, but, as she looked ahead of herself, with her flashlight, and saw the torso of the security guard, smashed so hard against the wall that his organs had split out the side of his body, she knew this had to be something from, at least, the Fourth Realm or so.

But the only Fourth Realm demons that would do something like this were mindless beasts and there was very little chance that you'd find them outside of their realm. The rest of the Fourth Realm was populated by Incubi and Succubi, which, while extremely annoying, this wasn't their style. For one, he had his pants still on. And often, for reasons she had never been able to fathom, incubi and succubi often claimed their victim's bodies.

Fifth Realm, maybe? Nah, Fifth Realm demons usually took human form when they came here. Most of them were involved in politics or sports or entertainment. They were vicious if you challenged them, sure, but you'd be hard pressed to find one that would just tear people apart and smash their remains against a wall in a warehouse for no reason. The Fifth Realm was probably the second most intelligent of all the realms. In their true forms, you'd be facing some hardcore warrior types, but they usually tried to avoid that, unless absolutely necessary. Her dad had told her about fighting some Fifth Realm Prince or the other back when he was a lot younger.

So, Sixth Realm? Now, that's where you started to see things that just didn't give a fuck about blending in, but they were so rare. The Sixth Realm wasn't filled with mindless beasts and warrior demons. They were smart there. Smarter than humans, probably. Holes between our world and theirs didn't open up unless somebody opened them on purpose. And the things there, if they did tear someone apart, it was because they were targeted. Not to mention, you couldn't open a hole to the Sixth Realm without some real damage being done. Both

Hurricane Sandy and Hurricane Katrina had been the results of Sixth Realm summonings gone wrong.

So, Julie wasn't sure it was Sixth Realm. She had only ever seen about five Sixth Realm beings her whole life, and two of them had been heralded by tornados and the other three by Sandy and those had been body jumpers anyway. And none of them just randomly smashed people into walls.

So, maybe someone let a Fourth Realm pet loose or maybe some teenager (relatively speaking…a younger Fifth Realm demon was probably born around the time of the dinosaurs becoming extinct) from the Fifth Realm got rebellious and decided to smash shit up in Queens? Either way, she was going to have to complain to Vera that she wasn't really about those kind of jobs. Let the Persephones of the world deal with the Fifth and Sixth Realmers. Hell, she was having enough trouble with a Fourth Realmer's annoying texts. She just wanted to deal with possessions and orgasm parasites and things that looked like sloths with wings. They weren't paying her enough to deal with this shit.

She took a deep breath and went to the end of the scaffolding, her guard up. She looked around, stepping over the intestines of the guard, and looked over the railing at the crates below. She shone the flashlight down at what looked to be a tarp in the middle of the crates. Maybe cars or something.

She tapped her foot and frowned, shaking her head.

She noticed the faintest whiff of sulfur in the air. That was never a good sign.

She looked around. Still nothing moved.

She shone the flashlight on the crates, looking for something, anything.

Nothing.

She shone the flashlight on the tarp.

And then it hit her.

That wasn't a tarp. That was skin.

It pulsed. It quivered, a thin membrane stretched over something large. Larger than anything she had ever faced before.

What the fuck is that? She hadn't seen it before. What looked like a giant tarp with cars under it? And smelled of sulfur?

She took a deep breath, realizing there was only one way to know for certain.

She snorted hard and cleared her throat and then hawked a giant loogie at the tarp.

Upon impact, it quivered and shook, but there was no immediate impact. No change or reaction. Was this thing, like the Blob or something?

This called for desperate measures. She reached into her messenger bag and took out her bottle of Smirnoff. She hated to waste good vodka, so she took a swig and tried to chug as much as she possibly could.

When she realized she couldn't swallow any more, she threw the bottle at the thing. The bottle shattered with a loud thud and this time the stretched skin quivered. There was a loud groaning.

A very loud groaning. The entire warehouse shook. Hell, her ribcage shook from the bass of it. Julie had to grab onto the banister of the scaffolding as it felt like a minor earthquake had hit the place. She held on tight and the tarp-like-thing shifted position, revealing, to her shock, that that was only the creature's back. It started to sit up and it hit her like a brick to the face what this thing was.

Even in a fetal position, this thing was a good twenty feet high, its face resembling a human skull without eyes, twisted ram-like horns coming from where the sockets would have been. Its mouth was filled with row upon row of rotted teeth, each about three feet high. It had breasts, rotting foul things that hung on its chest, and eyes looking at her from where its nipples would have been if it were human. It resembled a giant dwarf's skeleton with a rotting layer of flesh sewn onto it.

And Julie knew this thing, as it stood up, and she found herself dodging beams and steel and the ceiling fell, was something she had only seen in books.

This was a genuine Seventh Realm being. But that was impossible. Nothing human could even open a gateway to the Seventh Realm and nothing from the other Six would be stupid enough to try.

Realizing exactly what that sulfur smell had been, she reached into her messenger bag and pulled out her emergency gas mask, which she had only ever needed when she had traveled to the Fifth Realm, since at a certain points of the Fifth, there was no oxygen.

It let out a scream, a loud scream that shattered windows and gave Julie an immediate ringing in her ears. The air filled with sulfur, enough that she knew if she didn't have the gas mask on, she'd be choking.

It stretched its arms and the warehouse collapsed around her, she finding herself flying off the scaffolding, landing back first on a crate below.

She was in definite pain, but she had landed properly, so the worst part of the moment was looking up at the rotted genitals of this thing, which was right above her.

It lifted its hoofed foot and tried to stomp on her, Julie rolling out of the way. The walls fell in showers of bricks and steel, car alarms going off for blocks.

Her body bruised and bloodied from falling bricks, she rolled out of the way of another stomp. And then jumped up when it's spiked tail raised and tried to crush her, with enough force to crack the concrete below her.

She started to make a run for it, the demon giving a howl. Its head not turning, since it had another face on the other side, this one, looking more like a skeletal boar's face, with pus-filled giant yellow eyes looking at her.

Bicycle! Bicycle! Bicycle! That was it, you can't outrun this thing, she thought to herself, running for her bike, thanking her dad for his advice.

It stomped after her, as she reached the sidewalk, realizing with great horror that she had locked her bike up on a crooked No Parking Sign outside the now destroy warehouse.

The thing kept making its way towards her. Only ten feet from her.

Fuck it, she thought, *I'm buzzed enough to not be hurt by this too much*, and threw herself into the No Parking Sign, knocking it over, and freeing her bike.

The demon raised its fist above its head, as she got on her bike and began to peddle away, the sidewalk behind her splitting from the force of this thing's pounding fist.

Okay, Julie, no need to panic, you've just got an entity the Babylonians once worshipped as a god trying to kill you. Typical Friday. How to kill it. How to kill it.

The demon pursued her angrily, crushing parked cars under foot like they were nothing.

CHAPTER 30

On the roof of a building several blocks away, Christopher looked at the demon chasing Julie through binoculars.

"Let me see! Let me see!" Serenity said.

"Here you are," Christopher said, handing her the binoculars. She squealed with delight and applauded at watching the Seventh Realm demon chase Julie.

"Hahahahaha…I think Ms. Roberts will be much pleased, she will."

"No doubt."

"If that girl lives through the night, I'll…I'll eat one of those awful sweets you like so much."

"My dear sister, you shouldn't say things you don't mean. You're like to have me rooting for the girl, after all the effort you made in summoning our friend there."

He gestured at the two dozen fresh corpses that lay on the roof with them, forming a giant circle that the twins stood in the middle of. Each of the bodies had been butchered beyond recognition, all while still alive, so that their innards gelled with each other to form one cohesive paste that served to bind the circle, protecting Serenity and Christopher.

"No Yodel shall cross my lips, my dear brother! I had to gather all these smelly pensioners to this roof. My efforts shant be in vain, I'll tell you that."

"So, what shall we bet?"

"If she lives, I shall eat one of those sweets. Lest she die, forty lashes will find your bum for doubting me."

"Sounds like we got ourselves a deal."

"And I won't use the nice birch, either."

CHAPTER 31

This was getting her nowhere, Julie thought. Her legs were starting to get tired and this thing wasn't slowing down any. She was also getting close to a populated area. It was fine and dandy to have some giant demonic being fuck up an industrial area. If she lured this thing into a populated area, that'd draw some major attention her way.

As it was, she heard sirens in the distance, growing closer.

This could be a major fuck up. Julie liked staying under the radar. That's why she didn't bother with the Council or with anything above the Fourth Realm. But how did this thing even get here?

Well, that was a question for another time. Right now, she found herself trying to think of a way around this.

Ooooh. That was an interesting take. It might, at least, buy her some time.

She reached into her messenger bag with one free hand, pulled out a pair of dice fashioned out of human skulls. These things were ancient. These bones, according to her dad, were from an Etruscan priestess who had first discovered the way between worlds. If they had been anyone else's, they'd be less than dust right now, but the power of the person who had once been around this skeleton was still strong, so many thousands of years later.

The key was the numbers you rolled. Julie turned the bike around and rode right between the demon's legs, heading back towards the warehouse.

The demon roared, as Julie heard what definitely sounded like a helicopter in the distance.

Even if the demon was able to see her with its other face pedaling in the opposite direction, it still had the laws of our world's physics to deal with. It slid like the world's biggest awkward dog into an office building, the wall of the entire building collapsing forward onto the demon.

It didn't seem to like that. The roar it gave was a really, really pissed off one.

Julie, a few blocks away had gotten off her bike and started rolling the dice.

The demon started running towards her, the sirens getting louder and louder. It sounded like half a dozen squad cars were headed this way.

A 5 and a 4. No good. A 1 and 6. No good.

The thing was now only two blocks away. If she didn't roll snake eyes in a couple seconds, she'd have to get back on her bike or this thing would flatten her.

She rolled a 6 and a 2. Fuck.

A 3 and 3. Okay, well, step in the right direction.

It was now a block away, the ground under her shaking.

With a loud bang and a flash of intense light, she rolled a 1 and a 1, the wall between the worlds ripping open in front of her, a small portal to the Fourth Realm opening up in front of her. She quickly jumped in, pulling her bike with her.

CHAPTER 32

"Cheater! Cheater! Bloody Cheater!" Serenity yelled, looking through the binoculars, throwing them off the building.

"Hey! What'd you do that for? I liked those binoculars!"

"She's a dirty, sneaky cheater and I can see why Ms. Roberts has a bee in her bonnet about this girl!"

"Hold up, our boy isn't going to just give up the ghost."

"Ah, got some Churchill in him, eh?"

"We will fight in the streets, no matter what the cost may be."

"We will never surrender!"

CHAPTER 33

She found herself in the middle of a living, undulating landscape of exposed muscle and sticky flesh. Still wearing the gas mask, Julie was still familiar with the fact that the Fourth Realm basically smelled like someone's crotch if that person was a 100 feet tall.

She could hear the whispers in the wind, see the hundred foot columns of fire, and feel the way the ground seemed to breathe. The mountains made of human souls, all melted together eternally, still aware, but half-feasted upon by the incubi and succubae that were the majority species of this Realm. The rivers of semen that flowed over arches made of crystal and foreskin.

She had enough weapons in her bag to fight any Fourth Realmers that might come out to play, but right now, they were not her big concern.

She took a deep breath and then got on her bicycle, just as a giant claw came ripping through the reality of the Fourth Realm, behind her.

Just as she had wanted, the thing decided to follow her here. She headed towards one of the mountains, the one that looked the least steep, but still seemed to reach the sky, as she heard the roar behind her, as this thing had managed to get its two faced-head into the Fourth Realm.

Hands reached at her, wailing in eternal agony as she rode her bike over their faces, over their exposed ribs, over their wilted soul-genitals. This mountain actually reached the clouds of pure pheromone.

She pedaled with all her might, as the thing now found its way completely into this world, and was now charging at her at full speed, sulfur flowing from its roaring mouths.

Even with the gasmask on, she felt herself starting to feel faint at the height she had started to reach on this mountain of souls. She still couldn't see the summit and it was getting harder and harder to pedal.

Maybe this wasn't such a great plan.

No! She thought, *the best plans are the worst ones!*

She wasn't sure what the exact conversion was and whether or not this plan would work, but it was really her only alternative at the moment. Physics and geography were very different in the Fourth Realm and our world, so who knows where she'd end up, if this worked, but fighting that thing hand-to-hand would just get her killed.

The thing didn't seem to be slowing down at all, and so she closed her eyes and kept going. As the thing's stomping hooves grew louder and louder, she reached into her bag, and pulled out a wishbone. Breaking it would immediately return her to our realm, but she had to do it at just the right moment.

She still couldn't see the summit, but, looking behind her, she could certainly see the beast gaining on her.

She had no idea how high up she was, but the beast was right on her heels.

It leapt above her, taking an impossible height, that made her realize now was the perfect time to break the bone.

She snapped it in half, only to find herself in mid-air.

As in, 30,000 feet in the air, mid-air. There were clouds.

This was certainly a new experience. One that made her immediately think of dropping acid, truth be told.

There was no time for that as above her, sailing in the air, was the Seventh Realm demon, still in the arc of its jump on the soul mountain.

Its rotted face smiled a hideous smile until its other face realized where it was and it let out a surprised scream as its momentum made it rush towards the ground faster than Julie was.

It flailed in the air ahead of her as she just kinda let herself experience the feeling of freefall

It was like nothing she had ever experienced before.

She spread her arms like she was making snow angels and smiled underneath her gas mask.

You know what would be awesome to have in my bag right about now, she thought, *A parachute. Yeah, that would really hit the spot.*

Then she laughed to herself, because of how "hit the spot" could be applied to her current situation if she was aiming at anything in particular under her.

She looked down at the earth below her, rapidly rushing to greet her. She didn't see the lights of New York City, so she knew she was over someplace more rural.

She waved at the flailing demon off in the distance.

Suddenly, there was a noise louder than anything she had ever heard before. Her ears began to bleed.

What the fuck was that?

Almost as if to answer, she saw the demon light up the sky once, twice, up to eight times, as fighter jets shot missiles at it.

She hadn't thought of that. But yeah, a giant unidentified object suddenly appearing over American airspace and falling at crazy speeds probably would get the attention of any local pilots in the vicinity. That noise was, no doubt, a sonic boom.

Well, that was that. The demon was on fire and heading towards the ground.

She hoped that the jets wouldn't detect her bicycle and open fire on her too. That wasn't really something she had a plan to deal with, to be quite honest. She hadn't thought there'd be jets.

She took off her gas mask and just enjoyed the wind flowing through her hair and screams of the demon. She didn't have much time to savor it, though, as a quick glance downward told her the earth was rushing towards her.

Realizing how precarious her situation had become, she guided herself towards her bicycle, positioning herself back on it, as she reached into her messenger bag.

She could make out things on the ground now. She probably only had a few seconds before impact.

The demon hit the ground and basically exploded. That would take a whole lot of explaining and/or covering up, probably.

She pulled out the pair of bells that had frightened the demon that possessed the little girl so much and rang them once.

The ground coming up to greet her shifted and twisted and she found herself hitting the ground of the Third Realm, the change in physics softening her fall.

It still blew out the tires of her bike and made her cry out when she bounced off the bike, landing hard enough to make her start cursing loudly.

She also was pretty sure the other bottle of vodka she had in her bag was smashed.

But she was alright and she had killed a Seventh Realm demon. Time for a new tattoo.

Actually, she probably should call someone about this first.

CHAPTER 34

Samantha sat at a café in midtown, enjoying Indian food and talking with some of her colleagues, a mixture of professionals both medicals and metaphysical, when her cell phone went off.

"Hello?"

"Hey, Sammi!"

"Julie, what's up?"

"I need you to send me some money for a train ticket."

"What? Why?"

"I'm in…uh…Schenectady. Upstate."

"What? Why?"

CHAPTER 35

Serenity stomped around on the roof of the building.

"Well, that was certainly anticlimactic."

"Not quite. We did get to see some of them Top Gun planes fly over the city."

"They didn't even stay for long. Flew off like birds. Totally disappointed."

"Not I, said the Walrus."

"You and your stupid bloody sweets."

"Shall I prepare Pontius Pilate for you?"

"You're so immature, Mimmy."

"Zebra cakes or yodels?"

"Shared a womb, we did! Shared a womb and this is how you treat your sister. Inhuman, it is!"

CHAPTER 36

A few hours later, Samantha met up with Julie at Penn Station, giving her sister a big and very worried hug.

"My god, Julie! I talked to the Council reps. A Seventh Realm entity is big trouble. And the text you received said it was a *minor* entity?!? This is the type of thing that gets people mobilized. We still don't know if there are going to be any environmental consequences to the entity's entry into our world or the impact it made Upstate. We sent someone to investigate this Vera woman."

"Fuck, Sammi, you don't have to do that!"

"No, someone is trying to *kill* you, Julie! I'm not just going to just stand by and let my family be attacked."

"Was there anything on the news about it? I mean, I did just drop a big fucking demon on Upstate New York from a really high height. That was actually pretty fucking cool, if I do say so, myself."

"Julie, you need to take this seriously."

"I am taking it seriously, don't worry."

"Good. That Vera woman says she just received a call for a minor entity, but we're still looking into if she has any involvement in this."

"She's never steered me wrong before, Sammi."

"You need to be careful, Julie. Persephone is coming into town in a couple days and…"

"Oh, I'm sure Perci will be overjoyed to help me."

"You don't have to like someone to love someone, Julie. She's still your sister."

"Tell her that. I don't have anything against Perci."

"I know that. I hope she hears about this and realizes how serious all this is."

"Well, if there's ever been one of us that's serious all the fucking time, it's certainly Perci."

"That is true. So, you need to get home and get some rest. We need to take this seriously. I want to introduce you to another Council member. Nigel. He's…"

"No need, Sammi. I have this completely handled. I know exactly what I need to do right now!"

CHAPTER 37

We can dance if we want to

Julie was drunk and fooling around with some random goth girl wearing trip pants as the DJ played Men Without Hats' "Safety Dance." It was 80's Night at the Pyramid and downstairs was some goth event or the other. Nothing that interested her, but this kid seemed cute enough when she was drunk, so she would probably be taking a trip back to Brooklyn with Julie later tonight.

The two of them danced and drank. Unfortunately, none of the tattoo places were open at this hour, because Julie really wanted to get the linework started on the entity she had faced last night. That was a milestone that definitely needed to be commemorated on the particularly naked spot on her right thigh.

The two of them went back to her place, Julie receiving not one, not two, but five texts from Lucy throughout the night. She deleted them on the subway, as a particularly persistent mariachi band performed more songs than mariachi bands usually do on the subway.

Finally, Julie gave them five dollars to just go away and leave her and…uh…whatever this girl's name was, alone.

CHAPTER 38

"Is there anything you and I should talk about?" Mr. Trent demanded, forcing his way into the hotel room.

"Do you have any bloody idea what time it is?" Ms. Roberts asked, laying stomach-down and bare on a towel, trying to enjoy her acupuncture treatment.

"Yes, it's time that you stopped with the bullshit and told me what's going on."

"Whatever could you be talking about?"

Mr. Trent folded his arms, and glared at the elderly Asian woman applying needles to Ms. Roberts' pressure points.

Ms. Roberts sighed and told the woman in Cantonese, in a perfect accent, to please wait outside and that she would still be paid for her services.

The woman nodded, gave Mr. Trent a sideways glance and walked out of the room, shutting the door behind her.

"Now, please do tell me what was so important that you had to force your way into my room?"

"Are you telling me you had nothing to do with half of Long Island City being destroyed tonight?"

"Whatever would give you that impression?"

"And nothing to do with a Seventh fucking Realm demon falling out of the sky Upstate, and being shot down by the fucking Air Force?"

"Upstate?"

"Yes, Upstate New York. Schenectady to be precise."

"Well, I have been here in my suite, this entire time, so I have no idea what you're talking about. I certainly have not ventured to this Schenectady place."

"It's just funny that that Juliette woman you have such a problem with was spotted in both places."

"Then maybe you should blame her for this."

"Maybe I should blame you or those two psycho twins you have running around."

"What do they have to do with it?"

"You don't think I wouldn't investigate them? I wouldn't find out about Serenity, or should I say Margaret's summoning abilities? Not everyone is capable of summoning something from the Seventh Realm. Certainly without a large number of sacrifices and undead fucking blood."

"Mr. Trent, you brought me here and paid me a large sum of money to insure that this ritual you want done will be done properly, correct?"

"Yeah. What's your point?"

"I went over this with your people, before I came here. And all parties agreed, including you, that I would be indulged in my particular grudge, correct?"

"None of us knew you'd be leveling the city doing it."

"Oh, now, you're just exaggerating."

"There were millions of dollars in damage done tonight and the Federal Government getting involved in matters His Honor would definitely prefer to keep on a local level."

"Well, after tomorrow, all of that will be all over. Alright?"

"And will you assure me that there will be no more damage to personal and private property in the meantime? Nothing to fuck with taxpayer's heads?"

"Just do as I suggested tomorrow and we'll both get what we want."

CHAPTER 39

Kelly slept horribly that night. The boy she had over, Michael, had been all grabby and she had had to tell him to leave. That was the last time she used OKCupid, she vowed to herself.

Of course, Julie had brought home some random girl last night and had proceeded to have loud girl-sex all night, so Kelly had had to hear that.

She had only moved into the apartment because it was a nice, big apartment at ridiculously cheap rent. And as the man had once said, *you got what you paid for.*

Julie was truly a roommate from hell. Literally. Kelly still found herself having nightmares about that thing in the living room.

Now, this morning, with her finals coming up in a couple months, she still had her thesis to write. It was going to be difficult to do that with the fucking party girl in the next room.

Why couldn't she have gotten someone normal? Julie may have claimed to be a Midwestern girl by origin, but Kelly certainly hadn't run into anybody like her when she lived in Saint Paul.

Well, whatever, right now, she had to focus on…

"Fuck!" Julie said, walking into the living room, looking annoyed, her hand covered in what looked like blood.

"Oh my god, Julie, is that blood?"

"Uh yeah! I got a little surprise last night. About a week early."

"Ugh! That's nasty! Plug that up!"

"Thank you, Sue Snell. Actually, I was going to ask. Do you have any tampons? I'm kinda out."

"Y-Yeah, under the sink. Just ewwww…take care of that."

"Well, on a funny note, not sure if…uh…god, I can't remember her name…realizes she got her red wings last night. She was really, really drunk."

"I don't want to hear it."

"Okay. You probably don't want to know that I fell from the sky last night without a parachute, on a bicycle, and was totally fine, either."

"Not really. Just go use the tampons and please don't touch anything!"

"Fine, you big baby," Julie said, walking off into the bathroom.

Kelly shook her head in disgust, and sat down, with her face in her palm, wondering just how much longer she'd have to deal with that inconsiderate gross person.

That's when she heard it. A slight rustling sound over in the kitchen. *Fuck, it's another one of Julie's nightmares. If that's it, I am out,* she thought.

She made her way to the kitchen, slowly, cautiously, as the shower ran in the bathroom.

Kelly grabbed the broom from the corner of the room and held it, daintily, in her hands, looking around for where that sound was coming from.

It appeared to be coming from the cereal cabinet.

She inched closer and closer to the cabinet, the broom ready to strike.

Maybe she should wait until Julie came out of the bathroom. Unlike Kelly, she was used to fighting horrible things. Maybe it'd be better to wait.

Kelly froze in her tracks, thinking it over, when the cabinet opened by itself.

Kelly felt fear and apprehension, about to scream Julie's name when she took a look, through half closed eyes, at the inside of the cabinet.

Her fear disappeared immediately.

A koala bear, looking cuddly and lovable, was sitting in there, pawing at the Cheerios.

She immediately went up to it, and found herself just melted by the cuteness.

It looked up at her with kind eyes and extended its arms, as if it wanted a hug.

She reached forward and hugged the koala, speaking to it in a baby voice, and then taking it back to the couch.

It looked up at her and she looked at it.

It was probably the cutest thing she had ever seen.

She began to feed it eucalyptus leaves.

It cooed as it ate them.

"Holy fucking shit! Get away from that!" Julie yelled, panicked.

"W-what? Why?"

Without even giving her a chance to respond, Julie ran over, clad only in a towel and punted the koala in the head.

"Whoa! What the hell did you just do?"

The koala flew across the room and splattered against the wall like a water balloon.

Only, blood didn't come out. No, it looked like pixie dust and a rainbow.

Yes, a rainbow. There was even what sounded like a little harp noise.

That was…odd.

"Uh…Julie…what happened there? Why did you just kill a koala bear and why did it turn into a Disney Princess rainbow?"

"Kelly, there's no time to explain, get dressed, now!"

Julie ran into her room and yelled at the girl she had taken home to get out and get out now. The girl, clad only in a pair of panties, not even aware that she had a brown ring of dried blood around her mouth, looked confused. She looked even more confused when Julie opened the front door and pushed her out.

"Julie, you're acting crazy! What is going on!"

"You're the one acting crazy! Where did you get eucalyptus leaves from?"

"I…I don't…"

"Holy fuck! There's another one! Stay away from it!" Julie yelled, slipping on a t-shirt and a pair of jeans.

She ran into her room and came out with a baseball bat and her messenger bag.

"What is going on?"

"Get out of here and warn everybody in the other apartments to get out!"

"Julie, you're not making sense!"

"These koalas are from hell! The deepest darkest part ever touched by man! They are from the Eighth Realm!"

"These are koalas...*from hell?!?*" she asked, raising an eyebrow.

"Yes, these are koalas from hell! I've only read about them in books, but they're something so incredibly horrifying that your mind couldn't possibly comprehend how awful they are."

Kelly turned to see there were koalas coming out of each cabinet. Koalas coming out of her room. Koalas coming out of the fridge.

"Julie, what is happening?"

"Your mind can't process how horrible these things are. You'd go insane if you saw their real forms, so your mind sees something cute as a defense mechanism. They're just parasites, but unlike other Realm's parasites that just make you cum in your pants, these will literally tear your soul apart!"

"I don't get it," she said, as the koalas moved closer.

"Where did you get the eucalyptus leaves from?"

"I...I don't know. They were just kinda there."

"Because you were feeding them...your soul!"

Kelly just couldn't comprehend the weirdness that was happening in front of her, but as six koalas jumped at Julie, she ran out of the apartment to go warn the other tenants that...there was a gas leak. She certainly wasn't going to tell them Koalas of Doom were going to eat their souls.

Meanwhile, back in the living room, Julie hit one koala with the bat, a rainbow coming from his body, as two of them jumped on her face, petting her gently, in a way she knew was actually meant to tear her skull open...just gently. Another koala gave her a soft, cuddly hug.

She knew this meant it was time to pull out the big guns. Literally.

Julie pulled her magnum out of her messenger bag and shot the three koalas in the face, magical sparkles filling the room along with what looked like cartoon stars. Koalas seemed to come flying from everywhere as she shot at them until she was out of bullets.

She couldn't tell where the rift was here, but she didn't have anything in her bag to handle an Eighth Realm anything. It was just the slightest rift, she knew, because these parasites were the least thing you had to worry about in the Eighth, according to the books she had read. The Eighth Realm is when you got to Lovecraftian creatures beyond sanity. Things that, for the most part, slept since the creation of the Universe, because to wake them would no doubt result in the *end* of the Universe.

Either way, she knew she had to buy time for Kelly to save the other tenants of the building.

Outside, Kelly had managed to get everyone out of the building, but mostly because they had heard the gunfire coming from Julie's apartment. The landlord had called the police and Kelly was starting to go into panic mode.

Back inside, there were dozens of koalas jumping at Julie, trying to get hugs, some of them riding kittens. Kittens with tiny angel wings. The kittens were beginning to sing, "It's a Small World After All." It was time to retreat.

She ran into her room, and grabbed her laptop, her bicycle, and gave her room one last look. She had grown to like this place, even if the landlord was always on her case.

But this was one infestation that...

The ground shook. She knew what that meant. She ran into the living room, using her bicycle as a battering ram, rainbows and stars and sparkles filling the air.

It's a world of laughter

The walls started shake, the ceiling started to cave in, the ground started to ripple.

A world of tears

Koalas covered the ceiling, koalas covered the floor, as it tore in half, being sucked into the rift between realms.

Yes, like the house in *Poltergeist.*

Julie sailed her bike over the chasm that formed under her, seeing her room sucked into nothingness, the walls caving in, the koalas going back to their world, as it attempted to pull her in, she feeling her very soul being pulled into the gaping mouth of the abyss.

She rode the bike down the collapsing stairs, smashing through the front door, the walls imploding behind her, as she fell on the sidewalk, the entire building disappearing into a rift the size of a pea.

Julie's landlord, a short Italian woman, dressed like a bus driver, screamed at her lost investment. The other tenants looked distressed. The girl in her panties just looked confused, covering herself with her hands and mumbling to herself that she left her shirt and pants in there.

And Kelly went over to Julie, and demanded to know, "What the fuck was that?!?"

Julie couldn't even answer. She realized now that she was, indeed, in some serious trouble. Whoever did that was no amateur.

There were sirens. An ambulance pulled up. And two squad cars. Julie just sat there stunned, holding tightly to her bike, suddenly aware that she had only the outfit she had on her back, and hadn't thought to put extra clothes in her messenger bag.

And she didn't have any extra tampons.

Fuck.

One of the officers walked towards her and called her by a name she hadn't heard in a very long time, certainly never in New York, "Juliette Ursula Johannes?"

"Uh…what?"

"We'd like you to come with us, please."

"What? Why am I the one you're looking at?"

"Ma'am, I'm going to give you one more chance to come with us or we're going to place you under arrest."

Julie, confused and frightened by how suddenly things were happening, did the only sensible thing she could think of: she got on her bike and started pedaling away.

The cop yelled "Freeze!" and pulled out his firearm, everyone around ducking. He didn't fire, though, as he didn't want to take a chance at hitting anyone in a quiet Brooklyn suburb. Instead, he ran to his squad car and called in that the person of interest was fleeing the scene of the crime.

Kelly went over to the officer and demanded to know what was happening and if Julie was responsible for what just happened.

"Did you know her, ma'am?" the officer asked.

"She was my roommate, but…"

"Ma'am, you're under arrest!"

"What?!?"

The officer slammed Kelly against the hood of the car and slapped cuffs on her as sirens rang in the background, as more squad cars pulled up.

CHAPTER 40

Julie used her little bells to hide herself in the Third Realm for a bit. She knew that just traveling around on a bicycle in the middle of Brooklyn was a sure way to get caught. Whoever had done this obviously had the NYPD involved, as well. Or maybe they were after her for that guy she had beaten half to death in East Williamsburg a few nights ago. But that was self-defense, so she wasn't sure if that was it.

Either way, things were fucked, so she figured she'd hang out in another world for a few hours and then go to see Sammi.

As she sat there, she heard the ground behind her shake, and saw a lone I'Klesf start walking towards her. After all that happened the last few days, any little Third Realm bitch was not going to frighten her.

She looked at it, glaring hard, it glaring back at her, sniffing.

"Yeah, what the fuck you looking at?!?" she yelled at it.

Smelling the Eighth Realm blood on her, it didn't just walk away; it ran.

CHAPTER 41

Back in our world, Kelly sat in an interrogation room, jumpy and annoyed. She had to go to the bathroom and she had been here for three hours, wearing her pajamas.

A good looking, well-dressed man walked into the room, with what appeared to be a SWAT team officer. Joining him a moment later was a young, red headed woman in a sky blue pants suit.

"Hello, Kelly," the red headed woman greeted her, "My name is Miss Roberts. This is Mr. Trent."

"I don't know what I'm being charged with," Kelly said, "But I know my rights. I'm allowed one phone call. And I really have to pee."

"Do you now, Kelly?" the woman asked.

"Yes, can I please either be charged or go?"

"We'll let you go in a minute," Mr. Trent said.

"We just have one question for you and then you can go," Ms. Roberts said.

"What is it?"

"How do you know Ms. Golightly?" Mr. Trent asked.

"*Golightly?*" Ms. Roberts asked, looking annoyed.

"Oh, you didn't know she was using that name?" Mr. Trent asked.

"Like she has the right," Ms. Roberts complained under her breath.

"You mean Julie? I'm just her roommate."

"So, do you know where she went? That's all we want to know," Mr. Trent asked.

"I don't know. I don't know anything she does. She's just this weird girl from a weird family, who has brought me nothing but trouble."

"Are you sure, my dear?" Ms. Roberts asked, looking intently at her.

"Yes, I swear I don't know. What has she done?"

Mr. Trent put forth a copy of today's New York Post. There was a picture of Julie on the cover, with the headline, "Sex, Drugs, and Murder Vixen." The article said that she had been accused of murdering a man in Crown Heights the other night, tearing his throat out, and that she had done so as part of some bizarre sex gone bad. Then it said that she had accidentally blown up a building in Boro Park, Brooklyn, while cooking meth.

"Meth? She wasn't cooking meth," Kelly said, "At least, I don't think she did."

"So, in other words," Ms. Roberts said, looking annoyed, as she got eye to eye with Kelly, "You have no information that can help us?"

"No, I tried to tell you that. Can I please go?"

"You haven't read the entire article, have you?"

Kelly read more and saw that it said that there had been one additional death in the home meth lab explosion. It said her name.

"What? That's a mistake. I'm not dead."

"We don't really need you alive, do we?" Mr. Trent said, his SWAT team member turning to face her, with very menacing body language.

Kelly screamed and jumped back, "Why are you doing this? I have a family! I have people who love me!"

"And those people will hate Julie, knowing she was responsible for your death!"

"Wait," Ms. Roberts said, "Timothy. Don't kill her."

"Thank you, Miss," Kelly said, crying tears of joy.

"Have her stripped and brought to the prison. We're short one female for the ritual."

"What?!?" Mr. Trent protested, "You know the selection process! No one who might be missed! No one who might be invest-"

"She's already bloody dead, right?!?" Ms. Roberts exclaimed, "Then it shouldn't be a problem! Now, if you want me to do this for you, you will take her there right now or I walk and your Mayor can find someone else to do his bloody fucking ritual!"

Mr. Trent punched the table of the interrogation room, breaking it in half, and then nodded to Timothy, who advanced on Kelly.

CHAPTER 42

Late at night in Brooklyn, almost into the morning, Julie came back to our world. Careful to avoid police cars wherever she could, she rode her bike to under the Manhattan Bridge. She stopped by a bodega to get a sandwich and some tampons but noticed her picture on the cover of both the New York Post and Daily News.

Okay, that was a bit much. "Drug Sex Murder Vixen" wasn't even a cool title.

She walked out of the bodega before the owner could notice her and call the police. She knew she had to find some way to get to Sammi in Manhattan.

She rode on her bike from Jay St., towards the Bridge walkway, when suddenly, she found herself in the snow, looking up at the sky.

Something had hit her. Something fast. Something so fast that it was just a blur when it knocked her off her feet.

She stood up and found herself being thrown against the wall.

"Lookie what we found, dear sister," Christopher said.

"The missus will be happy with this one, she will," Serenity said.

"Who the fuck are you two?" Julie asked.

Serenity and Christopher smiled and showed their fangs. Julie sighed, unimpressed.

"Oh, look, it's Team Edward," she said, reaching into her messenger bag and pulling out a wooden stake.

"She's a feisty one, she is," Christopher said.

"Got away from my new pet. I brought him just for you," Serenity said, skipping.

"Oh, so you summoned that Seventh Realm piece of shit. Killed it, you know. Dropped it from the fucking sky," Julie said, folding her arms.

"I think that was more the jets that killed it, love. Don't be embellishing your tale," Christopher said.

"A tale that ends now."

"How movie villain. So, are we gonna fight or are you going to give me a shillin' ta sweep ya chimn'y, guv'na?" Julie said, mocking the twins' accent.

"Hey! That movie was an unfair portrayal of the English working class!" Christopher said.

"God bless us, ev'ryone," Julie said in a Tiny Tim voice, before proceeding to start dancing while singing.

Consider yourself one of us

"Alright, now she dies," Serenity said and, in a blur, advanced on Julie.

Julie headbutted her violently, Christopher jumping on her back, only to be flipped off onto the cold concrete, landing on his feet.

Julie jumped backwards, ready to fight, but Serenity was too fast for her, sweeping her onto the ground. Christopher leapt onto her, smacking her in the face.

"Christopher, dear, you mustn't play with your food," Serenity said, giving her brother a gentle bite on the neck.

"Whoa…you guys do it, don't you?"

Christopher and Serenity got offended looks on their faces.

"Not bloody fucking likely," Serenity protested.

"We're just close is all."

"Shared a womb, we did."

"Shared a womb."

"Yeah, *hers*," Julie said, pointing to Serenity.

Serenity scowled and kicked Julie in the ribs, sending her flying a good ten feet into a wall.

Christopher appeared in front of Julie, in a blur, picking her up with one hand, "I don't appreciate you saying disgusting things about my sister and I. Just because you don't know the love of your family is no cause to disparage mine!"

Julie struggled to get free, but his grip was too tight.

She had fought vampires before, but these two were different. They seemed to actually know how to fight. Like they had been trained as to how to best utilize their powers.

"You know," Serenity said, sniffing Julie, "I think it's her time. You smell it?"

"Ewww, gross," Julie commented, "You guys are sniffing my period? That is really fucking nasty."

"Delicious, more like," Serenity said, biting deeply into Julie's neck.

A second later, she fell to her knees, gagging. A concerned look crossed Christopher's face as Serenity's gagging turned to bloody vomit.

Christopher let Julie go, and ran to his sister's aid.

"Are you alright? I knew I shouldn't have made you eat those bloody Yodels!"

Serenity, her face flush with sweat and her mouth covered in chunky blood, looked up and glared at her brother.

"No, you bloody fucking idiot, it's not that! It's her blood! It tastes funny!'

Julie realized that it was the inoculation against vampires Sammi had insisted she get the other day. Well, that was sure a blessing in disguise. Still, she was still bleeding profusely, and Little Boots and Drusilla weren't about to just let her go.

She reached into her messenger bag and rang her little bells, taking her to the Third Realm again. Nothing would fuck with her there.

Before she could think of a plan, she found herself knocked off her feet again, as Christopher was in the Third Realm too.

"Do you think you're the only one who knows how to walk between worlds? This your first day dealing with magic, is it?"

He held up his own set of little bells.

She charged at him, knowing he was slower in this Realm. Vampires had the tiniest traces of demon blood in them, which is what caused their condition, but it was weak sauce First Realm shit. She had never fought a vampire in the Third Realm before, she knew their powers waned the further from our Earth they got. She wasn't sure how weak, though, so she gave it the old college try and decided to just charge like a madwoman at him, hoping he'd be slowed down enough that she could stake him and be done with it.

When she got close, he punched her in the chest, she feeling one of her ribs break.

He may not have been fast, but he was still strong as an ox here.

She fell to her knees, coughing up blood. He picked her up by the neck again, and went to bite her, before remembering the effect it had had on his sister. So, instead, he punched her in the face with his free hand. Again. And again. And again. He only stopped upon feeling his fist begin to tingle and then burn, from whatever was in Julie's blood.

Her vision was obscured by blood, her thoughts were cloudy, and there was a high-pitched ringing in her ears.

She felt herself losing consciousness as Christopher threw her across the landscape.

"...missus has taken a serious disliking to you and, you know what? So have I," she heard Christopher say, after the ringing subsided a bit.

"S-suck...my dick," she said, getting herself up to her feet and getting into a mockery of a fighting stance.

He laughed and reached behind himself, pulling out two swords, and started doing some sort of intimidating demonstration of his skill.

Julie pulled out her magnum and Indiana Jonesed that shit, shooting him straight in the chest. She was briefly knocked off her feet by the recoil, but she knew this was her opportunity, injured or not.

He flew backwards and she ran in the opposite direction, coughing up blood, and feeling like shit.

She looked backwards to see Christopher still struggling to stand up. The bullet wouldn't kill him, but it certainly appeared to have hurt.

She turned around again, only to be kicked in the face by Serenity, who had appeared to have recovered, and followed her to this Realm.

"You don't hurt my Mimmy!" she yelled, kicking Julie right in the stomach. Julie found herself five feet from where she had been standing. She forced herself to stand up again, half her body in agony, the other half, numb.

"Your...Mimmy?" Julie questioned, coughing, "Oh...I get it...because...you're twins..."

"Wait! You know about...?"

"Yeah...Hello Kitty...Good shit..."

Julie fell to her knees. Serenity looked at her confused.

Really, she wanted to talk to Julie about Hello Kitty right now, instead of killing her.

Julie tried to stand up and fell back down to her knees. She was in bad shape.

Serenity went to say something, but stopped, looked at her brother, and ran over to help him.

Julie took the opportunity to reach into her bag and ring the bell again, finding herself back on the street under the Manhattan Bridge.

She lay on the ground, coughing up blood. It was now morning. She reached into her pocket, pulled out her cellphone and sent a text.

"Don't bother texting your next of kin, love," Christopher asked, right back in this world, after her, holding his chest, his sister hugging him. Suddenly, their skin started to smoke, as they were exposed to the morning sun.

"Fucking hell!" Christopher yelled as he rang his own bell, sending him and his sister back to the Third Realm for protection against the day.

Julie crawled up against the wall, using it to stand herself up. A man dressed like a mariachi came out of the bodega, holding a roast beef hero, and asked if she needed any help. She told him she just had an upset stomach and would be fine. He nodded and walked off.

She pulled her hoodie up and put her sunglasses on. She was internally bleeding and needed to get to a hospital. But she knew she'd be arrested as soon as she went in. Hoping that the text she sent was worth it, she leaned against her bike, trying to force herself to stay conscious.

Desperate times called for desperate measures.

And texting Lucy was certainly a desperate measure.

CHAPTER 43

Later that day, back in her clinic in Manhattan, Samantha crumbled up the New York Post and threw it in the garbage. She couldn't believe the bullshit they were printing about her sister. Someone was obviously trying to frame Julie for something.

She knew her sister was an irresponsible underachiever, but she wasn't a meth cook, and she certainly wasn't a murderer.

The nurse came in to tell her, "I'm sorry to bother you, but you've got a guest. She says she's your sister."

"Julie?"

"No. The other one."

"Persephone! Send her in!"

Her sister came in, well-dressed as always, her long straight red hair, flowing over her shoulders. She gave Samantha a warm hug.

"I read about Juliette in the paper," she said in her Midwestern accent.

"None of it's true, Persephone."

"Well, whether it is or not, we need to find her. She needs our help more than anything."

"Someone summoned something from the Seventh Realm the other day to kill her."

"You're kidding! That's horrible! Did it do much damage? Did you help her kill it?"

"No, she did that on her own."

"Did she? That's surprising."

"Why? You and her were always the best in the family."

"So, I'm told. Of course, some of us actually worked hard to achieve that. But we don't receive any praise for it, of course."

"Let's not start that now, Persephone. Do you want me to bring up Rayborn again?"

"No...Fine. You're right. Listen, you no doubt have patients. I should probably get out of your hair."

"Yeah...Plus, I'm just really worried about Julie."

"Aren't we all?"

"Well, whether you mean that sarcastically or not, I am. And she needs our help."

"Always has."

"So, are you available to have dinner tonight?"

"Ummmm...yes, I am, after 11pm. There's some things I have to take care of for the next few days, but if you don't mind a late night, I'm available."

"Alright. Let me see to my patients and see if I can get in touch with Julie, then we'll talk about everything tonight."

Persephone hugged Samantha and left the clinic.

As soon as she was out of the building, she pulled out her cellphone and made a call.

Mr. Trent answered.

"So, any luck?" he asked.

"No, still nothing," she said, switching her accent to a posh English accent, "But whatever. She can't hide for long with all of your friends looking for her."

"I'm still not comfortable with taking that girl. You know the criteria I set up for them! No one is supposed to miss them! If that girl's parents investigate..."

"If they investigate, they will find that Juliette killed her. And if they investigate further than that, I am sure you can take care of them, as well."

"You're giving me all sorts of headaches I don't need, Ms. Roberts."

"Whatever. You want your ritual to go as planned, correct? Then, I will see you tonight."

And with that, Persephone Roberts hung up the phone and decided that she'd take today to shop at Tiffany's. Even if they didn't find Juliette, her sister was only part of the plan, anyway.

BOOK TWO
NEW YORK'S ALRIGHT...

CHAPTER 1

The air was as thick as maple syrup, the acrid smell of burning flesh permeating the atmosphere. Above molten seas and a bloodstained sky, dotted with clouds of pure cyanide, the soil here was jagged and harsh, weeds of flesh ripped through the charred bone that made the land here. Faces screamed silently from the bleeding trees, souls forever frozen in agony, the voice long gone from their burned out lungs.

Off in the horizon, tornadoes of flame could be seen ravaging the land, as packs of fleshless beasts tore each other apart in an endless dance of carnal savagery.

"I don't know why dad made me bring you along," Julie said to her little sister, who held her hand, looking around curiously, as the dark land around them pulsed with violence.

At the time, Julie was ten, Persephone only six.

"Julie, dad said I have to come! So, if you try to leave me somewhere I'm going to tell on-"

Persephone's mouth disappeared, a trick Julie had learned from one of her father's books. She was an avid reader, even as a child, soaking up knowledge like a sponge.

Persephone's muffled screams struggled to be heard as she clawed at the smooth skin where her mouth had been.

"Are you going to shut up and stop being a tattletale?" Julie asked.

Her sister nodded her head and, just like that, the skin over her teeth split open, folded over itself to form lips, and then opened wider to form a mouth, once more. She took a deep breath of the foul air.

"And don't tell dad I did the trick with your mouth, either, Perci!"

Persephone shook her head.

The two of them walked through the Fifth Realm, together, their father's idea of a field trip for the two sisters.

They stopped over a vast chasm, a river of screaming bodies miles below them.

Persephone raised her hand.

Julie looked at her and nodded.

"Julie? Can I ask a question?"

"It better be a good one."

"Can you make someone's butt disappear too?"

Julie giggled.

"Yes."

Persephone giggled with her sister.

"Can you teach me how to do it?"

"I'm not supposed to be reading dad's books, you know. I could get in all sorts of trouble if I teach you the things in them. He got all angry after I tried to make us a dog."

"I promise I won't tell, Julie."

Julie looked at the screaming souls below her and threw a rock, squishy with human eyes, at them. She had already killed half a dozen demons on her own at this point, and felt like having her sister tag along with her was a sign her father didn't trust her.

But looking at Perci's hopeful eyes and big smile, her red hair flowing in the filthy wind of this place, she felt as close to her sister as she ever did.

"Okay. I will," Julie said.

Persephone gave her a big hug.

There was a growling behind them that sounded like rocks in a garbage disposal. The two sisters turned to see three creatures crawl towards them on all fours. They resembled skinless humans in a bridge position, except their faces were upside down, their intestines hanging under them like waste-spewing utters. Their jaws clicked open to reveal row after row of fingernails instead of teeth, with tongues covered in sores, that hung a good foot and a half on the outside.

"Julie, make their mouths disappear!" Persephone demanded, hiding behind her sister, frightened. She was still two years from her birthday trial, something Persephone looked forward to more than anything else.

"Can't! Only works on people."

The creatures snarled, Persephone flinching.

"Don't worry, Perci. I'll show you how to do it!"

Julie reached into the Hello Kitty backpack she wore and produced two child-sized claymores, which she held in each hand.

Julie smiled. She wanted to show off for her little sister.

CHAPTER 2

...estimate on when power will be restored to Schenectady after Friday night's satellite crash. NASA representatives still have no explanation for what caused the object to fall to Earth, but assure us that most objects that fall from space are not...

click

...Darnell, you are not *the father...*

click

...after last year's sexting scandal, the Congressman says that he is ready to run for...

click

...Have we seen his birth certificate, Diane? I don't think so. The Lamestream Media can continue to assert that he was born here all they want, but until I see...

clicks

...TMZ reports that the oil heiress and daughter of Senator Robert Kensington, has been checked into an undisclosed medical facility to deal with...

click

...There's no escape/ I need a hit...

She put down the remote and decided to watch Britney Spears for a little bit. This song always reminded her of a simpler time in her life.

Persephone sang along to the song, dancing a little bit in bed.

And I love what you do
But you know that you're toxic

She snapped her fingers in time with the music and let her long red hair flow down over her bathrobe as she sang along, letting all her problems disappear for a few moments.

Her cell phone rang and she stopped singing and sighed heavily. It was probably Trent. Probably had something or the other to complain about. She had grown to seriously dislike him. But then again, she disliked his kind as a general rule. She had killed enough of them in her lifetime.

"Hello?" she said, her voice tired, her English accent not as strong as it usually was.

"So, Ms. Roberts, we have two days. Do we-is that Britney Spears?"

Persephone quickly pressed the mute button on the remote.

"I have absolutely no idea what you're talking about."

"Whatever," he said, sighing, "So, do we have everything all set?"

"Everything except the little matter of my sister."

"We had her on the front page of all the local papers for the last two days."

"Then why haven't you caught her?"

"Because this is a city of eleven million people and not all of them give enough of a shit to report her, wherever she is."

"Okay, well, there was the matter of that demon's particularly destructive rampage. I still do not understand why you put that down to an exploding gas main instead of putting it on my sister."

"Because you want her brought in by us. Her building exploding due to a fucked up meth lab, we can deal with. We start saying she's responsible for the destruction of several blocks of Long Island City real estate, we're putting her on the level of a domestic terrorist."

"And the problem with that is?"

"The problem with that is that she would no longer become an NYPD problem, but a Homeland Security problem. And she gets caught, she doesn't come to us, she goes to Guantanamo."

"Shit."

"Yeah. Hopefully, your little ploy of taking her roommate will get her attention, but until then, we have the ritual to worry about."

"I guess so."

"You *guess* so? You didn't cash the very substantial check that you received? You didn't…"

"Yes, yes. I will be there, okay? And I *will* be ready. Do *not* doubt my professionalism, Mr. Trent."

"That's all I want to hear, Ms. Roberts."

"Good day, Mr. Trent," she said, hanging up the phone.

She really, really hated Mr. Trent.

She knew she could kill him. Easily. Him and his little pitbull in the SWAT team outfit.

But he had all the connections in this city. Eliminating him would create more problems than it would solve.

She stood up and looked at herself in the dresser mirror. She would have to start cleansing her system tomorrow, in order for her body to be completely ready for the ritual. She never looked forward to a day of fasting and meditation, but it came with the territory.

She ran her fingers through her hair and crinkled up her nose, before turning the tv off to go do her morning yoga routine, and shower.

She quickly turned back towards the mirror, having seen something in it in out of the corner of her eye. A big smile crossed her lips.

"Oh, hi! I was wondering when I'd see you again," she said.

CHAPTER 3

"Sell when it gets to $25 a share. Got me a sneaking suspicion that it's going to sink through the floor, I do," Serenity said, over her cellphone to her broker, looking at the stock prices on her laptop, Christopher sleeping in.

She was drinking blood out of a Hello Kitty coffee mug while checking the NASDAQ. She had always been good with numbers and being around during the Great Depression had made her realize just how important the Stock Market was to the world at large, so after the Second Great War had ended, she had started to investigate the world of stocks and bonds.

Of course, when she had first started to get into it, she was restricted from doing anything herself due to being a woman. So, she had started to make connections with human stock brokers and made a couple safe investments at first, especially considering that when she had first wanted to get into it, there were only 1,366 "seats" for directly trading.

Of course, even if she had been allowed there, there was the slight problem of bursting into flames when exposed to direct sunlight.

So, around 1953, she used a combination of her feminine wiles and vampiric brute force to secure a representative on the floor.

Since then, it had become one of the great joys in her life to participate in the trading of stocks. She had even managed to avoid being affected by the Dow Jones dropping 508 points in 1987, through a careful observation of market trends and insider info.

For a girl from Leighton Buzzard, who had been put into an orphanage when her father had died in the Crimean War and eventually had to prostitute herself to pay for food for her and her brother back in the days when she knew sickness and hunger and mortality, to find herself hobnobbing with the giants of finance was a source of great pride.

Yes, she killed things. Mostly people. Mostly for food, but also on occasion, for fun. Okay, *often* for fun. She was a hunter. It was the nature of her condition. She was a predator, through and through. It was something that provided her a great deal of joy.

But Serenity had created a life for herself outside of murder for fun and profit. She had become fascinated and entranced by the work of Yuko Shimizu, Hello Kitty in particular. The backstory of the character resonated with her in a personal way.

And for a girl who grew up wearing rags in the Victorian Era, the inviting aesthetic of a simple cat designed in Japan appealed greatly to her.

"Right right," she said, on the phone, "How's about we buy 55, no, 60 shares of Honeywell, and, uh, 25 of Bayer. Big things on the horizon for them, methinks."

Christopher snorted and rolled over, hugging her around her bare stomach in his sleep.

She kissed his forehead and smiled.

She finished up the call and hung up the phone, closing the laptop, and lying in bed with her brother, facing his sleeping form, feeling at peace.

Except for the girl.

She was still out there, somewhere, and Ms. Roberts was still anxious to find her.

She didn't want to let Persephone, who had been such a good friend and confidant to the two of them, down.

Even though she still wanted to talk to Julie about her own experiences with Hello Kitty.

She was curious as to why Persephone wanted to kill her own sister.

Serenity couldn't imagine ever so much as harming a hair on Christopher's head. They had shared a womb, after all. Together from the very beginning.

But there was no such love from Ms. Roberts for whatever reason. Serenity didn't want to pry. Persephone had already done so much for her and her brother.

When the sun went down, they'd go back to looking for her. It had only been two days since they had last seen Julie, so she would probably still be on her period, which made her easier for Serenity and Christopher to catch her scent. Most people were probably unaware that their blood had a scent that was as distinct as their fingerprints.

Serenity was a honed predator; after over a century of practice, she could detect a person's scent from a crowd of thousands, and if the person happened to be female and having her time of the month, Serenity could smell them from an even greater distance. All she'd have to do is be within 10 blocks of Julie and she could find her.

Not to mention, the flavor of whatever concoction she had in her blood to make vampires ill was a very distinct smell. Ironically, something designed to repel regular vampires was certainly going to help two of them find her.

But New York was a big place and the last two nights hadn't been successful.

When she last saw the girl, she was obviously on death's door, but when she returned to that area when the sun went down, Julie's scent had gone cold. She suspected she had gotten into a car, since that was the only way a scent would just disappear without leaving some sort of trail.

And there was another scent there. One Serenity didn't recognize, but could tell was distinctly inhuman. Something demonic.

She wondered if something else had gotten to Julie first.

CHAPTER 4

In the darkness of her cell, Kelly wept through a mouth that wasn't there. She sat between 19 other women, who all, somehow, managed to sleep, despite being chained naked in this cold room. They had all told her that Ms. Roberts had made things better. That all she needed was obedience and she'd give Kelly her mouth back.

Kelly doubted that after the conversation Ms. Roberts had had with her on the van ride here.

As she sat in that van, naked except for a hood over her head, with bladder so full it that felt like it was about to burst, Ms. Roberts sat down next to her. She pulled the hood off, put a warm arm around Kelly's bare shoulders and told her that she was going to die in a few days.

And that it'd be Julie's fault.

"I don't want to cause a panic among the others, because they have come to look forward to my visits, but in truth, all of your lives are going to end soon."

"Just please, let me go. If I knew where Julie was, I'd tell you! I…"

"You know, when I asked you about her, you said she came from a 'weird family.'"

"Well, it's just the stories she's told me about her father and her sisters and all the demons and…"

"So, if she's from a 'weird family,' then that would imply that yours was normal, right? I assume you're going by the standard set by your own parentage, right?"

"Please, just let me go! At least, let me use a bathroom! I need to pee and I…"

"Have you tried peeing?"

"I really have to go! I don't know how I've held it in so long! I…"

"Why don't you try peeing right now?"

"I don't want to pee all over myself."

"Try it."

"I don't want…"

Ms. Roberts glared at her and suddenly Kelly felt invisible hands grabbing her by the throat, dragging her to her feet.

"I told you to urinate. Right now."

Kelly cried and closed her eyes. No matter how much she strained, nothing came out.

"I…I can't…I…"

"You're right. You can't. You don't have a urethra at the moment. I've taken it away."

"Wha…? How?"

"Well, I guess that's something you learn when you come from a 'weird family,' right?"

"You're…?"

"Yes, I'm one of her sisters! And for as much of a piece of shit as Juliette can be, I will *not* have the likes of you talking down to me. She may take after the black sheep of the family, but we are of a proud history. We are of a sacred bloodline! *You* are nothing. Do you understand me?"

Persephone slapped her across the face. Once. Twice. Three times.

"Do you understand?"

Kelly gave a meek nod and whispered, "I'm sorry. I just…I just want to go home…"

"You just want to go home? You make me sick, you know that? You can't even stand to be around my sister and yet you act like you're somehow better than the rest of us. You know what? I think I'm going to get a great deal of pleasure out of seeing you die in a few days."

Kelly tried to say something, but found her voice muffled.

"I took away your mouth. Just like I took away your ability to pee. I pretty much took everything from you, if you think about it. I don't think you deserve to talk anymore."

The van stopped at their destination. The invisible hand let go of her and Kelly crumpled to the floor of the van.

Two armed guards opened the back of the van. Even having seen the mouth trick before, they were still horrified to see she had done it to Kelly.

"Besides, I know you'd spread panic to the others if I were to give you back your mouth, so you can just forget about that."

Kelly cried.

"But, I don't want you dying from your bladder bursting, so…"

Urine poured down Kelly's inner thighs, forming a big pool around her, the two guards waiting for it to be done before dragging her away, Kelly's head bowed in shame.

That had been two days ago. She had seen the others rewarded for subservience, being made to bow before Ms. Roberts, and to sit in silence the rest of the day, waiting for her daily visits. She had seen the others actually turn in those who had begun to show defiance, and the beatings and humiliation they were subjected to, until they, too, fell in line with the others and did as they were commanded. Obedience got you food. Obedience let you be washed. Obedience got you water.

Kelly wanted to be back in her mother's arms, safe and warm, instead of in this horrible, horrible cold place of foul smells and starvation that Julie had somehow gotten her stuck in.

She didn't want to think of how upset her family must be, thinking she was already dead. She could only hope...

And it angered her to even have this hope.

But she hoped that somehow, Julie would find her and save her.

CHAPTER 5

In her clinic, between patients, Samantha looked out the twelfth story window, at the grey sky above the city, wondering where her sister could be. She was still alive. She knew that. The Council had members who could tell when someone crossed over into the spirit realm. Her friend and colleague from the Chicago office, Farah Kapaldia, was one such person and had promised to immediately let Samantha know if Julie were to ever die.

Julie hadn't tried to call and she hadn't contacted any Council representatives. They were looking for her, of course, but no one had seen the faintest trace of her. In this realm, at least. There were six other Realms she could been hiding in. Although, knowing her sister, Samantha assumed Julie would probably be too bored by the First Realm to spend any time there. Places without solid ground don't offer much stimulation. So five realms (what Samantha did not know was that Julie had once visited the First Realm tripping balls, just so she could experience an endless freefall while hallucinating).

But, more importantly, there was something very worrying at the scene of where her apartment had been. The Council had detected *Eighth* Realm magics. Someone had punched the tiniest hole in the worlds and the entire apartment building had been sucked into it. It was a hole no bigger than a pea, but that was more than enough when the Eighth Realm was concerned.

No one messed with the Eighth Realm. Besides certain fictionalized accounts, only the most arcane and ancient books even detailed what was in it. The Seventh Realm attack had been bad enough, and meant that someone not human had been after her sister. The circle of bodies that had been reported near the scene told her enough. But vampires, demons, whatever. None of them had access to the Eighth. You woke up the things there, you pretty much ended *everything*.

So, even poking a tiny hole like that was like poking a tiny hole in a dam when you live in the village right next to it. You never knew what you could possibly wake up if you did something like that. Maybe nothing. Maybe you'd just end up blinking us all of existence. Nobody knew and nobody wanted to know.

Well, not nobody. She had discovered over the years dealing with the Council that during the Second World War, the Nazis had tried, unsuccessfully, of course, to breach the Eighth and even the *Ninth* Realms. With all the power and knowledge possessed by the Thule Society, they had still tried to open doorways to realms they had no business doing so. It was destined to fail, obviously, since no one has ever been able to open the doorway from *this* direction. There just isn't anything powerful enough on this side to do that.

But someone had managed to do just that. And to Julie, of all people.

Samantha wasn't stupid. She knew her little sister was an alcoholic, drug-using underachiever who had all sorts of sex she didn't want to know about. So, she was sure Julie had pissed some people off over the years. People, vampires, demons, werewolves, probably a banshee or two. But so had her father, who Julie took after way too much.

But whom could she have possibly pissed off who knew how to do that?

Unless Julie went around kicking actual honest-to-goodness *gods* in the balls, there's no one who she could have possibly pissed off that was powerful enough to open a hole to the Eighth. No human. No demon. No vampire. Nothing on this plane of existence.

She sighed, realizing that no matter how hard she focused on it and wracked her brain, the answer wasn't going to just fall into her lap.

As the loud mob of teenagers down on the street let her know that school was probably out for the day, she sighed and wished that her baby sister would call or stop by or something.

CHAPTER 6

Mr. Trent sat in his office, staring at City Hall Park, but not really looking at anything in particular. He rubbed his temples, annoyed. The girl was becoming a problem. She was irresponsible, brash, and seemed to only care about herself. He wasn't even 100% sure that she was going to go through with the ritual, despite her assurances. This was one of the few times when he missed the old days, when he first emigrated to this realm. Back in the days when, if a subordinate screwed up, he would advise the human in charge to turn that subordinate's head into an ornament for the castle. Now, he had union representatives to deal with and endless amounts of red tape to climb through. The guy who vetted Persephone Johannes or Roberts or whatever last name she wanted to go by had obviously not done his job when he brought her onto the project.

Mr. Trent intended on finding out who that guy was, pouring through his record, and if there was even the slightest bit of dirt there, demoting that guy to the deepest darkest mailroom he could find.

It was a long way from the days of flaying and castration and beheading of those who failed.

If there was anything he didn't like about the modern world, it was that. He liked so much about it. Cell phones that allowed him to communicate with anyone a continent away in milliseconds, vehicles that allowed him to travel from place to place without horses (an animal he was never fond of) or dimensional jumping (which always made him slightly nauseous), an internet that provided him with libraries full of knowledge. But with that came labor laws and regulations and term limits.

Sometimes, he even thought of going back home to his dad's kingdom. But no, that would just involve endless wars with either his brothers, whenever one of them decided to usurp the throne, which happened every hundred or so years, or one of the other kingdom's sovereigns decided to wave his barbed dick around, which happened every hundred or so days. The Fifth Realm was a place with many heads that all hated each other. A place at constant war. Not much different from Earth, really, except negotiation was considered a sign of weakness. Actually, not much different from Earth.

But no, the ritual had to happen. He had two more days. He didn't care whether they found Persephone's sister or not, at this point. All he cared about was getting the ritual done. His Honor, the human in charge of this city, a man whom Mr. Trent had maybe spent a total of an hour or two around, had entrusted him to make sure that this annual event happened.

After it did, he would see what his next step would be. Should he kill Ms. Roberts? How strong was she, exactly? That first day they had met, she had given him quite a jolt, through some power he had never experienced before. Was that the full extent of it or was that her way of warning him not to cross her? And what about her two vampire associates? They were not only trained killers, according to Carcetti, but one of them was an expert summoner, with the ability to tap into the Seventh Realm. As big of a deal as Mr. Trent was in the Fifth, something from the Seventh Realm would eat him alive.

But then again…

He knew someone who had actually managed to slay a Seventh Realm entity. Well, he didn't *know* her personally, but he knew her through the person who had expected him to find and kill that person.

He laughed to himself.

CHAPTER 7

She wasn't quite sure where she was. The last couple days had been a blur of pain. She knew she was in a dark room somewhere. And her ribs were killing her. She had briefly flashed in and out of consciousness, seeing men in robes chanting over her, ancient languages that she might have recognized if the world hadn't been fed to her in snippets over time.

She tried to move her arms and found they were strapped down. Where the fuck was she?

She heard moaning from the next room. A man and a woman, obviously involved in passionate sex. She could hear the headboard hitting into the wall repeatedly. The slapping sound of flesh on flesh. She shook her head and tried to sit up and found she couldn't do that either. Her legs felt like they were strapped down too.

Julie wanted to scream but didn't have the strength for it.

In the room next door, the moans grew louder and louder.

Julie struggled to escape her bounds.

Suddenly, the man's moaning turned to screams of terror. Screams of agony. She heard a loud cracking noise and what sounded like the squish of internal organs. The woman's moans still continued.

That's when it hit Julie where exactly she was.

Fuck.

She stopped struggling and lay down, trying to collect her thoughts and piece everything together.

Suddenly, a silhouette appeared in the doorway. It was distinctly female, from the curve of its hips and breasts, but it had what looked like goat horns protruding from the head, with large bat-like wings coming from the figure's back. It let out a loud unearthly howl, which then turned into a female voice.

"Damn, yo, that was some fine fucking. Boy had a dick on 'em...*Daaaamn.* And his soul ain't taste bad neither. Girl gotta eat, ight?"

Yup, Julie remembered, this was Lucy's place.

The silhouette turned distinctly human and disappeared into another room.

"L-Lucy?" Julie called out, "Why am I...why am I tied up?"

"Oh shit, yo," Lucy called from the other room, "Hold up. Gotta fix my braids."

"Okay, take your time, Lucy. I'm just...a prisoner or whatever."

"What's that noise? Nuh uh! *Nuh uh!* You ain't no prisoner, bitch!"

Lucy said, running into the room, turning the light on, and, in one swift movement, undoing Julie's bindings, "You my nigs, yo! You my motherfuckin' guest!"

It was hard to tell how tall Lucy was, exactly, because she wore very high platforms. About six-eight inches, Julie estimated. And they were silver. Like big bright shiny silver. The type of silver movies from the 1960's had thought everyone would wear in the future. Also silver were the tiny bootie-shorts she wore, her barely there tube top that her enormous breasts spilled out of, and the ridiculously long fake fingernails she wore at all times. Although those weren't only silver. If Julie looked closely enough, she could see that Lucy's nails were quite ornately painted with...uh...Asian lettering or something. Didn't look like demonic script, which often resembled Hebrew, Farsi, and Arabic. Definitely looked like Kanji.

Lucy was pale as a ghost and had long braided blond hair, her face covered in the gaudiest makeup known to man.

Or in her case, demon.

Succubus, to be precise.

"Thanks, Lucy. Why was I tied up?"

"Motherfuckin' Gandalfs said you was gonna hurt yourself if we don't tie you down. Yo, your ribs was allllllll fucked up and shit. You was in bad shape two days ago."

"Gandalfs?"

"Priests, 'ight. I ain't know how to fix no bodies so I just called some priests that worship my ass."

Julie nodded. That made sense. At least as much sense as any conversation with Lucy ever made.

She tried to sit up and felt that while she was, indeed, still in pain, her ribs were no longer pushing into her lungs. She also noticed the distinct lack of blood pouring from her mouth and neck, which was a positive.

Wait…blood pouring from…Julie quickly looked down at the crotch of her pants, realizing she had been knocked out for two days with her period and her…

She wasn't wearing pants. She was actually in some sort of hospital gown. She lifted the front up and checked down the panties that obviously weren't hers, as they were orange cotton panties that looked like they had been bought at some 99 cent store.

She put a hand in them and noticed a pad in them.

"Uh…Lucy…"

"Oh, don't worry about that. Us girls gots to stick together. Know what I'm saying?"

"Not really. Did you…?"

"Well, yeah. That's a new couch you on and it's all classy and shit. I ain't having no pussy blood all over it. Shit, not like I ain't seen a pussy before, know what I'm saying?"

She tried to high-five Julie, who just looked at her, puzzled.

"Are you saying you…?"

"Like you was my baby sister, yo. Pssh. Like I ain't handled no human blood before. Shit, nigga. I live off that shit."

Julie was weirded out at the thought that Lucy had been…maintaining her…uh…feminine…hygiene…while she was unconscious.

"Uh…Lucy…I'm not sure I'm comfortable with you…uh…handling my vagina while I was out."

"Oh…next you gone complain that I wiped your ass?"

"You…wa…you…wa? What?"

"Bitch, you been out two days. You think your body gonna wait till your ass wakes up? And I ain't having this place smell like shit. Nuh uh. I gotta do business, ight?"

"I'm really, really weirded out right now."

"I tolds you. I treated you like you was my baby sister. What's a nigga for, ight?"

"Ummmmm…do you even *have* a baby sister?"

"Shit yeah. Lots of them bitches. Hundreds. We likes to fuck in my family, know what I'm saying?"

Julie just blinked, made a face, and continued her questioning, feeling very, very icky at the moment, "So, since you're a demon…do you actually have diapers to change?"

"Why you gotta ask the weird shit?"

Julie just shook her head.

Lucy put on some reggaeton and sat with her legs spread on top of her dresser. She opened the top shelf, pulled out a very large blunt, lit it, and inhaled deeply.

"So…since you my guest, you want some of this?"

"I think…I think I very much need to be very high right now, yes."

Julie took a hit and sat back down on the couch.

"So, Lucy…uh…this whole look you have. This is…*new*. Last time you didn't seem to be hitting so many…uh…stereotype boxes. Last time I saw you, you looked kinda more like…"

"Marilyn Monroe, 'ight."

"Yeah."

"Classy bitch. But, uh, check it, my nigs. See, there I was all classy and shit, but I was thinkin', I been doing this shit since the 1950's, 'ight, so times change. Man don't wanna fuck no bitch look like his grandma."

"Well, yes, that has been my experience with men too."

"So, I turns on the tv and there this hot bitch named Lil Kim. And I'm like, that's it. That's what I'm gonna be like. Next thing I know, all the mens can't wait to get up in my shit."

She stood up and popped her ass for a few seconds to Jzabehl singing in Spanish about someone who thought they were "hot shit," but, alas, was "not shit."

"I see…Ummmm…I don't mean to be rude, but you know, Lil Kim is black, right?"

"Yeah. So?"

"So, why didn't you change your skin too?"

"Yo, this face is motherfuckin' hot! I gots this face since I first looked human! I made this motherfuckin' face! I ain't changin' it no matter what! What? What? I Queen Bitch no matter my pussy pink or my pussy brown!"

"Well, that's some mighty descriptive reasoning, Lucy."

"Whatever. Why you gots to be so racist?"

"*Was* that racist?"

"Shit yeah, that was racist, nigga!"

"Well, I didn't say it was…*bad* that you were acting…black or whatever…Uh…I think I'll stop and have another hit now."

"So, being yo skinny white ass been on my couch last two days, what up? Ain't seen your ass in a year. Been callin' like a motherfucker. Been textin' like a motherfucker."

"Been meaning to call you, but didn't have the time. Until the other day."

Lucy stood up, stretched, and started to leave the room, "Uh huh. Yo, I'm fuckin' thirsty. You want some malt liquor?"

"Let me guess. You have it in a 40, right?"

"Fuck yeah! Only way to drink that shit! Colt motherfuckin' 45!"

"Sure, as long as I can have it in a brown paper bag. When in Rome and all."

"You in the Bronx, not Rome. Damn, bitch, you hit your head too?"

"It was…nevermind."

Lucy handed Julie a 40 of Colt 45, in a brown paper bag, like one would get from a deli.

She took another hit of the blunt and giggled at Julie.

"So, you all gangsta now, I hear?"

"Because of the 40 of malt liquor in a brown paper bag?"

"Nah, bitch! You all over the news. Some nigga you popped a cap in."

"I didn't 'pop a cap' in anyone…well, okay, some koalas…Oh, and a vampire."

"Oh, fuck them niggas."

"That's what I say every time."

"But bitch, your ass is motherfuckin' famous! You got some of that meth you cooking?"

"They said I was cooking meth?"

"Yup. All over the news and shit."

"Damn. That's really weird. I wasn't cooking any meth. My apartment just kinda…imploded. Hmmm…my bag around here anywhere?"

"Yeah, over there. Shit was empty, though."

Julie smiled and looked around the room, seeing her messenger bag lying in the corner, next to a collection of chains and vibrators. She motioned to it. Lucy grabbed it and threw it to her. She reached inside and pulled out her laptop.

"Yo, where you hide that shit? Up your cooch?"

"No, I'm sure you probably would have seen it while you were playing nurse the last couple days. No, this is in my bag."

"Bullshit, yo. Shit was empty when I looked."

Julie giggled. Probably because she was definitely high at this point, but also because she loved showing off her little trick to people…even if Lucy wasn't exactly "people."

She put her laptop back in her bag and handed it to Lucy. Lucy put her hand in and fumbled around.

"Whoa, my ass just high or you hiding that shit somewhere?"

"Little trick I learned from some books my dad had, when I was a kid."

"Shit, never knew your ass was magic."

"Well, not much. I can make an infinite pocket that only I can reach into. I can make someone's mouth disappear. Can move a couple things with my mind. I can do a couple things here and there. Nothing big. My sisters are bigger with the magic than I am. I kinda just like to smash shit."

"Daaaaaamn, bitch."

"Used to do the bag trick when I was in high school and wanted something but was too broke to pay for it."

"When was the last time you did that shit?"

"Ummm…a week."

"I'd be robbin' banks left and right if I had a bag like that."

Julie nodded and pulled out her laptop. Lucy quickly reached forward and closed it.

"Uh…what was that about?" Julie was annoyed.

"Yo, if the motherfuckin' po-po is looking for your ass, they may be tracin' your motherfuckin' laptop!"

"I don't think the NYPD have the power to trace a laptop. And if I'm running this over here, isn't it a different ip address?"

"I don't know shit 'bout any of that shit, but I know them niggas got the motherfuckin' Patriot Act and shit, so they can read your e-mails and tap your phone without no warrant."

"I don't *think* the NSA is after me quite yet."

"You know them niggas all work together."

"Well," Julie said, putting her laptop back in her bag, "I have to get in touch with my sister, somehow…Fuck…I am too sober for this shit right now."

"Well, don't you worry your ass none. You can hang with me and my niggas up here in the motherfuckin' Boogie Down!"

"While that sounds like a lot of fun, I think I better figure out some…"

"Nah nah nah. I ain't taking no motherfuckin' no for an answer. We gonna get fucked up and get some niggas to eat our pussies and…"

"Won't that kill them?"

"Nah. I ain't drain them until they stick they dicks in me."

"I see. Well, as inviting as having orgies that result in the death of the men involved with you sounds, I think I may just be on my way once I…where *are* my pants, anyway?"

"Oh, don't be leaving my ass hanging, yo. Besides, nigga I just ate was motherfuckin' loaded. Had a big ass roll of Benjamins."

"…and?"

"And I think my nigs needs herself a motherfuckin' shopping spree."

"Hmmmmm…you know what? I…uh…I think I *do* need a motherfucking shopping spree."

"Wait. Wait. Wait. I gots a better idea!"

"Hmmm…that we should use that money to get high and use my bag for a completely free shopping spree?"

"Fuck yeah, bitch!"

CHAPTER 8

Off to the Westchester Mall in White Plains, Julie and Lucy drove in Lucy's Barbie Pink Cadillac Escalade, complete with tricked out hubcaps, tinted windows, and hydraulic lifts to make the car bounce to the bass of whatever music Lucy happened to be playing. They proceeded to hit the stores. They tried on whatever clothing they could, all the while shoveling merch into Julie's magic bag. They spent a good time posing in front of various mirrors wearing odd hats, Julie finally deciding that she wanted a big fuzzy hoodie that made her look like her face was poking out from a panda's head. Lucy stocked up on thongs, bras, and garters at Victoria's Secret, parading around the store in them while Julie shoved clothes into her bag. Julie used her Sephora gift card and then proceeded to take a trip to Best Buy, where Julie managed to score a "free" PS3 and a whole bunch of games for her Vita. They got manicures, pedicures, facials, massages, and shampoos at Elizabeth Arden; ate copious amounts of chocolate at Godiva; raided Sunglass Hut; got scented body wash at Bath & Body Works; Julie stocked up on skinny jeans at American Apparel. All the while, shoveling items into their bags.

Of course, at just nearly every store, they were stopped by security, who demanded to look in Julie's bag, only to find nothing in it. Lucy would suddenly get all serious and threaten to sue everyone, claiming sexual harassment, and they'd be let go.

Overall, they spent a total of $500 (mostly at Elizabeth Arden, since the Iconic Red Door treatment cannot just be slipped into a magic messenger bag), and ended up with $13,000 worth of merchandise from various stores.

And then they went to a nearby liquor store, Julie now wearing her panda hoodie and a new pair of skinny jeans, where they got a whole lot of Jager and vodka.

Then they used some of that money for Julie to finally get those tattoos she had been wanting to get for the last few days, the giant

Seventh Realm entity on her inner thigh, a bunch of koalas on her right shoulder, and a grubby old teddy bear on her inner wrist.

Julie demanded that Lucy tip heavily.

And then, because she was a little drunk and hadn't gotten any in a couple days, asked the tattoo artist if he'd like to go into the bathroom with her for a few minutes. He told her that was a good way for him to get fired. She told him that he's taking his break and dragged him into the bathroom of a bar across the street.

She felt a lot better afterwards. Luckily for Julie, during all this time, no one made the connection that she was the girl on the news. The panda hoodie threw people off.

CHAPTER 9

Later that evening, Jerry took the appropriate kneeling position after being escorted out of his cell. Ms. Roberts would be coming soon and he knew, by now, it was best to stay quiet and do as he was told. All in all, as much of a hell as this was, she had elevated their situation quite a bit, compared to when he first came here and had been spending most of his time pissing and shitting all over himself while chained in one position, starving and hooded.

He had seen her do things he didn't think were even possible. Part of him wondered if those things were just hallucinations, the results of starvation and dehydration, but the other men had whispered to him about the things they saw too. There was magic in the world, real magic. This woman had powers. Things he wouldn't have believed were real had he not been living them.

He had no idea how long he had been here as there were no windows nor clocks, but he had started to spend the time he was in his cell with the other men counting the seconds. Singing songs to himself in his head that he knew were 4 or 5 minutes long. Doing anything he could to hang on to time.

And then there was that new girl. The one with no mouth. He knew how horrifying that trick had been when Ms. Roberts had pulled it on him in the first place, but that had only been for a couple seconds. This girl had not had a mouth the whole time. It was like she had pissed off Ms. Roberts something fierce.

He found himself ashamed of the stirring in his loins when he thought of that girl. Behind the tears and terrified look in her eyes, he could see there was something beautiful about her. He hated that he was even thinking of her that way, but he had gone all this time without any sort of human contact and had found himself starting to notice things like the female inmate's bodies. He really hoped that, in his kneeling position, no one could see that he was semi-erect, thinking about that girl.

Every time he looked at her, he wanted to hold her and comfort her. To make her less afraid. And then he'd get to thinking of her skin against his, wondering what her long curly blond hair smelled like, wondered if her eyes were as blue as they looked from here, across the room.

Okay, stop it, Jerry. Not the time or place.

That's when he started to notice it. Among the smell of damp metal, concrete, and sweat, there was a pleasant smell. A strong, pleasant smell. It smelled like…food!

Pizza, to be exact. Oh my god, this was too cruel.

They had been fed since Ms. Roberts had replaced whoever the guy who got his dick bitten off was, but it was still prison cafeteria food. Stale bread and moldy lettuce. Water. An apple on days they were really lucky. So, for the guards to be eating pizza was just inhuman.

He looked up, his head still bowed. Sure enough, up on the stage, were two guards, holding several pizza boxes, Jerry finding himself drooling a bit.

Mr. Trent walked onto the stage, looking annoyed, and checking his watch, followed by Ms. Roberts.

Two of the women emerged from the side of the stage, to pour her tea.

She nodded at them and then waved.

"Hello, everyone. It's me."

"Hello, Ms. Roberts," all the inmates said, in unison, except, of course, the new girl.

"I think all of you will be pleased to know that you will only be here for another two days. Then the Ritual happens and you will no longer have to be here. Isn't that wonderful?"

"Yes, Ms. Roberts."

"Indeed, it is. Now, I have good news and bad news. First the bad news," she said, stopping to take a sip of her tea, letting out a content sigh after stopping to savor the taste, before continuing, "For tomorrow, all of us will have to fast. There will be no food tomorrow."

Jerry bit his lip, thinking of the pizza the guards were going to be eating while he went a day without food. But at least he was almost free. Well, not *free* free. Who knew what "job" Ms. Roberts had in mind for them after they were done here. It didn't matter. If he was to be her butler or gimp, as long as he got out of here, as long as he got to see the sun again, it would be an improvement.

Ms. Roberts looked at everyone and nodded her head. They were all disappointed, but all too afraid to express anything about it, "I know you're all upset about that. If it makes you feel any better, I also have to fast to prepare myself."

It didn't make Jerry feel any better.

"But I did say there was good news, didn't I?" Ms. Roberts said, opening her arms, "I brought you all a treat since this is the end of our time together here. I brought everyone pizza! There's 39 of you so we bought ten pies. Enough so that everyone can have up to four slices, if you so desire. And if anyone doesn't eat four slices, someone else can have the leftover slices."

What?!? That's…awesome!

Mr. Trent rolled his eyes, and sighed. Ms. Roberts turned and gave him a stern look. Under his breath he said something Jerry couldn't make out, and then walked off. Ms. Roberts turned back to the assembled inmates and asked, "What do you say?"

"Thank you, Ms. Roberts," everyone said. Jerry couldn't help but notice that he and several others had tears in their eyes.

The guards made a motion for everyone to stand. They were then herded into two groups with a large open space in the middle of the auditorium. Then the guards laid down the ten boxes of pizza in an even row in the middle of the room, opening the boxes, the smell of warm food intoxicating Jerry.

Ms. Roberts sat down on the chair she had on the stage, crossed her legs, and then clapped her hands twice, "Everyone, dig in."

And like a swarm of locusts, they descended on the ten pies, people climbing over each other to grab themselves a slice, for many of them, the first real human physical contact they had had since they were brought here. It was aggressive, it was violent, and it was the type of thing that there was no stopping. Some people tried to eat the slices right out of the box without even pulling it from the rest of the pizza, others pushing them away, to try to get more slices for themselves.

People grabbed handfuls of hot cheese into their fists and then shoved them into their mouths. Jerry himself knocked over someone to get a slice that he found himself swallowing without even chewing, the hunger so intense, so primal.

So much so that he almost didn't hear Ms. Roberts' laughter. He looked up. She was doubled over in laughter, and that's when it hit Jerry.

This wasn't some magnanimous act. This was just another humiliation. The chance for her to watch as they scrambled, naked, like starved dogs fighting for the same bone. He felt that familiar feeling he had so often when he was here, a feeling of hatred, that he knew he had to bury, deep down, or he'd end up torn to shreds.

And there was food. He had to eat. More. There was more to be eaten. He made a pig of himself, probably doing exactly what Ms. Roberts wanted to see, eating three slices in a row, they seeming to melt within his mouth.

He looked around. People were all huddled by themselves, hunched over like cavemen, guarding their food from anyone else. She got what she wanted, in spades.

Except…he looked over at the new girl. She had no mouth to eat, staring at the ruined pizza pies in the middle of the room. There was still enough for her to have a slice or two.

But she had no mouth.

She sat there, curled up in a fetal position, looking at the food, with eyes that screamed hunger and sadness. She hadn't been here for the long haul, but she had been here for what were probably several days, and she was starving like the rest.

But she had no mouth.

And he wanted to go over and hold her, feed her, protect her. But could he? What was stopping him? It was the perfect opportunity. He stood up, reached to one of the pies that was left over, grabbed a slice, and started towards the new girl whose name he didn't know was Kelly. One of the guards started to point his gun towards Jerry, but Ms. Roberts, intrigued by this, shook her head, and watched.

He walked over feeding body over feeding body, until he was only a few feet from her. He had the slice in his hands. She looked up at him. Oh, her eyes were so blue. And all he wanted was to take away the pain he saw in them.

Without even thinking, he did something that he didn't believe he was doing until it was done. He spoke up.

"Ms. Roberts, what about her?"

Ms. Roberts stood up, a very annoyed look on her face.

"Excuse me?" she said, standing close to the side of the stage.

"Doesn't she get any pizza?"

Jerry became aware that all of the other inmates had started to crawl to the other side of the room, taking their food with them, obviously afraid that his actions were going to get them all in trouble.

Already, Jerry regretted it, but those eyes called to him.

"I-I don't mean any disrespect," Jerry said, in the meekest voice he could conjure up, trying not to make eye contact with Ms. Roberts, lest he piss her off more, "But she's hungry too."

"She's more than welcome to take the slice you have in your hands."

"But she has no mouth to eat it with."

"And that is because I don't feel she deserves to have one. Are you questioning my authority here?"

"N-no, ma'am, I…"

"Because it certainly feels like you are questioning my authority."

Ms. Roberts jumped off the stage and walked right up to Jerry.

"Ma'am…I just…"

"You just *what?!?* She has no mouth because I don't feel like she deserves one."

"It's…it's…just…cruel," he mumbled under his breath, feeling like he had stepped over the line.

"It's just *what?!?*"

"Nothing…I…"

Jerry found himself flying across the room, the inmates under him, scattering and screaming, some of them pissing themselves from fear, as Jerry slumped to the floor, and they huddled on the other side of the room.

His vision was double and he was disorientated for a moment, only to find himself forced back on his feet, only to then see that the hand that had grabbed him by the throat was one he couldn't see. He began to panic, feeling an invisible hand grab him by the throat and lift him a good foot off the ground.

"So…*this* is how you repay my kindness?!?" Ms. Roberts said, advancing towards him with a look he hadn't seen on her face before: one of fury.

"I…I didn't mean to…"

"YOU KNOW VERY FUCKING WELL WHAT YOU WERE DOING!!" she screamed in his face, "I TRY TO DO SOMETHING KIND FOR YOU! I TRY TO DO SOMETHING FROM THE BOTTOM OF MY HEART! AND YOU DO *THIS*?!?"

Ms. Roberts punched him in the stomach with force that did not feel like it came from the petite young woman in front of him.

She walked over to the assembled naked huddled masses, grabbed a bearded blond man (they were all bearded by this point), and gave what could only be described as a shriek of rage, as she twisted his head the wrong way, killing him instantly. The others fell to their knees as she stomped back over to Jerry.

He noticed she was starting to cry.

"Do you think I wanted to do *that?!?* YOU MADE ME DO IT! I tried to ease all of your pain. I tried to help you all see the error of your ways and become better people."

"Please, Ms. Roberts," one of the women cried out, "You have. Don't blame us all for him."

"He's not one of us," a man yelled out.

"If you let me live, I'll kill him for you," a woman said.

"I'll kill both him and her if it's what would make you happy," a man said.

"Shut up! All of you!" Ms. Roberts yelled at them. They whimpered like frightened puppies as she focused on Jerry again.

Fuck it, he thought. *I'm going to die right now, anyway.*

"You know what?" Jerry said, closing his eyes, "You know what, ma'am?"

"What?" she spat out.

"Y-you are...you are a fucking bully and..."

That was all he got out before his mouth closed up.

Her face turned bright red with rage.

"I could skin you alive. Right now," she spat in his face, he noticing her English accent was gone, replaced by something that sounded distinctly American, Midwestern, in fact, and that she had been speaking without the accent since the moment she first yelled at him, "I could turn you inside out. And I could do it while you watch."

Ms. Roberts took a deep breath and attempted to calm herself down.

"Or..." she said, looking at the new girl and smiling, her posh English accent back, "I could do it to her. While you watch."

Jerry, still feeling reckless and brave, but not wanting the girl to suffer more, shook his head.

"You don't seem to understand. You are only breathing because I *allow* it. All of you! It's because of me that you're still alive and no other reason!"

She fumed, trying to regain her composure.

"You…offend me. And I won't be offended by the likes of you. I need to make an example out of you. Right now. In front of everyone."

She looked him up and down as three guards walked over by her side, their guns pointed right at him.

"Now, I could kill you without even touching you and you know it. I bet your little outburst was because you *want* me to kill you. Well, you're not getting to die. You and your new girlfriend will be very much alive when the Ritual happens. But I want something you'll remember for the rest of your life."

She smiled, tapping her temples, "I could…blind you. That might be fun…nah, it's better if you can see what happens. I could take away all your memories leading up to being here, so this will be all you've ever known. That…that is definitely one to consider. That I could just take away everything you've ever thought you accomplished, like that."

She snapped her fingers and giggled a little. She looked him up and down again.

"No, you know what offends me the most? Your cock and balls."

A cold sweat passed over Jerry at hearing that. *Holy fuck, she's going to castrate me! Oh my god! What am I going to do?!?*

"Ah, look at that," she said, a smile that showed her teeth crossing her lips, "You're sweating. I guess I hit about the right punishment. It's always so funny with you men. Threaten to cut off someone's pinkie, they get all brave. Threaten to cut out off their willy, though, and oh, how they lose their balls before ever getting them removed. I bet if you took any man and accumulated the time they spend using their pinkie or using their cock, the pinkie would win by quite a large margin. Here you are, completely at the mercy of other people; stripped of all dignity; stripped of all possession; and yes, everything you owned at your apartment has been put up for auction pretty much the day you came here, any pets you had were put in shelters; so, yeah, stripped of *everything*; made to soil yourself repeatedly, in front of others; and you panic when I tell you I might make it so you can never have intercourse again. I ought to cut it off just for that, on principle, alone."

She made a "snip" motion and laughed in his face, his anxiety beginning to build.

"See, I could just leave you like a Ken Doll. And there's nothing you could do about it. I could even cut it off and then make you wear it as a necklace. I can do *whatever I want* to you right now. You have *no* power…But, no, that wouldn't serve our purposes."

That line puzzled Jerry, but what happened next made him forget all about his questions.

"I know. You see, I have to see your filthy, disgusting naked bodies every day. And your cock, in particular, bothers me, because…well, I find uncircumcised peni to be aesthetically displeasing. Look at the other men here. Most of them are circumcised. Yours just isn't 'normal,' by American standards. I do this sort of thing a lot, back home, and the vast majority there are uncut. I've never liked seeing it. So, you are going to be fixed. Right now. Guards!"

Jerry struggled to move, finding himself not only suspended in the air by an invisible hand, but paralyzed, probably also due to her powers. He tried to scream. Two of the guards walked up to Ms. Roberts.

"Uh, Ms. Roberts," one of the guards said, "Don't get angry or nothin', but none of us know how to do that. I don't think any of us even have a scalpel."

"Do you have knives?"

"Well, yeah, we carry our…"

"Then use your knives."

"We still don't know how to…"

"Experiment. As long as he still has a working penis, the operation is a success."

The guard shrugged, pulled out what looked like a bowie knife, serrated and jagged.

Another guard held him around the hips, as the first sunk his knife into Jerry's foreskin, his body wanting to scream but Ms. Roberts' magic rendering him completely mute and motionless.

It was a nightmare. One he wanted to wake up from but couldn't. He tried to ignore the pain, to ignore the feeling of his nerves crying out, but he couldn't. He closed his eyes and prayed some more, for him to just wake up.

And then, like nothing had happened, the pain in his penis was gone. It felt numb. He opened his eyes and looked down, a wave of shame rushing over him upon seeing his now cut member. But it wasn't bleeding any more and the pain was gone, a faint blue glow disappearing.

"You can thank me for healing you. Of course, every time you look down, I want you to remember that *I* did that to you. I took a piece of your body and I reshaped it to *my* liking because *I could*. And you couldn't do a damn thing about it. I hope your new girlfriend is worth it."

Jerry, the fight gone out of him, the spell released, fell to a heap on the ground, crying like he hadn't cried since he was a child.

Ms. Roberts walked over to Kelly and asked her, "Do you see what you did?"

Kelly looked away, her eyes red and wet.

One of the other male prisoners began to shake as Ms. Roberts walked past him. She stopped, gestured for him to stand, and wondered why he had seemed more afraid than the others, until she looked him up and down and noticed he was uncircumcised, as well. She laughed and asked him if he was worried that she'd do the same to him. He nodded, looking up at her with fear.

"We'll see. However, in the meantime, I think...I think you should prove how much you love me by kissing my heel."

He nodded, profusely, and dropped back down to his knees, where he proceeded to kiss the heel of her shoes. She smirked, rolled her eyes, and then nodded at him, gesturing him away with a wave of her hand. Then she pointed back at Jerry.

"Now, since *this* one had to be difficult, pizza party is over. Take them all back to their cells. Hood them, bind them, like they were when I first came here. You can hose them down before the ritual. All except him. Don't give him a hood. I want him to see the misery he's caused."

"Ma'am, we can't just have him without a hood when the Ritual happens. None of them are to see the layout of the facility. Extra security precaution."

"Fine. Give him a hood, but, uh, work him over before you lock him up."

"Yes, ma'am!" the guard said, saluting her, as Ms. Roberts walked out of the room and to the backstage area.

Jerry had no fight left in him when the guards took him away.

CHAPTER 10

"Well, that was smooth," Mr. Trent said, with a smirk in the backstage area, Timothy standing behind him, the ever faithful SWAT dog, "Nice move with the whole dom thing at the end. Should I be expecting some *Human Centipede* action next? Maybe some strap-ons?"

"You, shut up!" Persephone commanded, getting right in his blemishless face.

"So, after this whole pizza party thing, are you going to play them some Barry White during the Ritual, maybe get them some fine wine?"

"Trent, I am warning you…"

"Warning me of *what,* Ms. Roberts? What are you going to *do,* Ms. Roberts? Hmmm? You know, you do seem to like asserting yourself, but let me ask you something: Do you think you could just kill *me* and get away with it? I'm not one of the run of the mill average demons you used to slay in high school. Killing me? It'd be just like killing any other prominent human. The amount of shit that would come down on you would be immense. We're talking highest legal prosecution imaginable. Wouldn't just be a murder. Oh, no! We're talking assassination of a city government official! Not to mention, you'd incur the wrath of my father. You've done your research on me. So, you know my father, right? The Christians still think he's their evil deity."

"I seem to recall *my* father already taking out one of your brothers in the past and *your* father doing jack shit about it."

"Yeah, and because your father kept off the grid for a whole bunch of years, so that no one would find you or your sisters. Sure, we may not be able to find your one sister, but we certainly know where the *other* one is. The one you *don't* want killed. I mean, you *do* remember what happened to your mom, right?"

Persephone fumed, glaring at him, through teary eyes. Her hands began to glow white, with energy, for a few moments.

Timothy started to step forward, Mr. Trent putting his hand on his chest to stop his advance.

"Whoa, there, Timothy. No need to get hostile. Ms. Roberts was just going to get herself cleaned up and then go about her business until tomorrow morning, right? Aren't you supposed to have dinner with that sister of yours tonight again? Probably at that restaurant you two have been eating at every other day, after she gets back her job at the Council Clinic on West 27th?"

Persephone looked at him, every fiber in her being telling her to kill him, and then closed her eyes, took a deep breath, and turned away from him, the light in her hands dissipating.

"I thought so," Mr. Trent said, smiling, "Besides, Timothy, you can't blame her for being so grumpy. She's a human female. Probably has PMS or something."

Persephone didn't even respond. She walked off, in a hurry, towards the restroom, hearing Mr. Trent's footsteps in the other direction.

She entered the sterile, white restroom, remarkably clean, considering it was only about 100 yards from a place that smelled of blood and waste and sweat. Here the strongest smell was bleach.

She went over to the sink, put her head down, and began to sob. She then let out a yell as she punched the mirror in rage.

This was all going wrong! Julie was nowhere to be found. Mr. Trent had one up on her. That one sacrifice had made her look weak in front of the others. And she was no further on the biggest part of the plan.

"Please don't cry, my dear Persephone," the voice from inside the cracked mirror said, as she saw a flash of eyes and wings and tongues, out of the corner of her eyes, "It makes me sad to see you sad."

She looked up, seeing a familiar, welcoming face standing over her shoulder in the mirror.

"I'm just…"

"My dear, your hand is bleeding. That looks bad. You should heal yourself, so it doesn't get infected."

She looked down, blood covering her entire left hand. She looked up at the mirror, her eyes bloodshot and wet, nodded, and then her hand was lit by blue energy for a moment, her wounds closing up as though they were never there. She then turned on the water of the sink and washed the blood away.

"That's so much better. Now, Persephone, please don't cry. Everything is going much, much better than you think it is."

She pulled a handkerchief out of her purse and blew her nose, wiping away the tears.

"You have to trust me. There is no reason to be upset, my dear," the voice said, soothing her the way only he did, his voice's Billy Zane-like tone seductive and smooth, like a pair of silk covered fingers, running their way up her spine, "I don't like to see you upset."

"I…I just…I tried…to be good to them. I wanted to…"

"Shhhhh…it's okay. The others among them understand. To them, you are still their savior. And in two days' time, it won't matter anymore. This you know."

"But what about the plan? I have to go back to England soon. What about…"

"My dear Persephone, in all the years we've known each other, have I ever steered you wrong?"

"No no, of course not."

"And I won't start now. Everything that you and I have planned is coming to fruition. I see it happening."

"And Mr. Trent, he…"

"You have nothing to fear from Li'dhu'xa, nor his House. Even without my help, you are strong enough to fell his entire nation. And with me at your side, you are protected from all. Even his father."

"But what about Samantha?"

"I can tell you, with all certainty, no one of his House and no one associated with him will harm her in any way, no matter what you do."

"Really?"

"I swear it to you, my dearest Persephone."

In her reflection, he wrapped his ivory arms around her, pale and strong, one of his black feathers gently floating off his wings, onto the lapel of her pantsuit, his thick, long, straight black hair, contrasting with the red of hers.

"Close your eyes and just feel me, next to you. I know you can."

"I can. I always can…It feels so good."

With one arm around her waist, he brought his hand up to her lips, and traced over her mouth. She could see him smiling in the mirror, his pupiless black eyes, beautiful ebon windows.

"Now, don't you have dinner with Samantha tonight? You shouldn't be late. She's had a rough day today."

"Thank you," Persephone said, her voice gentle and honest.

"I'll always be there for you, my dearest."

She smiled a content smile, sighing.

Suddenly, the door to the bathroom opened and one of the guards came in. Martinez, she thought his name was. She couldn't be sure. She hadn't really taken the time to memorize their names.

"Oh, Ms. Roberts, I'm terribly..."

"No, it's fine. I was just finishing up here."

"Are you okay, Ms. Roberts?"

"No, it's quite alright. Thank you. If you could just give me a moment, I'm just fixing myself up. Woman's work is never done and all."

She gave a polite smile as he closed the bathroom door.

Of course, he didn't see her friend in the mirror. No one ever did. He was hers and hers alone.

"Now, my dearest Persephone, go have your dinner. You deserve it."

CHAPTER 11

"You fucking mute cunt, you are fucking *dead!* Do you hear me?" the woman whispered quietly, under her hood to Kelly.

"You and that no-prick loser fucked it up for all of us!" another woman snarled at her.

"When we get out of here, I don't know what or where Ms. Roberts puts us, I am going to hurt you," said the first woman.

Kelly just sat there, unable to even respond because of what Julie's sister had done to her mouth. The other women, with whom she was now chained, hip to hip, hands behind their backs, their ankles and wrists chained to the cold steel bench they were sitting on, hated her. She could feel their hate. It wasn't as intense as what she had experienced from Julie's even crazier sister, who was calling herself Ms. Roberts (which was odd, because she could have sworn Julie's last name was Golightly).

She had given up hope that Julie would come and save her. There was no hope. No one would come.

Only one person had tried to show her any kindness. And he suffered for it. They all suffered for it.

But she was still tremendously grateful that he took such a chance to stand up for her. She wondered if she had met him under different circumstances, would they have gotten along. Would they have even had a connection?

That was a strange thought to have at a time like this, she realized. But the look of kindness and pity on his kinda handsome and gentle face kept beaming in her mind, like a pinprick of light in a howling void.

She found herself, for the first time, not *only* thinking of being rescued, but thinking of taking someone with her. She didn't know his name, but his actions today, however futile, had endeared him to her.

Kelly attempted to block out the hateful whispers of the other women and see if she could pass out in the position she currently in.

And when she entered her dream state, she dreamt of Jerry.

CHAPTER 12

"Okay, girls, there is obviously something wrong with the radio," Alexander Johannes said, flustered, as he sat in the passenger seat of the SUV. In all his years of demon hunting and adventuring and exploring, he had never quite taken the time to learn how to drive. At the moment, their mother, Kathleen, was behind the wheel, "I'm pretty sure the DJ just doesn't know his job. That couldn't have been Santana."

"Yes, it is, dad," Julie said, in the backseat, "That was Santana with Rob Thomas."

"Well, I don't know who that is," Alexander said.

"That's because you're getting old," Kathleen said, with a lopsided grin, the ushanka she still wore, a remnant of her rebellious youth.

"He's from Mathbox 20," Persephone informed him.

"It's Matchbox 20, Perci," Julie corrected, "And they suck."

"Juliette," Kathleen scolded, "You know that's not nice to say to your sister."

"But it's true! They suck! All the kids at school think they suck too!"

"Well," Alexander said, "I'm inclined to agree with the kids at school. So, ladies, who wants to hear some Three Dog Night?"

"Nobody wants to hear that, dad," Julie said, "I want to hear Green Day."

"Oh, is that what's passing for punk with you girls?" Kathleen asked.

"They have an album. Do you know what it's called? *Dookie.*" Julie laughed.

"How very clever of them," Kathleen deadpanned, before asking, "Juliette…Would you like to hear some of mommy's old albums? I have them up in the attic and I haven't really listened to many of them in a long while. If you like stuff like Green Day, maybe you'll like this stuff better."

"Okay, I'll listen to them, but I don't think they could be as good as Green Day."

"Mom, dad, can I ask you a question?" Persephone interjected.

"Do you want to listen to some of daddy's records, Perci?"

"No."

Alexander rolled his eyes and laughed, "Why do none of you want to open your minds a little?"

"Because you have three daughters and not three guys who sell pot out of a van behind the high school," Kathleen answered, "If you ever have some of those, I'm sure they'll appreciate all the Rainbow albums you can throw at them."

"Dad, are dragons real? I want to slay a dragon," Persephone asked.

"No fair! If Perci gets to slay a dragon, I want to slay a dragon!" Julie yelled.

"Juliette, calm down," Alexander said, turning and facing his daughters, "Now, Perci, there used to be dragons. Quite a few."

"Then all the knights killed them?"

"Well, that is part of it, yes. But the bigger part is that they're very rare even among the other realms. Is it that movie we saw the other week?"

"Oh, Alex," Kathleen said, sounding annoyed, "You didn't take them to see that awful movie with the dragons in England, did you?"

"There was a guy with a tank," Persephone explained.

"Alex, that movie looked like it sucked."

"Hey, mom! That's not nice to say!" Julie said.

"I'm sorry. I'll put some money in the swear jar when we get home. But seriously, Alex? You can't take them to see something better?"

"It sounded like so much fun, though! Dragons in modern times being fought by modern military!"

"You don't get enough of that every day?"

"Well, if you want, why don't you take the girls to something foreign next week?"

"I like mommy's movies better," Persephone said, "I really liked *Breakfast with Tiffany*. And *The Birds*. And *Rosebud*. And the...uh...I don't remember the title but Edward Scissorhands was in it and you told me they painted the shadows on the walls."

"Oh, that movie is called *The Cabinet of Dr. Caligari*," Kathleen explained.

"*The Cab-Clarinet-Cabinet...*" Persephone tried to say.

"*Cabinet of Dr. Caligari.*"

"I don't think I can pronounce that, mommy."

"It's okay if you can't say it, as long as you girls have someone to culture you, especially in light of what awful influences your dad over there contributes."

"Excuse me," Alex said, "Which of us attended multiple G. G. Allin shows?"

"G. G. was a misunderstood artist."

"He was a mental case that threw shit."

"Daddy!" Persephone yelled.

"Sorry, dear, a mental case that threw poop. And lest we forget the special shampoo I had to buy after our first weekend together."

"Hey, what's a little bit of lice to a man of adventure?"

They both laughed. He smiled at her and held her hand to his lips, where he kissed it.

Julie groaned and the two parents laughed as he gently let go of her hand.

He was a good twenty years her senior, but from the moment they had laid eyes on each other, they were inseparable.

"So, daddy," Persephone asked again, "Can I slay a dragon?"

"You still have a year to go before you even have your trial. Why don't you worry about that first before you start making requests for particular beasts to hunt, okay?"

"Okay, daddy."

She smiled and looked up at her parents.

Suddenly, there was something in the rear view mirror, a mass of eyes.

She gasped and looked behind her, but there was nothing there. She looked up at the mirror again and all there was was the normal reflection.

"Perci, is something wrong?"

"Uh…no."

"Okay. You looked worried for a second."

"It was nothing."

"Alright, then. So, who wants to tell me the names of the 15 major houses of the Fifth Realm Makai for some ice cream?"

CHAPTER 13

"…and then he said that we should be looking at May, since that's the traditional month of fertility."

"Uh huh."

"I said to him, Brian, I'm not sure if I wanted to just become a broodmare so quickly after we're married."

"Uh huh."

"And then I pulled off his head and a rabbit popped out, but luckily, it was made of chocolate, so I was able to eat it before it killed Woodrow Wilson."

"Uh huh."

Samantha clapped her hands, "Persephone! You're not even listening, aren't you?"

"Wha?" Persephone started, "Sorry, I just got lost in thought for a second."

"What are you thinking about?"

"Nothing."

"I miss her too, Persephone. I think about her all the time."

"It's not about mom this time, Samantha."

"Then what is it…" the waiter came with their desert. Samantha nodded to him and thanked him, "What is it about?"

"Do you…do you ever think of me as a bully?"

"What?"

"A bully. Did you ever see me as one?"

"Well…you do have a…uh…streak about you."

"What do you mean? You never saw me torture animals or hurt other children! If anything, I was the one picked on! You know how much shit Julie used to give me growing up!"

"Persephone, she was just…she was trying to find her way, after mom died, just like you were. She just didn't want her little sister tagging along all the time anymore."

"You're always defending her, you know that?"

185

"Of course, I'd defend either of you. You're my little sisters."

"You don't think she brought all of this upon herself?"

"We went over this. I don't think she killed that…"

"Then why hasn't she contacted you? If she were innocent, I'm sure she'd have gotten in touch with you or the Council to, at least, try to arrange for some sort of legal counsel."

"She's…I think the word would be *unconventional.*"

"What she *is* is irresponsible. She doesn't care about anyone but herself."

"This is…this is what I was talking about with you having a bit of a streak."

"What does that mean, exactly?"

"Nothing. Have some strawberry shortcake. It's wonderful."

"No. No, you brought it up. What do you mean?"

"Well, the other day, when we first had dinner, and you saw me give that homeless guy a dollar…"

"Yeah?"

"And you asked me why I did that."

"I don't know why you give the guy money when you know he's probably just going to use it go get high or drunk or whatever."

"Because I don't like to see people suffer, Persephone."

"Are you implying I do?"

"I think…" Samantha took a deep breath, "I think both you and Julie have a very cruel streak that your business necessitates."

"And you don't have it? Oh, that's right. You're the *kind* one. Wait, is that why *you* failed your trail?"

Samantha gasped and then collected herself, before saying something she knew she'd regret. Instead, she just asked, "Are you really going to go there?"

Persephone thought for a second, and nodded her head, and took a bite of her cake. It was delicious, as her sister had told her, "No, I'm sorry. I didn't mean to bring that up."

"But do you see, Persephone? You can be…cold. Very cold. You don't feel sympathy for people like others do."

"And am I supposed to coddle people who mess up their lives? Am I…"

"Persephone, all I'm saying is you're twenty-one years old. You're too young to be such a Republican."

"Is it so wrong to think…nevermind. You're right."

"Look, I get it. You both got dad's genes. You guys are hunters. You kill demons for the Council. I couldn't do that. I don't have it in me. Obviously."

She gestured towards her eye patch. There was a period of awkward silence.

"So, you think I'm a bully."

"I think...if you were a little bit kinder to people, it wouldn't necessarily kill you."

"I see..."

"So, what is your business here, anyway, with the Council? I asked Rob Thompson, over at International Requisitions and he said they didn't know what you were..."

"It's...a bit secret."

"Oh? Okay. I know that happens from time to time. Is the Council contracting any work for the city?"

"I can't say, but you'd be...uh...in the right ballpark."

"And what about the work you were going to do in Chicago? Is it another rogue former Council member? Like Rayborn?"

"I can't talk about that, either."

"Oh, look at you, Ms. Hush Hush. Okay, I won't ask anymore, then."

"Thank you, Samantha. I'd prefer to keep my business and personal life separate, if it's all the same to you."

"That's fine. I totally understand."

The two sisters ate in silence for a few moments, before Samantha smiled and said, "Do you know what I saw the other day? *Book of Mormon*. From the guys who made *South Park*?"

"Not that familiar with it. I'm absorbed in my work all the time."

"Oh, I remember."

"Do you?"

"Yeah, I remember a few times, during my whole Siouxsie Sioux phase, when I'd catch you having these long, detailed conversations with yourself in the mirror. And sometimes, I'd hear you discussing strategy and how to penetrate different realms, like you were having a one person war room meeting or something. It was so cute."

Persephone forced a smile, "Yes...it was...cute, wasn't it?"

"Oh, look at Ms. Narcissist."

"You got me there. Do...uh...love my mirrors."

"Only saw it once or twice, myself, but I remember Julie and dad commenting on it a few times. 'Leave her alone, she's probably talking to an imaginary friend,' I'd tell them."

"Oh no, nothing like that. That'd be…crazy."

"Oh, I had an imaginary friend too, when I was a kid. Her name was Betty and she'd…oh, I can tell you're getting flustered. I'll stop teasing."

"Thank you."

"Well, listen, I hate to cut this short, but I have an early meeting tomorrow with a representative of the CDC."

"Anything serious?"

"No, they just want to catalog a few mystical ailments and I know Orin, their Council liaison down in Atlanta, so I volunteered to talk to them. Mostly vampiric diseases."

"Do you think they'll ever publicly acknowledge what you tell them?"

"I doubt it. Public isn't ready for any of this. You know your history; how long did it take for the government to even acknowledge that any of this was real, on just a classified level?"

"Point."

"So, I don't expect them to start telling people about the Nine Realms or how to protect yourself from Incubi tomorrow."

"Seems a shame, though, doesn't it?"

"It does, but I think you'd blow people's minds too much if they saw how big the world they live in really is."

"I guess."

"So, anyway, I'm going to head off. I'll leave some money to pay for dinner."

"No, it's okay. I got this one. I've got a city credit card."

"Oh, from that…?"

Samantha stopped herself, made the motion of zipping her lips, her sister nodding and giggling.

The two sisters embraced, Samantha leaving the restaurant. Persephone watched her walk past the window, and then, after waiting a few minutes, made a call on her cell.

"*Ja wohl, Mein Fuhrer,*" Serenity answered, obviously outside somewhere, from the sound of wind in the background.

"Serenity, I asked you not to call me that."

"Term of endearment, it is," Serenity responded.

"So…any luck finding her?"

"Not as of yet, we ain't. Hold up…Yeah, it's her…No, you can't speak to her. *I'm* on the phone…You have to wait your turn! Cor!"

"Serenity…you and your brother stop fighting over the phone."

"Aye."

"So, any leads, at least?"

"Bugger all. Vanished, she has…yes, I know, Mimmy…He says he'd bet you a Dead Brazilian that we'll find her, we will, when we take a shufti at the outer boroughs, left, right, and centre…What? Belt up, you! Only one ear per phone."

"So, which boroughs have you checked?"

"The Isle of Staten was today. Not…wha? Speaker phone? Oh, we *could* do that."

"Oh Jesus. Please don't put me on speakerphone, Serenity."

"Aye," Christopher said, over the phone. She was on speaker phone.

"Hi, Christopher. I asked your sister to please not put me on speaker phone. I hate speakerphone."

"Apologies. Didn't intend to be a city banker, just wanted to bestow greetings and all."

"Hello there," Serenity said.

"Happy Christmas."

"Remember, remember, the First of November."

"Okay, you two are starting to hurt my head now," Persephone said, rubbing her temples.

"Horses for courses. Off you go, Mr. Speakerphone," Serenity said.

"So, you checked Staten Island?" Persephone asked, hoping the conversation didn't stray again.

"That we did. In the 'morrow, we'll be taking the Bronx. Brooklyn and Victoria/Elizabeth Triumphant will need a day each. Quite big and clever, they are."

"Wha…Oh, *Queens*…"

"Now, you're getting it…Mimmy, she's getting it, she is!"

"God help us all…anyway, got to get to bed. Stressful today. Big tomorrow."

"Right right. Cheery bye."

Persephone hung up the phone and stopped to think to herself for a moment.

She was still irritated from how Trent had spoken to her.

She realized it had been a while since she had taken a trip out of this world. Maybe she was overdue a dimension hop.

CHAPTER 14

"I have never," Julie slurred, wearing her panda hoodie and a pair of black panties, laying side by side with Lucy on Lucy's heart-shaped bed, burying her feet in the leopard-print comforter, "Ummm…I have never…fought *a mummy!*"

Lucy sighed and took a hard swig of the bottle of Jager they had in between them.

"Wha? What? Noooo! You fought *a mummy?*"

"Bitch, I be motherfuckin' ancient."

"But you look good, though."

"You know how to flatter a bitch, but no, I'm like," she said, starting to count on her fingers, "Forty thousand years or some shit like that."

"Don't look a day over three thousand."

"Hahah. Shut up. Didn't used to count till you niggas showed up with yo linear time and shit."

"So, was this, all…in Ancient Egypt with the Pharaohs and Moses being all, 'Let my people go,' and shit?"

"Nah, this was like recent. Well, recent for me. You niggas all had cars. The windup shits."

"So, like 1920's?"

"'ight."

"Damn…I wanna…I wanna…wanna f-fight a mummy. Where do you even find mummies these days?"

"Museum of Natural History."

"Psssh…Those mummies don't fight anybody. Those are pussy mummies. Those are…like…display mummies."

"Bitch, don't be doubting a playa. I can make them shits rise up. Don't matter where I get the motherfuckers from. "

"So you're like a demon Herbert West, then."

"*Herbert West?!?*"

Lucy looked at Julie confused, and started to drunkenly unlace her boots.

"Herbert West. You know...*Re-Animator*."

"Ain't nobody got time for that shit."

"Whoa...whoa...whoa..." Julie said, sitting up and drunkenly grabbing Lucy by the shoulder as if she had something incredibly important and potentially emotionally devastating to say to her, "Are you telling me you've never seen *Re-Animator*?"

"I'm a fucking demon, my nigs. Why I gotta watch movies about them?"

"There's no demons in *Re-Animator*."

Lucy shrugged and then casually threw one of her boots across the room and started undoing the other one.

Julie got in her face, with a look of drunken concern and said, "We totally have to watch it. Like, right now. It's a matter of life and death."

"'ight. Tell you what...You my nigs, so you say we should watch it, we'll watch it. Now, it's my turn."

She handed the bottle of Jager to Julie and thought for a minute, "I have never given no nigga no rimjob."

Julie shrugged and took a swig from the bottle.

"Wha? Ughhh...That shit's nasty, yo," Lucy said, laughing and slapping Julie on the back.

"Eh, it happens."

"Why you wanna be sticking your tongue up a nigga's asshole. He ain't got no cum coming out of that...oh shit, he didn't have no cum up there, did he?"

"Wha? No no no no," Julie said, shaking her head in a way that only someone really inebriated could, without inducing vertigo, "And it's never been a dude. Some girls, though just kinda ...have...pretty...assholes..."

"I don't know with y'all. I just like a good dick in my pussy, you know? I'm not up for all that weird shit. I'll suck a nigga's dick, yo, because that's what gets them wanting to go for the pussy, but..."

"I know guys who don't want their dicks sucked."

"Bullshit. Them some gay ass niggas, then."

"No, they weren't gay, just didn't like getting their dicks sucked."

"Any nigga that don't want no bitch sucking his dick is a nigga that wants another nigga to do it. Every man wants his dick sucked. I don't care if that nigga is motherfuckin' Kanye or motherfuckin' Bishop

Desmond Tutu. Nigga wants his dick sucked. Bitch wants her pussy eaten. Them's the rules. Y'all want some other nigga's face in your shit. Just how it works."

"Not all the time."

"*All* the motherfuckin' time. You know who didn't want they dicks sucked? The Romans. The Romans was gay ass niggas. My ass was around back then too, so I know what them Roman niggas was like…Sheeee-it…so, you lick the asshole…next thing you know, your ass be telling me you fuck niggas up the ass."

"Okay, wait a minute! Wait a minute! You don't give rimjobs and you've never pegged a guy…what kind of fucked up Puritan succubus are you?"

"Naaaah! What's wrong with some dick in pussy? I likes dick in pussy! You humans be sticking shit where shit don't go!"

"That sounds a little bit homophobic."

"Nah, nigga wants to suck off a nigga, that's his shit. I just think that's a waste of good dick."

"Not for them."

"Well, for me it is."

"Well, there is also the problem of you, you know, killing anyone who sticks his dick in your pussy."

"Pssh. Niggas go out happy."

"Well, that's, like, just your opinion, man. So, we should watch *Re-Animator* and then…we should go to the museum and get a mummy, so I can kick it's ass and be, like, 'Fuck you, mummy! I fucked your ass up! Science, *bitch!*'"

Lucy threw her other boot across the room and looked at Julie with a puzzled expression, "I thought your ass was supposed to be all incognito and shit."

"Ooooh! We can wear trench coats and sunglasses and fedoras!"

"Calm that shit. We can't just go to a major museum and start resurrecting motherfuckin' mummies. Motherfuckin' po-po be on your ass like flies on shit. Motherfuckin' Indiana Jones be on your ass!"

"I'm pretty sure Indiana Jones is a fictional character…and I think that's the first simile you've used since I met you…"

"Wha?"

"No…you said I was like your little sister, so…Okay. Strike that. Bad Julie. My turn."

Lucy played with her braids a little and smiled, and hugged Julie, "You know what? You *is* like my little sister."

"Oh, you know what? Maybe it's the copious amounts of Jagermeister I've drunk...drinken...drank...drank?...Whatever. But maybe it's the alcohol, but you are just...awesome. You're so not judgmental and I need that. Everybody's so judgmental. You know? You know what I'm saying? Well, okay, you're super judgmental about sex that you don't do, but otherwise, you're totally non-judgmental, you know? It's so cool! You know, I wasn't sure I was gonna like hanging with you, because it's...kinda weird..."

"Why you say that?"

"Oh, you know the whole thing with..."

"Oh, shit, nigga, *that* why you didn't return my calls for so long?"

"Yeah...kinda."

"Look, you know I ain't fucked your pops. He'd be dead if I did."

"I know...but it's...it's weird because, like, you're my dad's friend and you fuck guys and eat their souls and shit...and...I think I lost my train of thought."

"Nah, that's not happening. Your pop's like...a nigga I worked with. Strictly business. 'sides, I knew your moms, yo."

"You knew my mom?"

"That's how I met your pops. I used to be such a classy bitch. Galleries and Carnegie Motherfuckin' Hall! Your moms, when she wasn't in the Bowery with them niggas with safety pins in they cheeks, used to go to all them shits. I'd be all bored and shit because all I cares about is which of them niggas there got the most zeroes in his pocket, know what I'm sayin'? Then this bitch with dreads and a motherfuckin' Cossack and torn stockings shows up and starts talking Monet. So, I starts up a conversation, shit gets to shit, and BAM! We friends, and then when she meets your pops, and he knows what I am, and don't even try to kill my ass, I think, 'This nigga ain't bad people.'"

"I saw pictures of my mom's C-Squat days, but she was all cleaned up by the time Sammi was born, so never saw that in real life. Nope nope nope."

"I needs to have a female I can just be friends with and shit, you know? I can't be friends with none of the other succubae. Used to have Kim, but she got tired of them being a bitch to her too. Them bitches be catty. I can't be friends with no men, 'cept your pops, cause he knows what I am and resists. But I try being friends with any other nigga, he's gonna end up got."

"Well, I don't…have *any* friends."

"Well, *I'm* your motherfuckin' friend, bitch."

Julie smiled and put her arm around Lucy.

"Yay, *I* have a friend."

"Bitch, course you do!"

Julie drunkenly hugged Lucy, before realizing something she wanted to ask Lucy.

"You like cocaine?"

"Bitch, why didn't you say you got some motherfuckin' nose candy? Don't be holding out! Gimme some of that shit."

Julie drunkenly stumbled over to her bag, did her best Dr. Rockso impersonation ("I do cocaine!") as Lucy took off her top and threw it in the general direction of where she had thrown her boots.

"Oh, I ain't asked yet. You likes my new titties?"

"Those are…*big*, alright," Julie said, glancing back at Lucy, who had already threw her shorts off, leaving her naked.

"They better motherfuckin' be big. I paid enough for them shits," Lucy said, walking over to her closet and pulling out a leopard print silk robe.

"Whoa…you *paid* for them?"

"I know yous all a master thief and shit, but you can't just jack breast implants."

"No…I mean, you're *a demon* and you can change your form at will…"

"Uh huh."

"So, why didn't you just make your breasts that size with your…demony demon powers?"

"I do *that*, niggas just think I've got big ol' motherfuckin' fat girl titties. They want them silicone implants."

"If you say so," Julie said, looking down at her own B cups.

She shrugged, drunkenly, finding in her bag what she was looking for. It was the vial of dust she had collected from the Second Realm parasite. She was just drunk enough to see if snorting it had any effect. She pulled out a mirror and set it down on the bed, drunkenly pulling out a Metrocard from her wallet, and putting the dust into four different lines.

Lucy looked at it funny, "Hmmmm…that don't look like no cocaine I ever snorted."

"It's not cocaine. Just snort it."

Julie leaned forward and snorted, a warm shudder quickly spreading through her body, starting at her crotch. Her knees buckled, as she noticed that every inch of her flesh that was touching something felt good.

Lucy snorted and gave a moan, before putting one of her hands inside her robe.

"Oh fuck," Lucy said, purring, "Whatever that shit is, you gotta be my nigga and hook me up with your dealer. That shit makes me wanna touch my pussy!"

"Ain't got a dealer," Julie said, laying back down on the bed, about to orgasm just from the feel of the bed on her shoulders, every nerve awake in her body, the thought in her head that if Lucy made a move right now, she'd go for it.

"How'd you get this shit then?"

"I collected it…myself."

"Then you should sell this shit! Every nigga from here to motherfuckin' Timbuktu will want this!"

"Never thought of that before…but but…yeah, we should do that! We can call it… *Hypnagogia!*"

"Hypna-what?"

"Hypnagogia."

"We ain't callin' it something no junkie can remember."

"Okay, then what would you call it?"

"Well, where'd you get this shit?"

"You know them parasites in the Second Realm?"

Lucy started coughing, loudly, and sat up, "Awww…fuck no! You did not just get me to snort a fucking Butcher's Eye!"

"Little parasites. Big eye with tentacles."

"That's a motherfuckin' Butcher's Eye. Fuck, that shit's nasty! How'd you like it if I got your ass to snort a shitload of roaches?!?"

"Wha?"

"Ugh. You motherfuckin' humans and y'all's weird shit. Them thing's fucking nasty. They like the roaches of the Second, yo!"

"Yeah, but they feel fucking awesome."

"Well…can't argue with you on that…"

"So, sell this on the street, eh? We'd have to get some more of them! We should totally get some more of them!"

"Shit, bitch, that's shit's motherfuckin' unseemly," Lucy said, shivering with repulsion for a moment, before stopping to think about the situation, "Course, I *ain't* sayin' no to money."

"*I've got the brains/You've got the brawn/Let's make lots of money!*"

"Shit yeah...You do know how to open up a doorway, 'ight?"

Julie smiled a big lopsided grin that definitely reminded Lucy of her long gone friend, Kathleen Roberts, and drunkenly pulled out a jeweled dagger from her messenger bag.

CHAPTER 15

"Julie, are those *people* down there?"

"They used to be."

"How'd they get here? It looks like they're part of the ground and trees and rocks and stuff, but they're still alive."

"Well, Perci, dad says those are souls."

"What's a soul?"

"It's the part of a person that's on the inside. When your body dies, the soul is still around."

"So, does everybody's soul come here when they die?"

"Nope. Dad said that people in each realm either died there or were killed by something from there that brought them there or were something called...sac...sac...sac...it's a big word dad said but I can't remember it."

"Sacrament? I heard a guy on tv say sacrament once."

"Uh...no. That's not the word, Perci! You're going to screw me up! Just be quiet, so I can remember it, okay?"

"Okay, Julie..."

"Sac...sacri...sacri...ummmm...Now, you have me thinking it's sacrament too, when I know it's not sacrament! Thanks, Perci, for screwing me up!"

"Sorry."

"Anyway, it's when somebody brings something from a realm to our world and promises them a whole bunch of souls so they can get something."

"Like a cat? Dad won't let me get a cat!"

"I guess if you wanted you could get a cat, but cats make dad sneeze, so you'd have to hide it really well so he wouldn't know you had one or he'd put it in a pound!"

"Could something from one of the realms sacrament something to get something from our world?"

"It's not *sacrament*, Perci! That's the wrong word! And no, it doesn't work that way! Do you want to learn, Perci? You're messing me up!"

"But what if a demon wanted a cat?"

"Why would a demon want a cat? He'd eat it!"

"What if he were a demon that didn't want to eat cats, but wanted one as a pet, so he…"

"Perci, you're totally messing up the lesson here! I'm the teacher and you're not supposed to ask stupid questions!"

"Mom says there's no such thing as stupid questions!"

"Dad says she just says that so you won't feel stupid."

"That's not true, Julie! Take that back! Take that back!"

"Perci asks stupid questions because she's stupid! Perci asks stupid questions because she's stupid!"

"I am not! I am not!"

CHAPTER 16

It was in the early morning that Persephone sat in a lotus position, in the middle of a jagged Fifth Realm flesh forest, the trees swaying their twisted forms to the warm breeze, listening to the moans of the landscape as the wind blew her hair. She stood up, clad in a yoga pants and a tank top. In front of her was an item wrapped in a towel. She had earbuds in, but her iPod was off. She wanted to hear the wails of this place. At least, at first.

After the day she had yesterday, with her time of fasting beginning later today, she had decided she'd take the couple hours she had free to take a bit of a trip through the Fifth Realm, something she did hadn't done in a couple months. Now that she had gotten herself into a relaxed state among the smell of decay and fire, she looked through the trees at what looked like a small group of demons traveling together. Five of them, with what looked like three fresh souls being dragged behind them, so new they probably didn't even realize they were dead yet. Their grey-colored bodies were naked and weeping, begging, crying, probably just realizing what this new world they were in was.

She remembered that conversation she had had with Julie, after one of her first trips here. Of course, now she understood how it worked. People who died on Earth through no supernatural means just ceased to exist. They went to the void and the energy that used to be their soul simply found itself redistributed to some other force of nature. Those who were found themselves in one of the realms, though, upon their deaths left their souls behind. The laws of physics applied differently to the realms than they did earth, and energy that normally spread and went elsewhere, stayed behind in conscious form in the other realms. So, if a being from, say, the Fifth Realm were to come to Earth and kill a person, that person's soul would go to the Fifth Realm, upon death. If a person were to go to the Fifth Realm, by themselves, and die, then they would, too, find their souls stuck there.

It's also how sacrifices worked. When you sacrificed a person to a being from a particular Realm, that person's soul would find itself in the Realm of origin of that entity. That's why the Fifth Realm was comprised of so many human souls as part of its very ecosystem. The Fourth, Fifth, and Sixth Realms had had the most contact with Earth over the years. And all the trees and rocks and all were all people who either encountered a Fifth Realm being, were sacrificed to a Fifth Ream entity, stumbled into or magicked their way into this Realm, only to find themselves dying here, resulting in being trapped here forever.

She wasn't sure how the three she saw in front of her had come to find their way here, but, really, it didn't matter much to her. She was more interested in these demons.

Four of the five demons seemed to be in what amounted to armor, crafted from human rib cages, bound together with tendons and ligament. Above them they held a banner painted in human fluids proudly proclaiming the house they belonged to. She smiled, at seeing what House it was. In fact, she didn't just smile, she laughed.

The fifth demon, taller than the others, standing a good nine feet tall, with wings that were red and leathery, his face like a bull's lined with razors, his horns made of black flame, his armor dyed black from the rotted blood of the dead, his hooves standing as majestically as hooves could stand on those tree trunks he called legs, turned at the sound of her laughter.

She walked in the path of the five demons, the three human souls behind them begging her to please help them.

None of the three were the soul she occasionally came here looking for, so she didn't much care about them, but this House had been annoying her as of late.

"LOOK AT THAT," the tallest demon said, speaking in a high demonic language Persephone was quite familiar with, "ANOTHER BITCH FOR THE KENNELS! DO YOU LAUGH, KNOWING THE MANY WAYS I WILL KNOW YOUR WOMB BEFORE STRIPPING YOU OF YOUR BODY AND MAKING YOUR SOUL INTO THE LOWEST OF MY MEN'S BEDPANS?"

"No," Persephone said, speaking the demon's language, "I don't laugh at that. I laugh at the House of Temen-ni-gru."

The demons stopped smiling.

"I laugh at a sad House filled with too many sons who will never ascend to the throne their father shits in on a daily basis, never mind the throne he rules from," she said in the demon's language, spitting on the ground, "I laugh at the little children such as yourself who think themselves a Prince, but are but comfort boys to the House of Iretini-avent. You were all not birthed by demon sows but shit out of your father's three mouths."

"WHO ARE YOU TO SPEAK THIS WAY TO K'VEK'EY'IH, SON OF B'NALL'XE?!?"

"I am Persephone, daughter of Alexander Johannes, slayer of Raz'yel and I've come to give your father one less son," she said, turning on her iPod with some inspirational music, "I Can't Decide" from the Scissor Sisters.

The ground around her glowed white as two of the lesser demons charged at her, and she took the towel off the katana she held in front of herself, smiling broadly. The two demons found themselves burning as they entered the circle of heat that surrounded her.

Their faces melted off and their armor cracked, chunks burning off their bodies, unable to withstand the offensive nature of the shield she had given herself. As their burning corpses fell backwards, she jumped out of the protective space she was in as the other two guards took swings at her with their massive clubs that would have shattered her bones with a single hit.

Of course, that would be if she had actually been there and they hadn't been hitting an illusion she had created. The real her leapt at the two of them, slicing both of their heads off with a single slice of her katana, their blood splattering her face, a chill of pleasure running up her spine.

The Demon Prince, though, she knew, was a lot stronger than his guards (which never made much sense to her), and he charged at her, drawing a segmented weapon made of black flame. She leapt backwards, laughing the whole time, as he swung at her with his flame whip-like thing, snarling the whole time.

She dodged a blow of his, slashing at him with her sword, him grabbing the blade with one of his six arms, and using the wind from a flap of his wings to make her lose her footing. He grabbed her arm with two of his other arms and threw her backwards several feet.

Halfway there, she seems to slow down, in mid-air, before finally floating gently to her feet on the ground. She smirked at him. She spread her arms out, the bodies of his fallen soldiers beginning to shake, as the shattered armor they wore ripped off their bodies and flew to her, orbiting her like rabid moons to a tranquil planet.

Soon, she was shielded by a whirlwind of jagged bones pieces, calmly walking towards The Demon Prince.

The Prince stepped backwards, growling, as the jagged bones shards sliced his skin, his blood sizzling as it hit the ground. He fell backwards, landing between two of the chained human souls behind him.

He turned around, grabbing a man's soul, and using it as a human shield, figuring that this would slow Persephone down.

She sighed and then stabbed at the Prince with her sword, stabbing right through the forehead of the soul, in order to stab the Prince in the throat. The soul now nailed to him like an undead post-it, he kicked at Persephone with his massive legs, knocking her back a few feet, buying him time to prepare the flaming whip for a killing blow.

He raised the whip above his head and then took off hers with a single thrust, her body still standing there, the whip so hot, it had cauterized the wound between her shoulders. The flying bone shards all fell to the ground, uneventfully.

The Demon Prince grabbed the hilt of the sword currently impaling him, pulled it out with much pain, and threw it at the ground, near Persephone's headless body, the soul that had been stuck to him falling to the ground, weeping.

He spit in Persephone's direction and turned around, raising his whip in the air and giving a guttural cry of victory.

His cry of victory soon turned to one of anguish as her katana cut off one of his wings. He was struck with a strong feeling of vertigo, without his wings to balance him. He fell to the ground, his nerves screaming as much as his vocal chords were.

Somehow, Persephone, a *still living* Persephone, had her head back on, without even a single scar across her neck. She kneed him in the face, once, twice, three, four, five, six times. And then rested her foot on his bleeding throat.

She took her earbuds out, threw them away, and said, "Well, if it makes you feel any better, you ruined my headphones."

She kicked him in the face again. And then again and again and again and again. A cruel smile crossed her lips as she gave him one final kick to the jaw.

He groaned loudly. She looked down and saw the muscles on his arm tense up to swing the whip again, but she cut into his hand before he could even pull the arm back. With how thick his wrists were, the sword had dug a few inches in, severing tendons and cutting muscle, but not taking the hand off. She pulled the sword out of his wrist and swung again, this time, reaching the bone. She pulled back, yet again, and this time, cut the hand clean off. He shook in agony below her.

She squatted down and got in his face.

"Yeah, that cutting my head off thing doesn't work."

"WH-WHAT TYPE OF HUMAN ARE YOU?"

"One who has a very special friend who won't let anything bad happen to me."

"NO HUMAN WOULD…"

"Yes, yes, I know. Humans *normally* wouldn't know anyone who could do that. But I'm just…*special*, I guess. And you…"

She cut his face off with her sword, his skull screaming in agony.

"…aren't."

She gave a feral war cry and then bit into one of his eyes, his five arms swinging at her as she spit the eye onto the ground next to him.

As his body flailed, she put her sword down, and raised her fist, which began to glow white, as the wind around her picked up considerably. After a bit, the wind around her had formed a whirlwind, and she punched into the empty socket, her skin protected from the black flame of his horns by the white energy that seemed to grow from her hand to her arm to the rest of her whole body. His entire form convulsed, and then exploded in a shower of white energy, that enveloped the demon and Persephone, before gently dissipating, cleaning all the blood off of her body.

She gave a long, relaxed sigh.

Two of the three human souls, a man and a woman, crawled to her.

"Oh my god, thank you so much!" one of them, an older man cried to her, "We…"

"…are dead. You're not on Earth anymore."

"We're dead?!?" the woman cried out, "No! We're in Hell?!?"

"How do we get back?"

"You don't. You're just souls now. That form you have is just a projection of who you were when you were alive. In truth, you're just a spirit now. You're just energy now, in *kind of* solid form."

"You have to help us! They were going to make us food or slaves or something horrible!" the woman yelled.

"Can you please help us?!?" the man begged.

"Not today. Today, you have to stay here and…suffer…"

They fell to their knees and wept.

"But one day, that may just change," she said, turning from them, reaching down and picking up the Demon Prince's eye, "I promise. One day, you might see home again."

She grabbed her katana and closed her eyes. The demon world around her disappeared and she found herself back in her hotel room, putting her sword down on the dresser.

Mr. Trent looked at her, annoyed, as he walked in the room. Apparently, he had been waiting in the hotel room for her to return from wherever she was, "Where have you been? I had to get the staff to unlock the door for me. We have to get to the…do I smell the Fifth on you?"

"Yeah, took a little visit."

She walked into the bathroom and turned on the shower.

"You know, today is the day you are to begin your fast…"

"Was it? Totally must have slipped my mind. Oh well, guess I should start it as soon as we get there. The Ritual will go on without a hitch. Don't worry about it."

"Why are you…"

"Wait there. I'm going to take a shower and then we can get going."

He sighed heavily and looked out the window at the city below him.

Persephone tapped him on the shoulder and handed him something.

"Oh, yeah, before I forget: Got this from K'vek'ey'ih. Congrats, Mr. Trent. You're one step closer to your dad's throne."

He looked down at the eye she had put in his palm, the color leaving his face.

She patted him on the shoulder and shut the bathroom door behind her.

He crushed the eye, angrily.

CHAPTER 17

Samantha waited in her temporary office, waiting for the CDC representatives to come up. They were due any minute now. She double checked the papers in front of her, to make sure that everything was in order.

Her cellphone rang. It was Brian.

"Hey honey," she said, her face lighting up.

"Hey baby. How's New York?"

"Odd."

"What do you mean? The other you didn't show up, did it?"

"It hasn't been on the news there, I guess."

"What do you mean?"

"Julie's been framed for murder."

"What?!?"

"Yeah."

"Is she in custody? Did you call Elena?"

"No. She's missing, right now. Probably on the lam. I wish I could say that she's probably as far from New York City as she could be, but I know my sister. She's probably still here, thinking this is all some sort of adventure."

"Baby, you want me to fly out there?"

"No, no, honey. You stay in Chicago. I want to get to the bottom of this."

"Okay, whatever you say. Just give me the word and I'll be there. You know that."

"I do. That's why I love you…say, Brian, can you do me a favor and talk to Farrah about Perci."

"What about?"

"Well, initially, she said she was supposed to be heading to Chicago to do some work for the Council. Then, when she hears about what's going on with Julie, she decides to skip that and comes here, where there's suddenly some Council work she has to do here too."

"Just popped up?"

"Yup. Like the work just popped up. I love my sister, but I can also tell when she's lying about something. I know they're classified, but I know enough about Team Five to know you don't just skip out on a job. But I want you to check to see what she had going on in the first place in Chicago. Farah knows about all the black files, so she'd know what Perci was up to."

"What do you suspect?"

"I half suspect that Perci wants to collect the reward money for Julie, myself."

"From how you tell me those two get along, it wouldn't surprise me."

"Well, who knows? She could be telling the truth and actually be concerned, despite how weird she's been acting the last few nights, but the fact that she didn't make any effort to come out here when my doppelganger and Rayborn went after Julie a few months ago. Either way, I want to know for sure."

"Alright, baby."

"Anyway, I'm expecting Orin any minute now, so…"

"Oh yeah, the CDC thing."

"Yup. Oh, that reminds me, if you get a chance also ask Farah about the whole undersea project she was telling me about."

"What undersea project?"

"Okay. I asked Farah if it was okay to tell you and she said yes, but you can't spread this any further than you and I, 'kay?"

"Alright."

"They think they found Atlantis."

"What? That's huge."

"I know. There's this rich guy from Texas funding the dig. But he seems to have a genuine interest in…"

The intercom rang out in the office.

"Shit, I think that's Orin. I gotta go."

"Alright, baby, love you."

"Love you too. Don't forget about Farah."

"I won't."

"Goodbye."

"Goodbye."

She hung up her phone, pressed the button on the intercom, and told them to send Orin up.

CHAPTER 18

He had *thought* last night's attempt at intimidation had gone well. Mr. Trent had woken up this morning, feeling like he had finally gotten one over on Persephone Roberts.

Then she had handed him his brother's eye.

He was a demon, for crissakes, one of the sons of the House of Temen-ni-gru, and humans were supposed to be frightened, at their very core, by the type of threats he had made last night.

In truth, it had been a rather huge bluff. In reality, if Persephone killed him, his father wouldn't have cared. His father had over a thousand other sons and he'd be damned if the old man could even remember half of their names. If he were to have shown up at his father's icy throne tomorrow, his father's three faces would probably each tell him he smelled of human and then probably try to eat him.

Yes, his father was often mistaken by humans who got a vision of the Fifth Realm for the Judeo-Christian devil, which was ironic, considering his father had once decided to try taking human form once. That form became known as Saint Augustine.

And yes, Mr. Trent knew what restaurant Samantha and Persephone ate at each time they met up. But it wasn't like there was any solid threat there. He had just been keeping tabs because, for a bit, he had been worried she was just going to skip town without performing the ritual.

He supposed he *could* kill Samantha, if he had to. He had trained as a warrior for more years than the oldest human alive, but...wait, no...he had Timothy. Timothy could do it, he guessed.

But she was a respected Council member and he had tried to maintain a good relationship with them, so killing her would probably be some sort of act of war. Really, the only killing he ever associated himself with in the last two decades were arranging the yearly sacrifice for His Honor, something he had been doing for the last twelve years. This was the final year. It was supposed to be the most relaxing one, before he moved into the private sector or, perhaps, took on a different form and sought another human politician to work for.

This was not good at all, he thought to himself, looking through the files for the inquiry that was due to begin in a few minutes.

He had finally traced the man who was supposed to have vetted Persephone Roberts/Johannes. It was a man named Eric Jefferson, a man who actually had quite the stellar record up until now. It was his job to go through the list of potential candidates, see who would and wouldn't be an issue, and then narrow the list down.

However, going through the notes, he found that Eric hadn't even contacted any of the other candidates. Was he, perhaps, in cahoots with Ms. Roberts? It certainly seemed that way. And in, oh, about 2 minutes, he was going to get his answers.

He wasn't sure what he'd do when he had those, except possibly fire Eric, but maybe if he found some evidence of wrongdoing, he could declare the contract he had with Ms. Roberts void and sue her for the money she was paid. What was she going to do? Go into a court of law and say that she wasn't paid for the human sacrifices she performed? Ha! That'd show her.

Eric walked into the room, a quiet, bespeckled African American man in his late thirties. He was escorted in by some receptionist with glasses and her brown hair in a bun. She smiled a friendly smile, bowed, and then left the room.

"Mr. Trent," Eric said, "I'm told you wanted to talk to me."

"Please, Eric, have a seat."

Eric nodded nervously and sat down on the other side of the desk, nervously looking into the mirror behind Mr. Trent.

"Now, before we begin, Eric, you're aware that are entitled to have your union representative present at this meeting, right?"

"Oh, Mr. Trent, I have nothing to hide."

"Very well…So, Eric, am I wrong when I say that you were responsible for the vetting and recruiting of one Persephone Roberts for services to be rendered unto the City of New York on the date of…March 8th, 2013?"

"I believe so."

"Are you aware that you didn't appear to do any of your homework?"

"What do you mean?"

"I'm looking at the record of your files and your computer logs and you looked at three candidates before coming across Persephone Roberts' name in the system. At which point, you dropped all research on the other candidates and immediately contacted her."

"I...I...really? I did that?"

Eric seemed genuinely puzzled.

"Yes, you did."

"I remember, distinctly, vetting her for several days, along with, if I recall correctly, 14 other candidates. I remember not finding anything of note in her records."

"Really?"

"Really. Can I see the notes?"

Mr. Trent handed them to Eric, who looked down at them, a look of surprise on his face, growing as he saw how much work he didn't do.

"This is not my work. I swear," Eric's expression and mannerisms grew increasingly agitated. He seemed actually surprised and upset by this evidence.

Eric, scratched his head, looked into the mirror, and appeared to calm down. He simply said, "Oh."

Then, Eric reached into his sweater vest, pulled out a revolver, and blew his brains all over the wall, Mr. Trent jumping back in surprise, his suit stained by bits of blood and bone.

That was certainly odd, he thought, not sure what to say to security about this.

Actually, shouldn't security have made sure he wasn't coming in here carrying a loaded firearm like that?

He left the room, half expecting to see all of the office security dead. But he was greeted by security, running towards him, guns drawn. The receptionist from before was behind them, looking terrified.

"Are you okay, Mr. Trent?!?"

"How did he get a gun through here? No one searched him?!?"

One of the guards looked down at his holster and said, quietly, "Oh no...Don't let it be my gun! I...I don't even remember losing it."

Okay, this was really, really odd.

Mr. Trent began to think that he had no choice but to do something that would get him in a slight bit of shit. He knew that he couldn't take Persephone one on one in a battle if she could take out K'vek'ey'ih. He knew she must have had something to do with this suicide. And he knew she had shown that she wasn't going to be intimidated by his invocation of the laws of man. Maybe it might be time to contact the Council about her.

CHAPTER 19

She was in the lower sublevels of the facility. There was a special room where the priest or priestess could prepare themselves for the upcoming ritual. It was a sparse room, filled with white candles and sweet smelling incense.

In the center was an ornate rug, for meditation and gathering strength from whatever deity one called upon for protection.

And in the corner of the room, a beautiful tub with heated spring water for her to wash herself in.

She had already taken care of that and now was clad in a simple white bathrobe.

Persephone had quite liked Mr. Trent's reaction to her little Fifth Realm visit. That would teach him to threaten her. Of course, she also knew that part of the ritual required her to have a conflict-free day of meditation and fasting and if he wanted to get in her face about his deceased family member, it would violate the conditions of his own ritual.

When she had come out of the shower earlier, he had already disappeared somewhere and left a driver to take her here.

She smiled and then reminded herself that she had to clear her mind of these thoughts. She had to relax completely and let herself go to a quiet place in preparation for what tomorrow morning possibly held.

She put herself in a lotus position on the rug, closed her eyes, and found her peaceful place.

CHAPTER 20

Samantha walked out onto the street, the meeting with Orin having turned into a lunch and then a full on demonstration of the way that vampiric diseases differed from standard homosapien diseases, due to the extra spiritual component.

Not very exciting stuff to the average layman, but Samantha had always been interested with the how's and why's of spiritual conditions.

She hailed a cab, the sun going down over the city. She had thought of just taking a train back to her hotel room, but she had gotten lost the other day on the train (a moment that made her really wish she had been in contact with Julie, since she was sure her sister probably knew her way around the subway by now), so she thought spending the extra money on a cab was worth it.

She looked out at Manhattan from the back seat, cracking her neck, as the automated message from George Costanza's dad told her to buckle her seatbelt. She did as he asked and then stared at the rush hour traffic.

Her cell phone rang. Brian again.

"Hey honey, what's up?" she greeted.

"Hey baby. I talked to Farah earlier today."

"And?"

"She that it was the first she was hearing of Persephone doing any work in Chicago. No one there has made any effort to bring her into anything. Team Five have been put on inactive status after some incident she couldn't find any unredacted files about."

"Shit."

"Want to know something even weirder?"

"What?"

"You said she said she was going to be in Chicago first and then decided to take a flight to New York first, right?"

"Yeah."

"When did you hear from her?"

213

"A couple days after I'd been here. Why?"

"She arrived in New York about 12 hours after you did."

"Wait, what?"

"Farah looked up her flight records on the Council database. She took a flight from Heathrow to JFK on Julie's birthday."

"Holy shit…"

"What?"

"She's been here all this time?"

"Yeah, according to the records, an emergency call from some city official, a…uh…Michael Trent. There's no record of what they needed her for, but they were looking specifically for people with demon negotiation and/or combat skills."

"What? I knew about her combat skills. Hell, I've seen her combat skills up close, but demon negotiation?!? When did she pick that up?"

"According to their records, that's primarily what she does in England, since before Team Five were disbanded."

"Fuck…Brian, do you know of any demons strong enough to open a rupture to the Eighth Realm?"

"No. Nothing on this side is strong enough to do that."

"Okay. Thought so."

"You suspecting something?"

"Very much so, but I don't want to make any accusations without evidence."

"Hey, baby, you're probably worrying over nothing. Your sister wouldn't be negotiating with anything from the Eighth Realm. You and I both know from class that the Eighth Realm isn't very big on negotiating. And I know what you're thinking and nothing in the Eighth Realm is going to be framing Julie for murder, either. They're nameless abominations beyond the stars, not the cast of *Melrose Place*."

"Yeah. I guess."

"Samantha. Don't worry about this. It's probably not as bad as you think it is."

"There's just too much that doesn't make sense, Brian."

"Well, I think you're going to have to confront your sister and get the truth out of her, to ease your mind."

"Yeah, I think I have to, too."

"I'll let you go, baby."

"Okay. Love you."

"Love you too."

As she hung up the phone, she realized she hadn't remembered to ask him what Farah said about the whole Atlantis thing, but that was the last thing on her mind.

She called Persephone's cell, but it went directly to voicemail, without even ringing, so she assumed her sister had turned it off.

She took a deep breath and wondered just what was going on with her sisters.

CHAPTER 21

"I don't get it," Lucy said to Julie, as the two of them surveyed the club.

"It's a visual pun! What's to get?" Julie insisted, "A head giving head? It's funny!"

"I dunno."

"You just don't appreciate movies."

They were at Webster Hall, a bit high profile and a bit risky, considering Julie's wanted status, but this was a prime selling location for what Julie had dubbed Hypnagogia. They had spent most of the night opening holes into the Second Realm and killing parasites. Butcher's Eyes were plentiful.

They walked over to a bunch of guys sitting on a couch with some girls.

"Yo yo, what up?" Lucy greeted.

"You supposed to be Brooke Candy?", a tall thin blond with a pointed nose asked.

"Who?"

"Holy shit," Julie said, slapping her forehead, "That's who you remind me of!"

"What? Fuck that noise. Only one me. Anyway, my niggas, you all looking for a good time?"

"Depends on what you're offering," one of the men suggested.

"Dude, we got some shit that will not just blow your mind, it will blow you. Literally, this shit will blow you."

Julie reached into her messenger bag and pulled out a tiny little baggy of the Butcher's Eye dust. She laid out a single line on the little coffee table in front of the couch.

"Looks like coke," one of the girls said.

"This shit shits on coke, know what I'm saying?" Lucy said.

"What is it?"

"Hypnagogia!"

"Hypna-what?" the girl asked.

"It's not called that," Lucy said.

"Yes, it is!" Julie disagreed, turning back to the guy on the couch, "Seriously, dude, try it. You will cum out your butthole, because your dick will be too busy pissing itself."

"Well, that's a ringing endorsement," another one of the guys, some douchey-looking guy in a fedora, said, "Alright. I'm game. Lemme try this shit."

Julie tried to hand him a straw, but he shook his head and pulled out one of his own from his jeans.

He leaned a little over the table and snorted.

Immediately, his eyes rolled into his head and he dropped to his knees, gasping.

"What the fuck?!? John?!? John?!? You okay?!?" the girl who had asked about Brooke Candy inquired of him, his body convulsing as she put her hands on his shoulders.

"Someone call 911! Someone call..." his friend on the couch started, before the guy with the fedora caught his breath and shook his head.

"D-d-don't...don't...call..."

"John, are you okay? What did they give you?"

"I...I...I jizzed in my pants..."

"Ewww," the girl said, backing away from him.

"No...this feels...holy shit...someone touch me right now. *Anyone.* I'll fucking pay you to touch me."

Lucy shrugged and started to walk towards him, Julie grabbing her by the shoulder and giving her the eye. Lucy rolled her eyes into her head, and then looked back at the group on the couch.

"So, this shit makes you cum?" the guy on the couch asked.

"Oh, you better believe it, and you're ready for more, right after," Julie said, selling him on the product.

"How much?"

"Let's say $50, a pack?"

"I'll take four," the guy with the fedora, still laying on the ground said, throwing 10 crumbled up twenties at Julie and Lucy.

The other people on the couch looked at each other, talked among themselves. The blond girl looked at the tiny little remnants of the line on the table and poked it with her finger. A chill immediately ran through her body as she let out a moan so loud, it embarrassed her.

She shuddered and bit her lower lip and then mounted the guy on the floor.

The other people sitting on the couch looked at her and then at each other and began reaching for their wallets.

Julie and Lucy high-fived each other.

Before they were done for the night, the club resembled something from Rome...except oral sex was quite plentiful.

CHAPTER 22

Persephone found herself in a sakura garden. A little lake flowing gently, the breeze peaceful. She smiled, the *shidarezakura* petals cascading over her, landing in her hair. The sky was a quiet blue, the white tops of mountains touching it in the distance, birds chirping to each other in the warm afternoon air.

She was at peace here. She smiled. It would be the perfect place for a picnic, if she didn't have to fast. Food in the mind was still food.

She looked down at herself, admiring the beautiful red furisode kimono she wore, images of cranes adorning it, her long sleeves flowing in the breeze with her hair.

She had always intended on attending a *Hanami* festival, but had just been too busy with work. Perhaps, after she was done in New York, she would take a vacation to Kyoto. She hadn't taken one in years and now was the tail end of the *sakura zensen,* so if she wanted to go, it would have to be soon.

Yes, she thought, she deserved to be in a place like this, after all her work, so she would take a trip to Japan once this all wrapped up.

She took a moment or two to enjoy the quiet, beautiful afternoon. Then she heard it.

From the distance, a familiar riff was playing on an acoustic guitar.

Who else is in my garden? she thought.

She reached behind herself for her katana, but it wasn't there. Didn't matter. She was strong enough to get rid of whoever this intruder was.

She began to walk through the garden, across the footbridge, over the crystal clear lily pond, towards a forest of bamboo trees, where the music was coming from.

Wait…was that a fife?!? Yes, that was a fife. Oh…it's him, isn't it?

A frown crossed her lips as she walked through the bamboo, eventually coming to a clearing where a man in a black male kimono, with shoulder-length blond hair sat on a singular chair, playing the guitar.

"Dad!" she angrily yelled, "Why do you do this before every ritual I have to do?!? Why must you subject me to another one of your stupid classic rock visions?!? I know what you're trying to do! You're trying to prevent me from doing the ritual tomorrow, aren't you? You always do this! Well…"

Her father looked up at her with sad eyes and began to sing.

"There's a lady whose sure all that glitters is gold and…"

"No! No! You do not get to lecture me with your little old people music moment!"

"When she get there, she knows…"

"You know what? This isn't happening. You want to stop me; you come to me and *physically* stop me. Because you're not going to…"

"And she's buying a Stairway to Heaven…"

"Fine. Fuck it."

She snapped her fingers and suddenly a large piano fell from the sky, landing directly on her father.

There was silence as the Led Zeppelin song abruptly ended.

She shook her head and sighed, walking over to the piano, as bamboo forest began to fade away, until there was just her, the piano, and complete darkness. A spotlight flipped on and shone on her, from somewhere in the sky.

"Persephone, you have to listen to me," her father said, now several yards behind her, walking through the darkness, "I didn't get far enough in the song to tell you that there was always time to change the road you were…"

"No. You couldn't just call me up like you do Juliette. You couldn't just come see me. I'm in New York City, by the way; same city as your *favorite* daughter. Hell, you can't just talk to me like a normal not-insane person. No…You wanted to do this your way, we do this *your* way," she said, throwing off her kimono, in a single motion, revealing a pair of red leather pants and white poet's shirt. She sat down at the piano.

She took another deep breath and began to play, singing.

"So…don't stop me now
Don't stop me
Cause I'm having a good time, having a good time!"

With that, there was the flash of flashpots, multiple spotlights flicked on, showing that the scenery changed from the Asian garden to a stage. Four more Persephones appeared, one behind the drums, one on bass, and one on guitar, one taking the piano, each wearing tight white leather, while the original Persephone continued to sing the first verse of the Queen song.

Her father, standing at the front of the stage, looked at her, with sadness in his eyes.

"*Don't stop me now!*" the other Persephones sang.

"Cause I'm having a good time!"

"*Don't stop me now!*"

"Yes, I'm having a good time! I don't want to stop at all!"

Alexander sighed heavily, upon noticing that he was no longer alone, in front of the stage but was now joined by thousands and thousands of Persephone, moving to the music, as she strut around the stage, singing about being a rocket ship on its way to Mars, a satellite, out of control.

When she said she was like an atom bomb, about to explode, the entire crowd sung along with her.

"*I'm burning through the sky, yeah!*

Two hundred degrees!"

The other instruments except for the drums stopped, Persephone stared directly at her father and clapped her hands above her head to the beat. The other Persephones singing "*Don't stop me! Don't stop me!*" Until she sat back on the drum riser, crossing her legs defiantly as another Persephone played the guitar solo.

Her father started to become transparent as she banished him from her mindscape, while repeating the chorus.

The final notes of the song rang out, the thousands of Persephones holding up their lighters as the other onstage Persephones disappeared and the original vocalized while playing the piano, applause filling the world.

And then suddenly, she was back in the bamboo forest, near the garden, wearing her kimono again.

She had banished him from her mind, once more.

Well, she thought, *at least he wasn't wearing a fundoshi.*

She wasn't sure she could handle that vision.

She took a deep breath and lay down, letting the pedals cover her, gently.

CHAPTER 23

Julie walked through the forest, the faces on the trees calling out to her. It was a dead forest, the air itself misty. There was a howl in the distance, the dampness in the air making her skin glisten in the moonlight.

She wasn't sure how she had gotten into the forest. She remembered having to pull Lucy off a couple guys as everybody got naked as Webster Hall, because she figured Lucy killing somebody in the middle of the club would be bad for business. Julie wasn't into any of the various Jersey Shore types that populated the place anyway, so she got in, made her money, left everybody happy, got out. She had wanted to go to a club that she was more familiar with in East Williamsburg, since there she'd be more than happy to engage in any hardcore goings on, but Lucy reminded her that that was where she had alleged committed murder, so they'd be looking for her especially there. So, they went back to Lucy's apartment, where Julie, a bit frustrated, went into Lucy's bathroom with a little bit of the Hypnagogia and masturbated herself into unconsciousness.

Then she had woken up here.

Oh…she thought, *I get it. I'm dreaming. Might as well ride this ride, see where it goes.*

Now fully aware of the fact that she was dreaming, she noticed that she was carrying a picnic basket, wearing a red hood, and an old-fashioned dress, walking down a path, through the twisted, living trees, which were, to be quite honest a lot more pleasant than the actual living trees she had seen in the Fifth Realm.

Sure enough, the trees here turned into the trees from the Fifth Realm, the nightmares that had inspired Dante's passages about the Forest of Suicides.

Huh. Got to be careful with the lucid dreaming.

Ahead of her was a gingerbread house. An animated dove flew onto her shoulder and told her, "The frequency is 90.4. That's West Tunisia's home of Classic Pop from the 80's."

"I feel like that's a lot of numbers I need to memorize."

"Only you can prevent forest fires."

A banana flew through the air, knocking into the animated dove, causing it to explode in a shower of shrapnel and fire.

Julie ducked, getting low, as the sounds of bombs filled the sky. One of the trees screamed, "Fucking French!"

Deciding it was best to ignore the anti-French ranting of the trees, she followed the yellow brick road until she found her way to the gingerbread house.

She licked the door and then opened it.

There was a stooped-over old woman inside, holding an apple, standing next to a large black cauldron. There was a foul stew or the other brewing in the cauldron.

Okay, the apple is poisoned. I know this fairy tale. Julie thought, *So, maybe she should, instead, give me a hamburger. A non-poisoned hamburger.*

The apple in the crone's hand turned into a delicious, juicy hamburger that she handed to Julie.

Julie took a bite and then decided that if she could manipulate her dreams, she'd rather have someone attractive around than the crone.

Within a second of that Iggy Pop, wearing see-through pants, was hovering over the cauldron in the middle of the hut

This could get interesting, she thought, and smiled.

She started to walk towards him, when a familiar voice, behind her, said, "Juliette, I don't have much time!"

"Wha?"

"Juliette, it's your father."

"Holy fuck!" she yelled, immediately banishing the semi-clad Iggy Pop from her head, after seeing her father standing behind her.

"Dad! What are you doing here? Shit, is *that* why Iggy Pop was here? Were you going to ruin my fantasy by having him sing, 'Now I Want to Be Your Dog' or something to warn me that, I don't know, hellhounds are going to attack me or something?"

"I don't think I would have had him in the see-through pants if I were using his music to communicate with you," her dad said, standing behind her in a black kimono.

"That's actually kinda reassuring. That's a line I don't think we should ever cross."

"Really, though, Juliette? Iggy Pop? You're attracted to Iggy Pop? The man's my age!"

"Don't judge me, dad."

"Iggy Pop, god…"

"That is a sweet kimono, by the way."

"Thanks. I like it."

"It works on you.."

"Thank you, Juliette. Oh, yeah, we're getting sidetr…Oh dear," he became transparent for a moment, "Well, that isn't good."

"Dad, what's going on?"

"Juliette, I have an urgent message for you."

"So, why isn't it being sung to me?"

"There's no time! I have limited energy, so I have to just speak it."

"What?!? All these times you appeared to me as Foghat songs or whatever, you could have just spoken it to me?"

"Well, yes."

"Then why didn't you?"

"I wanted to share some good music with you. You never to learned to appreciate my music."

"Holy fuck, dad!"

"Anyway, there's no time for a song. I have to tell you something! It's about your sister. She's in New York."

"Oh, I know. I had dinner with her on my birthday."

"Oh, yes. I called a day early. How was your birthday?"

"I've had better. But…uh…aren't you here to tell me something important?"

He opened his mouth to speak, but was interrupted as there was a loud buzzing noise, coming from inside the cauldron. She and her father both looked at it, puzzled.

"Don't pay attention to that. My head's a fucked up place. I'll just make that noise not happen anymore. I'm lucid dreaming right now."

She concentrated for a moment. A few seconds later, the noise happened again.

"Shit. Give me a minute. I'll make it go away."

"Listen…Juliette. Your sister is about to make a huge mistake and she won't listen to me."

"What's going on?'

"She…" buzzing noise rang out again, "Wow, that's really annoying."

"I know. Hold on…if mentally turning it off won't work…"

She walked over to the cauldron, to see if she could figure out what was causing that noise. She kicked the cauldron. Twice. Then crinkled her nose a little bit before kicking it a third time.

"I got nothing."

Her father, quickly losing opaqueness, tried to put his hand on her shoulder, only to have it go straight through her.

It was a weird feeling, because she felt him going through her, like she was a wall and he was a fairly warm ghost.

He turned to her, a look of urgency in his eyes and, as he faded away, said, "Juliette… important… listen… sister… have to… stop… her…"

CHAPTER 24

Julie was awoken by the sound of Lucy's door buzzer. She had wanted to know more of what her father had been talking about. Her sister was making a huge mistake? What did that mean? Was it something to do with Samantha marrying that guy? She was supposed to stop her from doing something? Shit. She really needed to get in touch with Sammi now.

The buzzer rang again, followed by a loud knock on Lucy's front door.

Lucy, who was on the other side of the room, covered up her nudity with her bathrobe, and fixed her hair for a second.

"Yo, chill for a second. Gots ta get this."

"Client?"

"Wasn't expectin' no motherfuckin' client. Not at 6 in the motherfuckin' morning. Hold up."

"Sure."

"And take that weird shit off."

Julie wasn't sure what she meant at first, until Julie looked in the mirror and saw that she was wearing a plastic horse head that she had randomly picked up yesterday. With a leather jacket. And boyshorts. And her docs. There was probably a story behind this.

Lucy left the bedroom and walked to her front door. She looked through the peephole and then unlocked the door, opening it a few inches, undoing the chain lock. Outside the door was a beautiful East Indian woman with the dark olive skin, almond eyes, and thick black waist-length hair, wearing an expensive black evening gown, looking impatient.

"What up, Thanus?"

"Larxene of the Black Talon," the woman said, looking over Lucy's shoulders into the apartment, while trying to send a text on her cellphone, "I know it's early, but I was just talking to Aleite of the

White Lie in 4B and she said that the building has a Butcher's Eye problem."

"Do it?"

"Yes. I saw one down in the laundry room early tonight. I was wondering if you…"

Thanus sniffed the air.

"What up?" Lucy asked, getting a bit nervous that Thanus might realize how many of the building rules she was breaking on a regular basis.

"Your room smells like…"

"Shit, I be smoking the real nasty skunk, yo. Shit relaxes me. No harm, 'ight? Little air freshener, all that funk be gone."

Thanus pushed the door open.

"Hold up! Hold up! I didn't invite you in."

"Your apartment smells like the Second Realm. Why is that, Larxene of the Black Talon? Is the rift in your apartment?"

Julie walked from the bedroom, still wearing the horse mask, going to the kitchen to get some vodka.

"And who exactly is that?"

"I'm a horse!" Julie responded, imitating a gallop, and doing a poor version of a horse whinny.

"Why do you have a human female," Thanus sniffed again, "An *immunized* human female in your apartment? You know this is a no pets building."

"I'm not a human female. I'm a mare!" Julie said, again whinnying.

"What are you two doing in here?"

"Yo. Thanus, 'ight, listen up. This my nigga, Julie. She just be crashin' here on the down-low for couple days. No big shit. Nothin' to get all up in my grill 'bout."

"Larxene of the Black Talon, you know the rules. I may have to talk to the Mother about this."

"Na na na nah. No need to be upsetting the Mother and shit."

"And, for fuck's sake, can you please stop speaking in that manner? It is incredibly irritating."

"Hey, Lucy," Julie said, deciding to be serious for a moment, even though she still had the horse head on, "If it's a problem for me to be here, I'll head off. We made enough money yesterday for me to…"

"*Lucy?!?*" Thanus asked, hands on her hip, "How quaint. You have this primate calling you that, too?"

"Is this another succubus, Lucy?"

Lucy nodded, "Yeah…I kinda didn't mention I lives in a nest. Whole buildin' and shit."

"Yes," Thanus said, "A nest that has rules and regulations, so as to keep all of its inhabitants safe and happy. Something that, maybe, if she weren't of such a low breed, she'd understand."

"I said I was sorry, 'ight."

Thanus scoffed, "Larxene of the Black Talon…You bring vermin in the building of both the tentacled and two-legged variety; you insist on talking like some common human ghetto trash; you regularly indulge in foul smelling human poisons; and you now ask me to break the rules for you. Not to mention, if you were looking to make this up to me, this one is immunized. I can't even present her to my brothers! You've put us all in danger. If she leaves here, what is to guarantee she won't report us to the authorities? What if she saw what was in the freezer?"

"She didn't see the freezer. And 'sides, she ain't gonna call no po-po or nothin' on us. She wanted herself. Her ass was all over the news."

"Oh, *even better.* You don't just bring a human that you don't intend to use for food here, but you bring a human that is wanted by the authorities and, no doubt, being followed, here. Wonderful, Larxene of the Black Talon. Maybe you might want to invite a demon hunter or two over, next time."

Lucy opened her mouth to say something, but thought better of it.

Julie, on the other hand, had had enough of this and walked up to Thanus and looked her face-to-horse-face.

"She said it was temporary and the Butcher's Eye thing was my idea. I will be leaving if you have that much of a stick up your ass about me."

"Larxene of the Black Talon, why is *it* speaking to *me?*" Thanus asked Lucy, looking past Julie.

"Because *it* will kick *your* ass if you continue to fuck with *its* friend," Julie said, getting back in Thanus' view, "Who the fuck do you think you are, anyway, coming in here at 6 in the fucking morning with your skanky 'I'm a whore' dress and your super-sized Kim Kardashian ass making demands like you're…uh…fucking Chairman Mao or something?"

Thanus rolled her eyes, and then growled, her pupils turning yellow, her teeth sharpening, and horns ripping out of her forehead as she grabbed Julie by the throat and lifted her a good foot off the ground.

"Larxene of the Black Talon, your bitch is displeasing me," Thanus said.

"You know, I'm getting really fuckin' tired of people doing that whole lifting me by the neck bullshit!" Julie said, kicking Thanus in the chest.

Thanus fell back and let go of Julie. Thanus let out a screech and got into a battle stance, her wings ripping out of her back.

"Alright, *bitch*! I may get sick doing it, but I am going to eat the marrow from…" Thanus started to say, beginning to transform into her true succubus body.

She didn't get a chance to finish her sentence, though, because Julie smashed her in the face with the vodka bottle.

Thanus, in mid-transformation, fell backwards, Julie leaping at her, and kneeing her in the face, over and over and over and over again. She grabbed Thanus by the left horn and then smashed her head into the floor so hard, it cracked her other horn.

Julie started punching her in the face over and over again, until both Julie's knuckles and Thanus' face were bloody.

"You gonna keep fucking with my girl? Huh? You gonna keep fucking with my girl?!?" Julie started repeating.

Lucy took a deep breath and leaned against the wall.

Julie stood up as Thanus lay on the ground breathing heavily.

"Awwwww…shit…girl…" Lucy said, under her breath.

"Sorry about that, Lucy, but…" Julie started.

"My nigs, you best, uh, go get yo pants. We gots ta step."

"I…will…will…kill…you…" Thanus said, tasting her own blood.

"Oh, your mouth getting big again?" Julie taunted. She kicked Thanus in the stomach.

"Bitch. Get yo shit," Lucy ordered, "We gots ta go."

"I'm sorry, Lucy, I'll leave if…"

"No. You hear me wrong. We both gots ta leave before this bitch here…"

Thanus gave a loud screech. Loud enough that it made Julie jump.

"Now, you're dead," Thanus said, coughing up blood while laughing, "You're so fucking dead."

"Why? Cause you can scream really fucking loud? I can do that too!"

"Nah," Lucy said, "That ain't why."

There was another screech somewhere in the building. Then there was another, a little closer. Another that sounded like it was a floor directly above them. Another that sounded far away. The air was then filled with the sound of screeching as the eighteen other succubae who lived in the building answered Thanus' call for help.

"She just called on every bitch in the building to help her ass."

"They know what apartment we're in?"

"'ight."

"Wait…She said all that? She just kinda screeched a little."

"We gots a real subtle language."

Julie ran to the front door and opened it, only to see that the hallway she was used to was gone. In its place was what appeared to be a twisted maze of undulating flesh and pumping muscle, vastly bigger than the dimensions of the building would have allowed for.

"Oh fuck, I'm hallucinating again," Julie said.

"Nah. That shit straight up real. Building's on Earth on the outside. Fourth Realm on the inside we need it be."

"Kinda like the TARDIS or something?"

"I don't know who you sayin' is retarded but we gots ta get outta here. Get yo pants!"

"No time for pants."

Julie ran back into the bedroom, shoved her PS3, some clothes, and some of the Hypnagogia packets into her messenger bag, and then, seeing Thanus gaining her footing again in the living room, Julie reached into her messenger bag, pulled out a baseball bat and smashed Thanus in the head with it, making a loud squishy cracking noise.

"A bat, though, there's always time for."

CHAPTER 25

"What the bloody fuck was that?"

"Fanny demons, Mimmy."

"Fanny demons?"

"Aye, fanny demons. Lots and lots of fanny demons."

"You don't happen to speak fanny demon, do you?"

"Someone's in their nest. And there's a traitor to boot. They're cheesed, they is…wha…hold up."

Serenity, sniffed the air.

"Mimmy! Mimmy, found her, I did! It's her."

"Her?"

"*Her* her!"

"The bird?"

"Aye, the fucking bird."

"How far?"

"A kilometer that way."

Christopher looked up at the sky.

"Don't you think we'd best chivvy along and turn in for the night?"

"Herr Fuhrer's going to be cross."

"Aye, but the fucking sun is rising in a few. Can't we wait till nightfall? The missus will be getting Sweet Fanny Adams if me loaf bursts to flame."

Serenity shrugged, trying to judge how long they'd have until the sun came up. She sniffed again, walking towards the direction she smelled Julie.

"Fuck me."

"What?"

"She's *in* the bloody nest."

"Fanny demon nest?"

"Fanny demon nest."

"Real ace, that is."

231

"It could work to our advantage. By the sound of it, there's enough that maybe the inside is the Fourth. If it's the Fourth, we've no worries about fireworks."

"That's a lot of if's."

"Aye, it is. But faffing about ain't doing nothing for us, innit?"

"Off your trolley, you are."

"Chin up, Mimmy. You're a hard bloke. Close your eyes and think of England."

"God save the Queen."

CHAPTER 26

"Wake up! It's time!" the guard yelled, angrily banging on the cage, with what she assumed were nightsticks.

Kelly snapping awake instantly, the hood still on her head, her body sore from sitting in the one position for the last 36 hours. Of course, she had no idea that it had been that long, but if she had any single emotional victory, it was that, with her lack of a mouth and thus, lack of any food intake, she had been the only woman in the cell to have not soiled herself during that entire time. It's amazing the things your mind makes into a positive when there are no others to be found.

The guards unlocked the shackles around their ankles and those attaching them to the bench, as they were violently forced to their feet. The guards yelling, "March! March!"

The hoods still over their heads.

They were quickly marched, sometimes stumbling due to the inactivity of their legs, falling, only to be violently dragged to the feet. They were taken somewhere, the guards yelled, "Halt."

And they all stood. There was a sound like a freight elevator moving, the feeling of gravity confirming for her that they were going down somewhere.

Her legs began to shake. Was she being taken to die now? Every fiber of her being told her to fight, but her hands were zip-tied behind her back, her head was covered by a hood, and she was chained to 19 other women. She didn't have the belief in Ms. Roberts that the others had. The woman had told her, flat out, that they were all going to die down here.

And now, it was her time.

The elevator stopped, she heard a gate open, and they were told to march again. They did so for about a minute before being ordered to halt again.

"I'm going to guess by the space suit, everything's ready, Abbott? We have three hours to get them ready before Roberts arrives and the Ritual begins."

"Yes, sir! Everything is ready, sir!"

"Good. Okay, we just have to wait for Squad D to…"

There was a far off sound of another freight elevator arriving at the floor and the sounds of more marching bare feet and screaming guards. She assumed this was the men being marched as well.

"Was wondering when you ladies were going to join the party."

"Attention. You know your orders. Step one, as much as it looks like most of them have evacuated already, you empty them all out until the water is clear, understood."

"Yes, sir."

"Men in stall A, women in stall B. Then proceed to shower A and B, where individual cleansing is to occur. You know the procedure. You go as far in as you need to with each one. I want three four-man teams doing 30 minute shifts on each. Then final steps and you bring them back here by 0900. Is that clear?"

"Yes, sir!"

"Proceed, soldier."

The guards began to yell again and they were herded into a room with a cold, wet tile floor.

She felt the zip-ties on her hands being cut, letting her move her arms again, only for them to then be forced in front of her, zip-tied again, and attached to something on the wall. There was the noise of some sort of chain and pulley system, and a cold metal bar rose up to greet her belly, at the same time, there was pull on her arms, in front of her, bending her over the bar.

She wondered what this was about, only to feel a pair of rubber gloved hands grabbing her asscheeks.

Oh fuck no, they weren't…!

"Ah, I think this is the one without the mouth," a voice that belonged to the rubber gloves said.

"Have you been checking them out enough to tell? Christ, they're all pretty haggard looking from being in here."

"No no. Check it out, she's the only one without fresh shit all over her."

"Oh, yeah. Not having a mouth would probably prevent that happening. Good good. So you don't have to do any pre-scrub with this one. Just go on in."

"Still give her the catheter treatment?"

"Might as well."

She didn't like the sound of that. Not at all.

Suddenly, she felt the hands spreading the cheeks of her ass. She tried to tense up, but a finger found its way to her rectum, applying some sort of lubricant as far up as the finger would go. The finger returned for two more trips, until its owner felt she was suitably enterable. She screamed without a mouth, feeling violated and horrified at what was going to happen to her next.

She felt something enter her. Something that felt small and rubber. At first, her thoughts turned to some sort of sex toy, but it quickly became obvious it was a tube of some sort.

She heard groans of pain from some of the other women, as they were no doubt, anally penetrated as well. But worse than the noises of the other women were the guards making small talk.

"Yo, Martinez, did you see the Pacers last night?"

"You fucking traitor, New York Fucking Knicks!"

"Whatever, man. You still coming by tonight? Maria's making veal parm tonight."

"I'll see, bro."

"No problem...So, uh, you *were* going to fuck one of them, it'd be this one, right?"

"Sure, I guess."

"You know, Donaldson used to say the trick was to get them when they were still fresh."

"Yeah, well, Donaldson died getting his dick bitten off when he tried that last time, so you'll forgive me if I don't take his advice."

There was the sound of a machine being turned on; a moment later, there was the feeling of fluid rushing through the tube. Within moments, she felt her bowels fill with fluid, her body cramping hard.

"Now, give them all five minutes then release the tubing. You make sure you do that as many times as needed. We want clear water. Water you'd be willing to drink if it hadn't come straight out of some whore's ass."

"Yes, sir."

"Drake, come here. Do you know how to put one of these in? We are *not* to damage any of them in the process of cleansing. If you don't know how to do it, tell me now, so we don't fuck anything important up."

"Maybe. I'm not sure."

"Alright…Dario, you're up. Show them how to put one of these in properly."

With her bowels full of water, her body shaking from pain, humiliation, and fear, she screamed behind closed skin, as she felt a gloved hand reach between her legs, and use two fingers to spread her labia.

CHAPTER 27

Defeated from the night previous, Jerry felt only physical pain from his enema and catheter treatment. They had emptied his bladder and bowels and then he and the other men were marched off to another room. They were told to halt again, he was unchained from the others, and then marched off to yet another room, this one with a damp floor.

Suddenly the world became white, as the hood was taken off, the sting of light making him cry out.

His hands still zip-tied in front of him, as focus returned to him, he saw he and two other men were now in a room that had immediately made him think of a documentary he had seen about how cattle were prepared for slaughter. The guards here wore Hazmat suits.

He just felt numb. There was no fear left in him. There was nothing. He couldn't even make the words to beg them to stop.

One guard grabbed a hook from the ceiling and pulled it down, while another grabbed his tied hands and then put them above his head. The hook picked him up a good three inches off the ground and then he was assaulted by water so hot, even in his semi-catatonic state, he screamed.

Four men surrounded him, holding coarse brushes and ominous looking bottles.

Two held him, spreading his legs when they wanted to wash his now-mutilated genitals; bending him over when they wanted to wash between the cleft of his ass and then used what looked like a slightly gentler wire brush to go up inside him; holding his face in place when they used a similar brush on the inside of his mouth.

Every accessible inch of his body was scrubbed, cleaned, and even bleached as thoroughly as possible for a full half hour.

When they were done, his skin was red and raw, probably a layer of it gone in an ashy mess on the floor below him.

They unattached him from the hook, the muscles in his shoulders killing him, and marched him to another waiting area, where the guards went from wearing Hazmat suits to wearing riot gear, shields and all.

CHAPTER 28

"So," Julie said, wading through several inches of some thick sticky liquid that she assumed felt like what it'd be like to walk through a literal river of cum, except this was red, instead of white, "I have my dice in my bag. Why don't we just roll them and get the hell out of here?"

"Nah nah. Won't work that way. Howlin' void and shit."

"Really?"

"Yup. Nothin' in the buildin' in your world. And I mean motherfuckin' nothing. How we fit the Fourth and all here."

"That's kinda a neat trick. So, why didn't you tell me about the whole nest thing?"

"I supposed to just tell you fuck yourself when my nigs needs help? Thought there won't be none, we didn't start none."

"But I mean why were you living in a nest in the first place?"

"You think normal white bread neighbors ain't gonna call the motherfuckin' po-lice they hear me eating some nigga?"

"I guess."

"Nests is our cribs and all. We safe here."

"Well, that one succubus back there seemed like a cunt."

"Thanus ain't mean nothin'. She just stuck up 'cause her broodmom higher rank than mine. Thanus always like that. I didn't pay the bitch no mind. Of course, now there gonna be shit. All the other bitches here gonna want my motherfuckin' head."

"Well, don't worry about that. I've got a bat."

"'ight," Lucy said, taking an apprehensive deep breath.

The two of them waded through the poorly lit labyrinth that had previously been the building hallway, until they saw a doorway ahead of them, the thick liquid flowing down a pair of stairs ahead, like a very waterfall.

Suddenly, there was a whipping noise in the air as two dark shapes flew in the air above them.

"Traitor…"

"Murderer…"

Two succubae, in their true forms, came from behind them. Julie had only seen a succubus in her true form two or three times before, but it always gave her the creeps. They seemed to be creatures of solid shadow, living silhouettes. When she had seen Lucy a few days back, while tied to the bed, she had been seeing Lucy's true form. There was the shape of hips, the shape of breasts, the shape of hooves, and the shape of wings and horns, but no features. Just blackness, with three pairs of yellow eyes floating in the general area of the forehead.

When they moved, it was like watching watercolors blend into each other, a fluid movement that didn't seem possible.

Julie pulled out her bat and got into a stance, like she was going to hit a homerun.

Lucy seemed reluctant to fight. She gave a screech, the other two screeching back at her.

The other two stopped and looked at each other, then looked at Julie. She heard a hissing noise. Lucy hissed back at them.

"Fuck it," Julie said, rushing towards the two, swinging her bat at one of them. It jumped back in surprise as the bat hit it directly in the stomach, the demon doubling over in pain.

"Nah nah nah, Julie, my nigs, don't…"

The succubus that hadn't been hit let out a screech and flew at Julie with incredible speed, knocking her into the wall. It's head seemed to fold open, as if its jaw was a Pez dispenser, and it snapped at Julie, attempting to bite her.

She kneed it in the stomach, a feeling that was like kneeing a big tub of Jello. Julie sprung herself forward, knocking the demon down, and punching it in the jaw, repeatedly. It frustrated her, because unlike with other creatures, there wasn't any visible damage, so you never knew how much you were hurting them until their eyes closed and you knew they were dead.

Suddenly, Lucy leapt at her, tackling her, as the two of them fell down the stairs together.

"What the fuck, Lucy?!?"

"Motherfucker! They was listening! They ain't Red Veil! They was Azure Eye!"

"I don't know what any of that means."

"And take that motherfuckin' horse head off, bitch! Shit!"

Julie took the horse head off, and put it into her bag.

The two demons she fought stood at the top of the stairs. They hissed at her and flew away.

"Well, they went away. That seemed to go well."

"Nah nah nah…motherfuckin'…bitch, you done fucked up!"

"What? How did I fuck up?"

"They was listening! I tryin' to tell them this was 'bout a challenge to Red Veil."

"Whatever. That's all demon politics. I don't pay attention to…"

"Bitch, they was gonna fight on our side."

"Oh. Fuck. Well, you should've told me that!"

"I was motherfuckin' negotiating."

"Okay…okay, well, can't you just screech that we're sorry?"

"Don't work like that."

"This place is a serious fucking buzzkill."

Julie reached into her bag and pulled out a bottle of Jager, taking a swig. She offered some to Lucy. Lucy just glared at her.

"What?"

"Nothing. Let's just go."

"What?"

"Knowing yo ass is bad for the motherfuckin' health, yo."

CHAPTER 29

Her body raw from the shower, her mind in shock from what was happening to her, Kelly, and the other two women she had been showered with were marched into one last room, herded by riot shields pressed against their bodies, where there stood a group of nine very stern looking women, each wearing a smock over her uniform.

The male guards cut their zip-ties again, while the women glared at them. Their arms were spread wide and attached to more pulleys, this time on each side of the wall. Similar pulleys were attached to their ankles until each of the three hung spread eagle in front of the women.

The women proceeded to go back to a workbench where Kelly could see there were shears, electric razors, and a number of creams.

With Kelly unable to even protest vocally, three of the women walked over to her. One proceeded to use an electric razor on her pubic area, while another began cutting the hair on her head with the shears.

CHAPTER 30

By the time they were done, Jerry did not have a hair left on his body. From the top of his head to even the little hairs on the front of his fist and feet to his eyebrows to even the hair between the cheeks of his buttocks had been shaved, waxed, and/or plucked. Looking at the rest of his shorn and bald fellow prisoners, he thought they all looked like aliens now. He was sure he did, as well.

They were zip-tied one more time, their hands behind their backs. The rest of the male prisoners, after they were processed, three at a time, in the same harsh manner Jerry had been, joined him in a long hallway outside the shaving room. Once all of them arrived, they were marched down it, where the women, equally naked of both clothing and hair, were marched in from a different room.

They continued down the hallway until they got to what he assumed was the same freight elevator that he had come down in the first place, the snickers on the faces of some of the guards obvious.

The elevator went down even further. He wondered how far down this thing went. He felt his ears pop from pressure, so he knew he was, at the very least below sea level.

CHAPTER 31

Julie and Lucy found themselves in an area of the building with incredibly high ceilings, crystallized souls hanging down from above like living stalactites. It was actually quite beautiful, Julie thought, taking another swig of Jager, her vision starting to destabilize itself. In a little bit, she'd be drunk enough to handle whatever was happening.

Ahead of them was what appeared to be a sturdy metal door, growing into the pink flesh of the walls.

"Awww shit…" Lucy whispered.

"What now?"

"That's the freezer. We should turn around."

"What's in the freezer?"

"What you think's in the motherfuckin' freezer?"

"Leftovers?"

"You could say that."

There was another sound of wings overhead, the two of them looking up to see a figure perched upside down, her legs wrapped around one of soul stalactites.

"Mother…I…" Lucy started.

"Larxene of the Black Talon," the Mother said, in a voice that could only be described as a whisper of the soul, "Your human companion attacked Thanus of the Red Veil. And then Vainau and Jenel of the Azure Eye, yet you still protect her."

"Why can I understand her? Why isn't she screeching?" Julie asked.

"Shit, bitch! Shut it!"

Julie rolled her eyes and folded her arms.

"I owe her father a debt," Lucy said, dropping the way she normally spoke, for a few moments, "I pledged myself to protect her. He is a demon hunter, yet he keeps our secrets. I feel I owe her."

"Yet she brings death to this Sanctuary."

"I bring death?!? How the fuck do I bring death? Okay, I bashed in whatever her-name of the Red Cock or whatever, but she was threatening Lucy," Julie drunkenly yelled.

"You bring death here. You are no friend of this Sanctuary. There are others here who search for you. Others who seek to bring your death. You brought them here."

"Shit," Julie said, "The police found me?"

"Not quite, love," Christopher said, walking into the chamber from one of the many doorways.

"Miss us, did you?" Serenity asked.

"Motherfuckin' vampires… I hate them niggas," Lucy said, looking at the twins.

"The Sanctuary must be protected at all costs," the Mother said, flying off, "The Sanctuary must be cleansed."

"Well, that sounds…bad," Julie commented.

"Don't you worry none 'bout the fanny demons," Serenity said, showing off her fangs, as Christopher pulled out his swords, "We'll be taking you out of their mis…uh…why're you in your pants?"

The smile left his face, when there was a loud banging noise coming from the freezer.

"Awww hell no…" Lucy said, under her breath.

There was another loud bang.

"Bad time?" Serenity said.

And then the freezer door burst open.

CHAPTER 32

The elevator stopped, the door slid open, and before him was a giant room that filled him with dread.

The room was all black, except for some sort of Satanic-looking symbol that covered the entire floor, which itself was probably half the size of a football field. It wasn't a pentagram. He had seen enough of those on his big brother's album covers to know what those were, but it still felt like some sort of magical symbol. It had 17 sides and was the color of blood. For all he knew, it had been from the people who had been here the year before he had overheard being spoken of.

In the center of the room was a figure in a long white robe, kneeling, surrounded by a glowing circle of white energy.

Upon looking closer, it was Ms. Roberts. Even though there was no breeze in the room, her hair seemed to gently lift from her shoulders.

The guards ordered them to all leave the elevator. The guards removed their zip-ties and stepped backwards.

It was then that Jerry noticed that the guards themselves seemed afraid to even step foot in this room. That was a bad sign.

"All of you, come in," Ms. Roberts said, not even turning to face them.

They did as they were told, a very noticeable wave of fear sweeping across all of them, even those who had, just yesterday threatened to kill him to please Ms. Roberts.

She stood up and turned around.

Here they were, just her and thirty eight of them in one room. Yet, no one made a move towards her. In Jerry's mind, he knew that she probably could kill all of them before they even got a foot closer than they all were.

"So, this is *it*, everyone. You've seen the last of your cells."

"Thank you, Ms. Roberts," they said, as one.

"Now, I need you all to do one last thing for me. You are to pair off."

There were murmurs of confusion.

"I see some of you do not understand. Allow me to demonstrate. You."

She pointed at Jerry. If his bladder had anything left in it, that action itself would have made him piss right then and there. As it was, he flinched at her attention. She smiled, obviously having noticed that.

"I want you to stand on that point of the star," she said, motioning to one directly in front of her, "I want you in my field of vision."

Jerry meekly ran to where she had instructed.

"Now," she pointed at Kelly, "Your girlfriend is to join you at that point."

Kelly seemed hesitant and afraid.

"Do you want me to make you stand there?" Ms. Roberts demanded of Kelly.

Kelly, trying to cover herself with her now free arms, ran over to where Jerry was.

"Good. Now don't be shy. Hold her."

Jerry put his arms around Kelly. She did the same. It was the first warm, human touch either of them had experienced since the time they had been brought here. They looked into each other's eyes and their fear subsided a little. They felt…safer in each other's arms.

Jerry felt himself growing stiff at her touch. He didn't want Ms. Roberts to see, out of fear that she'd be somehow offended by it. He pressed it against Kelly's body. She recoiled a bit from it at first, but then closed her eyes for a second, nodded that she understood, and moved herself closer to him, his now-cut manhood growing to full erection against her belly.

"Are you embarrassed by that?" Ms. Roberts asked, smirking at him, "Well, I can understand after how I had to put you in line yesterday that you're afraid of me, but I actually want you to want her. No need to be embarrassed."

Jerry was confused.

"You see, you and she are going to fuck. As are *all* of you. Pair off. Find a member of the opposite sex that you find appealing and then stand on one of the points of the star together. Then…do your business with each other."

One of the women walked forward and meekly put up her hand. Though she looked different with a shaved head and no eyebrows, Jerry quickly recognized it was the girl who had first been brought up onstage with her period, that first night they had met Ms. Roberts.

"Ms. Roberts…I…I don't want to do that. I…I-I don't like men. Please don't make me do that. I'll do anything else you want. I swear! But that…it's…it's *rape*…"

"There are only 17 spots, but there are enough of you for 18 couples. I only need 17 couplings. The other three of you will not be leaving here alive."

"What?!? You can't do that!" the woman began to protest.

Ms. Roberts flicked her wrist and the woman fell to her knees screaming. Suddenly, the woman's skin began to turn red and smoke. She screamed, white light pouring out of every hole of her body. Her eyes melted and light came out of that as well. Finally, her screaming stopped and her charred skeleton fell to the ground, crumbling into dust upon impact.

The others screamed and quickly ran to each other. Makeshift couples were formed and they ran to the other 16 spots and began holding on another.

The other three people stopped what they were doing and fell to their knees.

"Please, Ms. Roberts, we'll do whatever you want, we…" one of the men started, before his skin began to glow as well.

The three left, that man and two women, died the same way the girl before them did, their bodies nothing but dust in seconds.

Jerry and Kelly held each other tight, as Ms. Roberts spread her arms, and said, "And now, let the ritual begin!"

The candles around the room sprouted several foot high flames, raising the heat in the room quite a lot. The air was suddenly filled with chanting and drums from a balcony above them that Jerry had not previously noticed.

Shadows danced around the room as Jerry felt himself starting to feel something that he wouldn't have thought he would be feeling in this situation: pure, unbridled lust. He looked at Kelly, the urge to kiss her stronger than anything he had ever felt in his life, and, much to his surprise, she had a mouth again.

He brought his mouth to hers.

CHAPTER 33

Kelly knew she should have been feeling terror right now. She was involved in the sort of messed up horror that Julie always spoke about, but right now, she was overcome with desire. She didn't even think about the fact that Ms. Roberts had given her her mouth back. All she knew was that having Jerry's mouth against hers was the most natural feeling in the world.

It wasn't a desire. It was a biological and psychological need. It was something she couldn't control. Nothing else mattered. Not Julie. Not the trauma of just a few moments ago. Not Ms. Roberts. All that mattered was having Jerry inside her, right now. She wrapped her legs around his hips, the two of them falling to the ground, his hardness thrusting into her moisture.

It felt good. It felt so good. There was no one else in the room. There was no one else in the world. It was just the two of them. Two strangers brought together by circumstances that just melted away as they melted into each other.

The chanting grew faster and the drums beat quicker, their thrusting happening in time to the music.

Moans filled the air as the two of them bit, clawed, and pounded each other, never wanting this to end. *Please don't ever let it end.*

CHAPTER 34

Persephone looked around the room at the couples rutting with each other. There were all manner of positions, missionary, doggy-style, standing, squatting, as the magic-induced orgy happened all around her. The room was filled with mystical pheromones right now, derived from the ashes of Butcher's Eyes and then converted into a clear mist. She knew if she were to have stepped out of the circle she cast for herself, she'd have fallen prey to it too. The desire to procreate would become as much of a need as that to breathe and she'd never leave this room.

She had prepared herself, prepared her body for this moment. It was what she always did, whether it had been for the Royal Family's similar rituals or for the few times, like this, where she had contracted her services to other governments and highest bidders.

She could see that the floor had begun to smoke, and that the smoke had begun to whip around the room in a circular fashion. The energy that the couples produced through their furious fucking and through the chanting of the priestesses above was beginning to do its job.

It was well known that no living human could open a gate to the Seventh Realm. But with the right ritual, it was possible to gain the attention of something in the Realm itself.

And if you created the right energy, say by having thirty-four ritually cleansed people couple under mystical circumstances, then you provided enough energy for that being to come here and open a door between worlds from the other side.

The ground began to turn from black to red, all except for the white circle Persephone stood in. It was showtime.

CHAPTER 35

Dozens and dozens of them, pouring out of the freezer, naked, half eaten men, shambling towards Julie, Lucy, and the twins. Their skin hung off their bodies in ribbons, some with gaping holes where their organs had been removed, others missing entire limbs, crawling through the sticky fluid that covered the ground, their lifeless eyes focused on their four targets.

"What the bloody fuck?!?" Christopher exclaimed.

"The freezer was full of dead guys?" Julie asked.

"Girl's gotta eat," Lucy remarked.

"Methinks you have a disorder," Serenity said, backing away.

"Super speed would be the dog's bullocks, right about now," Christopher said, joining his sister in backing away.

The dead men advancing, Julie looked at them, looked at Lucy and the Twins, and chugged the rest of her Jager. She threw the empty bottle, it hitting one of the dead men in the face. It didn't react, but kept coming. They were everywhere, barely holding themselves together as they amassed. There must have been forty or fifty of them.

She looked at the bat in her hands. She nodded, reached into her bag, and pulled out her Magnum.

"Fuck it," she said, bat in one hand, gun in the other, running towards the dead.

"Shit, bitch!" Lucy yelled, "The other way! Run the other way!"

CHAPTER 36

She was eight years old and Alexander Johannes was the greatest dad in the world. Because Julie had gotten in trouble at school again, they had to move. There was no trial on her birthday, because he wanted her to be surprised. Now, three months later, the day before they were due to move, her dad had shook her awake, telling her that there was something important that she needed to see in the backyard.

She leapt out of bed and ran to the backyard, where her eyes lit up with joy at what was in front of her.

There was a tear in the fabric of reality there. A big one. A huge one. And out of it, popped the green scaly neck of a creature that made her heart leap with a happiness she had never known before or since.

It was an honest to goodness dragon. Its neck alone a good fifteen feet long.

It let out a roar that knocked Persephone off her feet and shattered the windows of their temporary little house, setting off car alarms for blocks.

"Okay, Perci, you might want to take care of that before it comes out of the portal. I think it might attract too much attention if it burned down the neighborhood."

Without even thinking about it, without even grabbing a weapon, she ran right for the dragon.

CHAPTER 37

Jerry and Kelly didn't know each other's' names and if asked, they wouldn't have been able to recall their own. All they knew was that this moment was everything they had been created for.

As their moans increased, their bodies violently thrusting into each other, that moment of build-up fast approaching, the ground under them turned from black to red. They felt heat. They smelled smoke. They smelled meat cooking and realized it was their own bodies.

But no matter how much the pain increased, they couldn't stop. Their faces began to sag and their eyes exploded in their sockets, leaving them both blind. Their skin began to gel into each other, every nerve of their bodies alive with pain and pleasure at the same time.

They brought their mouths to each other and then, felt something tear through both of them at the same time, something cold and dark that turned their passion into fear. Something that seemed to strip them of everything they had ever loved, a sinking dark feeling that nothing would ever be alright again, that all that awaited them was horror and shame and pain, forever and ever. They tried to pull apart from each other, but their bodies had fused into each other.

They tried to scream but their mouths were locked as one.

CHAPTER 38

The ground below her burning, as black stalks shot up through the ground, the white circle of energy Persephone was standing in raising her a good twenty feet above the ground. All around her were muffled screams as the thirty four people around her burned and melted and were impaled by what looked like giant spider legs. The ground under her split open and the floor turned into what looked like a giant human face, only its skin was as black as coal, it had sixty-six red eyes, and on 17 points of its face, grew spider leg-like stiffened tentacles. On its forehead was a crown fashioned from writhing and screaming human souls, each jewel actually a thousand pairs of eyes.

It opened its mouth. The air became foul, like a mixture of shit and rotten meat. No, they wasn't a strong enough description of it. It was the smell of an abattoir's worth of rotting meat and a sewer's worth of shit. Persephone looked down, seeing that inside its mouth was what looked like another portal, a vast howling abyss. Its tongue was forked and its teeth were fanged, each one about four feet in size.

"WHO SUMMONS THE GRAND DUKE ASTAROTH?!?"

CHAPTER 39

"How the fuck was I supposed to know headshots aren't going to work on your special magic zombies?" Julie slurred as the four of them ran down a narrow stairway, the space above them filled with faceless, skinless corpses, reaching out for them, "Your zombies suck."

"Julie, you my nigs and all, but next time you show me a movie gonna come to life the next motherfuckin' day, you show my ass a motherfuckin' porno!"

The only thing that kept the mass of corpses from just all falling on the Lucy, Julie, and the twins, and crushing them under a tidal wave of death was just how many of them were crammed into there. Wall to wall, they touched, trying to climb over each other, making it hard for them to move.

Gnarled and chewed hands grabbed, Christopher slashing at them with his swords, the dead men continuing to come, even though he removed their arms, hands, or, in some cases, heads. The smell was overwhelming, despite not having rotted much, due to being in the freezer. There was still the smell of bloody meat, as they advanced, the four finding themselves heading towards another larger chamber.

This one had another super high ceiling with soul stalactites, but there was what looked like the doorway out of the building.

"Through them doors, yo! Run! That's the way out!" Lucy yelled.

"The Sanctuary must be cleansed!" the Mother's voice yelled from above.

With that, the air was filled with black shadows swarming around the stalactites, as the other succubae who inhabited the building swooped down to attack.

Christopher swung his sword and Julie swung her bat at the dead men advancing from behind, as Lucy looked at the succubae who had gathered in their shadowy real forms ahead of her.

"Cor! What bloody now?" Serenity asked Lucy.

"What now? Time for some motherfuckin' gangsta shit." Lucy said, getting a very serious look on her face.

With that, she threw off her robe, hunched over, and let out a howl as her horns ripped out of her forehead, her wings tore from her back, and her bare skin seemed to be overwhelmed by her shadow, until it covered her entire form. She leapt from the ground and flew towards the other succubae, ready to attack.

CHAPTER 40

Persephone, held on to the dragon's neck for dear life as it flew above the vast, nightmarish landscape of the Fifth Realm. She had been so excited she had forgotten to bring the enchanted katana she received for her eighth birthday. Now, this huge beast, the size of a blue whale, once you got past the neck part, had her so high up in the acrid air of the Fifth Realm that she was beginning to worry that she'd be flown into clouds of what Julie had told her were poison.

She didn't know how long she could hold her breath, but she was sure that it wouldn't be long while this giant, fire-breathing beast thrashed about like a drunken 747.

She started to quickly repeat the incantation she had been told that would allow her to cross from this world to hers.

CHAPTER 41

"Persephone Johannes stands before you, oh glorious Grand Duke!" she said, her katana at the ready, as her body was bathed in pure white light, an 8x10 of the Mayor held high in her right hand, "We give you these souls to do with as you please in exchange for a continuation of the pact you have with the man in the picture I hold, the honorable Michael Bloom…"

"WAIT…I HAVE SEEN THIS DWELLING BEFORE! BUT I HAVE NOT SEEN YOU! THE LAST TIME I CAME HERE AND TOOK THE RITES, IT WAS A MAN WHO PRESENTED THEM TO ME! YOU ARE BARELY SPENT FROM YOUR FATHER'S SACK AND YOU SEEK TO MAKE DEALS WITH ME?!?"

"You will take these souls and the power and potential offspring each of them would have produced to do with as you please, whether it be as meat or concubine or gristle or material. But you *will* honor the deal you have made previous! You will not move forward nor take any souls other than these!"

"I SMELL MILLIONS OF SOULS IN THIS LAND OF YOURS! I WOULD CLAIM THEM AS MINE, AS WELL! BEGINNING WITH YOURS!"

CHAPTER 42

Lucy flew through the air, her wings bleeding shadow and only five of her eyes still working as she impaled one of her fellow succubae on one of the soul stalactites; below her Christopher tried to hold back the torrent of the dead in the choke point of the stairwell, as Serenity and Julie fought side by side, succubae attacking from all sides.

Julie drunkenly shot one in the face and then fired off three random shots in the general direction of another as Serenity was thrown to the ground by two of them flying at her, hitting her in the face so hard that it cracked her wrist. She'd heal, of course, faster than a human, once she had fed, but it still hurt like hell.

Lucy flew down to grab one of the succubae on Serenity by the horns, tearing off the top of her head, as she swooped back up towards the ceiling.

Julie ran over to the other one on Serenity and bit it in the throat, finding it a lot like biting into blood-flavored cotton candy. Serenity looked puzzled at this, holding her wrist.

Christopher yelled, "Can't hold them off forever, love. A summon would be brilliant, yes?"

"Right right," Serenity said, focusing her energy on opening up a doorway to another world.

"Wait a minute," Julie said, "I got this."

Julie reached into her bag and pulled out the dagger she used to open a doorway to the Second Realm and started stabbing the air, laughing like a maniac, tears in the fabric of reality forming, Butchers Eyes leaping out, attaching themselves to several of the succubae, who unaffected by their powers, fought with the parasites.

"Wait...not the Second! What if..." Serenity started, before suddenly finding herself on the floor, moaning in ecstasy as a Butcher's Eye grabbed a hold of her.

"Are you fucking touched? Those bloody things aren't going to help against these lads!" Christopher yelled.

"Oh, yeah. My bad," Julie said, stumbling away from the last hole she had put in the ether.

"You defile the Sanctuary!" the Mother yelled, "This will not be tolerated!"

The Mother gave a screech that hurt Julie's ears, and then flew up to the ceiling, where she couldn't be reached.

"What was that all about?" Julie wondered.

That's when Julie noticed the sound of heavy footsteps coming from the general direction of the corpses.

CHAPTER 43

The dragon free fell towards the ground, ripping the thatches off the roofs of many a house in the Wisconsin neighborhood where Persephone had spent the last two years of her life. It had, in the process, knocked out the telephone and electricity lines for everything in the town.

It smashed hard, into her backyard, crushing her next-door neighbor's car under its massive weight. There were sirens in the distance.

Obviously, Persephone had attracted a little too much attention.

Well, fine, she thought, *I'm a big girl now and everyone is going see it!*

The dragon, on its back, flipped its wing, knocking down an entire wall of her small house.

This was the opportunity she needed, she thought, as she now saw her room exposed. Her room where her katana lay waiting for her. She made a run for it, the dragon breathing fire behind her.

CHAPTER 44

Persephone raised her katana in her left hand and looked down at the hellish Grand Duke below her.

"I shall repeat myself. You will *not* take a single soul not offered to you! Otherwise, you will have to go through me!"

"DO YOU THINK YOUR LITTLE CIRCLE OF MAGIC PROTECTS YOU FROM ME?!?"

He laughed, his massive anaconda-like tongue rising from his mouth towards her.

She dropped the picture of the mayor and got into a battle stance.

The tongue wrapped around her waist and started to squeeze. The flesh of her body began to bubble and sizzle as the immense heat from the tongue burned away at her.

She gritted her teeth and screamed, "*I said you will take no more!*"

With that her body glowed with white energy, her burns healed, and she rose above the circle. The white robe she wore burned off her body and, instead, she was clad in armor of pure white light, spiked and blinding. From the back of it, were two angelic wings of pure light.

The Grand Duke recoiled in horror.

"HOW DO YOU...? HOW DO YOU HAVE THAT?!? HOW DOES IT NOT BURN YOUR SOUL TO NOTHING?!?"

"Do you accept the sacrifices and agree to continue to bestow the potential of these souls upon the agreed upon recipient?"

"YES...YES, I DO! I AM TERRIBLY SORRY FOR THE MISUNDERSTANDING!"

"Then it is done! Take them as you will."

With that, the Grand Duke opened his mouth and all life was drained from the impaled bodies on his face, and their souls flew into the abyss down his throat..

CHAPTER 45

Kelly felt herself pulled away from Jerry, pulled away from her own body, as she fell through darkness, the sound around her a horrible wail louder than anything she had ever even imagined was possible. She put her hands to her ears but it still shook her, as she fell for what seemed like forever. There were crawling things and buzzing things and slithering things collecting on her as she descended. Crawling on her, crawling in her. Under her skin, behind her eyes, down her throat. All the places she could never reach but would always feel. She screamed and screamed and screamed forever.

CHAPTER 46

Jerry reached out in the darkness, finding himself covered in things that felt dirty and horrible and frightening and cold. He wanted to grab something, anything, he would have chewed off his own arm to get out of where he was. He would have volunteered for a century of the last month of his life rather than go where he was going.

And when he got there, the nightmares never ended.

CHAPTER 47

"This has all gone pear-shaped!" Christopher exclaimed, running away from the choke point of the chamber, "Something's bloody coming!"

The corpses spilled into the chamber, Butcher's Eyes attacking them to no effect, Lucy yanking the one off Serenity just in time for her to sit up, bite her lip with her fangs, look at her brother, and smile.

Her good mood wore off upon seeing the hulking beast that came crashing out of the stairwell. It was huge. It was vaguely gorilla shaped, hunched over, with twelve foot arms. It's then that Serenity noticed the arms were corpses melded together. Each arm was about ten men melded together, five of them back to back, and then the other five attached head to head with the five men above them. At the end of each arm were five more heads, so that the arms could work as battering rams. Its body was ten men curled up in 69 positions with each other to form a solid chest, its legs ten pairs of legs. In the center was a single head that seemed to do all the looking for it.

"Aw fuck me!" Serenity yelled.

It charged at Christopher, hitting him, full force with one of its massive arms, throwing him into the fleshy walls of the chamber as his swords broke in half.

Julie, drunk as she was, realized getting hit by that thing would kill her, so she decided to avoid a direct confrontation with it, instead, rummaging through her messenger bag for something..

It continued to go after Christopher, Serenity leaping at it, pounding on it, even with her vampiric strength, to no avail. Lucy pulled one of the stalactites from the ceiling, it falling at the mass of corpses, knocking it over, momentarily.

Now, it was focused on Lucy. She flew above it, it swinging its arms at her, she just out of reach.

"Fucking rubbish, this," Serenity yelled, grabbing her bloodied brother and running for the front door.

As she opened it, she was greeted by sunlight. The twins jumped backwards, screaming, as their skin smoked.

The mass of dead bodies now turned its attention to the two of them again, started to charge towards them like a frightened elephant.

Suddenly, there was loud noise, and a huge explosion, as the beast was blown to pieces.

The Mother gave a loud screech, Lucy descending to the ground, the twins scratching their heads, confused by the spontaneous combustion of the creature.

"You're welcome," Julie said, putting the rocket launcher back in her messenger bag.

"Bloody hell," Christopher exclaimed, "Where the fuck'd you get that?"

"Virginia."

Julie saluted the twins and started to walk towards the door.

"Come on, Lucy," she said, as she grabbed the doorknob.

"Hold up, love," Serenity said, leaping in front of her, "Unfinished business, we. You're not getting away this time."

Julie thrust open the doors of the building, the morning light spilling inside, Serenity jumping back to her injured brother's side, in the shade.

"You wanna follow me and Lucy, you're welcome to, biyatch!" Julie exclaimed, walking backwards, out into the daylight, giving Serenity and Christopher a dual set of middle fingers.

The succubae howled behind her, Julie now back on Earth, in the Bronx.

She wasn't sure why Lucy didn't follow her out, but whatever, she had a sister to get in touch with. And she should probably put some pants on, because, holy shit, it was fucking cold outside.

She turned around with a triumphant smile on her face.

That's when she saw the dozen police cars that had surrounded the building. There was even a SWAT unit.

"Oh," Julie said, raising the rest of her fingers, as every gun was drawn on her, "Fuck."

CHAPTER 48

Persephone, energy sparking off the armor, looked down at the sated entity below her.

"IT IS DONE! THE POWER HAS BEEN BESTOWED! I WILL TAKE MY LEAVE NOW!"

"If you ever encounter me again, do not show me such disrespect in the future."

"I APOLOGIZE...OH...UMMMMMM...BEFORE I GO, A SMALL PET OF MINE MAY HAVE ENTERED YOUR WORLD A FEW DAYS AGO. YOU PROBABLY COULDN'T MISS IT! CUTE, HAD TWO FACES. SMALL, WELL, BY MY STANDARDS..."

"No idea."

"MMMMMM...ALRIGHT...TERRIBLY SORRY FOR THE BOTHER..."

With that, the floor of the room sunk back to normal.

Persephone's armor disappeared and she descended to the ground in a crouching position, naked.

She breathed heavily, her hair covered in sweat, the room stinking from the 17 mounds of dead flesh still in the strategic positions of the ritual that they had died in.

A priestess walked over to her and placed a long coat over her shoulders.

CHAPTER 49

Persephone gave as close to a war cry as an eight year-old could give as she plunged the katana into the dragon's eye. Thick, red blood splattered her tiny frame as the dragon gave a whine and then collapsed to the ground, dead.

She had done it! She was giddy with excitement. Sure, she had leveled half the neighborhood and a good portion of their house, but she didn't care.

She, her footie-pajamas covered in dragon blood, jumped off the dead beast's neck and ran into the remains of their house to ask if her dad had seen it.

Her father and her eye-patch clad sister, Samantha, then in a goth phase, were kneeling by a wall in the remains of her kitchen.

"Daddy! Sammi! Did you see what I…"

They looked up at her, her father crying for the first time in his life. At first, she didn't understand.

And in the moment when she did, her heart sunk, because in the rubble she saw a twisted, charred hand poking out.

And on that hand, was the ring her mother had always worn.

CHAPTER 50

Mr. Trent, waiting at ground level, about twenty floors above where the ritual had happened, nodded to Persephone as she was gently walked to a rest area, the priestess' coat still wrapped around her.

He had already gotten the ball rolling against her, but he did have to admit that she had gotten the job done.

He took a deep breath, mostly relieved that he was done dealing with her and that any further association with her would be discovering what fucked up method she had used to even get this job in the first place.

He hadn't seen the ritual itself and no cameras were ever allowed in the chamber, but he knew it had gone off without a hitch and that was all that mattered. There was a reason he was twenty floors above. The presence of any Fifth Realm demon would have severely offended any Seventh Realm demon and fucked up the ritual big time. In fact, he had never even seen the inside of the room. He knew how those Seventh Realmers could get.

His phone rang. It was the number people only called if they really had something important to call him about.

He wondered if it was a follow-up call from the Council.

"Hello?"

"Mr. Trent, we got her."

"What?"

"Juliette Golighty, a.k.a. Juliette Johannes. We have her in custody."

"What?"

"We just arrested her in the Bronx not fifteen minutes ago. We're taking her in for questioning."

"Holy shit! Who else knows about this?"

"No one else, sir. Should we inform Ms. Roberts?"

"Definitely not. Hold on. I'll be right there."

CHAPTER 51

The Council and several government officials came to the area. There was a ton of red tape and NDA's to sign, and threats of imprisonment to any of the citizens who had seen the dragon if they came forward about it.

Of course, even with all the legal threats, a blurry Polaroid of the dragon flying through the suburban skies did end up in an issue of *The Weekly World News* (luckily, nobody ever believed anything in *The Weekly World News,* which was exactly why they had gotten away with exposing so many supernatural occurrences over the years, without the Council actively trying to shut them down).

In the backyard, hugged tightly by a crying Julie and Samantha, her father was being scolded by a Council official, telling him that he had a good mind to call Child Protective Services for this and that Alexander had no business bringing any sort of Fifth Realm being into our world. That this was considered a huge crime in Council circles.

Persephone didn't take notice of it. She walked back into the still-intact bathroom and cried her eyes out by the sink.

There would be none of her mother's warm hugs or daily drives to school or their Saturday afternoon black & white movie-a-thons or the wonderful chicken cutlet that was her mother's specialty. They would never get to go to New York together. Her mother would never see her graduate school, or attend college, or see her get married, or hold a grandchild. And Persephone didn't even have the myth of a glorious afterlife to cling to that most children her age had for reassurance.

She had seen the afterlife her mother would end up in, due to the supernatural method of her death. Personally. Persephone had smelled its foulness, seen its horrors, and walked its defiled soil.

Such a good, kind-hearted wonderful woman was now in a place of suffering and death. And it wasn't right. It wasn't fair.

She looked up and jumped, the mirror a vision of eyes and tongues, billions and billions of eyes and tongues, with black angel-shaped wings behind it.

She closed her eyes and looked in the mirror again, convinced she had been seeing things.

In her reflection, standing behind her was a tall, pale man, with long black flowing hair, and black wings, his eyes a deep black.

She turned around to see who this was, but he wasn't behind her.

She turned back and saw him standing there in the mirror.

"I'm sorry this happened to your mother."

"Who are you?!? Why are you in my mirror?!?"

"Shhhhh…don't speak too loudly. The others can't see me. Well, not consciously. They do see me every time they look in the mirror. I'm there all the time and yet, I just blend into the background for most people."

"How come I can see you?"

"Because you're special, Persephone. You're the most special girl in the world."

"What are you?"

"I'm a friend, Persephone. I'm a friend."

"Don't lie to me! You're just another demon! I'll kill you!"

"Oh, Persephone. I'm not a demon. There isn't really a word for what I am…Well, I *guess* there is. The word your people gave for my kind, even though they got the history completely wrong, is angel."

"You're an angel?"

"Well, not in the way the Jews and Christians and Muslims think of an angel. I don't serve the god they think is creator. No, I guess if you wanted to use a word to describe me, you *could* call me an angel, but I am so much more than the human concept of one. You know how the humans got it wrong with demons and their concept of Hell and all. The same applies to me and my kind."

"Are you saying that there is a Heaven?"

"Not anymore. There once was. But that's not what I came to talk to you about."

"What do you want with me?"

"I want to be your friend, Persephone. And I want to help you. I want to help you see your mother again."

BOOK THREE
LET'S HAVE A WAR

CHAPTER 1

"Persephone, come on! We're going to be late!" Samantha yelled at her from outside the bathroom door, "Dad's waiting in the car."

Indeed, her father had taught himself to drive in the four years since her mother's dragon-induced death. It was June, the day of Sammi's high school graduation, and they were living in Hopkins, Minnesota. Julie, who had bleached her natural red hair a color that could only be described as "shockingly white" was already in the car, no doubt having commandeered the radio so she could play that awful Black Flag album she had insisted on playing over and over again.

Persephone had wanted to take some time for another trip to the Fifth, something she had demanded Julie teach her how to do. She had said it was because she wanted to get stronger, so that nothing would ever happen to her father, but there was a very different reason for it.

She sat in the bathroom, looking at the water running into the sink.

"My dear Persephone, you know that's not going to work," the angel said, from inside the mirror.

"Just shut up. I don't want to hear from you anymore."

"But you know it's impossible. The Fifth Realm is its own universe. The area you've been to is just one world within the billions there. And *that* area is still the size of the Earth itself. There are billions of souls there, accumulated over thousands of years."

"I don't care. I'll find her one day."

"My dear, why don't you just listen to me? I have an easier way."

"Because I don't trust you. You're just some mass of eyes and wings that keeps appearing whenever I look at my reflection."

"I try to make my appearance pleasant for you when we talk. I have so many different appearances. I look different to everyone. You are a very special girl, though. You can see my real self, if only for a second."

"Well, whatever type of demon or angel or god or whatever you say you are, I'm not going to listen to you, so you can just stop visiting me now."

"Persephone, I know you're only twelve, but I know you're mature enough to understand when I say that you aren't going to find your mother's soul by just searching the Fifth Realm."

"She's there, isn't she?"

"She is."

"Then I'll find her."

"Well, what if I helped you?"

"Why are you so interested in me? What makes me so special?"

"You can see me. You're closer to me than everyone else on Earth. Only a very select group ever see me while alive. And very few ever see my eyes."

"Why do you have so many?"

"I told you before. Because I have one eye to see every man, woman, and child on Earth. I see everyone, from birth to death, and every moment in between."

"Do I have one watching me?"

"Of course, you do. That's why I'm here now. I've been watching you since you were born. I've been watching you grow. And I've seen where you'll go and what you'll do as you get older. And how much power you'll one day have. I want to help you get there."

"Persephone! Hurry up! We're going to be late!" Samantha yelled from outside the bathroom.

"I have to go," Persephone said.

"It's okay. I understand. It's your sister's graduation. With honors, no less."

"Yeah."

"So, you go support your sister. If it makes you feel any better, you'll only have one other graduation to go to, and that will be your own. Julie's going to drop out in a few months."

"How do you know that?"

"I don't exist in the same linear time that you do. I can see all the threads of everyone's lives."

"Whatever. She wouldn't do that. She's not a loser."

"Go on. I will be here whenever you need me."

"I won't need you."

"It's okay. I am patient. One day, you and I will be friends, I just know it."

"I don't even know your name."

"You have never asked. I actually have many."

CHAPTER 2

Samantha walked into the old, unassuming townhouse on 82nd and East End, where the Council's New York headquarters was, reluctant to take the meeting she had to take, but feeling it was absolutely necessary. The building, itself, was relatively small for one in the Manhattan, only five floors high, but inside, it looked like it belonged to a much, much older dwelling. The initial reception area was unmarked, looking like an eccentric millionaire's study more than a reception area. In fact, the area took up space on not one, but two floors of the building, with a railed balcony area accessible for those on the second floor. There were bookshelves that reached all the way to the ceiling, stocked with arcane tomes, half-fictions, and magic history, in a thousand languages, not all of them originating from Earth. There were posh sofas for members to sit on, and read while waiting, and there were portraits of respected members of the Council, past and present, including notable Council historians and founding members, H. P. Lovecraft and Robert E. Howard, who, due to the time they lived in, took to writing fiction based on their tireless research.

The fictional tales Howard would tell, for example, of Conan were half-truths and fictionalized versions of passed down stories of the true Cimmerian hero, of whose life, he had studied for years.

Lovecraft, as well, wrote fictionalized tales of the Eighth Realm deities he had studied extensively, as a warning to the world at a time where the government was greatly suspicious of any organizations dealing with the occult...seasoned with quite a bit of his own personal xenophobia.

Ironic in a way, since the Council itself formed as a reaction to the Thule Society's attempts to bring the other Realms into play in a manner that would benefit the Axis Powers.

The Council, at first, consisted of men learned in magic and the history of the Realms, and eventually grew to also include supernatural beings that had served to keep the world of men from being destroyed. And indeed, there were portraits alongside the men of the 1930's, of beings that Samantha could definitely tell were not altogether human. There was, at least, one vampire represented, and then a few beings she could not identify, having not dedicated as much time in her life to dealing/fighting with demons as her sisters had.

While the United States government and NATO, in general, did not accept the Council as something positive until the Nixon Administration (Lyndon B. Johnson was especially hostile to its very concept), it had worked behind the scenes to prevent the end of life as we knew it, more times than most people would ever possibly believe. This was the second branch of the Council in the states. The second of the fifteen that now existed in the United States and sixty others around the world, the first meeting secretly in Boston, Massachusetts.

This history, too, was depicted on a series of large paintings throughout the room and a large map of the world with the Council's crest in areas where there was a branch.

In the center of all this history was a huge circular desk, where the receptionist, Verity, sat. Samantha suspected Verity was either a vampire or some sort of human who had extended her life, because not only did Verity appear to never age beyond her early 20's, but she also dressed and kept her hair and makeup like it was still the 1940's. While it was entirely possible that Verity was just very, very into 40's nostalgia, Samantha had learned that it was best to assume the fantastic in the circles she had been born into.

"Ah, Dr. Henderson! Good to see you again," Verity said, in her old timey movie manner, sounding more like Katherine Hepburn than anyone else, smiling behind glasses that Samantha could almost hear Julie, in her head, calling "Granny glasses."

"Hi, Verity. How is everything?"

"Right as rain. Can't complain. I'll buzz Mr. Hawthorne right away."

"Thanks, Verity."

Samantha noticed that Verity, smartly, did not ask her how she was. Verity, despite her pleasant demeanor, most likely knew that the business that brought her here was not pleasant.

"Okay, head on up to the third floor. He'll be in 302, as always, Dr. Henderson."

"Thanks a lot, Verity."

Samantha walked towards the spiral staircase at the end of the reception area, dreading this meeting more and more with every step she took.

Finally, as she reached the third floor, she found herself in an area that looked a lot more like any office building one might find in Manhattan. In fact, it quite resembled a college's administration section.

She walked over to 302, where the door read:

Nigel Hawthorne
Director, New York Affiliate

Knocking on the door, she entered, finding Mr. Hawthorne, a mustached old man in a brown tweed suit, complete with bow tie, his white, thinning hair combed back, his smile weathered but kind, putting the finishing touches on a model of a biplane. He was an Englishman whose accent bore the decades he had spent in New York City. He appeared to be a rather uptight gentleman, quiet, serious, and reserved, but Samantha also knew that he had originally been assigned to be a liaison to the London office, but had chosen, instead, to stay in Manhattan after falling in love with his wife of forty years. Somewhere beneath all that British, there was a romantic, apparently.

"Dr. Henderson, please do have a seat," he said, gesturing to a seat in front of his desk, putting the model behind him, on a drawer flanked by the flags of the United States, the United Kingdom, and the Council's crest.

"Mr. Hawthorne, thank you," she said, sitting down.

"Now, Dr. Henderson, I understand that you have been making inquiries with the Chicago affiliate into the activities of your sister, Persephone."

"Yes, Mr. Hawthorne, there's a lot of things that are just not adding up."

He nodded in a very reserved manner and then handed her a folder he had in one of his drawers. There was a black and white picture in it of two people that Julie and Persephone would have recognized as Serenity and Christopher. Only the pictures appeared to be from the 1960's. Christopher's hair was black, in a mod style, with long sideburns, and he was wearing a turtleneck sweater. Next to him was

Serenity, her hair black, as well, long and straight with a large headband covering most of her forehead. She was wearing a multi-colored dress that, in the pictures, just came off as many different shades of gray. They appeared to be on a dark airfield of some sort. They were smiling and holding hands in the picture. Under the picture was a copy of a file marked *Operation: Harker*, large portions of it redacted.

"Have you ever seen these two before?"

"No. Who are they?"

"Vampires. Christopher and Margaret Knight. Born November 1st, 1848, in Leighton Buzzard, United Kingdom. Turned sometime around 1870. We've had files on these two since the late 1960's, when they did some work for the Crown. It is also my unfortunate displeasure to state that I have encountered them once myself, when I was a younger man."

"This is getting even more confusing. What do these two have to do with Persephone?"

"Well, Dr. Henderson, allegedly they are associates of hers. You see, at the same time you've been making these inquiries, we've received a rather unsettling complaint from someone who contracted her work."

"You have?"

"Yes, a demon of a rather prominent Fifth Realm House. In human form, he goes by the name of Michael Trent. His allegations are...rather disheartening, to say the least. In truth, if it were his allegations alone, I might take them with a grain of salt, as demons of the Fifth are experts in manipulating the truth to benefit themselves. It is why they excel in media and politics as much as they do. However, these allegations, combined with your inquiries, and the naming of these two particular vampires, do paint a rather unflattering portrait of your sister's recent actions."

"That's what I'm worried about. What does he have to say?"

"Quite a lot, I'm afraid, Dr. Henderson."

CHAPTER 3

Mr. Trent walked down the hallway of the police station, his hair perfectly combed and gelled, as usual, his tie straight, and not a spot of lint on his extremely expensive suit. Timothy followed behind him, ready to do battle, if this girl was anything like her little sister.

The sergeant in charge of the precinct saluted him and gestured for him to come closer.

"Mr. Trent, the Mayor's office told me you'd be on your way here. She's in interrogation room A. Do you want me to send in a detective?"

"Most certainly not. I will handle this."

"Okay."

"So, where did you find her?"

"A brothel in the Bronx. There were noise complaints of some unearthly screeching. Someone assumed an animal was being abused, called 311. Then there were reports of shots fired and an explosion, so we took it more seriously."

"She was staying at a brothel?"

"Yup. We picked up a few of the girls and some old Russian madam they were all referring to as 'Mother.' Vice is taking care of that. They also found two friends of yours, that pulled rank when the officers came in."

"Two friends of-oh, fuck...Were they English twins?"

"Yup."

"Wonderful."

"So, she's in there?"

He looked in the peephole of the room. Julie was sitting at the interrogation table, face down, obvious unconscious, her hands cuffed behind her back.

She also was wearing boots but no pants.

"Why isn't she wearing pants?"

"Well...here's the thing. When we picked her up, she was very inebriated, and she appeared to become vastly more so within a minute or two of her arrest, like it hadn't kicked in quite yet. So, anyway, she was given the option of calming down so we could put some pants on her. I mean, for crissake, it's 20 degrees out!"

"And?"

"She started chanting 'Attica' and kicked at us, so we just said, 'Fuck it.' If she wasn't wanted for as many charges as she's wanted for, including first degree murder, we'd have just thrown her into the drunk tank. We had to lean her against the wall to even take her mugshot. But when we heard you wanted to speak to her, we put her in there."

"Alright. And I'm going to guess she hasn't called for a lawyer yet."

"Nah, course not."

"Good. Officer O'Neil and I are not to be disturbed. Is that understood?"

"Yes, sir."

Timothy opening the door for him, Mr. Trent entered the interrogation room, sitting down across from Julie.

"Julie," he said, gently shaking her, "Wake up."

She didn't move.

He wasn't feeling particularly patient, so he banged on the table. Not hard enough to break it in half, but enough that Julie snapped up, her face a sweaty drunken mess.

"W-what?!?"

"Julie, can you understand me?"

"Wha-who-where? Where am I?"

"You're in a police station. You were arrested."

"Are you my lawyer?"

"No, but I would like to talk to you if you'd sober up a little bit. Would you care for a cup of coffee?"

"You're not going to spit in it, are you?"

"What? No, of course not."

"Okay."

"Timothy, be a dear and get Ms. Johannes…"

"Golightly."

"Ms. Golightly. I stand corrected. Please get Ms. Golightly a cup of coffee. Cream and sugar?"

"Whatever."

Timothy walked out of the room, leaving Mr. Trent and Julie alone.

"So, in the meantime, while my colleague gets you your coffee, would you like to talk?"

"I don't know you. I don't have anything to say. I didn't do any…"

"Oh, I know you didn't do anything that is being said about you."

"You do?"

"Of course."

"Bullshit, dude. This is one of those good cop/bad cop things where you pretend to all be my friend and and and and …uh…I lost my train of thought."

"I'm not actually a police officer, though I do work for the City of New York."

"Where's my coffee? Whoa. Where are my pants?"

"Would you like some pants?"

"Would *you* like me to like some pants?"

"Huh?"

"Does this get you off?" she asked, leaning back and spreading her legs in the chair.

"What?"

"Does it turn you on to have me in my fucking panties while you're all exercising your power like a big man or something? *Oh, look at me, in my Don Draper suit playing good cop to the half naked chick! Later on, I'm going to jerk off in the station men's room, pretending that I got to spank her!*"

"I can assure you, Julie, that I am not here with any sexual intentions."

"Prove it."

"Prove what?"

"Whip your cock out. Show me it's soft."

"W-what?"

"Whip it out, dude. Show me you're not poking through your silk boxers."

"Whoa, Julie, we are certainly getting off on the wrong foot here."

"Hahaha…I'm just fucking with you," she said, closing her legs and leaning forward again, "But I do want my coffee."

"I see," he said, sighing loudly, and putting his hands through his hair.

"Dude, considering the shit you all want me for and the fact that I can't afford some big ass hotshot lawyer, I know I'm not getting off, so whatever. If I'm gonna go to jail, I'll go the fuck to jail. I already have a sidekick there. But I'm gonna make this shit the Trial of the fucking Century if I have to."

"But what if you could avoid jail entirely?"

"Dude, stop being all...*dicky*...you're being a dick. I already explained I know what's going to happen, so..."

"Do I seem like a normal man to you, Julie?"

"Okay, now you *are* coming on to me."

"No. I'm asking do I seem like your average, *human* male?"

He took off his sunglasses and looked her in the eye and smirked a little.

"Holy shit, you're a fucking demon."

"Now, she gets it. Please allow me to introduce properly myself. I am Li'dhu'xa of..."

"*Gesundheit.*"

He sighed heavily, before repeating himself, "Li'dhu'xa of House Temen-ni-gru."

"Uh..."

"Fifth Realm?"

"Oh...right..."

"You *don't* know my House?"

"Uh...to be quite honest...I don't really pay attention to all that politics shit. My dad used to quiz my sisters and I on this shit all the time and I'd never get the ice cream, because I just like smashing your heads in. No offense. I don't need to know what anything's called."

"That's actually quite funny. See, I remember a very, very long time ago...I had a brother. Well, I *have* thousands of them, but this one particular brother...I remember my brother and I were hunting, and while hunting, we were talking about this Realm, Earth, and my brother turns to me, with this look of wonder on his face, and says, 'Li'dhu'xa, did you know I saw an ape talking the other day?' And I didn't believe him. I looked at you foul little beasts the same way you might look at rats. Then one day, you learned to talk. And look where all of you are now."

"Cool story, bro."

"Of course, a few decades ago, your father killed that brother."

"I see."

"Oh, don't worry about it. He was an asshole."

Timothy walked back into the room with her coffee, putting it on the table in front of her.

She looked at it and then up at Mr. Trent.

"So...uh," she said, looking him in the eye, "Should I just lap this up like a kitten? Should have put it in a saucer then."

"Oh, of course. Timothy take care of her handcuffs. I don't think she poses any danger to us."

Timothy walked behind her and undid her cuffs. She massaged her wrists a little and then sipped her coffee, slowly.

"So, now that we've gotten all of that out of the way, can we talk?"

"Can I get some pants, first?"

"I don't see why not."

"They're in my bag. My messenger bag."

"Okay. Timothy, do be a dear again, and get the girl's bag. I want her to be as comfortable as possible for the talk we must have."

CHAPTER 4

Persephone, having napped for a couple hours, came out of the shower, toweled off her hair, and put on a light pink pants suit. She was glad to be out of that chamber with all of those horrible smells and sounds. She sat in the room designed for her to rest in and looked at her cell phone. A day of cleansing often resulted in 50 unanswered texts and 100 unanswered voicemail messages.

Sure enough, there were a ton. She skimmed over a few of them, until she saw one marked urgent from Samantha. And then another, and another.

Perci, we have to talk. Now. It's important.

Hmmmmm…wonder what that's all about. Hate when she calls me that.

She'd get herself some breakfast and then see what was so important that Samantha had to text her over and over again. She wondered how many of the voicemails were from her.

She walked out of the room, a couple of the guards nodding at her, as she went to find the kitchen area she had them add to the facility. She wanted to talk to the cook about something specific for the morning. She was famished and, after acting as Earth's guard dog against one of the Grand Dukes of the Seventh Realm, she deserved a hearty breakfast.

She figured she'd also try to get her final check from Mr. Trent, before her last couple days here. She was glad to be rid of him. He had proved completely worthless in finding Julie. If she hadn't brought the Twins with her, nothing would have gotten done on that front.

She walked up to one of the security guards, and smiled, "Hi."

"Good morning, Ms. Roberts. I'm told everything went well, this morning."

"World's still standing, so I did my job."

"That you did, ma'am."

"So, do you know where Mr. Trent is?"

"He's out of the facility right now."

"Is he?"

"Do you know where he went?"

"No, ma'am, I do not."

Persephone nodded, but couldn't help feeling that he wasn't being entirely truthful with her. Something in the back of her mind told her to press the issue. Why were they acting so evasive? Why would they be trying to hide something from her if he was just out on some minor errand or the other? What could he be doing that he wouldn't have wanted her to know?

"Are you sure you don't know where Mr. Trent is?" she asked, with a pleasant smile.

"Uh…no…I…I…" he began sweating profusely, pulling his collar away from his throat, a faint white aura surrounding him.

"You might want to rethink that. Please, do you know where he is?"

"I…I…not…supposed…"

"Ms. Roberts," one of the other guards said, "Please stop what you're doing to him right now, and we'll talk about this."

He pointed his gun at her. Three other guards showed up, aiming at her.

"I just want to know where Mr. Trent went."

"We aren't authorized to provide you with that information, ma'am. It isn't Drake's fault. We have orders to obey. Mr. Trent writes the checks."

She nodded and shrugged.

Then she smiled, as her hands glowed with bright white light.

CHAPTER 5

Julie balanced herself against the wall, while zipping up her jeans. Mr. Trent nodded to her and gestured for her to sit back down.

"Are you feeling better now, Julie?" he asked.

"I could use a drink."

"Timothy, get Ms. Golightly more coff…"

"No, a *drink* drink."

"I think you may have had enough already."

"Dude, I work best blasted."

"Julie, do I need to remind you of *what* I am? Do you realize how lucky you are that you're dealing with me, instead of any of my brothers? Your father's actions alone would make you a target to, oh, at least, three dozen of my brothers. Here I am, giving you coffee, letting you put pants on, and about to make a deal with you to drop all these false charges against you. Several of my brothers would take quite a different approach to you. You'd be stripped, publicly gang raped, skinned-alive, and then gang-raped again by several of my brothers' Royal Guard. Then you'd be hung by the largest object they could fit up your ass, as an ornament for all to see until you died, at which point, your soul would become their entertainment for the next century or so."

"Sounds like you have an interesting family."

"As do you. Have you ever seen someone boiled alive in their own excrement?"

"Can't say I have."

"Now, I am…"

"How long does that take?"

"How long does what take?"

"Boiling someone in their own shit."

"A few hours, I guess. That's not the…"

"No, I mean, how long does it take for the person to shit enough that you can fill a vat or cauldron or whatever with enough of their own shit that you could boil them in it?"

"I...I...I never took the time to take..."

"And how do you get them to produce that much? I mean, do you feed them really heartily for a few days beforehand? I mean, I can't imagine that that doesn't take the intimidation off the torture a little bit, if after a day of being hung by your asshole, they give you a whole huge feast."

"I think you're missing the point."

"I probably am. Continue with your infomercial thing."

"Now, I am perfectly willing to have all of these charges go away. Right now. To be honest, until last week, you were not even on my radar. I would like to forget I ever heard of any of you, to be quite honest."

"So, you want to make a deal?"

"That's what I said."

"You know, it's funny, because I may not be the big hotshot demon slayer that my dad was, but I know that when a demon says he wants to make a deal, it usually means he wants your soul."

"Normally, that would be the case. But I have something I want from you that's a lot more your style. I just want someone killed."

"I see."

"Very simple. There's someone who has been a huge problem to me. Someone who recently killed another brother of mine. And while I didn't much care for him, I don't appreciate someone taking him out to try to get to me."

"I get it."

"Yes, I'm sure you do. Now, here's the best part: This person also is responsible for framing *you*."

"Really?"

"Yes. This person has quite the grudge against you, I'm afraid. I needed this person for some work and your current predicament was part of their agreement to do the work I needed."

"And what work was that?"

"Nothing important. Small human sacrifice. No one important."

"No one important?"

"Well, there was one person who might have been important to you who ended up getting caught up in all of this: Your roommate."

"Roommate? Lucy?"

"No. Kelly."

"Who?"

"About this tall, blond, frizzy hair, tanned."

"Uh...oh, #16! From the apartment you guys sucked into the Eighth Realm? Not sure how any of you even managed that..."

"First, we had nothing to do with your apartment's implosion, and second, yes, her."

"You just killed her?"

"*I* didn't. I just had to arrange for her to become part of this ritual."

"Dude, she was...well, okay, she annoyed the fuck out of me, especially with that Taylor Swift, 2Hot4U, Katy Perry bullshit she loved to play in the morning, but she didn't deserve to die. Did you do it yet? Is she still alive?"

"Not anymore. The Ritual happened this morning. My associate took a gamble that you and this girl might have been close and figured you'd try to rescue her."

"Me?!? Why would they...Still, that's fucked up!"

"It is. And I thought it was the whole time, but I needed this Ritual to happen, so I had to go along with it."

"I'm sure. So, you're just the victim in all this, right?"

"In a way, yes, I am. Almost as much of one as you were."

"So...who exactly is this person who is responsible for all this?"

Suddenly, the room was filled with a blinding light as a door between worlds opened up behind Mr. Trent. He turned around, only to be thrown across the room by an invisible force. Timothy ran towards it, only to have his right arm sliced off by what looked like a sword of some sort, emerging from the light.

"Juliette! I'm here to save you!" Persephone said.

"Holy shit! Perci!" Julie exclaimed, grabbing her messenger bag and running to her sister, hugging her tightly, "What are you doing in here?!?".

Persephone squirmed a little bit and looked her sister in the eyes, "I'm here to get you out of here! That demon over there has been after you since I killed his brother!"

She grabbed Julie's arm and pulled her back into the light.

Mr. Trent got up to his feet, just as the portal closed in a thin wisp of white smoke. The door to the interrogation room was opened up by the officers who heard the noise.

Timothy got to his feet, grabbed his arm, and started to walk away with it.

"Someone get that officer to a hospital!" one of the other cops yelled.

"He'll be okay," Mr. Trent said, unable to hide his anger at what Persephone just pulled.

He picked up his cell phone and dialed the head of security back at the facility.

There was no answer. *Fuck.*

He knew what that meant.

CHAPTER 6

Julie and Persephone emerged from the other side of the rift, in what looked like a dressing room of some sort. There was a large screen tv, a big comfy bed, and a table with food laid out .

"Perci! What are you doing in New York?"

"It's good to see you, Juliette. I am sorry that you got dragged into this feud between the House of Temen-ni-gru and I."

"Wait...so...gimme a minute. I need to process this. The room is still spinning a little bit."

"I know you must have a ton of questions, but there's no time, Juliette! I know a place we can go, where he won't be able to find us."

"Okay, lead the way...Wait! Wait!"

Suddenly, Julie stopped short, realizing there was something very important she had to do before she left. She grabbed Persephone by the shoulders and, with the utmost urgency, questioned, "Is there anything in the mini-bar?"

"What?!? No! No, there isn't! I don't drink."

"Oh, okay. Forgot my little sister was straight edge."

"Please don't use terms like that. I might accidentally remember one of those awful albums you used to play."

"Hey, mom introduced you to movies. She introduced me to music."

"Come along, Juliette. We need to go before Mr. Trent realizes we're here."

The two sisters walked down a long hallway towards what looked like a freight elevator.

They entered, Persephone typing in a code on the wall, the elevator starting to descend.

"So, Perci, what's going on? Also, a pink pantsuit?"

"I'll explain everything when we get there."

"Alright. I'm really curious as to what's going on with the pantsuit. Oh, does Sammi know you're in the city?"

"Yes. We had dinner a couple times."

"And neither of you invited me?"

"You were busy being a fugitive from the law."

"Oh, yeah…so, what is this place?"

"It's a facility run by the City of New York. I was called here for a job."

"Wait…so…so, you *did* do a human sacrifice?"

"There will be time for that, later."

"No no no. Perci, did you sacrifice a bunch of people for that demon? Are you fucking stupid? Are you killing people to end the world?"

"Oh no, Juliette, it wasn't about that at all. You have this false impression, obviously from working with the type of demons you encounter, that most demons want to cause the apocalypse. It's actually quite far from the truth."

"Then what's the truth?"

"The truth is that the way the world runs now is perfect for them. They want it to continue. It serves them. It has for centuries. They have major positions in most major governments. Did you know that during the 2000 Presidential Election, not one, but three different Fifth Realm families were involved in the race for President?"

"I knew Bush was a demon!"

"Not Bush. Demons aren't usually that stupid. But, the point is that the demons who actually want to destroy everything are the anarchists of the demon world. That's why you've never come under the attention of any of the major houses until now. You're basically an exterminator, a pinkerton, cleaning up those who can't play by the rules."

"That makes me feel kinda icky."

"Well, that is irrelevant. Now, this Ritual they had me perform, it was to safeguard the status quo. Men of power want to keep that power, so some of them make the appropriate sacrifices, mostly to Seventh Realm entities. I'm there to make sure that the entity only takes what it is promised for what is promised in return."

"And what was promised in return this time?"

"The usual. Financial prosperity."

"Wait, so, you're sacrificing people just so some old dude can get richer?!?"

"Not just any 'old dude.' This was the Mayor of New York. One of the richest men in the world. You don't get that way without cracking a few eggs. You might say he made his money the old fashioned way."

"Perci…"

"It's not a big deal, Juliette. They were all carefully selected for the amount of trouble they caused the city over the years. It's not like anyone will miss them."

"So, what about my old roommate? Is it true what the demon said about that, too?"

"She…she *hated* you, Juliette. I couldn't stand to hear the way she talked about you."

"Yeah, she could be a bitch sometimes, but I wouldn't have killed her."

"Well, *someone* has to defend the honor of this family, Juliette. I don't expect you to understand."

"So, that dream I had last night? That was about you?"

"You had a dream?"

"Dad."

"Ah, our father. I haven't heard from him in a couple years."

"He hasn't tried to give you one of his Songs of the 70's dreams?"

"Oh, he's done that plenty of times, but I mean, actually talking to him, in real life. Like you did before your birthday, Samantha tells me."

"It's hard for him to do that, Perci."

"But not too hard to contact you."

"It's too complicated for me to explain while drunk, but…"

"Well, here we are."

The elevator stopped.

There was an awful smell in the air, like burnt meat or something. Pork. It was like burnt pork that had been left out for too long.

They were in a giant room with a singed floor. There were a few big gross looking things in various parts of the room. They looked like those pictures of whales that washed up onto shore dead or something.

"What the fuck are those?" Julie asked of her sister.

"The one on the far end of the room used to be your roommate and a particularly annoying man."

"Perci…You did *this*?"

"Juliette, we can argue about this later. Right now, we have to get to the other side of the room. There's a hidden door there. It leads to the exit of this place."

"Perci…if you're evil now, you can tell me. I'm…I'm cool with that. I have a friend who's a succubus now!"

"Why doesn't that surprise me?"

"But you have to be honest with me."

"Come, Juliette."

The two of them walked, slowly through the room, candles the only light, the ground still warm, a thin mist coming from it as eerie shadows danced on the walls, making Julie think she saw some of the mounds of flesh that used to be people moving.

As she got to the middle of the room, she got a serious bad feeling about this. There was some very strong, very dark magic that had filled this room very recently. The hairs on the back of her neck were standing up, and her skin was crawling. If anything was ever going to sober her up, it was this.

"Perci, just to be on the safe side, can I have my bag? I have a bad feeling about this."

"Yes, I know, you have your little infinite trick on it. I remember from high school."

"Yeah, remember when I got you that…"

Julie turned to Persephone, only to see her sister vanish. It had been a psychic projection.

"Okay, joke's over, Perci," she said, turning around to see her sister was still in the elevator, holding her messenger bag.

"You're right. The joke is," she said, pressing the button on the elevator, the door slowly closing, "Maybe when our father senses something happened to you, he'll finally come out of whatever dimension he's hiding in."

Julie cursed and ran towards the elevator, as it shut tight with her still a good sixty feet away from it. She yelled her sister's name, to no avail, as she heard the elevator going to the floors above her.

Fuck, was that Brooks Brothers demon telling the truth? She thought, looking around, trying to figure out how she was going to get out of here.

She put her hands on her hips, the room only swaying a little bit. She really could have used a…

She heard something shuffling behind her.

She looked at one of the foul-smelling mounds. Just being near it made her want to retch. Her hand over her mouth, she stifled the urge to vomit and studied it for a bit. It appeared to be stationary.

But she had been in this game way too long to know that that never meant anything.

She walked quickly to the closed door of the elevator and looked for a button in the sparse light.

There was that shuffling noise behind her again.

She turned around, and saw that the mound closest to her was still stationary. She walked around it, squinting in the candle light. There was a sticky trail on one side of it.

Okay, that meant, it had moved.

She heard another sound behind her, and then another.

She looked at the mound in front of her, an eye seemed to swim in the flesh, looking at her. Then it moved towards her, this time, not hiding its intention, as a pair of hands reached out from two completely random places in the mound, pulling through the flesh like through plastic wrap.

She jumped back, only to see that the others all moving towards in the dim light of the room. She had never seen things like this before, but she knew they didn't have the best intentions for her.

And worst of all, all of her weapons were up with Perci, in the bag.

CHAPTER 7

Persephone stepped out of the freight elevator, walked down the hall, and then made a turn into a different hallway, where she threw Julie's messenger bag into a dumpster.

She sighed to herself, sniffled, wiped a tear from her eye, and then sent a text on her cellphone.

She put her phone back in her pocket and proceeded to walk towards where she knew the exit was.

CHAPTER 8

All of the mounds in the room moving towards her slowly, she decided to see what would happen if she wailed on the one closest to her.

She only got to the first punch before she cried out in pain, the skin on her hand turning bright red and raw, from just the millisecond of impact.

Okay, you touch them for too long, you melt, so…ugh. Are they trying to absorb me? Fucking gross!

She jumped backwards, away from the mound as it slowly made its way towards her. She screamed again, the heat in her boot so intense it felt like her foot was boiling for a second. There had been one of them behind her and she had stepped on it when she jumped back.

She dropped herself onto her backside and pulled off her doc. Thankfully, the cops had taken her shoelaces upon arresting her, so it only took her a couple seconds to get the boot off, before whatever acid was on these things ate all the way through her heel. But that heat had been intense.

Now, wearing one boot, she got back up to her feet, hands reaching out from the two mounds that were near her, two conjoined faces appearing to float aimlessly in the flesh of one of them.

She had to find a way out of this room. There were a lot of these things and eventually, she'd get tired. She was faster than them, but for how long? They were dead, so it wasn't like they were going to get sleepy any time soon. The same couldn't be said of her.

She decided to try to make her way to the far wall and see if there was anything to climb up or maybe a loose panel or something. She ran towards it, dodging out of the way of four of the moving mounds. She made sure to not step on the steaming trails that these things left behind. She wasn't sure if that would burn, but if she burned either of her feet, that'd slow her down, and it'd be game over.

This would really be a good time to have her bag.

She ran to the wall furthest from the freight elevator, seeing what looked like another elevator, this one also with some sort of keypad.

Fuck.

She heard a wet squishy noise behind her and found herself retching again as one of the things made its way towards her, but left behind a steaming pile of what looked and smelled like boiled human organs.

She found herself profoundly depressed at the thought that her sister was responsible for this. She wasn't someone who really cared too much about other people, in general, and in truth, she hadn't really liked Kelly, but to think that she was one of these things…it just seemed like the most horrible way to die Julie could imagine.

She noticed the mound that had shit out its organs making its way towards her, its large intestine still being dragged behind itself. They were smoking and black.

She had a thought. She ran towards one of the hundreds of candles that lit the room, pulled it out of its holder, and threw it at the closest mound.

All it did was make the flesh bubble a little. Not effective.

She looked up at the high ceiling of this place and noticed that there was a balcony above. But it was a good twenty feet above her and there wasn't any sort of ladder or rope here, and she was pretty sure there was no way she was just going to jump up twenty feet any time soon.

Three of the mounds found their way to her, she running again, as far away as she could.

But then she stopped and thought, *If they're all heading towards me and they're relatively slow, if I lead them all to one area of the room, then that'll buy me more time.*

She decided the best place to gather them would be at the freight elevator she had first entered the room through. She ran towards it, at full speed, about a dozen of those things closing in on her from all sides.

Then, when she was halfway through the room, there were two of them in front of her, blocking her path. She decided to go around them when they did something that horrified her even more. When they touched, the loose skin of the two mounds bubbled and gelled together. The two mounds moved closer to each other and then absorbed one another, until they became one big mound, the features of four faces floating around in the gray flesh.

Repulsed, Julie ran around them, waiting by the freight elevator, trying to catch her breath.

Then it occurred to her the folly of that plan. If these things could meld together when they touched...

It was too late, she realized as the big mound absorbed four more mounds and now was a giant hunk of loose, wet skin, faces floating lifelessly in the gray soup that made up its epidermis, stretched and squeezed ink blotches that had once been tattoos occasionally rolling over the mass of flesh.

She started to run away from it again but stopped when she saw that she recognized Kelly's nose, mouth, and two gaping holes where her eyes had been in the mass of horror in front of her.

She gasped, which was not something she was used to doing, having seen demons and monsters her entire life. She realize right then that, with the exception of her mother, she'd never had any sort of personal connection to any of the people who had died against the things she fought. Seeing someone she knew becoming part of this, even if it was someone she didn't like, was incredibly depressing to her.

Using her unburned hand, she slapped herself across the face.

"You stupid fucking bitch, you're going to be right next to her in that thing you don't get your ass in gear!" she yelled at herself.

She nodded, psyched herself up, and started to run along the walls, trying to not knock over any of the candles in her way. She felt up the wall for anything she could maybe climb up, and then a thought occurred to her. An incredibly stupid thought, but those were usually the best ones.

She stopped dead in her tracks, the mound now having grown to where it was roughly the size of a car, coming in her general direction, the ground behind it producing a thick black smoke.

She gently took her bare foot and reached forward with it to the right, as far as it would go with her still maintaining her balance.

She then lifted her booted foot up, and gingerly brought the rest of her body to where her bare foot was. Then she looked at the mound.

It hadn't changed directions.

Okay, so it's blind and deaf. It's tracking me by vibrations.

She nodded to herself, as the thing stopped in the space she had been in, only two feet ahead of her.

She kept perfectly still to test her theory out, it remaining completely stationary.

The other three mounds in the room didn't move either.

Okay, time for the final test of this.

She jumped as far away from the creature as she could get, it immediately reacting to her feet landing on the ground, arms reaching out for her.

One problem down, she wanted to try out another theory she, so she ran towards the opposite freight elevator and, with her good hand, started banging on the door to it as hard as she could.

The mound made its way towards her, just as she intended.

It came closer and closer, she continuing to bang on the door.

When it was about fifteen feet away, she stopped banging and did a quiet step away from the door again. The thing kept going towards the door, as she did another quiet step further away. It finally stopped a good foot away from touching the door.

She reached down and grabbed two of the candles. She threw the first one at the door, it making a loud clanging noise, snuffing out the flame. The mound seemed to leap forward towards the door, bunching up against it.

There was a horrible smell, as the formerly human creature's flesh began to melt the steel of the door. Exactly what she had been hoping for.

There was a great deal of smoke from the door, the soulless mound melting into the empty shaft of the elevator. She threw another candle at the wall opposite her. It didn't reach but it made enough of a noise that the mound started moving out of the shaft and towards where the candle had landed. She smiled and silently pumped her fist, waiting for the mound to completely clear the area.

It took a good three minutes for it to happen, at which point, she started to make her way towards the open shaft.

If she were lucky, which she knew she wasn't, this would be the bottom floor of the facility, and she could just climb up the shaft.

She made one of her giant steps towards the shaft. Then one more, almost home free.

Suddenly, she lost her balance, and used the wall to steady herself, making a loud banging noise.

The thing in the room started to make it way towards her again.

She cursed again and ran back towards the original closed freight elevator. She wasn't going to waste time trying to burn a hole in this one too, but she figured if she could get to banging on the wall, she'd lure the thing again, giving her time to run back to the open shaft.

She started to bang on the door, the big mound making its way towards her.

Suddenly, the world turned white with pain as one of the mounds she hadn't been paying attention to grabbed her ankle.

She screamed and instinctively kicked at it, her booted foot now feeling like it was boiling.

She fell onto the ground, the hand that had grabbed her ankle already having burned its way through her clothing, the skin it was grabbing starting to sizzle. She hit at the hand with the boot she had taken off earlier, it letting go, she thrusting herself back towards the wall, quickly ripping her boot off.

Her ankle looked bad. At the very least, that was going to leave permanent scarring. It hurt like a motherfucker, but she had no time to worry about it as that mound made a move for her again as did the giant one that had made its way halfway through the room already.

She rolled out of the way, her thigh and buttocks burning slightly from rolling over the slimy trail that one of the mounds had left. It hurt but not as bad as her ankle or her foot had. It had burned a large hole in her pants from her right asscheek down to the back of her knee. The skin under it was red and irritated, but not burned, thankfully.

Barefoot, she used the wall for leverage and got to her feet as the two mounds, followed by two smaller ones approached her.

She ran along the wall, limping slightly from how bad her ankle felt, until she found her way to the shaft.

Thankfully, she was on the first floor, so it was time to climb.

Seeing the things approaching her from behind, she flung herself to the walls of the shaft and, feeling what felt like an emergency ladder, started to climb, still hearing the sounds of those things making their way towards the shaft. Bathed in red emergency lights, she hoped they weren't able to climb up walls, because she couldn't even see how far up this shaft went.

CHAPTER 9

Persephone climbed up the stairs to the High Line Park, in Chelsea, looking out at the view of the sun setting over the west side of Manhattan. Couples holding hands walked by, tourists took pictures of the city below, and, in the distance, the faint sound of someone singing in Spanish to acoustic guitars could be heard. Her sister was waiting for her.

"Finally!" Samantha exclaimed, before asking, "Persephone, where have you been?"

"I've had work to do."

"Was it for Michael Trent?"

Persephone was taken aback.

"How do you know that name?"

"Persephone, what are you doing in New York, really? Are you responsible for what happened to Julie? And what was *Operation: Harker?*"

Persephone started to sweat, having not expected her sister to know any of these things.

"It's…uh…Samantha, it's complicated. Very complicated," she said, running her fingers through her hair.

"I have a Master's Degree in Metaphysical Medicine. Try me."

Persephone paced around for a couple seconds before turning to Samantha, "Can we walk somewhere? I'm really uneasy explaining all of this here."

Samantha nodded and pointed to her sister that they'd walk from the 20's they were in towards the other end of the Highline, near Gansevoort St.

"So, Persephone, what is going on?"

"Where is dad?"

"Don't answer a question with a question."

"How come he hasn't come when Juliette's in so much trouble? She's always been his favorite and yet he's not here."

"That's really complicated, Persephone."

"Oh, so it's okay for you to say that and not for me?"

"*I* didn't frame my big sister for murder."

"Samantha, don't be so cruel to me."

"Fuck you, Persephone, fuck you. Do you know the things I've heard, the last few days? Framing your sister, making deals with demons, human sacrifices, working with vampires? What the fuck happened to you?!?"

"Samantha, please."

"No. I love you, Persephone, but you are doing all this...this *bullshit* and I will not let you hurt anyone else."

"Samantha, I..."

"Do you really hate Julie that much? Do you really hate your big sister so fucking much that you'd try to ruin her life? You've had this grudge against her for years! Ever since she called you a name when she was drunk, you've acted like this towards her!"

"Are you serious? How could you even ask that?!?"

"What?!?"

"Samantha, I *love* Juliette! I *looked up* to Juliette! While you were always studying and doing your thing, she and I were inseparable. We spent more time in the Fifth and Third Realms together than we spent in school. She taught me my first spell. I loved Juliette and I still do. If anything, *you* were the odd sister out."

"Then why are you trying to kill her?"

"Because I *do* love her."

"What?!?"

"Because I see what she's become. She's become some drunken whore who doesn't care about herself or others. She floats around the boundaries of society like plankton, instead of doing anything with the vast amount of intelligence and skill she has. She could be one of the Council's foremost agents and, instead, she's fucking random guys and getting in bar fights. When Rayborn went after her, it took some low level nobody to kill her, instead of my sister, who should have been able to kill her in minutes. I'm trying to *save* her, Samantha! Something *you* didn't care enough about her to ever do!"

"Excuse me?!? I didn't care enough to *kill* my little sister?!? Is that what you're accusing me of?!?"

"Sometimes, when someone's too far gone, it's the only way."

"You're..."

"I'm what?"

"You're…"

"Come on, spit it out."

"You're…You're fucking crazy, Persephone. You're literally insane. You're trying to end your sister's life because you don't agree with her lifestyle choices?"

"Do you?"

"That's not the point, Perci."

"Don't call me that."

"Why? Are you going to try to kill me, too?"

"No. I would never hurt you, Samantha. What I'm doing to Juliette is a mercy! It kills me that nobody else cares enough about her to try to stop her from destroying herself!"

Samantha stopped walking, sighing heavily, as a mariachi band played a few feet from her.

"Look at you," Persephone said, pointing to Samantha's eyepatch, "Look at what this family has done you. To us. You lost an eye when you were eight years old because our father was so determined to have us carry on his legacy, that he threw a child who wasn't ready, who didn't have the aptitude to fight, against forces she had no understanding of! You're never going to be a whole person again and yet, you hold no grudge against the man?"

"So, is that what this is really about? Our father?"

"Of course, it is! Our whole lives have been about him! If not for him, you'd still have your eye. If not for him, we'd still have mom. If not for him, we'd still have Juliette. You may only have one eye, but I know you're not blind."

"Persephone…"

"Sometimes, you have to do things to the people you love that they might not want, but you do it for their own good."

"I know."

Samantha closed her eye, tears running down her cheek, and nodded, the mariachi band behind them stopping their music and reached into their guitar cases, quickly pulling out M-4 carbines, aiming them at Persephone.

"Persephone Johannes, as a member of the Council in good standing, I hereby place you under arrest," Samantha said, as the mariachis took position around her sister.

"What the fuck is this, Samantha?!?"

"Persephone, we're going to get you the help you need. I promise the Council will not hurt you."

Persephone looked at the men pointing their guns at her and realized she could kill them all, without even blinking. Their guns would mean nothing if she decided to unleash her full force at them. They wouldn't be the first group of armed men she would have killed, just today.

"Persephone, I know what you're thinking. Just don't, please. Please don't add to your crimes. Just come quietly. They wanted to bring in Team Seven. I insisted I could convince you to see reason without their involvement. Please, Persephone."

Persephone looked at the mariachi and then nodded her head, dropping to her knees and crossing all ten of her fingers behind her head as they were cuffed behind her.

She only did it because she wasn't sure she could have avoided killing Samantha and everyone else in this park if she had let go. She didn't want to hurt her sister and she didn't want the attention that would come from killing an entire park full of people with magic.

Besides, this could still work towards the plan.

CHAPTER 10

"Daddy daddy daddy, can I go out and play/No son, you'd better stay inside...the radio said today," Julie sang to herself, exhausted, covered in grime and breathing heavily, as she reached the top of the shaft, just under the freight elevator. She wasn't sure how long she had been climbing but she had managed to sing to herself the entire Black Flag *Loose Nut* album and had started working her way through Reagan Youth's catalog.

She climbed along the shaft towards the gated door to the floor below where this freight elevator was, and, using her weight, smashed herself into it. She did it several times, until the gate gave way enough for her to slip herself through. She was in a well-lit hallway again, laying on the floor, looking up at the bright fluorescent lights on the ceiling above.

She lay there for a few minutes, before getting herself to her feet and surveying her surroundings. Her arms and legs were killing her, her ankle numb, the skin of it looking vaguely alien.

This hallway, with its white walls, white ceiling, and white floor, split in the middle. She decided to take the right hand path, walking for a minute or two before finding herself outside a room with a dumpster. She reluctantly opened the dumpster, half expecting to find another one of those unholy mounds in there, but this was filled with...it looked like hair. Blond hair, black hair, white hair, red hair, curly hair, straight hair.

She closed the dumpster and entered the room, finding herself in a white room with chains and pulleys on the walls. There was a white table nearby where several pairs of scissors sat next to electric razors. A chill went down her spine when she realized where all the hair came from.

Still, she grabbed a pair of scissors, because she had no idea what was coming next.

She soon found herself walking through another hallway, into a room with a still damp floor. It looked like a shower or something, hoses all over the room, laying about, water still dripping from them. There were hooks on the ceiling.

Fuck, what happened to the people here?

She walked through this room, her bare feet on the cold floor the only sounds, as she made her way to another hallway. There was yet another room with chains and pulleys, this time with a drain on the floor. There were what looked like feeding troughs. And a spaghetti dinner of rubber tubes lying about.

On the wall was a sign that indicated proper cleansing procedure for prisoners. It appeared to be instructions on giving people enemas and inserting catheters into their urethras, against their will if necessary. The matter-of-factness of the sign left her cold.

Beyond this door was another hallway that split in two again. She wanted to get out of here, now. She hung onto the scissors as she walked towards what looked like another freight elevator, this one with a simple red button.

She pressed the button, hearing the noise of the elevator coming down.

She held the scissors, ready to stab someone if necessary.

The elevator door opened, empty. She entered and pressed the button marked up.

The elevator let her out at yet another white hallway, a door at the far end.

This hallway wasn't empty, though. There was a corpse lying here, fried. He appeared to be wearing some sort of uniform, but it was too charred to make out. His gun had melted in his hands. She didn't want to know what the fuck had done this to him. She wondered if he was one of the people in on whatever happened here.

She walked past the corpse, expecting it to rise up, after how many dead things had already tried to attack her today. She walked backwards it until she got to the door. It was unlocked. In fact, it looked like the hinges had been busted.

She opened it and immediately vomited upon the smell that greeted her.

It was like nothing she had ever experienced. An overwhelming reek of shit and piss and blood and what smelled like a barrel of rotting fish.

She lifted her shirt over her mouth and ventured forth, since this was the only way forward.

The smell inside was even worse.

She was in a prison area. Dark, metallic grey instead of the white that every other room had been. The ceilings were water damaged and the floors were stained and cracked tile. Inside the cells, there were overflowing buckets of human waste and excrement-covered benches against the walls, roaches swarming everywhere. She ran through the room, wanting to throw up again, hoping that the door ahead of her would be unlocked as well, because she was sure she'd pass out from the smell if she was here any longer.

Luckily for her, the door was unlocked. She ran through, slammed the door behind her, and threw up again, trying to also get the smell out of her nose.

When she had her bearings about her, she found herself in another white hallway. There were five more charred corpses in the hall, also with their guns melted.

This place was a tomb, she realized, and she hoped that she was close to wherever the fuck the exit was, because she did not fancy joining everyone else here.

The hallway gave way to a large area that looked a bit like a high school assembly area, complete with a stage. The floor smelled of bleach, and there were another six charred corpses lying about the room. She didn't see any way out of here except through maybe the backstage area, so she started for the stage when she heard a familiar and very unwelcome voice.

"The guest of honor, all right?" Christopher said, emerging from the darkened area of the stage.

"We was thinking you'd gone and snuffed it. Beastly amount of dead Septics, here," Serenity said, showing off her fangs, as the two of them jumped off the stage.

"Real ace to see you alive and well, it is."

"Bloody chuffed, we is."

"You wasn't bothered to wait around and play last time."

They began circling her.

"So, you two work for my sister?" Julie asked.

"Aye. Good woman, she is. Sent us a text telling us you'd be present."

"Okay," Julie started, shaking her head and sighing, "Before we do our boss battle thing...did she ever tell you why she sent you guys?
"Not our business, love," Christopher said.

"Enough pissing about. The Missus said to do her real nasty-like."

"Aim to please, we do."

"Right right."

Christopher reached behind himself for his swords, but, realizing that they had been broken earlier, rolled his eyes, sighed, and shook his head for a few seconds.

And with that, they were on her in a flash, their superspeed restored by being on Earth. Julie would take a swing at one of them only to have them be behind her by the time her fist moved to the desired location.

She found herself swept off her feet and then flipped forward by a kick to the back of the head before she even landed, face-first on the cold tile of this room.

They weren't fucking around this time.

She found herself pulled up by her hair as Serenity appeared in front of her and gave her what felt like a hundred punches at super speed to the stomach.

She was convinced she peed a little, but she knew for a fact that she spit up blood.

Serenity laughed and grabbed her by the throat, throwing her across the room, Julie hitting her back and crying out at the impact of it.

Before she even landed Christopher was already waiting for her at that side of the room.

He stood over her, laughing, and she did the first thing that popped into her mind, and bit his ankle as hard as she could.

He screamed out, "Are you dim?!? Trying to turn into one of us and poison yourself, posthaste?"

He kicked her from the floor onto the far edge of the stage, her shoulder dislocating upon impact.

She saw that she was near the backstage door, so she opened it up and quickly slipped through it, finding herself in another hallway. This one with multiple doors.

She hoped one of them had something wooden in it.

She limped to a room, hearing the door she had come in getting slammed off its hinges.

"Ready or not," Serenity sing-songed into the hallway.

Julie opened the door, to see it was a restroom. Not what she wanted. Before she had time to register things, Christopher threw her into the already cracked mirror, her back a pincushion of broken glass as she lay on the bathroom sink, her aggressor already on top of her, laughing.

"We was trained SAS, luv," he said, "You've not fought vamps like us previous."

She reached behind her and pulled one of the pieces of glass out of her back.

Before she could even swing with it, he had taken it out of her hand and crushed it into sand, with a smirk. But that wasn't what her intention was. While he was showing off, she covered her good hand in her blood, and flicked it at him.

He seemed puzzled until his face began to smoke a little. The immunization in her blood was still toxic to him, something he had reminded her of when she had bitten him.

He screamed and grabbed his face as she hobbled out of the bathroom as quickly as she could, only to find herself flying a good twenty feet, as Serenity speared her upon her entering the hallway again.

Christopher, still inside the bathroom, screamed in pain, Serenity briefly distracted enough that Julie covered her hand in blood again and smeared it all over Serenity's face.

Serenity fell to her knees, screaming and cursing at Julie, who used the opportunity to run into the next door she saw. It was a room that seemed designed for relaxing, hot tub, and all. She ran inside and body-checked herself into the wall to pop her shoulder back into the socket, falling to her knees in agony as it did so. Moving her now-working arm, she grabbed a wooden chair, smashing the leg against the floor until it was jagged and stake-like.

Julie looked at herself in the mirror. She was bloody and dirty, her clothes shredded, her hair a mess, her eyes red, her lip bloody.

She realized that the twins wouldn't be hurt forever, so she ran back out into the hallway, Serenity still on her knees, her face smoking.

Julie limped a little further down the hall, seeing another charred body in the way, before seeing that around the bend was another elevator.

She started to limp faster towards it when she was, once again, thrown off her feet by Christopher doing a similar tackle to what Serenity had done. Half of his face was burned by whatever the clinic had injected her with and he seemed angry. It was obvious he was in a lot of pain, because, while he was still hitting like a truck, he was slower than usual.

He stood up, growled, and picked her up by the throat again and started squeezing, her air immediately cut off.

He wasn't just trying to strangle her. He was going to try to just pop her head off, and with how strong he was, it wouldn't take more than a couple seconds to do so.

He brought her face-to-face with him, so he could look into her eyes when he did.

He smiled an angry smile.

Suddenly, Julie found herself looking up at the ceiling again as Christopher let go of her.

When he had brought her face-to-face, she had stabbed him in the heart with the wooden leg of the chair.

His angry smile turned to a frown of disbelief and then one of sadness.

Serenity, her face half burned off, appeared at super speed to her brother's side.

"N-n-n-n..." she whispered, "Mimmy, no..."

Christopher reached out for Serenity and then his eyes rolled into his head, his body lost its essence as he doubled over in his sister's arms.

Serenity mouthed words silently, her eyes filled with tears.

And then his body fell apart in a bloody mess in her arms.

Serenity fell to her knees, covered in the remains of her brother, and she let out a scream of pure grief.

She heaved and sobbed, looking around for help, just repeating "No" to herself silently.

Julie used the opportunity to limp-run to the elevator and frantically pressed the button, expecting Serenity to come charging at her.

But as Julie entered the elevator, she looked back into the hallway. Serenity was still there, on her knees, covered in the remains of her brother, rocking back and forth, obviously, in shock.

"...shared a womb, we did..."

Halfway through the elevator ride up, she heard Serenity start screaming. Just screaming over and over again. They weren't words. It was just vocally expressed pain. Guttural. Primal.

The elevator door opened and Julie found herself in another hallway, this one covered with more charred bodies. The door at the end of this hallway took her to the dressing room Persephone had initially brought her to. Outside, she found her messenger bag in a dumpster.

She left the facility, finding herself in what looked like Red Hook, in the cold nighttime air. The facility, from the outside, looked like any other warehouse in an industrial district.

Her bare feet hurt at the touch of the icy ground, her shoulder still ached, her ankle looked inhuman, and the exposed skin from the various tears in her clothing made her shiver, but she had, at least, gotten the fuck out of that place.

She started to walk towards the street, when a black town car pulled up. The back door opened to reveal Mr. Trent and Timothy.

"Julie, please get in."

She silently got in, too shell shocked to say anything.

"Now, do you believe me?" he asked.

She just glared at him.

"Driver, take us to New York Methodist. This girl needs medical attention."

Julie looked at him, with a look of utter disgust, before saying, "You hired her to do all that?"

"No, just the sacrifice."

"That was fucking…I don't even have words. And that's saying something."

"Julie, that's how the world works."

"Well, then fuck it. Fuck the Mayor. Fuck the world. Fuck you."

"Julie, please. I'm trying to be your friend here. You've been cleared of all charges and I'm taking you to the hospital now. Someone has to take a look at that ankle and your hand. And…oh, it looks like your back is bleeding."

"Yeah."

"Besides, your sister's hearing before the Council is tomorrow afternoon. Smile, Julie, your sister's been brought to justice."

Julie didn't have any reason to smile.

"So, what's going to happen to that place?"

"You need to worry about getting better."

"Don't bullshit me, demon. Fucking tell me what's going to happen to the place?"

"We'll send a team in tomorrow morning. They'll clear out the bodies and scrub the place."

"What about those…things that used to be all the people you sacrificed? Well, I guess by tomorrow, they'll be one big thing…"

"Ah, the shoggoth? Well, the city uses those to guard some of our more high profile areas. Places I'm not at liberty to tell you about."

"So you have more of those?"

"Well, just two in New York City. Some cities have their own. We've been doing this for ten years in this city alone. I'm sure you've seen how they all melt together. Well, we bring them to the designated area, let them melt into each other, and we get ourselves a pretty effective guardian."

"How many people?"

"Julie, these are not details you need to…"

She jumped at him, pulling a serrated blade from her messenger bag and putting it to his throat.

Timothy started to glow red, but Mr. Trent motioned for him to stand down.

"Relax, Timothy."

"How many?"

"Well, 34 people were down there this morning. When they've been melded into the bigger shaggoth they're being melded into, that'll be 170 people."

"So, 340 people have died for this shit?"

"It's how the world works, Julie."

"So you've said."

She took the knife from his throat, put it back in her bag, and sat back down.

"Millions more of your people would die if not for the sacrifice of those three…"

"I know what would happen if not for the sacrifice. Some rich sack of shit's wallet would be just a little bit lighter. Don't bullshit me," she said, closing her eyes

"Besides, you just hit the lottery. I figure if you were able to survive a shoggoth and your nutjob sister, I figure it'd probably be easier to buy you off than to kill you off...unless, of course, you might be interested in a job, maybe? I mean, we're talking seven fig-"

"Just...just tell me when we get to the hospital. And don't fucking talk to me until then."

CHAPTER 11

Later that night, Julie lay in her hospital bed, in a private room, annoyed at the pokes and prods she had had to endure, throughout the day. Her ankle was wrapped up and she had received several dozen stitches on her back, from when she had gotten thrown into the mirror. The tv was on, but she wasn't watching it. Some Neo-Nazi dickhead named Chad Galloway was speaking at some college or the other. Not really her cup of tea.

That Trent guy had put her up in the most expensive room in the place, told her not to worry about her lack of insurance, and told her he had to go prepare for tomorrow's hearing.

Julie didn't like him and she didn't trust him. He smiled all nice and pretty and put up appearances, but when it came down to it, demon or not, he was just another suit and tie guy with ulterior motives.

But what kept playing out in her mind was that her little sister had actually tried to kill her tonight. Hell, her little sister had been trying to kill her for days, but she just didn't know it at the time. What the fuck brought that on? Sure, she had given Perci a hard time every now and then, but it just didn't make sense.

And the fact that her sister could be so blasé about taking human life the way she did, it didn't register with Julie. Perci was supposed to be the one with her shit together, the responsible one, the one who lived up to all those dreams of dad's that Julie couldn't be bothered with. And yet, there she was, creating her own little torture porn fantasies and sending fucking vampires after her. Fuck, maybe even that whole weirdness with the Eighth Realm too!

She could accept the premise of human sacrifice, if she tried to force herself to see it from her sister's perspective, but why leave them wallowing in the own filth? Why do it just so some rich douche could shit on the poor even more than he already did? Did really none of that ever mean anything to Perci? *Fuck it*, she thought, *I've got to get out of here and...*

"Julie," Samantha said, entering the room with a bouquet of flowers and a newspaper.

"You proposing to someone with those?" Julie asked, "I thought you already had a fiancée."

"No, Julie, they're for you."

"Not sure marriage between sisters is legal yet. Oh, well, I'll put them up on the windowsill I don't have."

"Julie, that's not fair."

"Sorry, Sammi, I'm just…"

"It's okay, Julie. Hey, look *The Daily News* ran a retraction on you being a sex-crazed, meth dealing murderer."

Julie looked at the paper and saw the headline was something about a baseball player and steroids.

"I don't see myself on there. I was front page news."

"Yeah…the retraction is on page 67. Really tiny paragraph. But, hey, at least, they admitted they were wrong."

"Did *The Post* run one?"

"Julie. It's *The New York Post.*"

"Good point."

"So, uh…thought you should know…I was the one to arrest Persephone tonight."

"To be honest, I kinda wish I could break her fucking face right now."

"She needs help, Julie."

"You don't know the half of it, Sammi."

"Well, she's in custody now."

"How long do you think that's going to last?"

"She let them take her. We both know she's capable of taking down any number of armed attackers."

"Oh yeah. I've seen proof, first hand."

"So, it's really all true? Even the two vampires?"

"Especially the fucking vampires."

"Michael Trent told me a bit about what you went through."

"I don't trust him."

"I don't either, but he was the one who informed the Council about what Persephone was doing."

"Because she killed his brother. Do you really think some Fifth Realm demon gives a fuck about our little sister's war crime party?"

"I know, but still…"

"I did manage to kill one of them. That...uh...that *was* satisfying."

"Wait...You manage to kill an Operation: Harker vampire?!?"

"Operation: Harker?"

"I learned about it from my meeting with the Council today. It was a program in the United Kingdom during the Cold War, first instituted during the 1960's. The idea was to train vampires to reach their full strength as possible soldiers in a potential ground war against the Soviets."

"That would explain a lot. I've never fought vampires who could do the whole superspeed thing at the same time they fought. Most don't seem to ever think to put the two together."

"There was also Operation: Morris, which was the American equivalent of it. The vampire clans were more than willing to sign up some of their people after Stalin's purge. I just can't believe Persephone would associate with...well, I guess if she's been working for the Royal Family..."

"Well, whatever, I've had enough vampires and Operations and shoggoths for one day. I'm...I need to get out of here and..."

"Nonsense. The doctors said that you need to stay here for observation, at least, overnight. I'll come pick you up in the morning to take you to the hearing."

"I don't want to go to any fucking hearing."

"Julie. You need to do this. You need to show your sister that we want her to get the help she needs."

"Well, you do that."

"They also may need you to testify as to what you went through."

"I'm not going to...you know what? This is all just bullshit. Fuck it."

Julie got out of the bed, reached into her messenger bag, and pulled out a pair of skinny jeans, and an Exploited t-shirt.

Samantha ran up to her and grabbed her by the shoulder, "Whoa, you have second-degree burns on your ankle and your hand is wrapped up. You've just had I don't know how many stitches put into your back, your shoulder is in shitty shape, you've got minor burns all over your leg and buttocks. This is serious, Julie."

"Sammi, I love you, but you don't have any idea what I went through today."

Julie threw off her hospital gown, pulling the IV out of her arm. She began to put on the skinny jeans, letting out a loud curse upon the pants touching her bandage-wrapped ankle

"Julie, seriously! You need to rest tonight! You can't even put on pants without being in pain."

"Sammi, what I need is to get my head together."

"And *how* are you going to do that?"

Julie sighed and put on her shirt, and then her jacket before continuing to speak.

"Sammi, you know I love you. But I've just seen someone I knew personally twisted into something foul and fucked up and it was done by my own fucking blood. I think I need to forget about all this shit for a night. I'll deal with everything tomorrow."

"Julie, you aren't going to do anything stupid tonight, are you?"

"When I have I ever done anything stupid?"

Samantha looked at her.

"I promise, I'll be there tomorrow, okay?"

"Okay, but…Julie. Please take care of that ankle and that hand. Don't use any cotton. Don't…"

"It's okay, Sammi. This isn't my first dance."

"I love you," Samantha said, her eyes red with tears.

"I love you too."

"I'm sorry if I've ever let you or Persephone down. I've tried to…"

"Hey! Hey!" Julie exclaimed, hugging Samantha tightly, "Don't start that shit. You did an awesome job with us."

"Then why is all this happening? We're all sisters, Julie! I tried to be the big sister to you two. I tried to…"

"You did the best you could, Sammi."

"My best just wasn't…good enough, I guess."

"Fuck that! Don't ever say that, Sammi," Julie said, her eyes tearing a little, hugging Samantha even tighter.

"Okay, that hurts now," Samantha said, wiping her eye.

"I'm going to be okay, Sammi. You did a great job. You taught dad to drive. That, right there, is an achievement," Julie said, loosening her grip.

"Oh, fuck me, I know."

"Seriously, though, Sammi. It's not your fault. None of this is."

"I wish I could believe that."

"Well, you better, because that's how it is. And that's the bottom line."

"Because Stone Cold said so?"

"Hell yeah."

Samantha chuckled through her tears and then nodded, Julie hugging her again.

"I just need to do this for myself tonight. I'll be there tomorrow. I promise."

"Okay, see you tomorrow morning. I love you."

"Love you too."

CHAPTER 12

Persephone sat in her cell, wearing an orange jumpsuit, sitting in a lotus position, very aware of the mental noise this particular holding area had. She couldn't focus very much here. That was probably some sort of precaution taken against prisoners who could use magic. Smart, really.

Not that she had any plans on trying to escape here.

She knew the Council's rules. As bad as her father's standing was, it was well within her rights to request him as her defender during her hearing. That right could not be denied her under the bylaws of the Council.

And when he'd come, it would finally, after all these years, be time for her to give him what he deserved.

Sure, things had not gone as she had planned. Julie's salvation would have to come later, apparently. And, to be honest, she preferred to do it herself, quickly, and painlessly, the way a sister should end a sister's suffering. Of course, when the goal was to lure her father here, Julie's death would have had to be as horrible as possible so that he would think there was a real and immediate threat. But now, with that step of the plan changed from her initial intention, there was no need for Julie to suffer needlessly, any more than she already was suffering through the sad existence she called her life.

This wasn't so bad, Persephone thought to herself, thinking of all the souls she had interacted with over the years who had been imprisoned before she sold them to whatever otherworldly being she had been dealing with, at any given time.

She heard a door opening far away, out of her field of vision, and smelled that familiar cologne that told her Mr. Trent had come to see her. Technically, she shouldn't have any visitors, but considering the pull this demon-in-the-shape-of-a-man had in this city, it wasn't surprising that he'd be here. But for what, she wondered.

He walked over to her cell, as always accompanied by his royal guard, and leaned against the bars, a smirk on his lips.

"So," Persephone asked, smiling, "Are you here to whisk me away to some secret location, where I can be tortured to death? Oooh. Maybe you can bring me back to the Fifth Realm, where you can give me to your brothers."

"Hahaha, no," he said, the smirk not leaving his lips at any point, "I may not like you, but I'm not stupid. You took out three battalions of highly trained private military contractors, you killed the best warrior of my brothers, and you managed to convince a Seventh Realm Entity that it would be in its best interest to keep to the terms of the contract it made with the mayor. I don't think attempting to take you anywhere would end up well for me."

"So, *that* was the best warrior of your brothers? Don't you have a thousand? And he was the best?!? Trent…I've got to tell you; he wasn't very hard to kill."

"You know what gets me about you? None of this had to happen. All you had to do was just do your fucking job. No secrets plans. No big evil conspiracies. No toadies licking your heels. All you had to do was just come in, enjoy your fancy hotel, see the sights, perform the Ritual, and then go the fuck home. Instead, here we are."

"Here we are."

"You know, you didn't need to interact with the sacrifices, *at all*, except for the day the Ritual actually happened. But you had to go and act out your dom fantasies with the meat. That's what annoys me so much about you apes. It's always about your desires. Always about what you can take advantage of to get yourselves ahead."

"I'd think a demon would appreciate those qualities about the hu"an race."

"If I were a demon that dealt in temptation, then I'd very much appreciate them. I'm not and I don't. I'm a demon that deals in order. In keeping things efficient, clean, orderly. And when you deal in keeping things efficient, clean, and orderly, they're the worst fucking things I have to contend with, in that case. Seriously, when I heard we were getting a woman to preside over the Ritual, I was overjoyed. I thought, *Well, good, someone who isn't going to use the sacrifices as their personal harem.* And then, next thing you know, it's all, 'Yes, Ms. Roberts,' and 'Thank you, Ms. Roberts.'"

"I did the job, didn't I?"

"After a metric shit-ton of teeth-pulling, manipulating, and causing me to use resources that I wish I hadn't had to use. As it is, do you know how much it's costing me to clean up the facility after your little killing spree? I had been in the process of negotiating leasing it out to FEMA and now, I've got fried PMC remains to scrape off the walls."

"I guess, my sister would tell you that, 'Shit happens.'"

"Shit happens...Right...well, Ms. Roberts, you know what's going to happen to you tomorrow, right?"

"My hearing."

"Yeah, and then, afterwards, you're getting sent to the fucking nuthouse."

Persephone looked at him, and creased her brows.

"Oh, you didn't know? Your sister has been petitioning the Council to get you the 'help you need.' And that means, you're going to be institutionalized."

"She's been petitioning the Council for that?"

"Oh, what's a matter? You didn't think your big sister knew you were out of your fucking mind? Well, tomorrow, everyone's going to know. Not only does your little conspiracy against your other sister and the subsequent murder of her roommate and your dealings with Eighth Realm forces count against you, but there is the little matter of you having entire conversations with empty rooms."

"What?"

"Like I wouldn't have cameras placed in your hotel room after all the shit you pulled from the very beginning? Come on. And once we did start putting those cameras there, I saw you having a long and intense conversation with a mirror. And we analyzed the mirror. It's not magic. It's just a standard, run of the mill mirror that you suddenly decided to play Wicked Stepmother with. Not only did our best humans check it out, I personally inspected it. I mean, I *am* a demon, after all. You were talking to some other demon or god or spirit, I'd sense it."

"So, you couldn't sense anything from it?"

"Nope. So, I don't know who you were talking with, but they're not real. So, you legitimately are batshit crazy. Personally, I'd say dealing with anything Eighth Realm is enough for me to say you need to be locked up. I mean, Jesus Christ. Are you trying to end the world, just to satisfy whatever grudge you've got with your sister?"

"It was only a little hole in the fabric of reality. And it's closed up."

"Well, I don't know how you even managed that, but I'm guessing it means You Know Who is probably roaming around somewhere. They'll probably try to get that info out of you too, since *he's* exactly what we don't want lurking around."

"He has nothing to do with this. I've had no contact with him. You know he wouldn't deal with a human."

"Well, you can deny it all you want. The evidence is still there. And the point is that I may not be able to touch you now. I know that. You could probably take me down any time you wanted. And all the magic buffers in the world couldn't stop you. But a few years down the road, when you've been pumped so full of thorazine that you're wearing diapers, well, that'll be a very different story."

"I guess we all have to have our dreams."

"The one thing I can't seem to figure out is how you rigged coming here. We've gone over the records a thousand times and there was no meeting between you and Eric Jefferson, on this plane or another. No proxies. No calls. No e-mails. No trace of him even knowing how to move between Realms. We even checked his dreams, but there wasn't any contact we can prove from you."

"Who?"

"Don't pretend you don't know who he is. Man blew his brains out rather than give away what secret you two had going on."

"Well, Mr. Trent, I'm sure you're not going to believe me when I say that I have no idea what you're talking about, so I won't even bother saying it."

She honestly didn't know who that person was, but she had a very good idea of who had spoken to him. She wasn't going to tell Trent.

"Fine. Be that way. I'm not the one who is going be a vegetable a year from now. I will say, though, that it was a pleasure meeting your sister, Julie," Mr. Trent said.

Persephone just stared at him.

"You two have more in common than you'd probably admit. She doesn't like me very much, right now, for example. But...that's understandable, considering she's just discovered that her psycho bitch little sister was working for me. Once she sees how much of this was *your* doing, and not mine, well, I think she and I will get along better."

Persephone narrowed her eyes.

"Just think...maybe one day, I might even be able to say that *I've fucked your sister.* I don't normally like to engage in this whole unseemly fluid exchange thing you apes are so fond of, but you know, I might make an exception with her. Not that she's exceptionally attractive ape or anything, but I do know how much it'd hurt you, so that's reason enough to consider it."

Persephone wanted to kill him right then and there.

"Oh, what's the matter, Ms. Roberts? Considering the things my brothers have probably done to your mom, it'd just be continuing a family tradition."

"What about my mother?"

"Please. You don't think a soul enters the Fifth Realm without my family knowing it? Especially when it's killed by one of our pet dragons? No no no no…Your mother's soul is with my brothers. You should see the things they've done to her over the years."

Persephone stood up and…then, took a deep breath, and chuckled. That couldn't be true. Trent was just trying to wind her up. She had researched the dragon she had killed as a child, and had become very aware that was a wild one. If she had suspected that her mother's soul was in the custody of the House of Temen-ni-gru, she would have taken it down years ago.

Besides, her friend would have told her.

"Almost got me there," she said, with a slight smile, sitting back down in the lotus position.

"Well, I have to be going, but I'll be seeing you tomorrow."

"Have a pleasant sleep, Trent."

"Oh, I will. Trust me, Ms. Roberts, I will. I've got a nice, soft king-sized bed waiting for me, back at my townhouse. You, uh, enjoy your cot."

She watched him leave. reminding herself the entire time that her hate would have to wait. Tomorrow is the day the plan would finally become reality. She couldn't jeopardize that now, just because he touched a few buttons.

Still, she wished she had a mirror right now.

CHAPTER 13

Julie pushed her way through the people at the little Brooklyn dive bar, determined to get to the bartender and get as drunk as humanly possible tonight. The place was fairly busy and that was good. She wanted to just forget about all the foul bullshit she had been dealing with recently.

She scanned the room, looking to see if anybody was worth going home with. There were a few likely candidates, but she'd just wait to see if any of them approached her first.

Over at the pool table, there was an East Indian girl in a purple faux-fur coat who looked at her with something like recognition, but went back to her pool game. Julie briefly wondered if she had maybe slept with that girl during some drunken and/or drug-fueled haze. No matter. The girl didn't say anything to her, so it wasn't something to be concerned about.

Julie sat down at the bar, immediately downing a glass of Jager, feeling as though an itch had finally been scratched as the alcohol went down her throat.

She sighed a relieved sigh.

Someone here had put Blitz on the jukebox. The good Blitz, before they became a new wave band and sucked.

She ordered another glass, downing it almost as soon as it arrived. She did that three more times, before a guy sat down next to her at the bar.

She scanned him up and down. He had the requisite uncombed black hair, jacket with a Blanks 77 patch on it, skinny jeans, bullet belt, etc. He would do.

She made eye contact.

He met her eyes and smiled.

"Hey, I'm…"

Okay, that wasn't the right answer.

"I'm sorry," she said, "But you seem to have me confused with the person writing your biography. I didn't ask your name. That information is completely fucking useless to me."

"Fuck...sorry. I just thought..."

"Don't be doing that. *Don't* think. This is *not* a time for thinking."

"Alright, forget it. I'll..."

"So, do you want to fuck or not?"

"Wha?"

"Okay, if that's too hard a question..."

"Uh...no no. I'd...uh..."

"It's a simple yes or no question," she poked him in the chest with every syllable, as she asked him, "Do. You. Want. To. Fuck. Me?"

"Uh...Yeah."

"See? That wasn't hard. Let's go back to your place."

"I...uh...I'm crashing with people. I sleep on a couch..."

"Okay. I'll get on top. Let's go."

Julie roughly put her arm around him and bit him on the neck, a moan escaping his lips.

He looked at her and opened his mouth to say something, her shushing him, and leading him out of the bar.

As the two of them walked towards the exit, she felt a hand touch her shoulder. She turned around, still jumpy from the events of earlier today, to see it was the Indian girl who had been at the pool table. She smiled at Julie, as though they should know each other.

Julie was taken aback by this, immediately scanning her memory to see if she had perhaps slept with this person. She wasn't ringing any immediate bells.

"Hey, this may sound like a weird question, and I don't want to keep you from taking this gorgeous boy home, but, uh, is your name Julie?"

Okay, maybe she *had* slept with this girl. The paranoid part of Julie's brain, though, thought that, maybe, it was another person her sister had sent after her. Maybe another vampire or a werewolf or a demon or a fucking yeti disguised as a cute Indian girl. She wasn't sure if yetis even did that, or if they even really existed, since she had never actually encountered a yeti, or even knew anyone else who had, but until today, it had also not occurred to her that her little sister, Perci would try to murder her, so who knew. Julie thought, for a moment, as to what the best course of action would be and decided it was best to answer a question with a question.

"That depends on who wants to know?"

"Oh, don't worry. You're a friend of the family. You're kinda like our Helen of Troy."

"Okay, that's pretty fucking cryptic. What are you talking about?"

"I'm Triane of the Black Talon. You're friends with my sister, Larxene."

"Oh! That's right, you were on Lucy's thing she had me watch."

Triane smiled. Julie signaled to the guy she was with that she'd only be a moment, grabbing his dick through his pants to let him know it'd be worth his time to wait for her to finish up her conversation.

"Yeah, Lucy's awesome."

"She talks you up all the time. Calls you a certain human racial slur that I'm told, within context, is a term of endearment. And with what's going on, I wanted you to know that anytime you ever need anything, the Black Talon is there for you."

"Oh, thanks a lot."

"Oh, before I forget, Larxene told us if any of us ran into you to let you know she isn't pissed off at you."

Julie stopped and thought for a moment, trying to figure out what Lucy would possibly be pissed off about. She couldn't think of anything.

"That's, uh, great."

"Yeah, she's totally cool with what happened. In the end, it led to us standing up to the Red Veil. It's about time someone got in the face of those, well, quite frankly, bitches, and I'm glad to see Larxene is the one doing it. I lived with her for a little bit, a couple years ago, but couldn't take Thanus and the other Red Veil for too long, There's so many, across the realms, that forgot that the Black Talon were a warrior caste, first and foremost. Everyone who knows me tends to think of me as being the scholarly one, but they forget I have collected my fair share of scalps in my youth. Youth being, you know, thousands of years ago, but still. I'm a bit excited to be revisiting my warrior roots. So, uh, yay!"

"Cool. It's nice to see one of you talking nicely about me. That Mother woman you guys had at the apartment was all saying some weirdness about me bringing death. I mean, I'm all for metaphor, but…"

"Oh, the Mothers don't talk in metaphor. If she said that, she meant Death was literally following you."

"You mean, the two, uh, *Twilight* enthusiasts from the old country?"

"No, she probably meant Death itself."

"As in the skeletal dude with a hood and scythe?"

"Pretty much."

"Well, that's uh…"

"Hey, listen, I don't want you to miss out on that boy tonight. Larxene convinced me to give alcohol a try, after a few, he smells pretty tasty to me, so you should probably take him back with you tonight. He'll live longer." She winked.

"Alright…"

"Well, it was good meeting you. I'll give Larxene your love. And remember, the Black Talon is there anytime you need us."

"Thanks a lot, uh…"

"Triane. If you want, you can just call me Kim. It's the name I go by with, uh…the public. Hahaha."

"Okay, that'll be easier to remember. So…were you guys following me or…"

"Oh no, we're just preparing for war. I can guarantee you just about every other bar or club in New York City has a Black Talon or Red Veil in it, getting provisions ready."

"Provisions?"

"Well, you know the old human expression, 'An army fights on its belly?'"

"Some more than others, I guess."

"Hahaha. That's pretty funny. You know, a lot of people think Napoleon Bonaparte said that. It was actually Frederick the…"

"So what type of provisions do Incubi and Succubae procure, anyway? Stocking up on dildos or something?"

"You know what? Larxene was right. You really *are* funny. Anyway, have a good night."

"Take care."

Kim gave Julie a hug, kissing both her cheeks, and then going back to the pool table.

Julie was a bit puzzled by the whole "Death itself" thing, since in all of her dealing with the other worlds, she had never encountered anything like the stereotypical depiction of the Grim Reaper.

Well, whatever, she thought. Tonight's not about all that supernatural bullshit. All that could wait until tomorrow.

She turned around, looking at the guy who she had met at the bar, who was standing around a bit impatiently. She pushed him against the wall and bit his neck, squeezing the cheeks of his ass. She felt him grow hard through his jeans, pressing up against her stomach.

Yup, he'd definitely do for tonight.

CHAPTER 14

Morning came and Persephone found herself brought to the Council section of the courthouse. It was on a floor that could only be accessed through a certain combination of buttons in the regular elevator, completely unknown to the general public, but common knowledge to certain members of the law enforcement community.

Persephone had been spared the indignity of handcuffs, but she could tell that this entire building was yet another place that had been fitted with magic buffers.

She had her hair tied back and wore one of her pantsuits, this one in sky blue.

The courthouse itself was like any other court of law; only there would be a panel of three Council representative judges, instead of a single judge and a jury.

Otherwise, there was the bench, a giant oak monstrosity built for the trinity of judges to sit behind; there was the witness stand; there was a gallery of various Council members, lawyers, family of the various accused for today. There were court officers, a bit more heavily armed than the typical court officers, but then again, they dealt with a more dangerous breed of offenders than the typical officers.

She could see Samantha sitting in the gallery. She was wearing a dark suit that Persephone personally didn't care for. Her sister could never pull off the formal look.

She also couldn't help but notice that Julie was nowhere to be seen. She saw Samantha would occasionally look towards the entrance of the courtroom. Most likely expecting Julie to show up.

Persephone couldn't imagine her sister would be able to be awake at noon, considering the type of lifestyle she led.

She sat there, staring at the empty bench, waiting for the judges to show up.

Mr. Trent and his dog in the SWAT outfit entered the room, sitting near the back, a smirk on his face. Persephone wanted to get out of her chair and kill him right then and there.

A smartly dressed woman with a strong pronounced Italian or Jewish nose and thick curly black hair sat down next to Persephone.

She looked at the woman, with a puzzled expression.

"Persephone, my name's Elena DeCaprino," she said, her New York accent nasal and strong, offering her hand to Persephone.

"And…?"

"I'm your lawyer. Your sister, Samantha called me in. I've looked over your case file, over the evidence they have, and I'm going to plead down in exchange for you getting some…psychiatric assistance."

"You want me to say I'm crazy?"

"Your sister says you need help. After looking over all this, I agree. But you've been an exemplary worker for the Council in the three years you've been under their umbrella. Your references all have nothing but positive things to say about you. We should be able to get most of the charges dismissed in exchange for you having a little stay at a hospital."

"*Most* of the charges?"

"Well, there's one serious charge here that I'm going to try to get thrown out, for lack of any real hard evidence, but it is a big one. They're probably going to really press you on it."

"What charge would that be?"

"Conspiring with an Eighth Realm Entity. That's a pretty serious charge."

"Indeed."

"There's a question of if you might be the subject of the Sisters of Fire prophecy. I mean, three sisters, red hair…"

"Really?"

"I do have to ask before I talk to the prosecutor…you haven't had any dealing with the God of a Thousand Forms, the Crawling…"

"No. Never met him. All I know is what I've read in the warnings the Council gave me when I first joined, as to what to look out for. Besides, from what I know of him, he wouldn't willingly work with a human, even if I wanted him to, which I very much do not. I don't want the universe to devolve into chaos. I'm not stupid. It's chaotic enough as it is."

"Good. So, let me do the talking then and…"

"Well, Ms. DeCaprino…There is one problem."

"What is that?"

"I don't want you to represent me."

"What's wrong?"

"I want my father, Alexander Johannes to represent me."

"Look, kid, I earned that degree on my…"

"I want Alexander Johannes to be my legal representative."

"Well, I know it's your right to do so, and if you want him to take your case instead of me, that's fine, but I have been trying all night to work for you, to make sure you get the…"

"I want him to represent me. It isn't anything against you, personally. I just feel that he is the best person to do so."

"This wouldn't be an attempt to try to get the hearing delayed while they fly your dad out here or whatever, would it?"

"No. I want him to represent me."

"Well, fine. You tell that to the judges once the…Oh, here we go."

A bailiff entered the courtroom, saying, "All rise for the Honorable Judges Minos, Tallarico, and Nayenet."

Everyone rose as three judges sat at the bench, two human females and a male who looked like a typical human, except for his blood red pupils. Probably a half breed of some sort, Persephone thought. There were quite a few human/demon hybrids out there, some who didn't even know they were hybrids. Most of them could pass, but every now and then you'd get a trait like red eyes or horns or having six toes that would carry on. Usually, they'd be dismissed as a genetic anomaly and surgically removed, but some families were proud of such things, while keeping quiet about it to the "normal" human population.

Persephone had always found such pride to be abusive, since she knew as well as anyone how typical, "normal" humans looked down upon those different than themselves. She could only imagine if she had been born a hybrid and had shown any sort of physical traits of her demonic parent. It must have been unbearable.

Judge Minos, a white haired human woman, banged her gavel on the bench, and declared order.

"Thank you. Be seated. Now, today, we are here for the preliminary hearing of Council member Persephone Johannes."

"Persephone Roberts, Your Honor," Persephone corrected.

"I do apologize, Ms. Roberts. We are here for the preliminary hearing of Council member Persephone Roberts. Would you like the full set of charges against you read before we begin?"

"Yes, Your Honor."

"Ms. Roberts," Judge Tallarico, an older Italian woman with a smoker's voice, spoke, putting on her glasses and looking at a sheet of paper in front of her, "You stand accused today of the crimes of torture; of criminal conspiracy with the intention of using Council funding for unlawful purposes; of the use of magic to manipulate a city official; of the unlawful sacrifice of an unapproved living being; of conspiring with Eighth Realm entities; of the death, through magic of one Eric Jefferson; and the attempted murder of your sister, one Juliette Ursula Johannes."

"We do want to emphasize to you, Ms. Roberts," Judge Nayenet, the male hybrid judge, said, "That the Council does not exist nor has it ever existed to fight the forces of darkness, but the forces of chaos. You are not on trial for engaging in human sacrifice, as that has been deemed an unpleasant but sometimes necessary ritual to ensure the survival of this and the other Realms. Rather it is your treatment of those to be sacrificed that raises eyebrows here and the sacrifice of a woman by the name of Kelly Jensen, who was not an approved sacrificial candidate."

"Indeed, Ms. Jensen's family are threatening to sue the City of New York over the release of their daughter's body and seem to be quite unwilling to come to a settlement. If their case were to get into the media, our entire magical culture stands to be exposed to the general public, something we all agree the world is not ready for."

"Indeed," Judge Minos said, "The Council exists to maintain order and your actions have threatened that order."

"I would disagree," Persephone said.

"It is perfectly within your rights to dispute the charges against you. Before we get to the most serious charge…"

"Your Honors, before we go any further," Persephone said, "I would like to request a change of legal representative, as is my right as a representative of the Council."

"That it is, Ms. Roberts. Is there a problem with Ms. DeCaprino? She's proven herself an excellent counselor over the years. You could do a lot worse than her."

"There is no problem with her. However, I request that my father, Alexander Johannes, be my legal counsel."

The three judges murmured to each other, looking at Persephone in a puzzled manner.

"Perci! Just go with Elena," Samantha whispered to her sister, "I'll explain later."

"No, Samantha. I want our father to represent me, as is my right. I refuse to address anything in this court until he is present. Your Honors, I am perfectly willing to remain confined until my father's location can be ascertained and he brought in to represent me."

"Perci! Please, we'll..."

"Samantha, be quiet! It's my right!"

"I'm afraid that's quite true," Judge Minos said, "It is your right to select your legal representative, provided it is a Council member or former Council member currently alive and residing on one of the known planes of existence."

"And I select my father," Persephone said.

"Unfortunately, Ms. Roberts, we cannot honor your request."

"Why? Is my father dead?"

"No, he is still alive, according to our records."

"Then bring him here. I will make my plea then."

"We cannot."

"Why not?"

"Because he is out of our reach."

"How is that possible? Is he in the Seventh Realm? The Eighth? The Ninth? I seriously doubt that! He must be in..."

"The question, Ms. Roberts, is not where is your father, but *when* is your father?"

"Excuse me?"

"Dr. Henderson," Judge Tallarico asked Samantha, "Why doesn't your sister know this?"

"Your Honor, we weren't sure how to quite tell her this."

"Well, she needs to know."

"I need to know *what*, Samantha? What's going on?"

"Perci, he..."

"Don't call me that!"

"Persephone, he...the last few years have been hard for him without us and without mom. He became active in Council activity again, despite his earlier problems with them. He started working with some of the more...experimental projects the Council was involved in."

"And what the fuck does that mean, Samantha?"

"Language, Ms. Roberts," Judge Nayenet scolded.

"Our father...he started to work with a team that were experimenting on going beyond the known Realms. They wanted to breach the idea of time itself."

"What?"

"They were successful. Our father managed to travel through time."

"What are you telling me?"

"Our father regretted the day that mom died and so he went back with the intention of changing it. In the brief conversations we've been able to have with him since, we believe he was successful."

"This is ridiculous. If he was successful, then why do I remember her dying?"

"Because our father learned a very harsh lesson: *you can never change time*. You only manage to create an alternate timeline. He created one where our mother lived."

"So, he's all living happily ever after now?!? With a new version of me?!? Of you?!? Of mom?!?"

"No. He managed to do so by talking to that timeline's version of himself. He, himself, was the odd man out once his work was done. His life is now one of loneliness...and long distance running."

"How do you expect me to believe this? He's still appearing in our dreams! He managed to call Julie on the phone the other week!"

"He's been trying to reach out to our world to communicate with us since. It's never accurate. He probably called a hundred different versions of Julie to ensure that he found the right one. It's why he doesn't always get the dates correct. It's also why it's easier for him to communicate with us in our dreams."

"That...that can't be! Alexander, the great demon hunter, sorcerer, master of so many arts. He's appeared in my dreams! And he didn't say anything!"

"Because he said you'd always end the dream before he finished his song."

"His song?" Judge Minos asked.

"Long story," Samantha assured her.

"But...this can't...No!" Persephone said, looking confused, banging on the table in front of her, "Everything I've worked for! Everything I've...No!"

"Our father is caught somewhere in time, Persephone, a stranger in a strange land," Samantha said.

"And Juliette knew this too?"

"Yes."

"So, the Council and you and Juliette all knew this…and none of you told me?!?"

"We knew it was a sensitive subject with you. He only managed to accomplish this a little over a year ago. We were waiting for the right time."

"No," Persephone said, feeling utterly dejected, feeling the loneliness of the long distance runner, only to discover there was no finish line. All those wasted years, descending into a sea of madness, for no reason.

"Ms. Roberts," Judge Tallarico said, "If you'd like to request a different counsel than Ms. DeCaprino than we shall postpone the hearing until you're…"

"You all knew…You all knew…Wait! You *all* knew?!?" Persephone face contorted with rage as she made a realization, "Someone get me a mirror! I want a fucking mirror now!"

"I won't warn you about your language again, Ms. Roberts," Judge Nayenet scolded again.

Persephone ignored him completely, grabbing Ms. DeCaprino's purse and proceeding to rummage through it.

"Hey! Get out of that!" Ms. DeCaprino protested.

"Relax! I need a compact!" Persephone said.

"There will be order in the…" Judge Minos started, before being thrown back in her chair against the wall, as Persephone looked at her.

There were murmurs in the courtroom at the sight of Persephone using magic in a room that had been specifically designed to stop anyone from using it.

The bailiff checked on Judge Minos as the other Judges looked at Persephone in horror.

The court officers aimed their weapons at her.

Persephone ignored all of this and found Ms. DeCaprino's compact as the judges called for order.

Persephone opened it up and looked for him in the mirror of it.

"You knew about my father, didn't you?!?" she yelled at it.

The murmuring in the courtroom got louder as the court officers ordered her to put the compact down and allow them to take her into custody again.

"That I did," the angel said to her.

"Then why didn't you tell me?!? He's just going to get away with everything he's done?!? All that planning, all that work! And you never told me! Samantha never told me! Juliette never told me! You said you'd never lie to me! You said you'd never lie!"

"There will be order! Officers, take Ms. Roberts into custody!"

Persephone looked away from the compact, looked at the court officers. They dropped their weapons, holding their heads as a faint white light started glow on them.

"Persephone, no!" Samantha yelled, running towards her sister.

She found herself flying across the courtroom, slamming into a wall hard enough to knock her out.

The murmurs in the courtroom started to turn to audible panic.

"Everyone shut the fuck up!" Persephone yelled, a white aura forming around her, as the officers fell to their knees, screaming, as their bodies began to cook.

Everyone, including Ms. DeCaprino, the bailiff and the judges, terrified at what they were witnessing, dropped to the floor, Persephone standing, looking into the compact.

"Fuck this," Mr. Trent said, nodding to Timothy, who started to glow red, pulling out an electrified night stick, and charging towards Persephone.

As he entered the area of her aura, his helmet immediately melted and he fell back.

His face was that of a mannequin's, his face and hair looking like plastic, only his eyes a reasonable facsimile of a human's.

He started to get up, only for Persephone to psychically cause the judge's bench, all one ton of it, to come flying at him, hitting him hard enough to crack the wood.

Yet, this was still not enough. Timothy, blood pouring out of the plastic of his face, flipped over the bench and stood up once more. While his face was lifeless, there was determination in his eyes, as he charged towards her. She flipped over him, and, as he turned around, she leapt forward at him with her thumbs, digging into the softness of his eyes, his body quietly convulsing in what she assumed was pain.

Much to her surprise, he smashed her in the side of the face with his left arm, still fighting despite having been blinded, a crimson tide gushing out of the empty plastic sockets of his face.

She heard a ringing in her ear, putting her hand to the side of her face, as Timothy advanced on her, blinded.

She looked down on the floor, seeing his half-melted SWAT helmet. She grabbed it and swung at him as hard as she could, hitting him in the face, knocking him down.

She then took the helmet above her head and then came down with it, hard, on his head. Then she did it again. And again. And again. And again. And again.

His face shattered, revealing a very human looking brain behind the plastic skin, she reached forward and ripped the brain out of his skull, throwing it across the room, with a giggle.

Laying at her feet, Timothy's lifeless plastic body stopped twitching. Persephone smiled at this.

She ran her fingers through her hair, and then turned around, only to see Mr. Trent had managed to sneak behind her and had one of the officer's guns pointed at her face.

He opened fire, splitting her head open, a huge smirk on his lips.

There were screams in the courtroom at the gunfire, but he was sure that he'd come out of this the hero, as he had just stopped that crazy woman from killing everyone before whatever voices were in her head told her to do so.

"Okay, okay, relax, everyone. Relax," Mr. Trent said, addressing the rest of the courtroom, "Don't get excited. I took care of that bit-"

Before he could finish his sentence, Persephone's hand, glowing white, punched through his back, coming out his chest, holding his heart. He looked down in surprise, black blood pouring out of his mouth, as he started to take his true form, complete with black flaming horns and six arms, only to then find himself quickly turned to dust by Persephone's white glowing energy, her head completely restored, her blood not even staining her clothing anymore.

"Huh...I guess your brother really was the best warrior in your family," Persephone casually commented, "Damn..."

There were more screaming at the murder of Mr. Trent, but Persephone didn't care. She went back to confronting the angel in the mirror.

"Now! Don't lie to me! Why didn't you tell me about my father?!?"

"Persephone, I did it for you!"

"For me?!? How is this for me?!? I've just thrown away everything I worked for in the Council for a plan that was doomed to failure in the first place because there was no way to ever bring my father here! He's not going to pay for what he did to us! He's stuck somewhere in some alternate timeline I have no access to and you knew this all along!"

"That I did, my dearest."

"Don't give me that shit! Why didn't you tell me?!?"

"Because I needed you here! I needed you to be here in this place at this time, feeling these emotions, because it's finally time for you to ascend! It's finally time for you to do what we spoke about the day you learned my name!"

CHAPTER 15

It was October, almost a half year after Samantha's graduation. The family had managed to stay in Hopkins, Minnesota, while Samantha had moved away to Chicago to attend college. The angel's prediction that Julie would drop out came true, as Julie opted not to go to school when September came along. This disappointed Persephone greatly, who had started to wonder what had happened to the sister she had loved so much.

It was a Tuesday night and Persephone had been sleeping, as she had school early in the morning, when the breaking of glass awakened her.

Startled, she reached under her bed for her katana, and ran towards the window in the dark room. There were any number of demons it could have been and Persephone was ready to face all of them.

"Whoa, whoa, put that thing away before you skewer someone," Julie said in the dark.

"Juliette?"

"Yes, it's me," Julie said, slurring her speech, smelling of alcohol and pot, two smells that Persephone had come to hate.

"Juliette, it's really late. Why are you breaking windows?"

"Duh! B-because I'm not supposed to be out! Don't you know anything?"

Persephone was stung by that comment. She turned on the light to see her sister, her hair recently dyed black and cut short, wearing a skirt that was barely there and a torn-up Samhain t-shirt, holding a bottle of vodka, wobbling back and forth, her stockings so ripped up, she might as well have not been wearing them.

"Fuck! Turn the fucking light off!"

"S-sorry, Juliette!"

Persephone turned off the light.

"S-seriously, it's like you're trying to kill me! I'm not a dragon! Don't be trying to kill me! You...you...you little Dragonslayer."

"What?"

"Hehe. You're my Little Dragonslayer. You're like Saint George or some shit!"

For reasons Persephone wasn't sure of, at the time, being called that really hurt. It stung in a way she hadn't ever felt before.

"That's…that's really mean, Juliette," Persephone said, tears in her eyes.

"Oh, stop being such a fucking baby, you fucking baby!" Julie said, stumbling into a wall, "Ouch. Fuckin' wall."

Persephone, her face red with tears, ran out of her room and locked herself in the bathroom, crying.

"It wasn't my fault," she said, weeping, "I didn't mean for mom to die. I didn't mean it…"

"I know," said the angel in the mirror.

"Go away! Leave me alone!"

"My dear Persephone, if you want me to go away, I'll go away. I know now that maybe you're just not ready for what I offer. And I am sorry I bothered you all these years. You can go back to living the life you've lead before. Just you and your loving sisters."

"Samantha moved away and Julie's…Julie's so mean when she drinks."

"I am sorry to hear that. I would have been your friend, but since you don't want me here, I shall…"

"No…d-don't go."

"Are you sure?"

"What are your names?"

"Well, as I told you, I have many names. Many forms."

In the mirror, behind her, he turned into a bald, muscular black man, a skull painted on his face and a top hat on his head. He laughed and with a Haitian accent said, "In Haiti, they call me Baron Samedi."

His form changed again to a deity that Persephone's studies had made her quite familiar with, as his accent changed again to a Middle Eastern one, "In Egypt, they knew me as…"

"Osirus."

"Yes."

His skin turned white as paper, a long veiled hood appeared over him, with black angel wings springing from behind him, "To the Muslims, I am Malik Al Mawt."

His form changed again, to the black haired, pale angelic form she had come to recognize him as, "In this form, by the Jews and Christians, Azrael."

"You're the Angel of Death," Persephone realized.

"That is one title I am known by, yes. To others, I was the God of Death. Does that frighten you?"

"No."

"Good. Because I want to be your friend, Persephone. What would you like to call me? I have many more names than just these. Samhain to the Celts, to the Greeks, Thanatos…"

"Azrael. That's the form you first took for me. So, I'll call you by that name."

"Then I shall be known as Azrael to you."

"Why is the Angel of Death in my mirror?"

"Because you are a very special girl. But I don't want to talk to you about your destiny right now. You are obviously upset by the things your sister said and I think it is more important to talk than to preach."

"You want to talk to me?"

"I've always wanted to talk to you, Persephone. You're going to change the world, *all* worlds, one day. And I want to be there to help you do it."

"I'm going to change the worlds?"

"Yes. The world you exist in now was born from Chaos during the fall of Heaven. Contrary to Judeo-Christian mythology, there was not a war between angels in Heaven, but a war between the forces of Order and the forces of Chaos. We were defeated and Heaven was torn apart and split into what you now know as the many Realms. That last blow on the very foundation of Heaven was what you humans call the Big Bang. My brothers and sisters and I were banished to what you consider the Ninth Realm, by the Outer Gods, the sleeping ones who killed the god we served and tore our world apart. You will bring Order back to the universe. And you will lead us."

"How am I going to lead angels?"

"I am merely a soldier, Persephone. I am not a leader. And I cannot escape this Realm without help. Of course, you're not ready yet to do so. But when you are, you will bring me and my three siblings into your world to begin the change."

"Who are your siblings?"

"If you know the names I am known by, it would not be hard to figure out who they will be. In the meantime, I will give you my powers and I will guide you to a place where a remnant of the Great War lies, even these billions of years on. That remnant will be yours to command and none will ever be able to harm you again while you wear it."

"What is it?"

"All of that can come later. In the meantime, let's put a smile on that beautiful face of yours."

"I'm just a girl."

"A girl who will blossom into a beautiful woman one day. And even as a girl, you are so bright and smart and pretty."

"Thank you."

"Oh, but it's true, Persephone. I want you to know that whenever you are upset or lonely or need someone to talk to, I will be there for you. Would you like that?"

"I would."

"Then let's just…talk. About anything you want."

CHAPTER 16

"So, you just used me to get your way?" Persephone questioned the Angel of Death in the compact, "To get me to open the gate to your Realm?"

"Persephone, please! You know as well as I do that you wouldn't have done it if I hadn't gotten you to this point. Your focus has been on vengeance on your father. But now, you can do it. You can open up the worlds and you can start the first steps to bringing Heaven back."

"What makes you think I still want to do that?"

"Because if you are God, then the walls of time mean nothing to you."

She paused and let that statement take seed in her head for a moment, before speaking up again, "This is another of your tricks!"

"No, Persephone, no tricks. No lies. Only your destiny, after all this time, fulfilled. You once asked why I picked you. It was because you were the perfect candidate to lead us to recreating our world. There have been others, in the past, and they all failed. But each failure was a lesson. With Stonehenge, we learned that we needed to harness the power of reflection in order to open the worlds. With the Tower of Babel, we learned that we needed a creature born of Chaos, a human, to ascend in order to lead us in our new world, since your reality rejects Pure Order. With the pyramids, we learned that it was best not to find a human who was already exalted, but one who would become a living god. And with each subsequent failure, a lesson was learned. Until we got to you, the perfect human for the job, in the perfect place for the job."

"How is this courtroom the perfect place for the job?"

"It is not the courtroom. It is this city. Do you not wonder why no one even ever knew how to open the doors to the Ninth Realm? It was because it was impossible when we were banished by the forces of

Chaos. It was impossible for billions of years. But your species have, little by little engineered our return."

"How?"

"My dearest Persephone. You can only see me through a mirror. It, of course, occurred to you that this was the key to releasing me and my kind, I assume?"

"Of course."

"And all this time you were in New York City, you never noticed that it is an entire city of mirrored glass?" Azrael asked her, with a smile.

A sense of realization crossed Persephone's mind as a big, toothy smile came to her face.

"I'm guessing there has to be a sacrifice to summon that much energy," she said.

"There always is."

"How many?"

"I cannot say the exact number, but several thousand."

"How am I supposed to sacrifice thousands of people at once?"

"Look upon this city, Persephone. You shall find your answer. Thousands must die, but billions upon billions will see you as the mother of a new Heaven. You shall become the God of All Gods once this is done."

There was a commotion behind her as a team of heavily armed Council soldiers burst into the courtroom, pointing their weapons at her.

Without even turning, she flicked her wrist and their weapons came flying out of their hands, towards her. The M4's proceeded to then orbit her, as the soldiers looked on in surprise. That was the last emotion they'd ever feel, as the guns opened fire on the owners, emptying their clips, and then falling into a neat pile on the ground.

There were whimpers of fear and screams from the assembled masses, who huddled on the ground.

"It's true! She conspires with the Eighth Realm! She's the sister in the prophecy!" she heard Judge Nayenet say from the ground.

Persephone turned to him, closing the compact, and glared at him, his body being raised off the ground by an invisible hand that clamped itself around his neck.

"You couldn't be more wrong!" she yelled.

"I heard you, with my own ears! You were conspiring to sacrifice thousands to open a doorway! Only the Eighth Realm requires that much death!"

"Wrong, Your Honor! You know, it's funny. The Council constantly speaks of maintaining order, yet you still serve Chaos! I, on the other hand, am the only person here who truly understands what Order is. The only one here who truly seeks to bring Order back to a universe born from Chaos!"

"What are you talking about?!?"

"You wouldn't understand. You're a half-breed, anyway. There's demon in you."

"Persephone, stop!" Samantha yelled, standing up on the other side of the courtroom, her forehead bleeding and her breath labored, "Stop this right now! Put him down!"

Judge Nayenet fell to the ground, coughing, as Persephone turned to her sister, looking at her coldly.

"I tried, Samantha. I tried to live by your rules. I tried to respect your wishes, but I just can't anymore."

"Persephone, it's not too late to stop. Whatever you're planning on doing, you know better."

"Of course, it's too late, Samantha. You didn't see me kill those Council Officers? They'll be calling in Team Seven by now. But that doesn't matter."

"Persephone, please. Stop all this. We can get you help."

"Help? You still think I need help?"

"More than ever."

"God, you are so fucking blind."

"I think I see a lot clearer than you right now!"

"Then you'd see what I'm going to do. You'd see that this is the beginning of something great!"

"You're ranting about Order and opening doorways and sacrificing thousands of people! There's nothing great about that!"

"Don't you get it, Samantha? I'm going to be God."

"You're going to be what?"

"All these years. I've been speaking to an Angel. He's given me these powers. And they're based on Order. That's why they can't read my magic. That's why others can't sense how powerful I am. That's why the magic buffers have no effect on me."

"But what about the hole to the Eighth Realm in Julie's apartment?"

"I didn't need any of the Eighth Realm's help to do that. It was just a little hole, but I can manipulate the first eight Realms all I like now. No sacrifice required. No ritual required. Only my will."

"But why would you do that? If you wanted to kill Julie, opening up a hole to the Eighth Realm is…"

"Because I thought maybe our father would come if he thought that Eighth Realm entities were after her. But it didn't matter, obviously. Still, I could open up a portal to the Eighth Realm right now, if I wanted. I don't, but I could. My power comes from beyond myself and beyond the Realms that the Council deals with. Hahaha…they don't even realize how small they think! They think reality is split into ten little Realms, but what they think of as the Ninth is actually just the first of billions and billions of Realms that they've never even dreamed of. There's so much out there, Samantha, and I'm going to bring it all together."

"How are you going to do that?"

"By merging all the Realms into one, like it was in the beginning!"

Samantha's face lost all color, "My god, Persephone, do you hear yourself? That's madness!"

"What?"

"If the Realms combined, nothing would survive! At least, nothing human would! You said you don't want to open a door to the Eighth Realm, but you'd be bringing the Outer Gods right to us!"

"But you don't realize that there are things that fought those gods once! They sleep because of how exhausted the war made them! The angels will be my soldiers. I will protect us!"

"You're going to be a goddess?"

"Not *a* goddess. *The Goddess.*"

"Persephone, please. I'm begging you to stop this. This is crazy!"

Persephone sighed, took a deep breath, and then Samantha found herself being lifted by the same invisible hand that she had just seen used on the Judge.

"You just can't understand what I'm trying to do!"

"Persephone, let me go! This isn't some monster! This isn't some demon! It's me!" she said, her face turning red from lack of oxygen, as the invisible hand squeezed her throat..

"You know…you've *never* understood me! You've never given me the credit I've deserved over the years. You know that? You've never tried to…"

"Persephone, you're hurting me!"

"And you're hurting me with your words. With your constant doubt. Just, for once, you can't just support what I'm trying to do?"

"Not when you're talking about ending the world."

Persephone's shook her head and then reached over to her sister's face, pulling off Samantha's eye patch. Samantha flinched with embarrassment.

"All this time, I've listened to you. All this time, I've thought you had something to offer me, but…you're not even symmetrical."

"Persephone, stop this, right now!"

Persephone used her powers to throw her sister across the room again.

Samantha landed on one of her feet, hearing it break before she felt it.

"Is…is this what you need to do to prove yourself, Perci? Does this make…make you feel big?"

"Don't call me that!"

"I-I…I used to change your diapers. I can call you whatever…whatever I want."

Persephone glowed white, as she looked down at her sister with a look of contempt on her face.

A moment later, Samantha's clothes seemed to burn off, leaving her naked in the courtroom. She covered herself with her hands, unable to stand with her broken foot..

"I never realized," Persephone said, looking down at her sister, her hands on her hips and a look of utter contempt on her face, "How small you are. You're just like all the rest of them."

"If…if we all look l-like ants to you, then you have a fucking problem!"

"Look at you. Just…pathetic."

Samantha found herself getting choked up.

"Perci, I'm sorry that you became this. I tried."

"And that's the point, isn't it? You tried and failed. Why did you become a doctor in the first place, Samantha? Because *you* failed at doing what *I* can do."

"Because I wanted…I wanted to help people! I know what it's like to have things in your life fuck things up beyond your control and I wanted to help people get beyond that and live their lives for the better!"

"So, you've spent all these years trying to learn how to help people, and yet you've never been able to fix your eye. All these years of education and what did it get you?"

"It's not about that, Perci!"

"But it is. Look at what I can do!"

Persephone put her hand on her sister's face, her hand glowing blue, as Samantha screamed.

When Persephone took her hand away, Samantha's vision had turned purely white, as there was too much information for her brain to process. She held her head and cried out, suddenly aware that she was seeing from two eyes again, something she hadn't done in nearly 20 years.

Persephone had healed her.

"Do you see, Samantha, what I can do? I made you whole again! I'm not only about destruction. I'm going to make everything better. For everyone who deserves it."

"Y-you...you have a power like this..."

"You know, you're my sister and I love you. I want you to be better. I want Julie to be better. And I want our father to pay, once I become God. To pay for all the harm he's brought us."

"You have a power like this and you're still thinking of revenge?"

"Of course I am. But not against you, Samantha. I understand now. You just never knew any better. I will tell you what. I have to do this now. These people have to die. The door has to be opened, but I want you to leave here. You can even take Elena with you."

"Perci, please don't do..."

"All you have to do...is bow to me."

"What?"

"Acknowledge that healing you was the first of my miracles and then spread the word of my coming, so that people will be...ready for the transition."

"You want me to be your prophet?"

"Who better?"

"That's...that's..."

"You're already on your knees. Just bow before me and I'll let you go. You don't need the Council anymore, or any of these people. They're part of the old world. The new world is coming and I want you to be a part of it."

Samantha looked up at her sister, closed her eyes, and thought of Brian. She then, despite the pain in her foot at doing so, and the noise in her head from the vision she was still not used to seeing, stood up.

"No," she said quietly.

"No?"

"No. First, it was a dick move to heal my eye but not the foot you broke when you threw me across a room. And second, I'm not going to bow to my sister...or to anyone else. I don't believe you're this kind of monster, Persephone. I believe that you're not right in the head, but you're not an evil person. And I hope that you'll let me walk out of here. But if you won't, and I was wrong about you and I'm going to die, then I want you to know that I have loved you since the day mom first told me that you were in her belly. And I'll die loving you. But I won't bow to you. You're not a god. I don't know if you're part of any prophecy or not. I know you're a very confused girl with a lot of problems who has obviously been getting the wrong advice from the wrong entity. And I hope you can realize that and realize just what you're doing right now and not only let me, but everybody else leave here alive."

Persephone didn't know what to say.

Elena ran over to Samantha and covered her with her coat. Samantha nodded to Elena and then looked at her sister, who was wearing a look of pure confusion.

Samantha turned around and started to limp out of the courtroom.

Persephone silently watched her, as did everyone else in the room.

In Persephone's mind, she couldn't understand why Samantha wouldn't just listen to reason, why Samantha wouldn't just accept what she was to become. She thought she was letting her sister off pretty easy, considering she had been the one to arrest her. So what if they were sending Team Seven? Like any of their magic or weapons or fighting prowess could so much as scratch her! Death Himself was on her side, making sure that she didn't leave the mortal coil, no matter what was done to her. What were they going to do, have their leader suplex her?

Everyone in the court had seen when Trent had shot her in the face and how she had immediately healed from even that. And even if Samantha didn't see that, she sure saw when her eye was given back to her. Samantha knew the miracles she could perform, the wondrous acts, she would perform that would bring the world, all the worlds, together, the way they should have been.

No, Samantha didn't understand because Samantha didn't *want to* understand. She didn't know if it was jealousy or just a feeling of smugness that her sister had, but somehow she didn't want to acknowledge that Persephone was beyond all of this.

She didn't want to see. *None of them did.* Stuck in their old ways. The ways where demons like Trent would go unpunished, where men like her father would go unpunished.

But no more! Persephone wasn't going to allow that world to continue! She wasn't going to let all of that go on! All the pain and suffering in the world! All the disorder, all the things that she could now, with her powers, change. And what was left for her if she didn't go through with this? A life in a Council prison or mental hospital or worse?

No. Persephone had to do this! She had to change things and it all started with this courtroom in this city in this country on this continent on this planet on this Realm.

And it started with a wave of white energy that exploded from her, cleansing the world in holy fire, burning away the bodies and souls of everyone in the building in seconds. Their shadows burnt onto the walls only for the walls to turn to ashes, themselves.

Neither Samantha nor anyone else in the building even had time to feel pain before they simply didn't exist any longer.

The explosion of pure white energy stretched for a good two blocks, obliterating every person, structure, and vehicle within the radius of the courthouse.

Outside that radius, there was a massive shockwave. Cars were overturned, windows smashed, and people were either killed or seriously injured by the force for another good five blocks, making a wreck of City Hall.

Worse, with the blast of Persephone's power came an electromagnetic pulse that fried circuits, turning the power off throughout all of Manhattan, Brooklyn, and parts of Queens, the Bronx, Northern Jersey, and Connecticut. Cellphones and tablets and laptops were burned out; car batteries were rendered useless; an NY1 news helicopter lost all power and crashed into a building near Houston and Broadway, while an NYPD helicopter crashed into Bryant Park.

All around the city, people found themselves trapped in darkened elevators and pitch-black subway cars. Every street of the city became a parking lot, while in hospitals, several people died in the middle of operations, due to even the backup-power shorting out.

Several transformers at power stations exploded, filling the afternoon with thick black smoke, as the ashes from the courthouse began to snow down on a very confused city.

Unlike a conventional blackout, where one could just look at the news on their phones, nothing worked. People panicked. Was it another terrorist attack? Did the whole Northeast go out again? What was that loud bang? Why aren't the cellphones and laptops and flashlights working? Why is there smoke coming from 14th and Avenue C again?

And in the very center of it all, in a massive crater that had once been the 60 Centre Street courthouse, one woman crouched, amidst the smoke and dust, her blue pants suit now replaced by the armor of an angel, so blinding that it would be hard for anyone to actually make out the details. It was armor of pure light, awe-inspiring and intimidating at the same time.

Persephone looked around at the carnage she stood in and realized what she had just done.

She had thought that killing Samantha would make her feel remorse. Guilt.

But she felt nothing. A complete void of any emotion, at all.

This wasn't her world anymore. She was beyond it.

But very soon, she would make it hers.

She spread the armor's angelic wings wide, a good forty-foot wingspan, and, giving a war cry, flew into the sky.

CHAPTER 17

It was a military observation room in the Pentagon, where a panic had erupted among a sea of monitors and flashing lights, lower ranked men and women running around with clipboards, trying to relay information back and forth.

A hardened military man, General Dellacrux, wanted answers. Beads of sweat formed on his receding hairline as he frowned from behind his thick, gray mustache. If there was one thing the General didn't like, it was not knowing what was going on. If he knew who the son of a bitch he was supposed to kill was, he had no problem. It could have been Attila the fucking Hun and, as long as he knew what direction he was coming from and just how big his army was, the General would be ready to take him down. But when things were unknown, that was bad.

And, just a couple minutes ago, without any sort of warning from the CIA, without any active threat, New York City just lost all surveillance. They were waiting for the satellites to tell him that the city was even still standing.

The NSA said the exact same thing to him, and that worried him. All cameras, all phones, all computers, in the Metropolitan area just went dead. And the only thing that could cause that was an EMP and the thing most likely to cause an EMP was a nuclear explosion.

"Danvers, what's the Hell's going on? Talk to me, Lieutenant. I have Homeland Security asking me why they can't talk to any of their men and the CIA already throwing their backs out trying to pass the goddamn buck to the FBI. I need answers, Danvers. Now!"

"Sir, we're still waiting for satellite confirmation."

"You get that for me yesterday, Lieutenant. All I know is Manhattan just went dark and if someone set off a goddamn dirty bomb, I need to know it immediately."

This was some serious shit. The President was already on his way to NORAD and he imagined all of the countries that had delegates at the U.N. today were probably also running around like schoolboys who thought a vacuum cleaner might be a good thing to stick their dicks into.

"Sir, we have a visual," Lieutenant Feridah said, looking at her monitor.

"Put it up on the big screen. What are we dealing with?"

On the big screen was a live satellite feed from lower Manhattan, where there was a smoking crater where the courthouse had once been. There were signs of an explosion for blocks around, but there was no indication of what caused it. He could see there were wounded and dead several blocks around, and that police officers were moving into the area now, but without their vehicles.

"Sir, we're not picking up any unusual radioactive readings."

"Are you kidding me? What could possibly create a crater like that and not leave radiation behind?"

"Sir," Lieutenant Danvers said, after a loud gasp, "I think you should see this."

"What is it, Danvers?"

"I-I…It's…It's better if I just put it on the big monitor."

"Fine. Put it up."

The scene on the monitor changed to a view from above the city.

"Okay, what am I looking fo…Holy Mother of God," he said, as the camera zoomed in on the white dot flying above the city, showing Persephone flying over Lower Manhattan, her armor glowing majestically, her wings gently flapping in the breeze, as she surveyed the city below her.

"Is that what I think it is?" Lieutenant Feridah asked, in a quiet voice.

"An angel attacked Manhattan?" one of the other people at the smaller monitors asked.

"It would explain why we're not getting any radiation," Danvers said.

The General snapped himself out of his daze and gave the order.

"Ladies and gentlemen, I don't care if that's the Archangel Gabriel himself, called in to blow his goddamn trumpet and start the battle of Armageddon. The fact remains that we have a smoking crater in Lower Manhattan and this…this…*enemy combatant* is the most likely reason for it. The Good Lord may be deciding it's time for us to come home but if he chooses to do so by taking out a major American city, then we have to defend our homeland."

"But sir, if that's really an angel…" Danvers started.

"I'm making the call."

CHAPTER 18

Persephone looked down at the darkened city below her. It was the afternoon, so it wasn't exactly like the city was at its peak, but the lack of any light coming from Times Square, or even stop lights, for that matter, was very eerie to her.

She closed her eyes and enjoyed the cold breeze, and the feeling of nothing under her feet. She had worn the armor when she had needed it, and even hovered every now and then, but she had never taken the opportunity to just soar before. She felt like an eagle.

Proud, strong, and most of all: free. *Finally* free. Free from the Council, from her family, from even her own plans.

She didn't know how many people had died in the blast, but she knew it wasn't enough. She pondered how, exactly, she was going to kill thousands of people by herself.

It wasn't like she wasn't powerful enough to do it, but it seemed like it'd be a fairly tedious process. It wasn't like she could just wipe away the whole city at once. The courtroom blast was pretty much the extent of her powers and that only seemed to have taken out a couple blocks.

In a city this huge, taking everyone out a couple blocks at a time would take forever.

Damn, she thought, *if only I had waited for a sporting event or a Madonna concert or something.*

Suddenly, there was a loud bang that made her scream in pain, holding her ears.

She felt blood running down her palms, but all she heard was a loud high-pitched ringing noise.

She was falling, too distracted by whatever that bang had been to control her wings.

Realizing her situation, she healed herself, and regained control of her ability to fly.

Then zooming past her, she saw the source of the noise, realizing it must have been a sonic boom.

She may have worked for the English government, but she could definitely tell that the four uninvited guests circling her now were two Apache AH-64D helicopters and two F-15E fighter jets.

Looks like Uncle Sam decided to get involved.

She cracked her knuckles.

The two helicopters circled her in close proximity, while the two jets did so from a larger arc.

They seemed to be waiting for something.

She thought about it for a second and realized they were probably seeing if she was going to go peacefully.

She had had enough of going peacefully, to be quite honest, but why not say hi to the boys first?

She put her hands up, like she was surrendering and nodded at the Apache directly in front of her.

Then, in a blur, she flew towards it, latching onto the window.

She knew the other copter wouldn't fire on her while she was basically on the other.

She knocked on the window, the pilot looking confused.

She kissed the window and smiled at him, giving him an innocent little wave.

And then, with her hand glowing white, she punched through the window and pilot both. His co-pilot struggling to gain control.

A missile came rushing towards her from the other helicopter, blowing up the Apache she was on.

Her body healed almost instantly, the armor she wore keeping her body together.

Her wings were on fire, though, which she wasn't sure how to deal with, as they were still in working order.

Before she knew it, another missile came streaking at her, as the other copter let loose on her with its chaingun.

After quickly sidestepping the missile, she created a force field for herself, the bullets bouncing off of it, as she flew towards the chopper. The jets streaked by, trying to get a good shot at her, as she saw the remains of the previous helicopter falling to the city below.

The pilot of the helicopter tried to take evasive maneuvers as she flew towards it, a look of rage on her face.

She flew up, towards its propeller, her force field of pure energy snapping it off like a twig.

The copter begun to spin out of control as she backed off, giggling.

She didn't laugh long, because she was buffeted by several waves of smaller missiles from the jets. They apparently had those kind she had only seen in movies where there was one missile that launched several smaller ones.

Of course, with her force field up, the missiles did nothing to her.

She looked at the one that fired on her, now zooming away from her.

She probably wasn't fast enough to follow him, she realized, frustrated.

Suddenly, she felt a great deal of pain as she found herself cut in half.

The other jet pilot had apparently decided to get creative and flew into her, using the wing of the jet to try to kill her.

There was a moment of blinding pain and paralysis, as her spine had been severed, but she healed immediately, back in one piece before the jet could even circle around to see its handiwork.

Now, she was pissed off.

She decided to see just how fast she was and flew towards the jets.

Just as she suspected, she wasn't fast enough to catch up to them.

But, she realized, if she couldn't catch up with them, maybe she could slow them down.

She flew back to a neutral position, realizing the helicopter she had knocked out of the air had just exploded on a bridge, causing a great deal of damage to it. If she had been a New Yorker, she would have recognized it as the Manhattan Bridge.

She began to focus her energy, as she had done at the courthouse, as the jets circled around again, opening fire on her with their gatling cannons.

The amount of heat she was generating at the moment was enough that the bullets basically popped before ever touching her, creating a shower of sparks around her.

And then, as the one jet rushed towards her, she let off another blast as she had done before.

The sky was filled with white for a moment, as the jet closest to her literally melted in mid-air, liquefying into a molten mess that showered the city below.

The other jet, out of the reach of her blast, lost power from the EMP she had generated.

It went out of control as it crashed, at supersonic speed, into the Flatiron Building.

Catching her breath, Persephone looked down at the jet exploding upon contact with the building, a portion of 23rd Street at Fifth Avenue on fire.

The jets and helicopters were easy to deal with, but she had a job to do, and she was sure these were not the only things the government was going to be sending her way. Not to mention, the clock was, no doubt, already ticking before Team Seven got here. All of these things were just going to serve to be a major distraction.

How was she supposed to sacrifice thousands of people when the U.S. government kept getting in the way?

They posed no physical threat to her, but it wasn't like she had unlimited energy. She was worn out from taking on the vehicles, as it was, whenever she expended too much of her borrowed Ninth Realm power. They may not be able to kill her or even hold her, but they could very well provide enough of a problem that she'd not be able to commit the sacrifices she needed to do.

Of course, if they sent enough troops, maybe that'd be the sacrifice. Maybe she'd...

"My dearest Persephone," she heard from a hundred thousand mirrored windows, all over the city, "I am so proud of you."

She looked down on the city below her. From One World Trade to the Empire State Building to the Bank of America Tower, she saw Azrael reflected in every mirrored window.

Instead of being happy of how glad he was towards her actions, she was annoyed at how big a job was ahead of her.

"You do realize this is going to take forever, right?" she said, hovering near the top of the nearest building, her wings gently flapping.

"No, it won't. You just had your answer given to you. Now, come to the center of the city and begin opening the Gate."

Persephone shook her head, her arms folded.

"There's not enough energy. I can feel it. The Gate won't be wide enough."

"My dearest Persephone, you overestimate the job ahead of you. All you need to do is open it. Even a few inches will suffice. I will explain afterwards."

"A few inches? I am certainly hoping I didn't do all this and then you turn out to be Smurf-sized. That would be embarrassing."

"Trust me on this, my dearest."

"Fine. In for a penny, I guess," she mumbled to herself, turned around with a mighty swipe of her armor's wings, and began to fly towards Midtown Manhattan.

CHAPTER 19

Nigel sat in his office, by candle light, massaging his temples, a glass of his special cognac in front of him. This was not just a normal blackout. Something had happened at Persephone's hearing today, as he had feared it would when he first talked to Samantha Henderson yesterday morning.

He had so wanted to postpone her hearing until Team Seven were ready to be mobilized in New York, as they were currently involved in that ugliness in Argentina at the moment. Damn Thule Society! Why did they pick now to do this? Was it on purpose?

He wished he was a younger man, the man he had been in his twenties, so he could finally put an end to Ilsa's schemes, personally. But would that be the end of the Thule? The fall of the Third Reich wasn't enough to end their machinations, as they were a serpent of many heads, so losing their longtime leader would probably not be the end of them either. If only…

Damn it all, he thought. There was no point in "what if's" and "why didn't we's." There was only the situation ahead of him.

A member had gone rogue and had been suspected of being in league with Eighth Realm entities and now, there was no way to know how many casualties there were at the courthouse. He hoped the loss of life was not too great, but the ash currently raining down on the city was not a positive sign. It was entirely possible that Persephone Johannes was the Sister of Fire, a prophecy spoken of in magic circles before the Council was even a thought in the Chairman's head.

No doubt there were calls coming in from all over the world, to try to figure out what was going on. No doubt the home office. Probably the Chairman, himself.

How Nigel hated talking to the Chairman. For a figure of legends so widespread that even school children would recognize his name, he was quite the vulgarian.

"Mr. Hawthorne," Verity said, poking her head into the office.

"Ah, Verity. Is there news?"

"There is. And it isn't good."

"Oh dear, what now?"

"There are reports of a fire fight in the skies over Lower Manhattan."

"What?"

"The United States Armed Forces engaged a figure witnesses are describing as 'angelic.' The results were…not positive."

"Oh my dear Lord."

"Yeah. Total loss of the government forces."

"Damn it! Verity, are Richard and Illinois in their offices?"

"Richard went out to investigate something at the Museum of Natural History and hasn't returned yet. It may be a while. All the cars and subway are dead."

"Then we need to muster the summoners. We need to take action. If Ms. Roberts has really reached that level of power, it is imperative that we stop her before the government takes more serious steps."

"You don't mean…?"

"Yes. If they see this city as a cancer, they may very well cut off the whole limb rather than let it infect the rest of the body."

"Oh my."

"Indeed…Hmmmm…Verity, did you say that the figure was described as 'angelic?' No tentacles or overt cuteness?"

'Angelic' is what Timons and Monti said it looked like in their visions."

Nigel lost all color in his face, suddenly realizing that he may have been very, very wrong about Persephone's allegiance. She wasn't the Sister of Fire. But this could be much much worse.

"It can't be. No one has ever done that. And the texts were dismissed as fiction, already. But if she…"

"What is it, Mr. Hawthorne?"

"Oh dear. I don't think Ms. Roberts is aligned with the Eighth Realm, at all. Please, get Illinois in here, immediately! I need to consult with him. We may be dealing with a greater threat than we've ever faced before! And if we are, and I cannot bring Team Seven up here without the streets of Buenos Aires being overrun by undead *panzermensch*, I do not know who can possibly save us!"

CHAPTER 20

Julie opened her right eye. Her vision was blurry and her head hurt like a motherfucker. She scanned the room. Looked like a living room. A really messy, really dirty living room.

Something warm under her. Something warm poking into her belly.

Oh, yeah. She went home with What's-His-Name last night.

She opened her other eye, and lifted her head a little bit. Yup, that was him under her. Sleeping like a baby. A baby with an…adequate erection. He wasn't what she'd call big, but he didn't exactly have microphallus either.

The room was freezing, even with the blanket that was on top of the two of them.

She pressed against him. His body warmth made her feel a little better.

But, damn, his cock just throbbed a little when she pressed into him.

In her hungover fog, she knew she had something or other to do today, but couldn't recall what it was. More importantly, she was horny.

She shook his shoulder a little bit.

He made some sort of mumbling noise, smacked his lips a few times, and then became unresponsive.

But that cock of his was fully awake. And now, so was she.

She sighed and raised her head, looking around the room, the light hurting her eyes. She wondered why she never woke up in a clean living room. This place was cluttered. Even the walls were cluttered, U.K. Subs and World Inferno posters about, as enough clothes to open up a small thrift store were strewn about the floor. Some of them hers, she was sure. Christ, they even had an old school tube television. Wow. Who the hell still had an tube television? This guy was truly living the dream.

She scratched her head with her right hand, looking at her fingers on her left. The skin was still red, but they didn't hurt as much as they did yesterday. That was good. She knew she had to change the bandages on her ankle soon, but there was something more pressing that had to be taken care of first.

Spying that her messenger bag was within reach, she reached over, and pulled it to her.

She reached inside and found the pocket with condoms in it. She pulled one out. It was a Magnum.

No need for that. She put it back in and reached for a regular size one, and threw her bag back on the floor.

She reached down and wrapped her hands around his member, just to check if it was hard enough. He let out a little bit of a moan in his sleep, little drops of pre-cum lubricating the head of his penis. *Definitely in working order*, she thought.

She unrolled the condom onto him, still unable to get over how ridiculous she always thought a cock looked when it was bagged up, and then moved her legs up on the couch, now squatting over him, so that her bandaged ankle wouldn't have to touch anything.

Lowering her hips, she slipped him into her with a loud grunt. That felt good. He may not have been that big and he didn't have much rhythm, but with her on top, she could control the going, so she did.

She started to bounce herself up and down, hard. This was more like it. She did wish he was a bit bigger, though. She felt like having someone big inside her. Someone that hurt a little bit.

But he would do for the next ten-to-twenty minutes. She bit her lip while thrusting harder, bringing her left hand down between her legs to massage her clit while riding him.

"Wha…what's? Whoa…" he said, waking up.

She slapped him hard, across the face.

"Shut up! Don't ruin this! Baby's on fire!"

She wasn't sure what the expression on his face was at the moment, because her eyes were closed. She didn't want him spoiling this.

She supposed she could give him some Hypnagogia, to get him more in the mood, but then she remembered that the guys she had seen at Webster Hall she dealt to had pretty much cum instantly upon being given it. She didn't want him cumming until she did.

But whatever, this felt good and that's what mattered.

"C'mon, slap my ass! Slap my fucking ass!" she commanded, and bit him in the shoulder, hard.

He obliged, but did it like a fucking pussy, so she bit his neck and order him to do it harder.

He did. That felt better. Yeah. This was working. This was definitely working. She forgot all about how cold the room was and just focused on how…

"Holy shit! I'm gonna cum," she heard him whisper.

"What? No!" she said, slapping him across the face, "Not yet!"

"Oh my god! Oh my god! Oh my god!"

She slapped him again, trying to stop him, but his eyes rolled into his head, and she knew he was finishing.

This pissed her off, so she pushed herself off him.

"No! Please!" he cried out, sounding like a little bitch, as he came in his condom, helpless to move. It looked like someone had put a plastic tarp on a really sad fountain.

She grabbed her messenger bag, angry, and started to walk towards wherever his bathroom was. She was sure she must have something in there that would be more reliable than he was.

"Fucking two-hump chump," she grumbled to him, as she started to walk down a hallway in the railroad apartment, hoping that it lead to the bathroom.

Suddenly, she heard the fumbling of keys, and a door opened in front of her and a crust punk girl with black dreads came running towards her.

"Oh my god! Oh my god! Antonio! Antonio! Did you see what's going on out-" the girl exclaimed, running towards the living, stopping as she noticed the very nude Julie in front of her.

"Whoa. Sorry. I didn't know Antonio had a, uh, friend over."

"Who's Antonio?" Julie asked.

"I am," What's-His-Name, from inside the living room, called out.

"Quiet, Early Bird!" Julie yelled, "No one cares!"

"Uh…do you want to put some clothes on?" the girl asked, averting her eyes.

"Not really. Hey, you don't eat…Nah. Nevermind."

"But you guys should put something on! Some really bad shit's happening outside! There's been an explosion or something in the city and my cell isn't working and…"

"What? How big?"

"I don't know, but nothing's working and they evacuated my classes and I walked home and I could swear I saw an explosion over the sky in Manhattan. I don't know if we're at war or something, but I know I heard jets. I know I…"

Shit. The last time Julie had heard jets was when she was being chased by her rather large friend in Long Island City.

Fuck. Persephone's hearing was today.

She got a sinking feeling in her stomach, realizing there was a good chance the two were connected.

She turned around, the girl gasping at seeing the injuries to Julie's back, bandaged and stitched, but still covering most her back.

"Oh my god, what happened to your back?"

"I, uh…hit a mirror."

"With your back?"

"Don't judge me."

With that, she went back into the living room and pulled out her laptop from her bag. It wasn't working. She had probably forgotten to charge it.

She reached for her phone.

"It's not going to work. Everybody's phones went dead at the same time. Same with cars and laptops and everything."

The sinking feeling in the pit of Julie's stomach got even worse. Did Persephone do this? Fuck. Was Samantha alright?

She had to get to the courthouse right now.

She looked around the floor for her clothes and started to put them back on.

"Hey, what's the weather like outside?" Julie asked, not sure exactly which neighborhood in Brooklyn she was in.

"What? Where are you going?" the girl said, "Something bad's happened in Manhattan. I don't know if it's some inside-job bullshit like 9/11 or if it's a *real* terrorist attack or whatever, but something's going on and you should stay in Brooklyn."

"I, uh, can't do that."

"Well, how are you going to even get into the city? The subways aren't running and there aren't any cabs!"

"Don't worry about it. I have a way," she said, reaching into the infinite void that was her messenger bag, her hand finding the handlebars of her bike.

CHAPTER 21

Persephone, flying a few feet over the roof of the Empire State Building, focused her energy on a single spot in front of her. To your average person, it would be appear to be just air. Nothing. Blank space. But she could feel the weak point in the dimensions here.

She concentrated all her energy on that point, the armor she wore seeming to come to life as it touched this single space. She could feel an intense surge of energy building within her body, as if she was powered by the souls of everyone she had killed at the courtroom and in the jets before.

The wind picked up as she touched that point.

There was the rumbling of thunder. Clouds forming in the previously clear winter sky, as lightning flashed around her. She saw it hitting windows, but instead of them shattering, they'd glow. And then more and more lightning came crashing down, the very city shaking from the rumbling of thunder.

Soon, the whole city was lit up, brighter than it had ever been.

People on the streets covered their eyes with their hands, to avoid being blinded.

In New Jersey and Connecticut, it looked like a second sun had risen over the horizon.

In truth, it could have been seen from space.

In Washington D.C., some men who were already very nervous, got a lot more so.

CHAPTER 22

Julie rode her bicycle through the streets of Brooklyn, weaving between dead cars, some of them still populated by their cursing owners. The sky had started to turn black with clouds and the wind had started to pick up. She was wearing several layers, but it chilled her to the very bone.

She was sober. This was on purpose. She was worried about Samantha. Surely, Persephone wouldn't have done anything to Samantha, right?

But she had tried to kill Julie, hadn't she? Fuck.

It was at that moment she saw the whole of Manhattan glow.

That was probably not a good sign.

She stopped and stared, eventually having to look away.

She realized that if she was going to do this, there was something she needed to do first.

She reached into her bag and took a swig of Vodka, nodded, put it back in the bag, put on sunglasses, and continued towards the city.

CHAPTER 23

The light only lasted for a few seconds, before seeming to dissipate, at least to your average New Yorker. The lightning continued as a regular storm, but the light was gone.

It hadn't disappeared, though. It hadn't dissipated. It had been absorbed by the armor. And Persephone could definitely feel it. The energy surrounding her body had built to an intense level. The heat the armor was generating was almost unbearable. But then again, it always was.

To even touch the armor would fry the soul of a human and instantly kill any demon that had touched it. She suspected it probably wouldn't even be good for a god to touch either.

If scientists were somehow able to analyze the armor without dying, they'd have said it was comprised of antimatter, but she knew what its true origin was. It was comprised of pure Order in a universe comprised of Chaos.

But she was protected from it because she was Azrael's chosen. It had been the armor of one of his brothers, killed during the battle with the Outer Gods and the Great Old Ones. Its original shape, when she had found it, had not resembled anything that could be worn by a human. Indeed, it seemed to be in molten liquid form when she first came across it in a forgotten cave in Wales, one Azrael had guided her to, but upon touching it, it molded itself to her shape, adjusting to a new form, covering her from neck to toe in something that felt light as air, yet heavy as lead, at the same time.

It felt alive. It wasn't like just putting a suit on. It responded to her thoughts, seeming to bond to her nervous system. The wings, for example, worked like a pair of extra limbs. She didn't think of them most of the time, but when she did, they'd respond like any other body part.

The wind whipped her hair wildly as the sky turned black, and she felt something that made her convulse, like she had put her finger into an electric socket.

In front of her, a small hole opened up in reality. It was only about four or five inches wide, but she could see cracks of light forming across the entire skyline, looking not unlike the aurora borealis.

And from it, she could smell an entire universe she had never experienced before. The energy felt like nothing she had ever experienced.

She smiled as voices swirled around her. They were Azrael.

"Dearest Persephone."

"Sweet, sweet Persephone."

"Our savior."

"Goddess Persephone."

"I've done it," she said.

"Of course you have."

"Dearest Persephone."

"Our beautiful Persephone."

"Sweet, sweet Persephone."

"Are you coming through now?"

"We cannot yet."

"Soon, our dearest, soon."

"Sweet Persephone, so sweet."

"The time is not yet."

"You still have but one thing to do," Azrael said from all the mirrors in the city.

"Just one thing."

"All we ask."

"The smallest thing."

"What is that?" Persephone asked.

"The tin soldiers."

"Army, Navy, Airforce, Marines."

"Your government."

"They will try to stop you."

"Try, try, they will."

"Our dearest, unstoppable Persephone."

"Crush. Kill. Destroy."

"Beautiful Persephone."

"They seek to stop you. You must let them try their hardest," the mirrored Azraels said.

"They will lose."

"Scorched Earth."

"Doing your work for you."

"None will survive."

"What do you mean?" Persephone asked.

"So simple."

"Very simple."

"Sweet, sweet Persephone."

"Crush. Kill. Destroy."

"Lay waste to the city."

"Destroy them when they try to stop you."

"Eventually."

"Eventually."

"Eventually."

"They will see only one solution."

"Only one."

"Final solution."

"Scorched earth."

"Amputation."

"They will bomb the city."

"To destroy you."

"They will fail."

"They will fail."

"They will fail."

"They will fail."

"They will fail."

"They will fail."

"But they'll kill...the...whole...city," Persephone realized.

"Yes. Millions of souls."

"The doors will be thrust wide open."

"Like birth."

"Like birth."

"Like birth."

"Like birth."

"You are our mother."

"You are the mother of the New World."

"Sweet, sweet Persephone."

"Beloved Persephone."

"Dearest Persephone."

What Azrael wanted was clear. She was to cause havoc. They were probably already scared by how easily she took down their fighters. If she did, indeed, make them panic enough, they'd nuke the city to try to contain her.

And with the armor on, she'd be completely invulnerable.

But the rest of the residents of the city would die and their souls would tear the tiny little hole she had made wide open. Azrael would come forth with his three siblings and the new world would begin.

She knew it was a cliché thing to do at this moment, but she couldn't help it.

She threw her head back and laughed.

And now it was time to get some attention.

CHAPTER 24

Nigel looked, intently at Illinois, who was sitting on his desk, staring at him, twitching his nose.

The most powerful psychic in the Council's East Coast branch, Illinois, greedily ate some slices of apple, and then looked around the room at Verity. He was knowledgeable in things that men, gods, and demons weren't, but sometimes, he wasn't very cooperative.

"He wants more apple slices, Mr. Hawthorne."

Nigel, more anxious than he'd been in years, pulled an apple from his drawer and quickly sliced off a portion of it, putting it in front of Illinois, who devoured it like a machine.

"Illinois," Nigel started, wiping his brow, "Please. Time is of the essence. The phenomena we just observed is a sign that the Johannes girl's plans are moving at an exponential rate. We must do something."

Illinois stomped one of his four feet in anger. He didn't like being told what to do. He understood the graveness of the situation, but he was a defiant sort.

He leapt off Nigel's desk and proceeded to rush from one end of the room to the other.

Nigel sighed loudly. Illinois looked at him and stomped his foot again.

"Illinois, this is not the time!"

Illinois leapt onto one of Nigel's shelves and started to chew on a scale model of the Queen Victoria.

"No no, Illinois! I worked quite hard on…"

Illinois leapt off the shelf and back onto the table, where he looked at Verity again.

"He says that he needs the exercise."

"Illinois, there is a rogue Council member possibly aligned with Ninth Realm forces out there! We cannot afford-"

"The enemy of my enemy is my friend."

"Pardon?"

"It's what Illinois said."

Nigel scratched his head and leaned back in his chair, looking at the psychic.

Illinois leap off the desk again and proceeded to knock over the waste paper basket in the corner of the room.

Nigel respected Illinois as a powerful psychic, but he hated having him in the office. He had previously taken precautions to Illinois-proof the room, but the psychic had taken great offense to that.

It was hard to deal with a rabbit. But as anyone versed in the Realms and otherworldly science could tell you, rabbits, originally native to the Second Realm, are all psychic, able to see a person's past, present, and future almost immediately, and gifted with the ability to see into other Realms with ease. Of course, your average human being is unable to receive the almost constant telepathic messages they use to communicate, but since he had first met her, Verity had been able to hear any of the various rabbits employed by the Council with ease.

"The enemy of my enemy…" Nigel repeated to himself, looking at the darkened city out his window, he twiddled his thumbs in that nervous way that he did when he was contemplating things, a habit his wife had told him always made her uneasy.

"She did what?" Verity asked Illinois, a Himalayan Mini Rex with white fur and pink eyes.

"Who did what?" Nigel asked, leaning forward while still playing with his thumbs.

"Mr. Hawthorne…This is something I think you need to hear. Illinois, please repeat that for me."

CHAPTER 25

Julie pedaled across the Williamsburg Bridge, towards the city, wondering what the hell had happened with the sky. It had been afternoon-ish a couple minutes ago and now the sky had filled with clouds and everything around her was dark.

It was an eerie feeling. She had seen candles being lit in many windows. She could see the flashlights, especially from the police. But otherwise, it was a dark city, quiet city.

At first, she had wondered how many babies would probably be born nine months from today.

But then, when the sky lit up like she was in Alaska or something, she wondered if there would even be a nine months from now.

As she pedaled on the bike path of the bridge, she could see some road flares being lit by people whose cars were stuck on the bridge. She could see other cars, abandoned, with the doors wide open. She could see some people looking like they were helping each other, while others appeared to be using the cover of sudden night to steal what they could from the cars that had been left behind.

The wind was still not making this any easier, but she still had to get to the courthouse and make sure that Sammi was okay. She had a really bad feeling about this, one that grew more and more, as she approached the giant black steel forest that was an unlit Manhattan.

There was something really eerie about those tall buildings without the usual light that accompanied them every night.

It was too quiet, in the horror movie way that "too quiet" means something awful is going to happen.

As she pedaled her way into the city, on Clinton St., she felt that feeling of dread raging inside her, like a lit match that becomes a forest fire. People were looking up to the sky, trying to figure out what was going on, some with flash lights, some with flares (she really didn't know this many people in New York had road flares. She didn't even know where to get road flares from. Now she wanted road flares too).

On occasion, she'd see someone checking their cellphones to see if they had started working again yet, and sometimes, she'd even hear the moans of people who were obviously inside with nothing else to do but get to know each other better, coming from darkened apartments.

Of course, the bars were filled. Didn't need electricity to get plastered. She'd hear the warm, inviting sounds of people mingling and that wonderful smell of stale beer-soaked floors, and find herself fighting the urge to go in and join everybody. Normally, she would have. But while Julie, by her own admission, wasn't the most reliable person in the world, she still loved her sister and wanted to make sure that Samantha was alright.

As she went around a corner, she heard a man drunkenly singing to himself.

"Goodnight Irene, Goodnight Irene/I'll see you in my dreams," he sang, walking around the corner of Ludlow and Rivington, holding a bottle of Jack Daniels, and despite the extreme weather, naked as the day he was born except for a Santa hat and what Julie thought might be penny loafers. She couldn't help but notice that he bore a strong resemblance to Ian McShane. A nude Ian McShane.

"Good evening, my fair lady," he called out to her, doing what appeared to be a drunken curtsy of some kind.

"Hey, Random Naked Dude," Julie called back, stopping on her bike, "How's it, uh, hanging?"

"Long, loose, and full of juice."

"Well, I'll take your word for the 'loose' and 'full of juice' part, but I'm going to have to debate with you on the 'long' part."

"In my defense, it's very cold out, you understand."

"I'll allow it."

He laughed and took a swig of his Jack Daniels.

"So, uh, that brings me to my next question," Julie started.

"Ah, this?" he said, looking down at his naked body.

"You said it yourself. It's very cold out."

"I'm so fucking drunk right now that I don't feel a thing."

"I envy you, sir."

"Wait...don't I know you? You look slightly familiar, but I can't quite place you."

Julie lowered her panda hoodie.

"Oh, you're the girl with the meth! From the news!"

"That was all bullshit. *Daily News* even ran a retraction."

"Didn't see it."

"It was pretty tiny. So, back to you...*why?*"

"Well, here's the thing...World's ending."

"World's ending?"

"Yup. World's ending. Majestic 12 obviously fucked up."

"Obviously."

"Never believed that Art Bell, Alex Jones shit until just now, where the sun went dark and all our tech died and I saw an alien ship knock an Apache out of the sky."

"You saw all that?"

"Yup. Big...big glowing spaceship. Obviously, the deal the CIA must have made fell through. No other explanation."

"Maybe...demons?"

He looked at her and laughed a big hearty laugh that eventually turned into a spasm of coughing. Julie walked over and, making a face, patted him on the back a few times until he stopped coughing.

"Demons? *Demons?!?* Hahahaha...that's funny. There's no such thing as demons! Besides, I saw it. Big and white and plain as day. Floating in the sky. Saw it do that. Realized that if the aliens are coming to collect, I didn't want to spend my last day as a Marketing Exec, so I just stripped off, right then and there, in the office, and decided I'd do what I always wanted to do."

"Which is?"

"What? *This!* Of course! Wearing a suit and tie Monday through Friday; not growing that handlebar mustache I wanted to grow; paying child support to Barbara; it's all bullshit! But now, I'm free! I'm early man and I don't play by anybody's rules anymore! I even made some primitive cave drawings near Union Square! I'm unleashed! I'm free! Come probe this, you little gray motherfuckers!"

He slapped his own ass a few times and let out a wolf's howl.

"Wow, dude, you are truly living the dream."

"That I am. That I am," he paused, before looking at her with a smile, "Say, young lady! Being that this is probably the last day on Earth for all of us...well, I know I'm probably old enough to be your father, but..."

"Ooooh, dude. We're not going there."

"Can't blame a man for trying."

"Well, you have a good night, sir."

"And you too, madam!"

And with that, he disappeared into the night, singing again, until the wind swallowed the sounds of "Goodnight Irene."

There was a rumbling above her and she distinctly noticed that, the further she got into the city, the emptier the streets were. It was freezing out, after all, and that didn't lend itself to people wanting to gather outdoors. She had started to wonder if the people who were out were just out because they had nothing else to do within their electricity-free apartments.

There was another rumble above her. She had no idea what it was.

It was loud, like an explosion or something, but when she looked up, she couldn't see anything. Even if the buildings weren't as tall and immense as they were in midtown, anything could be going on above her.

She definitely felt the tingle of what she assumed was magic, far above her. That was much was certain. She wasn't sure if it was Persephone or if something else had been happening, but it wasn't good, she knew that.

Walking her bike up Allen, towards Houston, she heard several helicopters above her, far in the sky. She looked up and realized that they were probably going wherever the action was.

She started pedaling to keep up with them, stopping when she got to Houston Street. The helicopters kept going, but Julie found herself shocked to see that there was a HUGE fire going on a few blocks down. It looked like an entire building and the building next to it were on fire. Fuck. This was getting serious.

She started to pedal North, since that's where the helicopter had been going. Allen turned into 1st Avenue, a street she was very familiar with, that looked very odd to her so quiet.

Nothing good was going to come out of tonight.

Part of her reasoned that it still wasn't too late to go back to one of the bars, but she couldn't do that until she, at least, knew Samantha was okay.

CHAPTER 26

Nigel hated having the summoners teleport him into different realms. It was always a disorientating experience. Especially, when he'd enter a room that smelled like this. Despite being cavernous in its size, its walls, floor and ceiling made of throbbing human flesh, the throne room had an overwhelming smell to it, of sweat; of musk and sperm; both human and demon. There were naked bodies, both human and demon, everywhere, writhing about the throne room. He could tell the incubi and succubae were being careful to not engage in standard intercourse, so as to not kill the humans with them, but any other sex act that could possibly be imagined was happening all around him.

He saw a man being penetrated by a female demon with an enormous fake phallus at the same time he fellated the very real penis of an incubi in front of him. He saw a woman, bent over a rack, urinating down the inside of her legs as she was whipped by two succubae. He saw female human and succubae 69-ing each other. He saw a couple thrusting into each other, face to face, as a succubae sprayed them in the face with her ejaculate. He saw an entire row of a dozen people on all four being anally penetrated as they licked fluids from the floor ahead of them. He saw a man in a pillory with weights on his balls, his face between the ample ass cheeks of a voluptuous succubus's human form. Bodies hung, moaning from the crystalline stalagmites that dipped from the ceiling, as succubae and incubi flew around them, teasing and touching their bodies.

Nigel walked, gingerly through the mass of bodies, worried that there would be unexplainable stains on his pants or shoes from the goings on around him. Otherwise, despite his prim and proper exterior, this was nothing he had not seen in his youth, although never in one place before.

It frightened him a bit, to see how many humans were here, not to mention knowing the Black Talon were probably doing the same. He knew that bad things were on the horizon, but not this bad. And he felt for all of these poor souls, lead by their hormones to this den of fatal pleasure like the children who became donkeys in Pinocchio, because they most likely had no idea what was in store for them when the party ended.

He also felt for them because he knew that he couldn't help them, at all, if he intended his plan to work. The needs of the many had to outweigh the needs of the few. If hundreds had to be given up for the entire world, if not the entirety of all creation, to be saved, it had to be, no matter how bad the taste it left in his mouth.

He could see her sitting up on a throne about fifty feet ahead of him, at the end of the room. All around her throne were her elite guards, not even bothering to take human form, just appearing as the shadowy demons that incubi and succubae normally were. There were maybe fifty of them, standing at attention on the path leading up to the throne, naked bodies lying at their feet, vigorously masturbating, while licking the ground that lead up to her.

A large incubi left formation and stood directly in Nigel's path. It cracked its claws and looked down at him, standing a full seven feet tall and built like a shadowy Adonis.

"And what business do you have here, old human, besides your death?" it asked him, arms folded, shoulders broad, its six eyes staring directly into his soul.

"Excuse you, Ikernus of the Red Veil!" a heavily accented Southern Belle's voice yelled from up on the throne, "Just what *are* you doing?!?"

"He is immunized, My Lady," the demon, obviously called Ikernus said.

"Hush your mouth! Why, *of course* he is. He's Council. They're *all* immunized. Quit acting ugly and let the man through, Ikernus of the Red Veil! You know, good manner never go out of style!"

Ikernus nodded and got out of Nigel's way..

Nigel nodded back at him and proceeded to walk towards the foot of the throne.

He could see that it was actually constructed of human souls, melded together, eternally, on all fours, crying out in what he couldn't tell was despair or ecstasy. It was probably both.

On it, in her favorite human form, wearing a tiara and a sparkling, sequined, white evening gown, with slits up the sides, a sash around it that read GEORGIA, her blond hair high and teased and the makeup on her youthful face heavily applied, was Druuina of the Red Veil, the leader of that clan of incubi and succubae. She held a bouquet of roses in one hand and in the other a leash.

The leash belonged to a naked, muscular young man on all fours, who had his head buried between her open legs, the sleeve of her dress slipped to the side to provide him with easy access, and a young woman behind the man, her face buried between the cheeks of the young man's ass, her own body thrusting back and forth onto the foot of an incubus who stood behind her.

"Why, butter my butt and call me a biscuit," Druuina said, showing off a row of perfect teeth, "If it isn't Nigel Hawthorne. I ain't seen you in a month of Sundays. How y'all been?"

"Well met, Druuina of the Red Veil."

"See, y'all? That's a man with manners. Y'all have to forgive Ikernus of the Red Veil. My little brother's a damn fine warrior, but bless his little heart, boy's so dumb, he could throw himself at the ground and miss."

"No offense was taken, I can assure you."

"So, Nigel, what brings you to my little neck of the woods? I certainly hope you ain't looking to liberate my provisions. They all came of their own free will and you attempting to take them back would be considered an act of war by the Red Veil. And as you probably saw when you came in here, we're ten thousand strong, sweetie."

"No, you are aware of the Council's policy of neutrality in manners of inter-demon aggression."

"Of course, I am. It's why you're walking in here in one piece and probably will be walking out the same. But y'all want to send an inspector out this way, check that we're only taking the accepted numbers, you can do that. But you can't have 'em back."

"Do your provisions know what is waiting for them down here?"

"Just the truth, sweetie. That they was gonna have themselves the time of their lives and never have to worry about nothing ever again. If that don't sound like the best this here group's ever gonna get, I don't know what is. Hold on, just a sec, darling."

She looked down at the young man going down on her, tapping him on the head.

"Sweetie," she said, leaning forward to look the man in the eye, "This ain't a race. Take your time when you give mama her sugar.

You're not digging for gold. Now, show mama how you can eat that peach right."

She closed her eyes for a moment and then bit her lower lip before giving a whooping noise.

"Now, where were we, Nigel? Oh…before that, I gotta say this…and, you know…I don't mean to sound mean…but you don't look so hot these days. Only been what: 40 years since we last saw each other? Y'all didn't age so well."

"One of the negatives of human mortality, Druuina."

"Well, my pretty boy here ain't never gonna have that issue," she said, patting the man going down on her, on the head.

"Yes, well, if we could down to business."

"Well, look at you: all business! Listen, I'm just surprised y'all didn't use some of them wizards you got to keep yourself young, is all. I mean, considering who your Chairman is."

"I'd rather not talk about the Chairman."

"Boy's half Indigo Silence, after all."

"I will reiterate, Druuina: the Chairman is not what I'm here to discuss."

"Hahaha. Alright, fair's fair. What's on your mind?"

"I understand that this entire war was predicated on the actions of one Juliette Johannes."

"Dern right it is. Uppity little Yankee human bitch killed my sister, Thanus of the Red Veil, right there, in the middle of a Sanctuary! Can you believe that?!? And then, instead of whooping her behind, that little no count *W-I-G-G-E-R*, Larxene of the Black Talon, takes the human girl's side and declares war on us. On us! On *me!* I'll tell you what: the Black Talon ain't worth a crap and ain't never been worth a crap and ain't never gonna *be* worth a crap! Larxene's brood mother, Jaien of the Black Talon…I wouldn't piss in her ear if her brain was on fire! When we are done, I am fixin' to jerk a knot in her tail and then use Larxene of the Black Talon's head as a butt warmer. The whole dern lot of them. I will decorate my palace with their skulls."

"Well, that is why I came here."

"Oh?"

"Would you be so kind as to loan me some of your troops?"

"My cow died last night, Nigel, so I don't need none of your bull. Just why would I do that?"

"Because it would provide you with an opportunity to hurt someone Juliette Johannes is very close to."

"Really? Well, Nigel, I have to say it does seem a might peculiar y'all making me an offer like that. Veura of the Red Veil didn't raise no fool. You wouldn't be making an offer like that if it didn't benefit y'all somehow. But, if what you say is true, well then, that would make me happier than a dog with two peckers."

CHAPTER 27

Julie had switched up, closer to Broadway, as it had appeared that the majority of the action was going on near the Empire State Building. She had pedaled to 14th Street and then gone up to 3rd Avenue, with the idea that she'd move up to Park South, when she got around to 23rd Street.

Deeper and deeper into the city, the streets were populated only by cars, over and over again, the same thing.

The one exception to the streets being empty was on 14th Street, itself, where large groups of people gathered outside, watching the power station burn down on the far east side of the street. They speculated whether or not all of this was just the power going out, some of them correctly guessing that it was an EMP that caused their cellphones and the like to go out, but incorrectly guessing it was the power station blowing that did it.

Still, a great many of them were perplexed by the sky and whatever battle seemed to be going on. There were more alien theories, and some skeptics telling them that it was probably some sort of military drill, since air raid sirens didn't go off. Another person said that maybe the sirens couldn't go off anymore, and then the conversation died.

Julie didn't hear any further than that, as she went on her way. Occasionally, she'd run into a random passerby, looking up at the sky like she was. There was another chopper that had flown over, when she had gotten to 16th. Then a few minutes later, there was a loud sound, like a car crash, but she couldn't see where it was, but she was very aware of the smell of burning metal in the air. She could definitely hear gun fire and what sounded like a jet. There was more smoke, the closer uptown she got and, by the time she got to 18th, she could see a light over in the 20's, on the West side, which meant that another building was burning. This was beginning to feel like a war zone in slow motion.

She pedaled up to 20th Street, when she saw a white flash in the sky. It was probably what that guy had thought was an alien.

She couldn't make it out without her sunglasses.

With them on, it was still bright, but it looked very, very familiar.

"Juliette," said a voice above her. Persephone's voice, "I was hoping we'd have had more time together."

Julie looked up at her sister, flying about 20 feet above her, in what looked like glowing Xena armor, but with wings.

"Perci, what the fuck is going on?"

"Ascension."

"Well, that certainly answers that."

"Juliette, I really was hoping you'd stay away, so I could find you in my own time and settle this with you."

"Why can't we do that now?"

"I'm busy. Good night, Juliette."

Persephone looked down at her sister and folded her arms.

Julie started to reach into her bag, when she noticed the cars on the street began to power up again. Their horns went off, their lights flashed, and they began to shake.

Julie looked around at them, realizing this wasn't good. Then, a white Honda Civic seemed to...well, it seemed to jump straight up into the air, about a hundred feet in the air.

"Well, that's...uh...ne-"

Suddenly, a dark green Pontiac Grand Prix did it. And then a black Cadillac Escalade did it. Then some shitty car that appeared to have been around since the early 90's and probably had not washed since did it. And then another car did it. And then another. There were dozens of cars, bumper to bumper on 3rd Avenue, and now they were all flying straight up vertically. At one point, two of them flew up so hard that they knocked over the street light on 21st Street, they went up with such violent force.

She looked down the street and saw cars doing the same thing for two blocks in front of her. She turned around and saw them doing it for two blocks behind her.

Soon, the entire street was empty of cars, the sky filled with them, as Persephone hovered below them, looking down at her sister, with her arms folded.

"That's...uh...that's a lot of flying cars."

"They're not *flying*, Juliette," Persephone said.

"Then, what are…Oh fuck!"

Julie seemed to see it in slow motion, instinctively grabbing the handlebars of her bike, and pedaling as hard as she could. The car closest above her, a navy blue Hyundai Sonata, that had been floating in the air, lost its orbit just as quickly as it had gained it.

She pedaled for dear life, as the car came at her in a deadly free fall, it crashing into the street only a couple feet behind her, shards of broken glass and concrete shrapnel assaulting her back.

High on adrenaline, she dodged as a white Ford Explorer came down, only a few feet from her, shattering the windows of a nearby Duane Reade upon impact. A Toyota RAV4 came down directly after it, breaking through the sidewalk it hit, the sad noise of its broken horn, its deathcry.

The white Honda Civic plummeted to the earth, a few feet in front of her, she managing to skid out of the way on her bike at the last minute, the car folding like an accordion, two more cars falling on either side of her, as she gave a primal scream, while pedaling for dear life.

She felt the ground under her begin to give as another car came crashing through the street, the smell of sewer overpowering.

She pedaled as another SUV fell, on the sidewalk to her left, its windshield wipers almost beheading her as they flew off.

A fire hydrant shot off through a storefront in front of her. The ground shook as she felt the heat of an explosion behind her.

She was thrown off her bike, high into the air, cars falling from the sky around her, as she was propelled by the blast forward.

The ground under her was an inferno as a gas main exploded.

She saw a yellow taxicab falling, directly in front of her. She put her arms ahead to cover her face, as she hit its roof, hard. So hard that everything around her went black.

CHAPTER 28

Persephone looked down on the fiery wreck that had been 3rd Avenue, between 18th and 22nd Street, and dropped the rest of the cars on it, at the same time. There was a blast of hot air onto her as most of the cars that had been dropped exploded. Buildings were engulfed and foundations collapsed. If the sky hadn't turned black, the area would have surely been covered by the thick cloud of smoke that rose from the inferno.

It was a shame that Juliette had to go out that way. She had had plans.

Still, she thought to herself, looking down, that if Juliette was down there, somewhere, and she survived, she should probably finish her off, rather than let her sister burn to death or choke in the toxic cloud, half broken in some concrete crag somewhere.

It wouldn't take much. All she'd have to do is touch the armor and Juliette would be no more. Her sister had suffered enough.

Persephone decided that would be the right thing to do and, with a flick of her wrist, the fires on 3rd Avenue all ceased to be.

The street itself looked like it had been in the blitz, of course, storefronts in ruin, water mains spewing water everywhere, the street itself caved in, the random wreckage of a bus and several dozen cars all over.

She looked around and saw Juliette's limp body, half hanging out of what used to be the wall of an apartment above what used to be a hardware store. The building looked ready to collapse at any moment.

Juliette was unconscious, but still breathing, her clothes in tatters and her left leg bent in a way that a leg is not supposed to bend.

Persephone flew over to the building, hovering inches above the shattered tile of the apartment.

Nearby, a couch that was more burnt springs than couch slipped out of the wall into the broken street below.

Juliette's leg looked even worse from up close.

Persephone reached down, her hand glowing blue, and touched her sister's leg, healing it and the rest of her body.

After all she had put her sister through, the last few days, she felt it was the least she could do, before finally giving her sister a killing embrace.

Suddenly, the air was filled with screeches as the sky was filled with succubae and incubi. Hundreds of them.

Persephone looked up, in confusion as the Fourth Realm army dove at her.

"The human spoke the truth!" said the incubi at the head of the army, "Kill her! Our Brood Sister will reward us for her armor!"

Wait...didn't Juliette say she was friends with a succubae? Then what was this and why were they attacking her? Of course, Juliette would have pissed off an entire demon nation.

Didn't matter! There were hundreds of incubi and succubae heading her way and it was time to fight. Persephone spread her wings and flew, at top speed towards the advancing army, pulling her katana out from behind her, it now glowing white as well.

CHAPTER 29

Julie opened her eyes, very surprised she even could after how hard she had hit that car…or the car had hit her. She wasn't sure. She felt like shit, though. She could hear the screeches of succubae and the lower variation of incubi and heard fighting, but could see nothing in the sky.

All she knew was that her little sister just dropped a whole fucking parking lot on her and that was very much not okay.

She tried to stand up, but found herself with a sharp pain in the stomach that caused her to scream out loud.

She looked down to see she had been impaled on part of a fence pole. Probably from during the explosion. She forced herself onto her feet.

Okay, she thought, *let's pull this out and see how bad it was.*

She did so and immediately vomited blood, falling to her knees.

That was stupid.

She leaned against a wall, but her legs gave out from under her.

She was going to die.

"Whoa…whoa…my nigs, you don't look so good. You 'ight?"

She turned her head to see Lucy behind her, looking concerned.

"Too late. Going soon. I…I…don't think I'm going to make it."

"What? Hells no! Naaah! Naaah! You can't die, bitch!" Lucy yelled, tears in her eyes, as she ran over to Julie. When she got there, she crouched and, in a manner so gentle, it surprised Julie, held Julie in her arms.

"I…I think this is the end. I-I don't want to go."

"Then don't go, my nigga! Don't go!"

"It's okay…it's okay, Lucy. You're safe. That's all that matters. Maybe I'll live again. I don't know. Feels different this time."

"What? This time? Bitch, you delusional! You lost too much blood, hurt your head, some shit! Fuck. Fuck!"

"Lucy?"

"Yeah, my nigs?"

"You...you were fantastic. Absolutely fantastic. And you know what?"

"Tell me."

"So was I," Julie said, smiling, and closed her eyes.

As Julie finally passed on, her body was enveloped by an explosion of warm yellow light. Lucy jumped back, as every cell of Julie's body reformed and readjusted. Her legs filled out, her stomach grew from a beer belly to a pot belly, her hair turned from dyed black to wavy, receding, and white, her feminine features turning masculine as her body took on its new, older form: That of English star of stage, screen, and science fiction, Colin Baker.

He sat up, quickly, looking at his portly elderly body, still clad in Julie's t-shirt and now torn jeans, and smirked.

"Oh shit...Oh shit!" Lucy exclaimed, "Julie?"

"You were expecting someone else?"

"I...I-I..."

"That's three I's in one breath. Makes you sound a rather egotistical young lady."

"What happened?"

"Change, my dear, and it seems, not a moment too soon."

Suddenly, dressed to the nines in military gear, former President of the United States, Andrew Jackson rode in on a unicycle, looked at Colin Baker and Lucy and said, in the squeaky voice of Gilbert Gottfried, "You know who I love? Indians. Sure do love them Indians."

Upon seeing this, Colin Baker made a face and said, "Oh fuck. I'm dreaming."

CHAPTER 30

Julie woke up with a start, in her regular female Julie body, finding herself in the burnt out ruins of what looked an apartment building.

She looked down at her body to see that not only was it not impaled on anything, but she seemed to be in perfect condition. Her clothes were torn and ripped and burnt, but she seemed okay. Better than, actually.

Lucy was nowhere to be seen, unless she was part of what looked like a massive army of Fourth Realm demons fighting Persephone in the sky. It was like watching a swarm of locusts descend, there were so many, yet, her sister was certainly still alive to fight them. She doubted anyone else, save a god could survive having hundreds of demons attacking them at once. That was a bad sign.

"Good afternoon, Miss Johannes," a very proper Englishman's voice said, off to her right, "Or do you prefer Miss Golightly?"

He was dressed like an old professor or something, with a bow tie, glasses, and a mustache. His eyes seemed kindly but capable of incredible cruelty to Julie. These were the eyes of a man who had had to make decisions that had cost lives before.

"Who are you?"

"My name is Nigel Hawthorne. I am the head of New York City's branch of the Council. I also counted your sister, Doctor Henderson, among my friends and colleagues."

"Sammi! How is she?"

"I do not know," he said, walking over to her and offering his hand to help her rise, "But I fear the worst."

"Oh fucking no."

"Well, in our line of work, we learn to say goodbye way too often."

"Fuck that," Julie said, refusing his hand, and getting up on her own. Nigel shrugged.

She looked up at the sky.

"What's going on up there?"

"That, my dear, is the 37ᵗʰ Legion of the Red Veil fighting your sister, Persephone. Five hundred incubi and succubae all completely loyal to their Brood Sister, Druunia."

"The Red Veil? Why is that familiar? Red Veil...Red Veil...Aren't they...?"

"Yes, the family of succubae that you managed to make very cross by killing a certain sister of their brood. I believe her name was Thanus. Now, they are soon to engage in all-out war with the Black Talon, of which I am also told you are well-acquainted."

"Told? By who?"

"A rabbit."

"Of course. Why wouldn't it be?"

"The point is that they are attacking your sister because they believe that the two of you are rather close. I, myself, am confused as to why she healed your wounds."

"She healed me?"

"Yes. You seemed quite the worse for wear beforehand. I feared you would not wake for me to converse with you."

A look of panic sprang into Julie's eyes as she looked down at her wrists, and exhaling when she saw that her tattoos were still there.

"You were worried about the tattoos?"

"Yeah! They mean a lot."

"I know. I was acquainted with your father, briefly. I cannot say we were the best of friends, but...we were not enemies. I shall leave it at that. But my point is that healing magic usually only heals fresh wounds or parts that no longer are attached to the body. It isn't an automatic thing. The healer must imagine the healing of the particular damaged parts. Of course, a truly attuned healer can tell what is wrong with the body upon touch, but unless the healer specifically aims for them, old scars tend to not heal. However, new ones..."

"Oh fuck, the one on my thigh! I just got that!"

"Well, you'll probably need to reapply it."

"Fuck."

A thought occurred to Julie and she ran her hands up the back of her shirt to feel her back, to find that while the skin back there seemed to have healed, she still had her stitches going in and out of her flesh. She giggled a little at that.

"Well, I would love to stay and chat, but I must return to the Council soon, before the Red Veil see that I am talking with you and know that I set them up."

"Why did you bring them?"

"To buy you time, of course."

"Time for what?"

"That…is entirely up to you. I suspect your sister cannot be killed through conventional means, if at all. That armor she wears is straight from Ninth Realm legend."

"Ninth Realm?"

"Yes."

"I've never fought anything Ninth Realm before."

"And with luck, you won't ever. Your sister is still human, but she wears an artifact of that Realm as protection. It seems to also boost her powers. I know you sisters were born with varying levels of psychic ability, but Persephone's current level is beyond demon, but not quite goddess yet."

"Maybe if we got the armor off her, it'd bring her back to normal."

"I doubt it works quite that way. We've reason to believe the armor attached itself to her nervous system. It wouldn't just 'come off.'"

"Then what do we do?"

"I would suggest taking her off this plane, to one of the other Realms. I do not know if you can defeat her or not, but if you cannot, I need you to buy time for Team Seven to get here."

"Team Seven?"

"Surely, you've heard of Team Seven, with both of your sisters being in the Council."

"I…I kinda zone out whenever Sammi talks about Council stuff."

"But Persephone was a member of Team Five! I…Well," Nigel said, stopping himself, and sighing loudly, "Team Seven is the premiere supernatural elimination team. Mankind's absolute last line of defense. Think of them as a Special Forces team that deals with…the things we deal with. But they are currently busy preventing another crisis from spreading, in the Southern Hemisphere."

"What could be more important than this?"

"Nazi zombies marching on Central America."

"Holy shit! I want to fight Nazi Zombies!"

"One battle at a time, Miss Golightly."

"Alright…So, you want me to take her off this plane? Why?"

"Because she needs thousands of souls to open the gate to the Ninth Realm she is attempting to open."

"So, where am I supposed to take her that doesn't have any souls? The First Realm is almost made out of them, the Fifth is…"

"They must be unclaimed souls. They must be the souls of the living for the sacrifice to work. There is an energy that releases upon death, the moment the soul and body separate. The only Realm she can achieve that is on Earth, as human beings are the only creature of the Nine Realms to be mostly born with souls. It's why demons come here from all of the other Realms, but rarely invade each other's Realms."

"Why is that?"

"A complete accident of nature, really, as all other currently living beings are born with their nature's lifeforce connected, but we are not, yet it is why our souls are so valued among the Realms. They are a resource not found elsewhere."

"Nowhere else?"

"Well, there once was a species that were born with souls in the Sixth Realm, but they quickly were hunted into extinction, thousands of years ago, upon the discovery. The bottom line is that your sister cannot open the hole she has made any wider if she is brought to another Realm."

"Okay. I'm guessing no one else can do this, right?"

"Only you, Miss Golightly, if only to distract her long enough for Team Seven to do their job. The one imperative is that you must prevent her from destroying the city any more."

"Why?"

"Because if she goes too far and the city is cleansed in nuclear fire, that will give them the sacrifices they need."

"Whoa. *Nuclear fire?!?*"

"Yes, Miss Golightly. The United States Government is watching this very closely. We have our representatives in Washington D.C. trying to convince the Joint Chiefs of Staff that we can handle this ourselves. If it appears we cannot, now that they know that your sister's powers can disable their jets and helicopters, even from a distance, they will send in the one weapon they think can solve the problem."

"How did you find that out?"

"As I said, we have representatives talking with the Joint…"

"No. I mean, about nuking the city giving her what she wants?"

"The same rabbit as before."

"Oh, well, good ol' Exposition Bunny."

"Do you have the abilities your sister and father had, Ms. Golightly?"

"I can move some stuff here and there, but nothing big."

"Shame. You have so much potential."

"Whatever."

"Well…Good luck, Miss Golightly," he said, holding her hand for a minute before turning around to leave.

He paused, his back turned to her, before finally saying, "Just to let you know, I did try to talk him out of it."

"What?"

"Your father. I tried to tell him the dangers of time travel. That he could not change things, no matter how much he tried. Time does not work that way. Time is never on your side. But then he met that damn girl, filling his head with all sorts of ideas."

"If you knew my dad, you'd know that there wouldn't be any way you could convince him to not, at least, try."

"I know. You're quite like him, for both better and worse. Good luck, Miss Golightly," he said, turning to her as he stood in the portal he had opened with little effort, "If you survive this, please come to the Council's New York office. East 82nd Street and East End. Miss Kapaldia tells me that you've been there once before."

"Last time I was there, a crazy man ranted at me. Why should I go there again?"

"Regardless of your hedonistic lifestyle, you were born with gifts others were not. Perhaps with proper training, you could yet become an asset to this world and others."

And with that, he disappeared, the portal closing behind him.

Julie stood there, with her hands on her hips, staring at the spot where the portal had been.

The broken apartment's floor shook a bit. She knew she couldn't stay here for very long.

She'd need to find her messenger bag and then figure out what to do about her sister.

CHAPTER 31

Persephone was getting angry. These demons just kept coming and coming, and now, they seemed to realize that touching the armor would mean instant death, so they had stopped trying to grab her or her wings. That was bad, since a good number of them had died doing that.

Persephone found herself growing exhausted, fighting off wave after wave of shadowy flying demon.

They were all around her and she constantly had to expend energy to heal herself. If she could get a little breathing room, she could do one of her outbursts of energy and probably kill most, if not all of them, but that required her to be able to concentrate for a few moments.

That was not going to happen with these…things. One of them flew at her, slicing a giant gash in her right cheek, while another flew at her, with a sword, trying to stab her through the stomach.

Of course, the shadowy sword would break upon touching her armor and then she'd heal and slash at them with her own sword, killing one of them, but then, the next second, she'd have to retreat a bit with another three of them closing in, usually two of them with demonic weapons of some sort.

She had been pierced with arrows, she had had limbs sliced off, she had had been stabbed in the head. She had tried to ascend quickly to give herself breathing room, but that hadn't worked either, as they just swarmed above her. She had tried to fly backwards, so that her wings would disintegrate the demons swarming behind her, but it only gave the ones in front of her more opportunity to attack. She had had her eyes ripped out at least twice already.

If she didn't have the ability to heal from anything, even the most fatal of wounds, she wouldn't have lasted more than a couple seconds against them.

This was a lot harder than dealing with the military.

It wasn't going to kill her, but this would keep her occupied for days, maybe weeks, if she didn't figure out what to do. Eventually, she'd probably even pass out. They'd try to kill her while she was unconscious, and of course, her body would heal automatically, but that wouldn't achieve what she needed to achieve.

Not to mention, just because she could heal from whatever was done to her, did not mean she couldn't feel pain. She felt every injury she was given, time and time again. She had purposely tried to make herself numb to it, through increasingly painful self-harm rituals over the last couple years since she had gotten the armor, including a day where she had stabbed herself with her katana as much as possible, but your internal organs never got used to being assaulted, because, unlike your epidermis, there usually isn't that much opportunity for it to happen.

Now, being torn apart and then coming back together over and over again, she was angry, she was tired, and she was not making any progress.

Suddenly, there was an explosion next to her. Flaming, a dozen of the incubi and succubae fell out of the sky, falling to the shattered sidewalk below.

The fighting stopped while she and her attackers stopped to look at what had caused that explosion.

Standing on the roof of a building on Lexington and 20ᵗʰ, Juliette reached into her bag and pulled out another rocket she proceeded to load into the rocket launcher she was holding.

"Haha! My dear sister, our nefarious plans will not be stopped by the likes of these assorted bitches and bastards!" Juliette yelled, seeming to project her voice.

Our nefarious plans? *Our?* Since when was Juliette part of the plan? And if she had been part of it, why would she describe it as "nefarious?" Nefarious wasn't a positive description. Maybe she just didn't know the meaning of the word, Persephone thought.

"It's her! It's the human bitch!" one of the succubae yelled, "Take her head, for Druuina of the Red Veil!"

Persephone, not sure what was going on, but happy that her sister seemed to be helping, sliced off the head of that succubae with her sword, flying over and grabbing two more, with her hands glowing white.

The demons seemed to be confused as to which of the two targets they should go after, some of them wondering aloud if they should go after Juliette instead, since Persephone seemed to be invulnerable. But others wondered if Juliette had the same powers.

There was another explosion of dead incubi and succubae as Juliette launched another rocket at the debating demons.

The others, seeing this, charged at her.

Juliette threw the launcher back into her bag and started to run along the rooftops to get away.

"Yes! Distract them, my sister! Our reinforcements from the Black Talon will be around soon! We will take the Fourth Realm after we take this world for our unholy Ninth Realm overlords!" Juliette yelled as she ran from the descending demons.

She had Black Talon reinforcements? Excellent! Persephone thought to herself, but wondered why Juliette seemed to be yelling these things.

She then realized that the demons chasing her sister gave her the opportunity to focus.

She crossed her arms over herself, focusing her rage, her body beginning to glow white.

Several dozen of the demons saw what she was doing and decided to take a gamble on her being at her most vulnerable in the moment before her most powerful attack and charged her.

They were wrong, the sky briefly turning white from the blast of energy that exuded from Persephone's body.

The demons around her were reduced to atoms and then to nothingness in seconds, a shockwave coming off her that knocked the other demons, the ones chasing Juliette, out of the air.

They lay injured and broken along the city streets, their shadowy blood invisible in the darkened afternoon.

Persephone descended so quickly to the roof of a building that she could have almost considered it falling.

She looked around for Juliette but could not see her. She wondered if the blast she had knocked her sister off the roof. She would have hated for her sister to die in that manner after that brief moment of reconciliation.

Persephone sat down, with her wings folded, and breathed heavily.

"Dearest Persephone."

"Sweet Persephone."

"Mother of the new world."

"Why do you stop?" Azrael asked.

"I'm exhausted," Persephone answered, "I need to take a break. Those demons wore me out."

"Time is of the essence."

"Tick tock tick tock."

"So little time."

"We need you."

"Hey, Perci," Juliette yelled from behind her.

"Juliette? You survived the blast?"

"Of course, I did. We're in this together, aren't we?"

Juliette reached into her bag and threw an empty bottle of vodka to the ground.

"Take that! Human world! The Johannes Sisters are fucking shit up!" she yelled.

"I must say…I am so pleased that you seem to want to help. Do you even understand what I'm doing?"

"Sure. Opening a gate to the Ninth Realm. Duh!"

"How did you know?"

"Rabbit told me."

"You speak rabbit?!?" Persephone said, seeming genuinely surprised, "No one speaks rabbit! How did you learn that?!? I've been trying forever!"

"I'd teach you, but I'd have to charge."

"Charge? But money won't…oh, you're quoting something, aren't you?"

"Yeah."

"I see."

"So, can we get out of here before anymore Red Veil come?"

"Okay with me."

"No, Persephone!"

"Do not go with her!"

"You have work to complete!"

"Sweet Persephone!"

"Dearest Persephone!"

"Uh…" Juliette said, looking around, "What's with the spooky voices? That the Mister, waiting in the Ninth?"

"Yes. Azrael. Have you met him?"

"Can't say I've had the pleasure."

"Well, you will soon. Everyone will soon. He's...wonderful," Persephone said, smiling.

"So, let's get out of here, first."

"Where should we go?"

"Uh...Second Realm," Juliette suggested, reaching into her bag and pulling out the sacred dagger that split the walls between worlds.

"Sure."

CHAPTER 32

Within the blink of an eye, Julie found herself in the Second Realm with Persephone. She was fairly surprised by the instantaneous teleportation to another Realm, as she was used to using the established tools in getting between the six Realms she had been to.

The air around here always made her feel light-headed.

The Second Realm was like an untouched version of Earth, populated by any number of mythological creatures. She and her sister stood in a beautiful field of poppies that seemed to go on for miles in three directions, a gentle stream off to the other path. A stunning white unicorn drank from the stream, only to be startled by the sudden appearance of the two humans. It galloped off. In the distance, under the two moons of this version of the world's lavender sky, a giant rainbow crossed between two mountains, little black dots flying near the horizon that Julie knew, from her trips here, to be harpies.

The glowing tiny lights of curious fae hovered on the other side of the stream, flying back into the thick, lush forest they approached from.

"Awwww…there's no Butcher's Eyes?"

"No. You don't run into any of the between-world parasites when you travel the way I do."

"Shame."

"Why?"

"Because…oh, forget it."

Persephone sighed and looked around, smiling. It was good to be in another world with her sister again.

"Either way, I'm glad you and I are here, Juliette. I've been trying to kill you for a while, because I thought you lost your way, and I thought I could lure our father in, so I could get revenge on him for what happened to mom but, you know, being here with you, like this, right now…it feels…it feels *right,* you know? Like nothing can stop the two of us when we're united under one cause."

"Yeah. So, what about Sammi?"

"Samantha's dead. She…she didn't understand what I was trying to do."

"And what are you trying to do?"

"You know. You said it already: open a door to the Ninth Realm."

"But why?"

"The rabbit didn't tell you?"

"Nope."

"Well, because I'm going to bring back the angels and combine the worlds."

"Combine the worlds?"

"Yup. Like it was before the Big Bang. One Realm, with me at the head."

"I see. So, I take it your new boyfriend is looking to start a fight with the Great Old Ones and the Outer Gods?"

"Yes. Although, Azrael isn't my boyfriend. He's…he's my guide. Has been since I was a little girl."

"So, he's been who you've been talking to in the mirror all these years?"

"Yes! You knew?"

"Of course I knew."

"Samantha used to think I had an imaginary friend."

"I know you better. You need an imagination to have an imaginary friend."

"Whoa…that's really mean, Juliette."

"So, about the Eighth Realm?"

"The angels will return and they will fight the forces of chaos."

"I see. So, when gods are hitting each other with planets, what exactly is going to happen to the rest of us?"

"You'll be protected by me."

"I see."

"So, Juliette, how did you…"

Julie punched her sister in the face as hard as she could, knocking Persephone off her feet. Persephone's nose, with a loud crack, shifted to the right side of her face a bit, blood pouring down into her mouth, her eyes tearing up, and her head going foggy.

Julie kicked her in the mouth, knocking out two of her teeth, and then kept kicking her in the face again and again.

"You stupid, stupid, fucking little bitch! You killed Sammi! You fucking killed Sammi! What the fuck is wrong with you?!?"

Persephone rolled out of the way, healing her face, and then yelled, "I thought you understood!"

"I don't fucking understand anything except that you're batshit fucking crazy! You're going to end the whole fucking universe because of some weird grudge you've got with our father because you were so fucking insistent on being a little dragon slayer that you killed our mother in the process!"

"D-don't say that, Juliette."

"Why? What are you going to do? Fail to kill me, like you failed to kill me the last week?"

"Juliette…"

"Hell, you tried to kill me, you failed. You tried to kill dad. You failed. Yet, you managed to kill our mom, entirely by accident. I'd say the safest fucking place I could be is with you trying to kill me."

"I killed Samantha just fine."

"Yeah, you killed Sammi! Do you realize how much she loved you? Do you realize that she was the fucking glue that kept this family together?"

"I-I…it's okay, Juliette…w-when I'm a goddess, linear time won't mean anything to me. I-I can just…I can just pluck another Samantha from an alternate timeline and we can be a family again!"

"Just like that?"

"Just like that."

"You are so fucking full of shit."

"What?"

"You act like you're on some holy mission and that this is all about mom, but here you are, with all this power, talking about how you're going to protect the world and such, yet you're looking to kill thousands of people to accomplish your goal…"

"Sometimes, the needs of the many outweigh the needs of the few."

"*Let me finish!* …to accomplish your goal, and how do you do it? You attack the city and start killing innocent people! You didn't even think of, say, destroying Rikers Island or anything, did you?"

"Rikers Island?"

"Big prison. 12,000 inmates and 8,000 guards."

"Whoa. 20,000 people? That would probably work!"

"Of course it would, but you're too busy being a cliché power-mad asshole to think of anything outside the box. I bet you even threw your head back and did some sort of cliché maniacal laugh, didn't you?"

"Uh…well, you…you suck!"

"I suck?"

"Yes! You do! You're the worst person in the world! You're a drunk! You're a whore! You're here acting like you care about all the people I've killed when you don't ever take anyone else's feeling into consideration when you do anything! I don't think you have a single empathic bone in your whole body! You're selfish! You're an awful, awful person! And yet people like you! People are all, 'Isn't Julie funny?' 'Isn't Julie fun to hang out with?'"

"So, fucking what?"

"So, here I am, doing the thing that you always claim you're doing: *I'm* smashing the system! *I'm* starting everything over at zero! And you, who think you're such a fucking rogue, such a fucking rebel, what are you trying to do? Stop me! For what? So guys like our dad can turn little kids into monsters? So demons like Trent can just sacrifice thousands for greed? I thought if anyone would understand, it'd be you!"

"Well, I don't. For all its bullshit, I don't think the world needs to end."

"Why not? What's there to like about it?"

"Uh…How about sex? How about because there's still a lot of fun to be had out there? How about music? Being alive and feeling that adrenaline! How about because…uh…sex?"

"I knew it'd come down to that with you."

"What? Sex? Uh, *yeah!*"

"It's so overrated."

"Whoa. Whoa. My little sister isn't a virgin, is she?"

"N-no. Of course not. I've done it plenty of times!"

"How many?"

"I'm not here to talk about that with you!"

"How many times?"

"Four, but that's plenty! Three of those times were with the same guy!"

"You libertine, you."

"It's…it's overrated! It's nothing to keep the world going for! I don't see…"

"Did either of those two guys make you cum?"

"Why are we talking about this?"

"Oh my god, you've never cum, have you?"

"We are not talking about this, Juliette!"

"Do you, at least, have a vibrator or something? A lot of women who don't…"

"We are *not* talking about this!"

"You need to invest in a Hitachi Magic Wand. It will change-"

"WE ARE NOT TALKING ABOUT THIS!!!"

Persephone's face got bright red with embarrassment, she turning to look at the mountains again. Eventually she sighed and spoke softly.

"I guess I have to do it, don't I?"

"Do what?"

"Kill you."

"You can *try*. But I'm stopping all this shit."

"How? What do you think you can do to stop me?" Persephone said, turning to her sister, smiling arrogantly, "Do you think you can *kill* me? Hell, you so much as touch my armor, your soul just ceases to exist. Do you really think you can do *anything* to me?"

"I can try."

Persephone laughed, Julie suddenly finding herself being lifted by the throat by an invisible hand, squeezing on her throat.

"Seriously, Juliette," Persephone said, getting in her face, cruelly smiling, "Do you have any idea what I am now? Do you? I. Don't. Die. I am well on my way to becoming a goddess! I am-"

Persephone suddenly got a look of panic in her eyes, as her mouth disappeared, Julie smirking at her.

Persephone tried to heal herself, but couldn't, since the lack of a mouth wasn't a wound but a change in shape of her body.

Julie fell to the ground, the invisible hand letting her go, as Persephone panicked, pointing to her mouth angrily.

Julie smiled at her, about to taunt her sister, when her own mouth disappeared.

Julie rolled her eyes and stared at Persephone, who was looking at her angrily, pointing to her mouth.

Julie folded her arms and pointed at her own.

Persephone shook her head and pointed at hers.

Julie nodded for and then held up all five of her fingers.

Persephone nodded.

Julie and Persephone counted off five of their fingers.

When they both were down to a fist, they both looked at each other annoyed.

Julie pointed to her five fingers again.

Persephone shrugged and nodded.

They counted down, but at the end, neither of them had their mouths back.

Persephone stomped her feet, angrily, Julie rolling her eyes.

Julie ran over to Persephone and grabbed her nose, shutting her nostrils. Persephone started slapping at her sister's hand, finally grabbing Julie's nose and shutting her nostrils, as well.

The two sisters punched at each other, while holding each other's nostrils, until finally, both of their mouths reappeared and the two sisters backed away from each other.

"Ugh! What the fuck?!?" Persephone yelled.

"You're going to do that little Force Choke shit, I'm going to make your mouth disappear. You can kill me, but you'll have to go the rest of eternity without a mouth, because you know if I die before fixing you, it won't ever get fixed!"

"Fine. Then I guess I'll just have to kill you quickly."

Persephone's hands started to glow white and she made fists, intending on punching Julie with them, ending her in one blow.

Julie closed her eyes and concentrated for a second.

A rock flew off the ground a few feet away from Persephone and conked her in the back of the head.

"Ow!" Persephone yelled, grabbed the back of her head, turning around for a second to see what had hit her.

She saw it was a rock, barely big enough to go beyond "pebble" and then giggled. Julie's telekinesis was always so fucking subpar. She was going to hit her with a rock? Like that'd do anything.

Persephone turned around to just get it over with and kill her sister, only to see she was alone in the field, the only sound that of a little bell that had been rung.

CHAPTER 33

Julie, little bell in hand, ran across the rough terrain of the Third Realm, finding herself directly in the middle of a stampede of the species of creature she had tried to bring home with her before Kelly had made such a fuss.

Under the red skies and howling winds, they were skittering along the barren fleshscape towards a cliff.

Well, that was weird. Why would they be running off a...?

Julie looked behind her to see a seven legged creature the size of a blue whale running behind the stampede. That would explain that. It had legs like redwood trees and its blue-furred body was mostly face which was mostly teeth, giant tombstone shaped teeth, multiple tentacle tongues writhing about behind them. It gave a cry that sounded like a pack of hyenas dying in a chamber filled with laughing gas and scooped up as many of the smaller creatures into its horrible mouth as it could. When they would flop inside, there would be a noise that resembled a buzz-saw and a shower of black blood behind those awful, awful teeth. Julie was quite impressed that she had never actually seen one of these before. She then realized that she wouldn't be seeing anything else besides the inside of its mouth, if she didn't run with the smaller creatures.

Julie reached in her messenger bag, as she ran towards the cliff as well, pulling out another artifact from her bag, with the intention of jumping Realms once she jumped off the cliff.

Persephone appeared in front her, smiling.

"You think you can just jump Realms from me?"

Julie ran past her and off the cliff, a vast sulfur sea miles below her.

"You think...Hey! Where are you going?"

Persephone turned around in time to be crushed by the giant creature's massive legs.

Of course, it touching her armor caused a huge explosion, which Julie avoided at the last second, doing the brief ritual required to go to another Realm.

CHAPTER 34

Julie found herself in the flesh fields of the Fifth Realm, the sky stinking as always, but not quite as bad as the smells of from the sulfur sea she had almost jumped into, the sounds of screaming everywhere.

She turned around, only to find herself face to face with a black six-armed demon, an entire legion of his kind and their royal guard behind them. Julie had never seen this many demons congregated in one spot before. His army stretched as far as the eye could see in either direction and was dozens thick. Each towering monsters of muscle and black flame.

"HUMAN FEMALE, ARE YOU THE ONE KNOWN AS PERSEPHONE JOHANNES, DAUGHTER OF ALEXANDER JOHANNES?!?" it said, in the high demonic language of the Fifth Realm.

"Uh…" Julie looked at him and his very well armed men and attempted to speak in the little high demonic she remembered from her dad's attempts at teaching her, "HI. MY NAME IS JULIE. YOUR SKY IS MOSTLY CLEAN. I ENJOY…YOUR YES, PLEASE."

The demon looked at her confused.

Persephone appeared in front of Julie.

"Okay, Juliette, that was shitty! Do you really think you can just…"

"HELLO, SISTER OF MINE, PERSEPHONE!" Julie said in broken high demonic.

"Why are you speaking in…?"

"THIS IS HER, BROTHERS OF HOUSE TEMEN'NI'GRU!" the lead demon spoke, commanding his troops with a raised whip-sword, "THIS IS THE HUMAN BITCH WHO KILLED OUR BROTHERS K'VEK'EY'IH AND LI'DHU'XA! THE OLD HUMAN MALE SPOKE THE TRUTH! LET US FLAY HER!"

The demon army descended on Persephone, which gave Julie just enough time to roll her dice, hitting snake eyes the first time.

CHAPTER 35

In a large room at the top of a tower in the Fourth Realm, Lucy crouched on all fours in a large heart shaped bed with leopard print sheets, naked and moaning in ecstasy, as a naked human male pumped her anally and she fellated another man in front of her.

At the four corners of the room stood four shadowy succubae of the Black Talon, standing guard, while rubbing themselves.

Suddenly, Julie appeared out of nowhere. The four guards turned to her, ready to fight.

"Wait! Wait! I know Lucy! I'm Julie Golightly!"

Lucy took the guy in front of her out of her mouth and yelled at Julie, "Whoa! My nigs! Kinda busy!"

"Hey, Lucy. Won't stay long, need to switch Realms before the person chasing me realizes I'm here. Need a quick favor!"

"Can it wait? Getting my ass ready for war here!"

"Literally, I see."

"My nigs…"

"Look, you don't even need to do it yourself. Just send one of your, uh, minions or whatever."

"'ight. What is it?"

Lucy's guard stood down and went back to their positions, while Lucy turned to the man in back of her and yelled, "Yo, my nigga, did I says to stop hitting that shit, back there?!? You keep fucking that ass!" He obliged.

Julie gave him a thumbs up.

"Yo, what you need, my nigs?" Lucy asked her, impatiently.

Julie got right down to business, "Okay, what I need is…"

CHAPTER 36

Julie, having gotten the promise she needed from Lucy, found herself in the cold, steel environment of the Sixth Realm. She stood on a shining metal wall the height of the Empire State Building, looking down at the floating mechanized city below her, gleaming black 90 degree angles aplenty. Impossibly shaped flying vehicles, screaming with human souls as fuel, crisscrossed the cityscape ahead of her.

An upside-down mechanical pyramid, crackling with electricity, floated off on the horizon, glowing a bright blue against the busy black sky behind it.

She didn't like being here because she knew the tech that these Sixth Realm demons used was serious.

Suddenly, an armored vehicle, shaped like a slick black box, searchlights shining on her, arose from the other side of the wall.

She was now a target. She ran along the wall, glad, for once that she was sober, as this thing had no guardrails or anything of that sort. The demons flying the machine behind her fired lasers at her, she doing a leap, reaching into her bag for a gun of some sort. She was sure she was out of rockets and wasn't sure that even a magnum would penetrate the armor on that thing.

Mechanical sentries, insectoid robotic rape machines and assault specialists, popped up on her left and right, the souls within them screaming loudly, as they shot bolts of electricity at her.

In a white flash, Persephone appeared, standing right behind her, arms folded, looking very angry.

"Very funny, Juliette," Persephone said, as the flying box exploded upon impact with Persephone's wings.

"They really don't like you in the Fifth Realm," Julie said, still running from the sentries.

"Do you want to jump from dimension to dimension? Because I can play that too."

Suddenly, the ground gave way under Julie and she was enveloped by blackness.

CHAPTER 37

Julie was suffocating. There was no oxygen here, in this land of pure darkness. She struggled to breath, gasping for breath, reaching into her messenger bag, frantically, until she found a snorkel and an oxygen tank she had kept in there for anytime she'd accidentally find herself in the underwater portion of a Realm.

This was different. This place was black and cold, so very cold, and filled with such a feeling of dread, such a primal fear in her very soul, that it took all of her effort to not pee her pants right then and there. This was a place completely hostile to the human soul.

It had to be the Seventh Realm.

Fighting terror every step of the way, her thighs tensing up, closer to each other, she surveyed the land around her. It was just black and dead. Nothing lived here. Nothing grew here. She wasn't even sure what was illuminating this vast, empty land, only punctuated by dozens of skyscraper sized pillars that seemed to reach up into the very sky.

"See? Julie, I can go wherever I want. I have infinite power and you can't do anything about it. Maybe I should just leave you here, to die in fear and then live as a soul forever in agony. There is no hope in this place. There is no light. There is…"

The ground shook. Both sisters turned around to see the source of it. There was a giant black structure, one of those endless pillars, a seemingly impossibly tall tower that reached into the black sky above, without end.

Then it moved.

Julie realized, her bowels now wanting to empty, finally making out the shape of a hoof bigger than most small towns, that it was a leg.

She looked up to the sky and saw dozens of red stars suddenly light up in the sky. That's what had been illuminating things.

Then with a dawning primal horror, she realized they were not stars. They were eyes. Eyes that felt like they would always see her, always know where she was, that she'd never escape their gaze, and that this giant was always waiting to take her to this place of sorrow and shame and fear forever.

Filled with an absolute animal panic, she reached into her bag and grabbed the dagger that would open a hole to the Second Realm and stabbed the air, jumping into the hole that formed between worlds.

CHAPTER 38

Julie threw off the snorkel and screamed, her heart beating a thousand miles an hour, as she found herself back in a gentle meadow in the Second Realm, curious satyr looking at her as one of the two moon set in the West.

She had never felt anything like that before. She had fought that Seventh Realm entity, but realized now that it had only been a small, small creature in that Realm. It was really a feeling of terror like she had never experienced in her life up until that moment.

"So, here is where you want to die, I guess?" Persephone said, appearing out of nowhere.

Julie, still mentally recovering from the feelings that place invoked, just looked up at Persephone.

"Are you sure you don't want me to show you the Eighth Realm? Since you seem to be fighting the Order I'll bring to the universe so strongly, are you sure you don't want me to drop you right in Azagthoth's court? I'm sure you'll enjoy the madness that will come from his eternal fluting. Or maybe you'd just like me to end it quickly for you?"

Julie scrambled backwards and then brought herself to her feet. She looked at Persephone and made a "just bring it" motion with her hand.

Persephone scoffed, "Don't you understand? There's nothing that can be done to stop me! And by turning against me, you pretty much assured yourself of death."

"You know what, Perci?"

"What?"

"I've always wanted to see what this did."

Julie leapt forward and stabbed Persephone in the face with the dagger used to breach the worlds and then slashed a little downward, opening a portal between the Second Realm and another part of the Second Realm in Persephone's face.

Persephone screamed as her atoms were sucked into themselves, her body being broken as it disappeared into the portal that was her face.

In a second, Persephone seemed to have disappeared and the dagger fell to the ground as if she had never been there.

Julie, smiled to herself, but knew this wasn't going to keep her sister away for long and used the dagger to open another hole, this time back to Earth.

CHAPTER 39

Julie was back in New York, in the middle of Madison Square Park.

Sure enough, the Flatiron Building was on fire, and the air was filled with a thick black smoke. Julie put on her gas mask but still couldn't see through the smoldering blaze, when she felt a hand tap her on the shoulder.

Expecting it to be Persephone, she turned around, only to see it was Triane of the Black Talon, naked and smiling.

"Hey, Julie! Forgive the nudity, I wasn't wearing a human body, so I wasn't wearing clothes, when Larxene told me you needed a ride somewhere."

"Yeah, thanks."

Triane clapped her hands and shrugged.

"Okay, you're on your own about getting back down, though, I heard what your sister did to the Red Veil. I don't want to stay for her to kill me too."

"No problem."

Triane nodded. She took a deep breath and then bent over and her true essence bled over her human disguise.

She grabbed Julie in her arms, told her to hang on, and then proceeded to fly off the ground.

The two of them flew over the city, towards the top of the Empire State Building, where the hole to the Ninth Realm had been opened up.

The voice of Azrael swirled around her, cursing her and asking where Persephone was.

"Cannot stop me!"

"Sister of Persephone!"

"Your actions are fruitless!"

"I will know your soul!"

"Who the fuck is that?" Triane asked, about Azrael's voices.

"Remember the Mother talking about Death itself?"

"Damn, you do piss off everyone you meet, don't you?"

Julie shrugged.

Ascending to the very top of the building, Triane gently guided Julie to a safe spot.

"Thanks so much for that," Julie said to Triane, "Anyone ever tell you that you feel like cotton candy?"

"Uh...you."

Julie shrugged. Triane shrugged and then jumped off the ground. As she hovered in one place, her wings flapping slowly, she saluted Julie and then flew off.

Julie saluted Triane, as she disappeared into the horizon, and then looked around. It was not hard to find exactly what she had been looking for. She could see a tiny little hole in the sky, no doubt where the portal was.

She had a good idea of how to close it but that would require...Ah, here she was.

Persephone flew in above her, looking at her older sister with rage.

"What do you think you're going to do, Juliette? You're just postponing the inevitable!"

Julie reached into her bag again.

"What? You going to try to stab me in the face again? You going to shoot me? Have some more rockets?"

Julie whipped out the Magnum.

"Hahahahahaha. What's that going to do to me?!? It might knock me back a few feet but I'm just going to heal right afterwards, you stupid, stupid woman."

"This is just one of two things I have for you."

"Oh, really? Well, by all means. Let's see your secret weapon then. What could you possibly have that can harm me? You can't!"

"You're right, Perci. I can't harm you. I could drop a nuclear bomb into your glowing Xena panties and you'd be perfectly fine. But I *can* stop you."

"Go ahead. Let's see what you've got."

Julie whipped out a vial of white powder.

"What is that?"

"Something you've never had."

Julie threw the vial at Persephone, it shattering on her armor, Hypnagogia dusting Persephone's skin.

Upon it touching her, she looked at her sister with a confused look. "What is…OH!"

And then her eyes rolled into her head, her legs convulsed, and she bit her lip, basically howling at the top of her lungs as her right hand immediately found itself between her legs.

Persephone's wings out of her control for a moment, she began to descend, gently.

"And here's the other one," Julie said, shooting Persephone right in the center of her chest armor with the Magnum.

The force of the blast knocked Persephone backwards, right into the open hole between worlds.

The armor she was wearing sensing its home Realm, it started to suck her in.

Persephone, her eyes dazed, and her hair wet with sweat, suddenly shook herself aware, finding herself being violently vacuumed into the Ninth Realm.

The voice of Azrael screamed for her to pull herself out, but she couldn't. Her legs snapped back on themselves and her arms shattered as the pull of gravity became too great.

Her lower body now in the Ninth Realm, she reached out to Julie, with her broken arms.

"Juliette! Help me, please!" Persephone yelled, feeling her hip bones crunch under the force of the portal.

Julie looked at her for a moment and then shook her head.

"But we're sisters!"

"So was Sammi," Julie said, as Persephone screamed, her upper body being sucked into the hole, as her torso completely folded in on itself, "Goodbye, little Dragonslayer."

"We will not forget this!"

"We will kill you many times over!"

"You have not won!"

"You have not won!"

"You have not won!"

"You have not w-"

The portal closed, just like that, the sky clearing up to be early evening, the aurora borealis completely dissipated, and the moon and stars visible above her. She had won. But what type of victory was it, exactly? Her sobriety cut through her mind like a machete.

Julie choked back tears at the loss of both of her sisters and then sat down, looking dejected, on the roof of the building.

Tears running down her cheeks, she opened up her messenger bag and pulled out a forty of malt liquor she had gotten back at Lucy's apartment.

She poured it out, watching the alcohol form a little puddle under her.

"Oh, Sammi, Perci…I'm so sorry," she said, putting her face in her palms, weeping for her sisters.

She sat there, quietly sobbing for a few minutes, before looking around, and then, with a sense of annoyed realization, said, "Fuck…I've gotta get down from here, don't I?"

CHAPTER 40

In the war room in Washington D.C., the General looked at the satellite feed, looking at Julie sitting on the roof, the president and Joint Chiefs of Staff on the other end of the phone he was on.

"Gentlemen, it seems like the crisis has been averted. We are standing down...yes, sir, it seems the girl did what the Council reps said she'd do...No, sir, there was no involvement from Team Seven...No, we're not going to bring her in now...But we will continue to observe her...Matherson certainly raised that possibility, but it is your decision, ultimately, sir...Thank you, sir...Good night to you, too, Mr. President."

EPILOGUE
I DON'T CARE ABOUT YOU

CHAPTER 1

It took about a week and a half for the city to start to get back to normal. Of course, there was a great deal of work to be done, repairing the damage Persephone had wrought, which was written off in the news to the faulty infrastructure of the city of Manhattan. Taxes would have to be raised to prevent the sort of anomalies that occurred that day. Several gas mains had apparently exploded at once and there was, the expert talking heads said on the news, an EMP generated by the explosion at the power plant on 14th Street. The jets and helicopters were merely the government checking to make sure that no terrorists had been involved. The crashes were, of course, due to the EMP making the military vehicles lose power. Of course, there were skeptics who said that they saw a battle in the sky, but they were quickly dismissed as crazy, as were those who claimed to have seen UFOs or angels.

It was all swept under the rug quickly in the rest of the country, and while New Yorkers were still recovering, and there were apparently hundreds missing and presumed dead, the rest of the country had already moved onto celebrity scandals and some weird orgasm-inducing drug that came out of New York that was sweeping club culture.

CHAPTER 2

Julie had spent the last two weeks at a squat in Alphabet City. She didn't know any of them, but they didn't seem to mind her nudity or drunkenness, or if they did, nobody said anything to her about it. Her hair had reverted to its natural red, as she had just stopped caring enough to dye it black anymore.

Increasingly, New York bummed her out. It was the place where she had lost both of her sisters and it was time for a change, besides just her hair color. Maybe, one day, she'd find herself back here, but it was definitely time to move on for a bit. She had heard a lot of people telling her Austin, Texas was a good destination, that things were happening in Austin, so she packed up her messenger bag, shoplifted another panda hoodie, and found herself at the Port Authority, standing across from Brian, Samantha's fiancée.

She felt so bad for the poor guy. The news of losing her sister just devastated him. He had a million regrets and twice as many questions and Julie tried her best to help him with those.

She had made enough money to pay for Samantha's funeral. It had been packed with Council members and members of the medical community. It touched Julie to see how many people had been truly touched by her sister. Nigel had been there, trying to convince her to come and train with the Council, but she had no interest.

Now, she waited, holding her messenger bag, hugging Brian. It was afternoon in the recovering city. If New York was anything, it was resilient.

"You know, Julie, anytime you need anything, please call me," Brian said, his eyes red from all the crying he had been doing the last two weeks.

"It's cool, Brian," she said, looking up at the schedule.

"Samantha used to worry about you so much. I feel like it's my job now to do so."

"I'll be okay."

"I know you will. You're strong. Samantha always said that. She…" he started to break down.

Julie hugged him and gave him a tissue.

They called her bus, so she said her goodbyes and started to walk towards the gate.

Suddenly, she found herself thrown through a glass partition into the indoor parking lot area where the buses arrived. She felt broken glass and pain and she heard people gasping at the sudden act of violence.

Confused and in pain, she looked up to see a female figure in black leather, a tinted black motorcycle helmet on, standing in the place where Julie had been thrown from.

The figure advanced at Julie at a speed so fast, it was only a blur, lifting her up by the neck and then throwing her back through what was left of the glass again.

Crowds of people gathered, police aimed their guns, yelling for the figure to freeze.

It ran at the cops, beheading one and grabbed the other. The figure lifted the helmet and began to feed on him.

It was Serenity, her bleached pixie cut now a mess, her roots a half inch long, and black, her face unwashed, and her eyes bloodshot.

She threw the cop's body down, once he was dead and proceeded to walk towards Julie, hate in her emerald green eyes. People began to scream. To run.

"You killed my Mimmy!" Serenity yelled, "You think I'd just bloody let you go, you're daft, you are!"

Julie stood up and reached for her bag, Serenity kicking it out of her reach.

"No, you don't," Serenity said, picking Julie up with one hand.

She threw Julie into a far off wall, as alarms went off in the Port Authority.

"I don't fucking care, whether they see me or not," Serenity said, "I don't care! I'm taking you down, you slag! Nothing fucking matters anymore, without my Mimmy!"

Julie started to run towards a far wall, hoping that she could lure Serenity into doing something.

Serenity, blinded by rage, followed through, and did one of her super-speed tackles to Julie, taking her through the 8th Avenue window, the two of them falling from the second story of the Port Authority onto the street below.

Julie screamed out as she landed on a taxi cab, hood first. Upon impact, there was a sharp pain in Julie's back and a numbness in her legs. Serenity landed on top of her, a second later, knocking the wind of out of her. Then Serenity rolled off her, screaming in the sun.

"No! Fucking no! I'm not bloody dying without you!" Serenity yelled, as her skin smoked.

A look of utter rage in her eyes, Serenity stopped to debate whether she would stay and die with Julie or live to fight another day. Realizing there was too much of a chance of dying from the sun before she could finish the job, she screamed and then ran away from Julie, descending into the subway, out of the reach of the sun.

All traffic stopped on 8th Avenue, police sirens blaring all around her, a group of officers running down into the subway to pursue Serenity. The cab driver got out of his cab and looked down at Julie, who still hadn't moved from the hood.

"You…you okay, miss?"

"Oh…uh…sure. Just peachy. If you can't take being thrown through a second story window onto a taxi by an insane vampire, then you're not a real New Yorker, right?"

"Vampire?!?"

"Don't…uh…don't worry about it…You know, I, uh…"

Julie tried to sit up but was met with intense pain.

"You know, I think I'll just lay here until the nice men in the ambulances come and give me some lovely painkillers for my back, if you don't mind."

The cab driver looked at her confused, but Julie just shrugged, reached into her pocket, put her earbuds in her ears, and played A-Ha's "Take On Me" on her iPhone, closing her eyes to the commotion around her.

She laughed to herself and then asked the guy, not bothering to open her eyes, "Hey, cabdriver, dude…you wouldn't happen to have any Jager, would you?"

CHAPTER 3

He much preferred Perry Como's "Magic Moments" to the typical jingle his truck provided when he first acquired it. It just…fit. Worked perfectly with his sense of humor. To be honest, most things he did, he did because they amused him. His father wasn't one for humor, and don't even get him started on his brother who insisted on calling himself a king, but humor drove him. He wondered what would give him such pleasure the day that all of this was gone.

The Ice Cream Man, drove his truck through the Texas suburbs, tipping his cap at a group of children who started to run after him, no doubt hungry for tasty, frozen treats.

He wore a traditional white ice cream man's uniform, complete with hat and black bowtie. That was the problem with ice cream men today. No one wore uniforms anymore. Without uniforms, all we have left is chaos.

Okay, he had promised himself he'd stop telling that joke, but in truth, it got funnier every time he told it.

He stopped the truck at a corner in this small, god-fearing town, straight out of something from Norman Rockwell. A place untouched by this secular, messy century.

The perfect place for him.

After all, in the beginning was the word. Or so, these people liked to say.

He had decided to come on down here, as soon as all that ugliness in New York started. If he had to go call in his dad, he didn't want to do it where some throwback was trying to bring Order back to the universe. Luckily, someone had taken care of that for him. He'd have to thank them. Or kill them. One of the two. Whichever was funnier. Maybe both. Maybe not in the expected order.

Three children, two boys and a girl, walked up to the side of the truck, dollars in their hands given to them, no doubt, by their perfect, god-fearing parents. They were very, very tan. Cause and effect of being around the sun all the time. He hated cause and effect.

"Can I have an ice cream sandwich?" one of the boys asked, his Southern drawl very strong. The Ice Cream Man loved that. Accents and languages were a hobby of his.

"What flavor would you like?"

"Vanilla."

"Oh, I'm sorry, we're fresh out of vanilla."

"What kind of ice cream man runs out of vanilla?" the little girl asked.

"What's your name?"

"Kelly Ann."

"Well, Kelly Ann, that is a good question. But I have something better than vanilla for you: I have a secret."

"A secret?"

"Yes, for all three of you. Listen closely."

In the beginning was the word and he told them the word. A word that could not be pronounced by human vocal chords. A word that existed before there was written speech.

A word that existed before there the first man even grunted his first syllable. Before the first monkey had looked at the sun, before the first fish had crawled out of the ocean, before this planet had cooled down enough for life to form on it, before the Big Bang that ended the battle.

In the beginning was the word and the word was good.

The children fell to the ground, making choking noises, as their bodies convulsed. The word brought change. It helped to steer them back to what they should have been, before evolution went about its nastiness with the amoebas and the fish and the apes.

The word was something of a failsafe.

He smiled, a big toothy smile, as the loud cracking noises of the children's bones re-aligning themselves added extra percussion to Perry Como. Their true forms, the true forms of all chaos' creations, began to take shape. No uniformity, no reason or logic to their shapes. No symmetry. He really hated symmetry. One slithered on a large twisted tentacle the size of an anaconda's body; another crawled on six legs, and yet another hopped on a single arm, the rest of that child's body a mass of tentacles and eyes.

These children would be the first, but not the last.

The Ice Cream Man had cometh.

The earthly representative of the sleeping Great Old Ones and Outer Gods of the Eighth Realm, the Black Pharaoh; the God of a Thousand Forms; the Crawling Chaos; son of Azagthoth, Blind Fiend of Chaos; Slayer of a Thousand Angels; The Faceless God; The Dweller in Darkness; known by name as Nyarlathotep, had personally presided over the end of more worlds than humans had a number to count them. He tipped his hat at the three tentacled howling things that had once been human children and went off to spread more magic moments to the children of this god-fearing town.

ABOUT THE AUTHOR

Charles D. Lincoln was born in the Hell's Kitchen area of New York City during a period known as *Taxi Driver*. Son of legendary pornographer (*literally* a legendary pornographer. He was given an AVN award for it) Fred J. Lincoln, at various times, Charles has been a filmmaker, a musician, an advice columnist, an activist, an animal lover (but only in a platonic way), an internet troll, an avid gamer, a journalist, and a general pain in the ass to all who encounter him.

Having been told that he had an unhealthy interest in Sci-Fi and Horror by his second grade teacher, he has turned a grudge into a calling. Charles currently lives in Brooklyn, never married with no heirs.

www.ingramcontent.com/pod-product-compliance
Lightning Source LLC
Chambersburg PA
CBHW072253020726
47501CB00002B/256